MISTER NIGHTINGALE

ALSO BY PAUL BOWDRING

The Roncesvalles Pass

The Night Season

The Strangers' Gallery

MISTER NIGHTINGALE

A Novel

PAUL BOWDRING

Vagrant PRESS

Nimbus Publishing Limited
3731 Mackintosh St, Halifax, NS B3K 5A5
(902) 455-4286 nimbus.ca

Printed and bound in Canada

NB1210

Cover art: *Dissolving Images II*, lithograph, jacquelinebarrett.ca; tree image from iStock
Design: Jenn Embree

Library and Archives Canada Cataloguing in Publication

Bowdring, Paul, author
Mister Nightingale / Paul Bowdring.
  Issued in print and electronic formats.
  ISBN 978-1-77108-379-9 (paperback).—ISBN 978-1-77108-380-5 (html)
  I. Title.

PS8553.O89945M57 2016   C813'.54   C2015-908196-3
                                              C2015-908197-1

Nimbus Publishing acknowledges the financial support for its publishing activities from the Government of Canada through the Canada Book Fund (CBF) and the Canada Council for the Arts, and from the Province of Nova Scotia. We are pleased to work in partnership with the Province of Nova Scotia to develop and promote our creative industries for the benefit of all Nova Scotians.

For Glenda and Julia,
with love and gratitude.

At Regensburg he crossed the Danube on his cloak, and there made
a broken glass whole again; and, in the house of a wheelwright too mean
to spare the kindling, lit a fire with icicles. This story of the burning of the
frozen substance of life has, of late, meant much to me, and I wonder now
whether inner coldness and desolation may not be the pre-condition for
making the world believe, by a kind of fraudulent showmanship, that one's
own wretched heart is still aglow.

       –W. G. SEBALD, THE RINGS OF SATURN

And if poetry is not to be the agency of his transfiguration from ignoble
to noble, why bother with poetry at all?

       –J. M. COETZEE, YOUTH

CONTENTS

1: NIGHTINGALE COUNTRY

It's been a long day for Mister Nightingale.

Up at four to catch a six o'clock flight from Halifax, delayed till ten, I arrived in St. John's on a cold and snowy morning in May—a foreigner's, not a native's, notion of the place, a *mise en scène* for the prodigal son. Last night, my flight from Toronto had been unable to land in St. John's. On its third attempt, it descended to within a few hundred feet of the ground, then rose straight up like an elevator in a shaft. It was diverted to Halifax, and I spent the night in a generic hotel near the airport, a "Worst Eastern," as a disgruntled fellow traveller called it, having had a second shower in the morning while drying himself after the first. Water from the bathroom in the room above had poured down through the ceiling.

I'd inquired about the Lord Nelson Hotel—it seemed fitting that I stay there and hang out in Mr. Ray Smith's tavern; our first novels had appeared the same year—but I was told by the Air Canada receptionist that they didn't have "corporate arrangements with that facility." "Icon," I corrected, but was met with a blank stare. Smith's *Lord Nelson Tavern* and my (much less heralded) novel *The Ropewalk* had been published in 1974, the year I'd left Newfoundland for good. *The Ropewalk* was now being reissued by my first publisher, the notorious Alonzo "the Virus" Grandy, one of several reasons for my visit. It had barely been *issued* when it first appeared, merely allowed to crawl unaided out of the slime of literary oblivion and find some insecure foothold in the marketplace.

Landing in St. John's had been routine the second time round, and I immediately took a taxi into town, post-haste to a luncheon hosted by the Lieutenant-Governor for the university's spring crop of candidates for honourary degrees. "A shower of snow last night…just a few blossoms…Sheila's Brush…moved from March to May this year," said the man on the radio. "VOCM, the voice of the common man, first with the news in Newfoundland." No news of the royal visit, however, the return of the native, back from mainland exile to receive the laurel crown; doubtless no publicist's dispatch to announce the event. I imagined a small, loyal notice in the hometown paper: "Prophet finally honoured in his native land." Maybe a glossier notice in *enRoute*—I'd once had a prize-winning story in there—but no doubt just scornful copy in *Mill & Mire*, the Canadian publishing industry rag, sort of a punning prelude to an obit: "Mid-list author, listing fast, shored up a degree at home on the Rock." Perhaps, instead of a cab, I should have taken a donkey. "You will never get the crowd to shout Hosanna," said the philosopher, "until you ride into town on an ass."

Sheila's Brush. An omen, perhaps. No doubt a brush with sister Sheila was in the cards in the next few days. In the matter of our father and his erratic behaviour, his failing powers. The taxi had a chain-link steering wheel cover. I'd seen leather, fur, and rubber–even a wood steering wheel–but never chain. Another omen? The driver had a shaved head, a leather jacket, and an earring, and was concerned about the price of fish. He had been a fisherman, like his father, but "got the hell out of it," he said, after the cod moratorium in '92.

"The fishers and the processors still can't agree on a price for crab," said the earnest *Open Line* host. "The season is now open, but the fishers have refused to fish, the processors are refusing to buy, and the government is refusing to step in and help resolve the dispute. What do you think?"

"They don't care about the price of fish," the driver replied. "They don't care about the fishermen, either. What about the *moratorium?* Fifty thousand jobs lost—the largest layoff in Canadian history. All they care about is oil. But when one of them offshore wells blows—and you can be sure it will—we'll see about the price of oil. We'll see about the price of everything."

Moratorium, mused Mister Nightingale. The very word was like a bell. I still hadn't quite finished my acceptance speech, and now I had an inspired, if belated, notion. They had asked for, and I had sent along, a first draft two weeks ago. But we all know what becomes of first drafts. Perhaps a taxi was the best choice after all. I have a writer-friend in Toronto who takes a cab ride every week, whether he has to go anywhere or not. Cabbies, he claims, have been his best source of inspiration.

It was too early to check into the Bed o' Roses, the B & B I'd booked for my first night in town, though it was just down the road from Government House. In any event, it was well past noon, and the prodigal son was late for luncheon, the prelude to the afternoon session of convocation and conferral of my honourary degree. You'll be late for your own funeral, my poor mother used to say, but, as it turned out, I was late for hers. Worse than late—I had missed it altogether. She'd been dead for five years, and I still had not visited her grave.

∽ ∽

Yes, it's been a long, long day for Mister Nightingale. After the formal pre-convocation luncheon at Government House with my fellow honourees, at which Her Majesty's representative had unexpectedly, and embarrassingly, singled me out, patronized me in his after-dinner speech by saying how pleased he was to finally see his favourite *Canadian* writer on the university's honourary roll, and then referred to the title of his favourite book by his favourite Canadian writer as *Latitudes of Malt* (surely the Freudian slip of the century, the malt fancier's unconscious translation of *Latitudes of Melt*; not one of my books, however, but a friend's); after the Oxbridge formalities of the convocation itself, complete with Elgarian and Purcellian imperial marches, Processional and Recessional; after the crowded post-convocation reception in an airless sardine can of a reception room, shrimp and scallop hors d'oeuvres notwithstanding; and after the very late dinner and post-dinner brandies in the faculty lounge, I was finally relaxing in a different lounge at the other end of town with long-time friend and fellow writer Thomas Kevin Keough (Kevin to his friends, or TKO, as he was known in his younger, more pugnacious days). The day was done and I was glad to be almost alone. That is the feeling I have in the company of close friends. Not a negative one—on the contrary: a feeling of comfort and ease, a complete absence of self-consciousness, as if I were alone.

But Kevin was being rather antagonistic this evening. A tall, craggy, mis-shapen old pine of a man, but with the small, delicate hands of a sapling (*Nobody, not even the rain, has such small hands,* said his favourite poet, e. e. cummings, he of the small letters), TKO would always get into fights when he was drinking, though *skirmishes* might be a better word—abrupt, mercifully short, avian-like displays with acknowledged, if unwritten, rules of engagement to protect puffball-fisted, good-natured, comradely cowards like him. His presence, though, at any social gathering was still capable of creating, on an interpersonal scale, what newspapers sometimes referred to as widespread unrest, tension, or at least unease.

I was, quite unexpectedly, feeling it now. Kevin had taken a rather dim view, not just of my accepting the honourary degree, but of the content of my convocation address. Not for fouling the nest, about which I myself had worried aloud—no doubt Kevin was proud of me for doing that—but for sentimentalizing the noble craft and sullen art, the workworkwork of art, in which we have been sullen lifelong companions. I had strayed into the latitudes of malt myself at the rather lively and lengthy Government House luncheon, and perhaps I had strayed from the first draft of my speech as well.

∽ ∽

Professor William Mowbray, Public Orator: "I will finish my introduction, and my brief disquisition on the nightingale as the great traditional symbol of creation and inspiration in Western literature, with a phrase from Plutarch, now used to signify empty words, an empty threat. He tells the story of a man who plucks the feathers from a nightingale, hoping to discover, perhaps, the source of its beautiful voice. Finding that its miserable, featherless body is so small, he declares: '*Vox et praeterea nihil*,' 'a voice and nothing more.' But what a voice! I would add, as I present to you, for the degree of doctor of letters, *honoris causa*, a writer whose work can truly be said to *sing*: Mr. James Nightingale."

Flanked by a large roster of university officials, my fellow honourees and I were seated in a wide semi-circle facing the audience, and I stood up and walked to the rostrum accompanied by the sort of mild and uncertain applause one sometimes hears between the movements of a piece of music in the concert hall.

Thank you, Professor Mowbray, eloquent Public Orator. Your standard is way beyond my powers, a hard act to follow, as they say, but I will try my best. Thank you for your most kind introductory remarks, and for your learned and pithy disquisition on the nightingale. I have been allotted about ten minutes to speak and, being a gentleman, I will stick to it. As Mark Twain said, "A gentleman is someone who knows how to play the banjo, but doesn't." Likewise for giving long speeches.

Mr. Chancellor, Mr. President and Vice-chancellor, graduates, ladies and gentlemen...besides the generous tribute of the honourary degree itself, it is a privilege to be invited to address you here today at my alma mater's fifty-seventh spring convocation. To have an honourary degree conferred upon you by the university you attended as a student is a great honour—especially as I got a dishonourable discharge the first time round. But I have very happy memories of this place, and the people I met here, some of whom, students and teachers, have become lifelong friends and influences.

I think especially, and often, of the late Dr. Noel Eagleton, whom we all loved dearly, perhaps the first Albertan to emigrate to Newfoundland, who taught in the English department here. It was a *very* English, i.e., British, department at the time. In his famous, or infamous, Twentieth-Century Comparative Literature course—more a curse than a course, in the view of some faculty members—Dr. Eagleton generously accepted our poems and prose, our juvenalia, as substitutes for essays, a radical departure from professorial formality, academic rigour, for the time. He taught us that literature was nothing less than a matter of life and death, a way, if a strange way, of loving the world, and you have to love it, in the end, he said, you have no choice in the matter. Of course, we were so very young—you may not have learned that yet, yourselves—much too young to have any idea what he was talking about, though we knew instinctively that it was true, and believed, lived by, every word of it. He got himself fired in the end, of course. But I digress, and I haven't even started my speech.

I want to talk to you today about literature, writers and writing—specifically, the literary calling, the writing life. Surprise! I'm sorry to be so predictable, but I don't know much about anything else. "Bon qu'à ça," "All I'm good for," as Sam Beckett said when asked, "Why do you write?" It is very presumptuous of all of us who stand here, I guess, to think that we can say something in this short time that will make a difference to your lives. But so we must, as I feel that this is what is expected of us to some extent. But I'm uncomfortable with it, all the same. Fiction writers are always uncomfortable with ideas and beliefs, afraid to be didactic, imposing them on you, our readers. As one of J. M. Coetzee's characters, a writer, a stand-in for the author himself, perhaps, said, "Writers have beliefs but we don't really believe in them." Our characters do, however, and we have to believe in our characters…because we want you to believe in them. Think of me as a literary character, then, Shakespeare's Polonius perhaps, in that scene in *Hamlet* where he is giving advice to his son,

Laertes, on his going away. I'll think of you all as my sons and daughters. (Coincidentally, I have a daughter of my own who is sitting among you here today, attending this university but not graduating yet. She's just finished her first year. She's the one sliding down in her seat now, mortified. The first honours I ever received, in fact, were the gold and silver stars she removed from her scribbler and stuck on top of the scribbled pages I'd left on my desk while I was out for my habitual afternoon walk. Hope you're still out there, Sweetheart!)

I went to this university in the late sixties and early seventies. I wasn't sure exactly what I wanted to major in, so I majored in everything, i.e., I settled on English literature, or literature in English. Shakespeare alone, our greatest, contains everything. We sometimes forget that our greatest writer was a playwright. A poet too, of course. Shakespeare had so much disguised advice, wisdom, to give. In *Hamlet*, Polonius describes the players, the actors, who have come to entertain the court: "The best actors in the world, either for tragedy, comedy, history, pastoral..." I've always thought of the novelist as a poor player, an actor, a performer, an imitator, an impersonator. It's hard for many readers to accept, of course, that the writer is a mere performer at heart, a trickster. The critic John Ciardi has related an anecdote about one of these readers, a poetry lover who chastised poet Robert Frost after a reading he gave in which he made mention of his personal bag of tricks.

"Mr. Frost," she said, "surely when you are writing one of your *bee-oo-ti-ful* poems...surely you are not thinking of *technical tricks!*"

"I *revel* in 'em!" Mr. Frost replied.

Trickster or not, the poet, the fiction writer—and we tend to forget that the poet is also a fiction writer—is always sincere, of course; or I should say his characters, his narrators, his voices are. He adopts personas; he does imitations. As a human being, he has opinions, ideas, and beliefs, but as a writer, as I said, he doesn't necessarily believe in them. Sounds like a paradox, but it isn't. Perhaps Oscar Wilde was saying the same thing: "The truth of a work of art is that its contrary is also true."

Now where does all that leave us? I said that my subject is the literary calling; and if a novelist named Nightingale can't reflect on this, who can? The nightingale, as Professor Mowbray pointed out, is an Old World bird; it has never been seen in Newfoundland, in what he so kindly called "Nightingale Country." It reminded me of something I'd seen long ago in the Old World, in Edinburgh—a Scotch tartan blanket branded with the label "Burns Country," and, coincidentally, I thought at the time, young and arrogant that I was, that someday every patchwork quilt in Newfoundland might bear the label "Nightingale Country." Lest old acquaintance be forgot.

The New World, of course, is about speed, the conquest of space and time—cars, trains, planes, spaceships, computers, cellphones, satellite radio and TV. But literature, the writer's voice, the voice of the nightingale, has been conquering space and time for a long, long time. *The Odyssey*, the *Inferno*, *Don Quixote*, *King Lear*, *Bleak House*, *In Search of Lost Time*, *Ulysses*—*The Odyssey* come round again. The conquest of space and time is child's play in the realm of literature.

What, then, is literature, and what is the literary calling? What is literature's place in today's world? Why do we persist in writing it? Big questions, and ones that perhaps are only asked inside hallowed halls like these. What makes a person do what I do? I don't profess to know the answer for certain, but I have an answer for today, and I will probably have a different one tomorrow.

The only calling ever mentioned to us when we were young was the collar or the veil. But I heard another voice, and it was from much farther away. *I heard a voice; I heard voices.* It was my namesake's voice, given human form by the writers that I read, that I heard, sometimes from way across space and time, across the centuries, the millennia.

What is the place of literature now in the writing and publishing *industry*, as it's called, the literary marketplace, and the groves of academe—the whole book-based commercial/academic/industrial complex? This includes not just writers, the primary producers—more about them in a moment—but publishing houses, agents, editors, accountants, marketers, lawyers, book distributors, bookstores, libraries, arts councils, writers' associations, festivals, readings, prizes, poetry faceoffs, battles of the books, Canadian Literary Idol (it's coming!), university departments of literature and creative writing—a humongous hive, a perfervid anthill of industry that is three parts showbiz circus and one part dignified, serious literary pursuit, though how much dignity there is left in the whole enterprise is difficult to say.

Now, as you all know, we've had a cod moratorium here for more than a decade, and the fish still show no sign of returning. I heard that more than fifty thousand jobs were lost, the largest layoff in Canadian history. What would happen, I ask you, if we had a manuscript moratorium, if the primary producers stopped working, stopped producing fodder—manuscripts—for the gigantic literary machine I just described? I will here and now, before your very eyes, transform myself into the Honourable so-and-so, Minister of Canadian Culture, and declare—empty threat!—a manuscript moratorium. But what would be the result?

I will tell you. I will, on this most auspicious occasion, dispense with all humility—and all dignity perhaps—and, at the risk of being judged indiscreet, arrogant, lacking in gratitude and insulting to my hosts; at the risk of fouling the nest, I will point out—it is no exaggeration to say this—that this whole busy literary hive, edifice, infrastructure, vertical mosaic or horizontal patchwork quilt, whatever you want to call it, would no longer exist. It would topple, flatten, combust, disintegrate, deconstruct, unravel, vanish into thin air, without the primary producer, the writer, and his humble manuscript—his novel, in my case—just as the Newfoundland cod fishing industry could never have existed without the primary producer, the fisher, and the now endangered cod. This may seem obvious; but how often is it publicly, or even privately, acknowledged?

Their take, their monetary profit—the writer's and the fisher's—from the whole enterprise is, was, roughly equal—a few cents per pound, a few cents per word. The fisher may have gotten even more. Safe to say, I'll never have to hire an investment counsellor. Why does he do it then, the writer? (I can't speak for the fisher.) We are back to my theme—the literary calling—and to answer the question let us consider fish, or a type of fish, one that I've never been able to eat—I'm allergic to it—the bivalve, or mollusc. You'll know them as clams, mussels, scallops, oysters, which can produce a pearl. And pearl fishers, or farmers, as they've become—as cod fishers no doubt will as well—produce so-called cultured pearls.

If, for a moment, you can think of the great literary industry I've described simply as pearl harvesting, or pearl farming, then the writer is the mollusc, and his manuscript, the pearl inside it. If a foreign object—a piece of grit—happens to get inside the two halves of the mollusc's shell, it will act as a nucleus. The mollusc will coat it with a protective layer of nacre, which is what the inside of the creature's shell is made of, and produce, after two to six years, a beautiful pearl (coincidentally, about the same range of time it takes to produce a book).

But most pearls produced today are cultured pearls; a foreign object is artificially implanted in the bivalve. They are the equivalent of farmed fish, as are most novels, some critics say, the result of universal art care, state subsidy, creative-writing farms, and so on. What about natural pearls? (That is where the literary calling truly comes in.) No nucleus needs to be introduced, no starter, no foreign object; the starter, the piece of grit, settles in naturally. Molluscs create pearls all by themselves, but rarely a gem, one perfect enough for jewelry. Perhaps one in a million. Think of this pearl as a work of art, a work of literature in the purest sense, and let us ask ourselves: what is the calling, the need, the desire, the impulse, the compulsion, the driving force that produces it? For it is the writer's own tissue that is used to create the book, as it is the mollusc's own tissue that is used to create a natural pearl.

What is this bit of grit in the writer's soul and what is the writer's response to it? First, let's start with what it isn't. It is not merely an irritant, as it might be for the mollusc, and writing is not an act of revenge, anger, bitterness, resentment, or aggression. Writing is not about martyrdom, being famous for your pain, your suffering, your angst. It is not about fame at all. It is not a cure, consolation, therapy, or balm. It is not about messages, beliefs, and ideas, psychological and philosophical ruminations on what this grit might be—what's wrong with you and the world. If you have an *idea* for a novel, a well-known, anti-CanLit curmudgeon once remarked, lie down until you feel better. Writers have beliefs, but we don't really believe in them.

I could go on, but I won't. (I think I hear my banjo thrumming.) You want to know what it is, not what it isn't, which brings me back to my dear mentor, Dr. Noel Eagleton, who said, professed, that literature is a way of loving the world. Perhaps he had in mind more the reading than the writing of it, but writing,

I submit—and remember, children, sons and daughters, this is just Polonius speaking—writing is also a way of loving the world. No more, no less. The world is hard to love sometimes, but it's even harder to hate. "What thou lovest well remains,/the rest is dross," said Ezra Pound.

And as you go out into this world now, as you "launch out into the deep," as our university's motto instructs us to do, with whatever knowledge and wisdom your time here has given you, remember this as well. (It has nothing to do with writing—or perhaps everything!) And this is the real Polonius, so to speak, advising you this time, good counsel to any departing son or daughter:

> This above all: to thine own self be true,
> And it must follow as the night the day,
> Thou canst not then be false to any man.

Or woman.

Our revels, Frostian and Shakespearean, now are ended. I'm sure I hear my banjo thrumming. Thank you all very much.

2: THE SOUTHSIDE PRESS

Kevin and I had hastened to his favourite drinking spot, though by default, he made clear, the no-name bar of the new Newfoundland Hotel. A good fit, he said, for his literary reputation these days. All his favourite bars were gone, long gone, including the bar of the old Newfoundland Hotel, the Admiral's Keg. He recalled the others, with nostalgic pique, and I fondly remembered a few of them myself. Though I had lived in St. John's for only seven years, having happily escaped the confines of small-town life, I remembered them as some of the best years of my life. It was the end of the sixties—1967 to 1974, to be exact—the famous decade that began at the far western bookend of the North American continent, the legendary San Francisco, but arrived late and finished late at the far eastern bookend of St. John's. Another "City of Legends," as the signs and tourist brochures referred to it now, which once included some legendary bars, though cannabis, not alcohol, was the drug of choice in those heady, carefree days.

"There was Milt's," Kevin said, beginning to count on his fingers, but his left-hand index stayed hooked on the little finger of his right, and he merely tugged on it as he made his list, "the Tudor, the Stardust, the Cochrane, Bridget's, the Grad House, and the original bar without a name—Kearney's—where you had to ring the doorbell and wait, until Kearney himself found time from tending bar or performing—he played the bass—to appear at the door and size you up through the teardrop windows, which made his mournful, hangdog face look even sadder. If he liked the look of you, you got in;

if not, he would disappear without a word. If the place was full, he wouldn't come to the door at all. Kearney was shorter than his stand-up bass, but he was a tough old guy. He would shut the place down if he smelled the wrong kind of smoke."

"Where *was* that bar?" I asked.

"In a house on King's Bridge Road, just up from the hotel. It looked like Kearney's living room. He might not even have had a licence."

"Oh, yeah…I remember that place. He stocked a lot of European beer."

"Yeah…you had fancy tastes even then."

He poured the last of his Old Stock and stared at me with that ironic, pursed-lip look, as if always holding a grin in check.

"James," he said, "to get back to this honourary degree thing, and your little speech. As I said, I'm beginning to worry about you. It's too late now, but don't forget: my good friend You Know Who had the good sense to refuse. And not only that, but to keep quiet about it."

"Jesus, Kevin. It's not exactly the poisoned chalice, is it?"

"No, I suppose it could have been worse. You could have been annointed by Oprah, prelude to a belletrist shunning, or you could have won the Leacock Medal for Humour. If you don't watch it, you might yet, and they'll have you touring with Stuart McLean. Our way of loving the world, eh? I thought you were going to give us the papal blessing there today. I thought you were going to make the sign of the cross over us at the end. Jesus, I said to myself, he's finally listened to his mother and taken the collar after all."

"You didn't love it, did you," I said, echoing Kevin's standard confrontational response to anyone who was in any way equivocal, lukewarm, or evasive in their response to a new book of his. "You didn't love my little speech. They were children, Kevin, going out into the cold cruel world. What did you expect me to say? You think I should have told them the truth, warned them off the writing life? 'Writing and publishing books, kiddies, is like sending letters to the North Pole at Christmas. There is no Santa Claus.' Suffer the little children, the suckling saints, you cold-hearted son of a bitch. Besides, it was great fun being Polonius for a day. What a great role! I revelled in it, as Ol' Frosty would say."

"I think you were serious, James. I'd say thirty-plus years of that Ontario humidex has made you soft in the head. You weren't equipped to handle it. You need gradual, sustained exposure from birth, like you do to viruses, bacteria, and parasites—not to mention publishers. I see you even found a way of loving that virus we were both exposed to all those years ago. Suffer that little fucker. I caught a glimpse of him at the reception, stuffing the hors d'oeuvres into his fat face. Luckily, I was on the other side of the room. When I see him I get the same feeling of anal angst as I do before my annual DRE—the original digital technology, as my doctor calls it. So Grandy's reissuing your first book, is he? Now that you're famous—a famous *Canadian* novelist. Now that no one but Olympic curlers and Canadian idols will give him anything to *publish*. I use the word loosely. Jesus…when I think about it…I knew from the start he couldn't be trusted."

"Don't think about it, Kevin…please," I said, as he drained his glass and planked it on the table.

"Another one?" he said, his hands gripping the armrests of his chair, ready to propel himself toward the bar, to gather more fuel for the fire in his head.

"Sure…why not," I reluctantly agreed, knowing that refusal was futile, and comforted by the thought that the Bed o' Roses was just a five-minute walk away. Tomorrow I would be moving to our friend Grim McGillvray's vacant house, which was on the other side of town.

⁐ ⁐

Almost lockstep with me and my seven novels—my seven dwarfs, as I like to call them—Kevin had published seven books of poetry, all with different publishers, and all with different degrees of conflict and distress. His first experience, however, with Alonzo "the Virus" Grandy, had been the most heavily fraught, had embittered him, it seemed, at an early age, and made it impossible for him to get on well with any publisher thereafter.

Grandy had published Kevin's first book of poems, *The Rags of Time* (the title from a poem of John Donne's), at about the same time as *The Ropewalk* (my so-called Newfoundland novel, though there was another, more obscure one). Young and naive though I was, I had insisted on a written contract with Grandy and the Southside Press, and finally received a sketchy, one-page document. Kevin, on the other hand, had signed on with a mere handshake, a nod and a wink.

Yes, he looked like someone who could never be trusted. That was how I myself had felt about Alonzo Grandy when I gave him my first novel more than thirty years ago. From a hillside perch on the Southside Road, there was a panoramic view of the city and the harbour from the big bay windows of the three-storey heritage house that was the home of the Southside Press. With three turrets on the roof, ornamental, wrought-iron fences over the eaves, and the tri-colour nationalist flag, the Pink, White, and Green—"the Renaissance flag," as Grandy called it, and he claimed to be the first to revive it—drooping from a cantilevered flagpost over the front door, a Newfoundland Historic Trust Heritage Award plaque on the doorframe, the house looked like a misplaced, fortified mini-castle. I had delivered my manuscript in person to the sculpin-like figure sitting on his tail behind a huge inlaid oak desk that squatted on an authentic Persian rug, on a burnished oak hardwood floor, in a spacious, high-ceilinged, ivory-white room with spotlit paintings all around the walls. Was he running an art gallery or a publishing house? I wondered. Perhaps Art was what they talked about at the book fairs, instead of what you would expect.

"We never talk about *books* at those things," he had pompously remarked during our very brief meeting, in reference to the Frankfurt Book Fair, from which he'd just returned that week. No publisher, he suggested, would be so gauche as to talk about *books*. The corollary, of course, was that no one but me would be so gauche as to assume that they did. What *do* you talk about? I was about to politely and meekly inquire, but the phone rang in the middle of the conversation, leaving me to browse, for ten minutes or more, through the Southside Press books arrayed conveniently in front of me on the desk, and I forgot to ask what they *did* talk about, not that I was even vaguely interested. Perhaps cocaine or porn—we'd heard rumours. Or "estates." Grandy had been an "estate agent," as he used to call himself, adopting the more prestigious, or pretentious, British term, before he became a publisher.

There was something—a certain tone, one that didn't need a finely tuned ear—about the way Grandy pronounced the word *books*, that said *units*, that said *product*, that said everything I felt—suspected, distrusted, feared—about this man, my prospective publisher. In the way Grandy said *books*, I heard the hostile hiss of a snake—though the man looked more like a fish than a snake—an unconcealed, if perhaps unconscious and impersonal, contempt for the objects of my abiding, uncompromising, yea, everlasting, love. And Kevin's as well. Especially Kevin's. Parents and foster parents had failed him. Friends, girlfriends, teachers, so-called Christian brothers and priests had failed him. But books never had, and he was sure they never would.

My gut feeling about Grandy had been confirmed when he failed to publish my second novel, on which the mini-contract for the first had specified an option, after holding on to the manuscript for over two years and saying several times that it was "perfect," needed no revisions at all, and was being "readied for the press." Even now, after he had reissued my first book and it would soon be given a special launch—it had never been launched at all the first time round—with hors d'oeuvres and drinks and a glitterati of guests (or at least this is what Grandy had told me), I didn't feel much different, and this conversation with Kevin wasn't helping any.

∾ ∽

When he came back from the bar, however, a bottle of Old Stock in one hand and an India in the other, I was glad that, for the moment, there were other things on his mind.

"You've heard about The Rooms, then, have you?" he said. "Our new arts and culture *mausoleum*."

"Yes, there was a piece about it in the *Globe*, and a photograph. At first I thought they'd bought another one of those Expo 67 pavilions. You know…the ones Smallwood bought to use as arts and culture centres across the Island.

It reminded me of Habitat 67—remember that? A building made of concrete blocks piled one on top of the other."

"Yeah…architectural brutalism, they called it, and they do have that in common. But The Rooms is all triangles instead of blocks, and it's a new building, though based on so-called heritage architecture—fishing rooms, large sheds, on stages. Habitat 1667 or whenever. *Our Place. My Place. Your Place*—as The Rooms Corporation marketers put it. But try having a book launch in there. There's *no place* for that. Everything is a money-grubbing corporation these days, even the church. Anyway…the reason I asked…I figured you must have heard about The Rooms because of this manuscript moratorium you announced this afternoon, though you made no mention of it in your little speech."

"What do you mean?"

"There's no *library* in there, you may have read in the *Globe*. *No place* for books. I thought that might be where you got your bright idea. Fits right in with their long-range plan, on a go-forward basis, as they say in the government press releases. Why produce books if there's nowhere to put them."

"No, I don't recall reading anything about that. Bit of an oversight, to say the least."

"I'd say no one even thought about it, though there's enough empty space in that building to host the Calgary Stampede. There are new libraries going up all across the country, but it's the last thing they think about here. The Rooms has art gallery *rooms* for scrawling novels on walls—you should ask for an exhibit in there—archives *rooms* for merchants' ledgers and diaries, museum *rooms* for rotting dories and stuffed puffins, but no library *rooms* for books. No *rooms* at The Rooms for us. And I forgot: no *rooms* for theatre either. I hear Grim has a new show on the go. He doesn't perform much these days, but when he does he's still entombed in the Basement Theatre in the old Arts and Culture Centre—forty years old but still not christened—where you gave your performance this afternoon. You were lucky to be upstairs on the main stage. The main public library is in there as well, but half the books are stored in the basement, and it's leaking like a sinking ship.

"But to get back to our man Grandy…Have you forgotten what he put us through? And you're giving him your book *again?*"

"The Devil made me do it, Kevin, i.e., my agent. Grandy sent him a letter."

"A prick agent, obviously. Fire the fucker. Didn't he let you know?"

"I think he did, but I had other things on my mind at the time. My marriage was falling apart, for one thing, and there seemed to be one family crisis after another."

"Well, let's remind ourselves what Alonzo Grandy is capable of. Lest we forget…"

⟅⟆

Lest we forget, indeed. I'd heard this war story so many times, I felt almost as if it were mine, and, in a way, I suppose it was. But I had dealt with Alonzo Grandy at a distance—I'd left Newfoundland before my first book came out—and Kevin had dealt with him, literally, face to face.

I had first heard all the pathetic details of Kevin's confrontation with Grandy, his almost physical tête-à-tête, in the fall of 1977, when Kevin had stayed with me in my bedsitter on Sunnyside Avenue in Toronto. It was a tale oft repeated in other seasons of other years—if with subtle and revealing variations—and I had perhaps created a conflated version of my own. Time and distance had not dulled the unpleasant memory of my dealings with Alonzo Grandy, but I had sequestered it, perhaps, as is my wont, along with Kevin's much more traumatic experience, in the hold of my imagination. For possible future use. Had my friends' lives become mere *material* for my sport?

Kevin's war with Grandy had started with a simple query about royalties, about a year after his book had come out. There were no royalties, Grandy had told him on the phone, because there were hardly any sales—only about three dozen copies from a print run of five hundred. He said he'd given away the same number for publicity and promotion. What was worse, though, Kevin said, even more hurtful than the sales figures, which he later found out were false, was that Grandy had implied that he'd done him a big favour by publishing his book. It would advance his academic career, he said. Now he'd have a better chance for tenure. Kevin reminded him that he was a poet, first and foremost. He wasn't interested in an academic career. He pointed out that he was just a sessional. He didn't even have a permanent job, let alone a tenure-track one.

Grandy had offered him some freelance editing work, generous fees for manuscript evaluations, etcetera. The work did indeed come along in due course, but without any money for that, either. The crux came when a friend of Kevin's just happened to mention that he'd seen two of his poems in a new high school literature anthology that his son was using. Now, Kevin didn't know much about the business of publishing, but because of his teaching experience, limited though it was, he suspected that educational publishing—expensive textbooks for schools and universities, a captive market—was probably the most lucrative of publishing ventures, at least for publishers.

Kevin was working as a chicken catcher at the time—a dirty, exhausting job—there being no teaching jobs available, and he was under a lot of stress. This time he didn't bother making any telephone calls. Like any self-respecting virus, Grandy was always ready for business, but dormant—"unavailable"—when the secretary's "May I ask who's calling?" query flushed out unimportant solicitors. (It had taken weeks, if I recall, to secure my one and only "appointment" with Grandy.) He didn't bother writing any letters. Grandy's assistant always responded evasively to those. He found a used copy of the anthology he'd been told about at the Second Page bookstore—the manager made most of her money from textbooks as well, she told him, after he'd very discreetly inquired—checked to make sure that his poems were in it, and then drove right on down to the Southside Press on the backside of the harbour. A pustule on the backside, he used to say. He drove right on down and he marched on up the steep steps to the solid-wood door with the large, old-fashioned knocker instead of a bell. He pulled open the door and marched up the stairs to the second floor, past the secretary and her high-pitched objections ("Excuse me, sir"), up the stairs to the third floor, past another sentry ("Excuse me, sir"), and straight into Grandy's inner sanctum.

The secretary followed him in ("Excuse me, excuse me"). Grandy was talking on the phone, but he put his hand over the mouthpiece.

"*Kevin*," he said, with a big disarming smile, as if he'd been expecting him, as if Kevin were the one and only person he wanted to see just then. Kevin guessed that he was always expecting someone like him, someone who'd been wronged, and more than once, and he wasn't going to take it any more. And this way of disarming him—faux graciously making him feel as if he were part of the inner circle of the Southside Press's publishing world—to his own guilty dismay, vain collaborator that he was, had always worked. But it wasn't going to work this time—he wasn't called TKO for nothing.

Grandy gestured him to the antique wingback chair in front of the antique desk, waved the secretary away, but continued talking on the phone. Kevin ignored the chair and thumped the heavy anthology down on the desk in front of Grandy's face. He winced and drew back but kept right on talking. Kevin turned away and began to stomp around the room. Everything looked the same as it did the last time he was there, in early December, looking for pre-Christmas charity. But now there were different paintings on the walls. Last time it was Pratts; this time, Blackwoods.

After touring the Blackwood exhibit—all icy death and disaster and mourning—Kevin's mood was now even blacker, and he forced himself to sit in the wingback chair and fold his arms straightjacket-like to control and comfort himself. Just as he was beginning to gather his hostile thoughts, to consider what he would do in the next few minutes if Grandy didn't get off the fucking phone, he ended the conversation quite abruptly, though with his usual jovial insincerity, after a long stretch of quite antagonistic talk.

"All right, then, my good man, we'll have to leave it at that," Grandy said. "I've got an important visitor here right now. Yes, that'll be fine. You're good as gold. Talk to you tomorrow."

Then, even more jovially and insincerely, he said, "Kevin, my boy, what can we do for you? That goddamn federal gov'ment crowd are as tight-lipped as a nun's cunt. And the province still hasn't come through with a cent. We'll be down the tubes within a year if this keeps up. Why did I ever get into this business? I keep asking myself. Anyway, you don't want to hear about any of that. What's on your mind?"

Kevin had heard this poor-mouth routine so often he felt like breaking into an impersonation right then and there. And what was on his mind felt so heavy that, instead of wasting his time trying to articulate it, he wanted to just physically lift it off and drop it like an anvil right on the head of the lying, scheming son of a bitch who sat in front of him.

"This anthology," he said, as calmly as he could, but giving the book he'd dropped on the desk a threatening rap with his knuckles, "when did it come out? It's got two of my poems in there."

"Yes, two beauties," Grandy said. "From your book. 'The Poet in the Bank (Poor Tom)' and 'The Rags of Time.' I picked them myself. I told the selection committee they had to go in. It might help your sales a bit. I don't know why that book's not selling. But, you know…poetry. Even T. S. Eliot had to work in a bank. I love that Eliot poem, by the way. Masterful. When I read it again I realized you were writing about yourself."

"Well, no one told me they were going in," Kevin said, refusing to be distracted by Grandy's fawning pleasantries. "Shouldn't I have been told about that? And I haven't been paid."

"You will, you will," Grandy said. "We're sending out letters, contracts. This is just a pilot. The textbook won't actually be out till the fall. Everyone will get paid then."

"This looks like a book to me," Kevin said. "I bought it in a second-hand bookstore. A friend's son is using it in school. I need the money now. I don't have a teaching job this term. You owe me two thousand dollars for editing work. And I'm going to sell that poetry book myself, at readings and such. I want a tour."

"Well, I wish we could do something for you there," Grandy said. "But the money just isn't available. You and me, Kevin, the poets and the publishers, we're financing this fuckin' renaissance they're talking about all on our own. Not with money, but with blood, sweat, and tears, talent and time. We're the main investors in all this. But if gov'ment won't put some capital into it soon, it's going to go tits up just as fast as it began. This is *our time*, Kevin, our

1922—*Ulysses, The Waste Land, Remembrance of Things Past,* all in the same year. That's when Pratt's first book was published—I'm reissuing it this year. I've got Duley, Janes, and Horwood being readied for the press. There was your book last year…and Nightingale's. We're on a roll."

It was a clever strategy, and a new one—us against them, co-opting Kevin in the great honourable struggle for Art—but just another variation of the same old game of evasion and deceit, nothing he hadn't heard before, and he wasn't going to be taken in this time. There was *capital* all around him, he noted, as he considered his next move: thousands of dollars' worth of paintings on the walls; antique furniture; a real Persian rug, from Morocco, on the floor (Grandy had once bragged about it to him); a three-storey heritage *estate* worth a million or more (acquired for a song when he was in real estate, no doubt, and perhaps he still was); and a brand new BMW in the driveway. Not to mention free, taxpayer-funded vacations to European book *schmoozes* to get away from all this tedious talk about books of poetry that didn't sell and to avoid confrontations with aggrieved poets walking in off the street looking for actual money for their poems.

"Pratt's book was *1923*," Kevin said. "And didn't Proust *die* in 1922? The *Reader's Digest* was first published that year, too. Maybe that's why he died… but never mind. Listen, Grandy, *I need that money now*. I'm behind in my rent. As I told you, I don't have a teaching job right now. Want to know what I'm doing to pay the bills? I'm working as a chicken catcher—the late-night catching crew. A thousand chickens an hour is our quota. Want to know what that's like? You want a job description? Eight hours a night in a cesspool of a barn grabbing squawking, flapping, clawing, biting, pissing, and shitting chickens by the legs and flinging them into cages for shipping to slaughterhouses. Piss and shit all over you, mouthfuls and eyefuls of it. I've got a permanent case of pink eye—here, take a look. They are absolute shit-launchers, those chickens. But there's not half as much shit flying around in that barn as there is in this room. *I want a cheque before I go.* Two hundred dollars for the poems in the anthology, two thousand for the editing, and I want an advance, retroactive, for my book of poems, which I'm going to take on the road and sell myself."

"Kevin, my good man," Grandy said, "as I said before, there's no money in the till right now. I'm waiting on those gov'ment grants. I just got off the phone—you heard me. They won't even tell me if the money *might* be forthcoming."

Kevin jumped up out of his chair. "I don't give a sweet fuck about your grants," he shouted. "I got to live—like everyone else. I need some money and I want it now. How about this?" he said, making for one of the paintings on the wall. He lifted it off, only to find that it was attached by a heavy metal wire.

"Be careful there, my son," Grandy shouted, standing up but staying behind his desk. Kevin tried to put it back but couldn't, so he just let it dangle from the wire.

"How about this, then?" he said, reaching down with both hands and grabbing the fringed edge of the Persian rug, which he rolled up all the way to the wingback chair. "How about this chair? Looks like an antique." He tipped it over and out of the way, then reached in over the desk and grabbed Grandy by his fisherman's cable-knit oatmeal cardigan and looked right into his big, fishy, bloodshot eyes. For a moment, he even considered head-butting him in the face, cracking his conniving con man's conk, but just as quickly thought better of it, suddenly became aware of what he was doing—or what he was capable of doing—and simply pushed him back into his swivel chair.

Kevin rushed out the door, past the empty desk and down the stairs. It was lunchtime, and the secretary on the second floor was gone as well. When he reached the first floor, he didn't go out through the front door but on down to the basement, where he knew the stockroom was located, having been down there once before.

Eric Stoyles, the stockroom clerk and delivery man, had shown him around one hot afternoon the previous summer, when he had gone down on his way out to pick up the dozen free copies of *The Rags of Time* that his handshake contract had allotted him—a baker's dozen, actually, for he had taken an extra one. Eric hadn't bothered counting. He wrapped them in heavy brown paper and tied it up with twine, a packaging method he'd learned as a store clerk at Foster's Famous Sausages, he said, where he'd worked for ten years before getting a job at the Southside Press, which was just up the road from his house.

Eric was not there this time, probably gone to lunch, but being familiar with the layout of the stockroom, Kevin quickly found his book on the two-foot-deep shelves all around the walls. He wondered if Grandy had called the cops, but he doubted it. That might mean that his books—his ledgers, that is—would be examined by the court, and he surely wouldn't want that. Kevin's car was in the parking lot at the side of the house, and the stockroom loading door led out to the lot. He filled one large, empty box with his books and carried it outside, found a place for it among the junk in the trunk and went back inside to get the rest. Counting them later, he discovered—no surprise—that Grandy had lied to him again. Out of a print run of 500 copies, there were only 300 books left. With a baker's dozen for him and three dozen for reviewers, *maybe*, that meant that about 150 books had been sold. He had visions of a national bestseller—500 copies of a book of poetry, he was told—and he was eager to get the show on the road.

3: DOOMS OF LOVE

There was another story that Kevin had told me even more often than that one—the genuinely pathetic Funeral Home Saga, as I thought of it—but one that I had also taken too lightly, until, in my desultory reading, I accidentally came across a rather lengthy essay entitled "The Wound and the Bow." It expounded a theory of childhood trauma as suffered by sensitive literary types—a *very* sensitive group, I grant you, Marcel Proust perhaps being the most notorious example, "a man born without a skin," as one of his friends had described him. He had spent half his life in bed, in a cork-lined room, with the windows closed and the curtains drawn, but, nevertheless, had found enough time to write one of the masterpieces of world literature (as even Alonzo Grandy was aware).

In late September of 1977, Kevin was on the second leg of his cross-Canada tour in his Ford Falcon—the Visa Tour, as he first called it, but changed its name to the Keep-on-the-Sunnyside Tour after he left my place on Sunnyside Avenue and moved west for the third leg of the journey. I had been living in Toronto for about three years by then, and I arranged two readings for him in my west-end neighbourhood, one at a café that had an informal poetry-reading series and provided a bottomless cup of coffee as payment to the poet, and another at my local library. Kevin had sold only two or three books at each event, but seemed cheerful and optimistic nonetheless. Alonzo "the Virus" Grandy was, geographically, at least, if not emotionally, far behind him; not out of his system, so to speak, just dormant. And though still loaded down with a large bundle of *The Rags of Time*, Kevin was happy to be on the road, on the sunny side of the road, to bestseller glory.

But he would become much less sunny, increasingly antagonistic, gloomy, and bitter as the years went by, and as I saw him only sporadically, every few years, I was always surprised by the intensity and depth of it. I could hardly look at the expression on his face in the photograph on the French flap of his most recent book, a picture not just of doom and gloom, but of *ressentiment*, that most ignoble of emotions, as Nietzsche called it. Could it be, I thought, that Thomas Kevin Keough had been a victim of the Wound? A propensity toward darkness of spirit had been exacerbated by the emotional turmoil of his early years, and perhaps by one painful experience in particular. I was sure, though, that Alonzo Grandy, despicable as he was, had very little to do with it.

Though the argument of "The Wound and the Bow" seemed like such a simplistic notion, it had been advanced by one of my favourite writers, Edmund Wilson—a *critick*, mainly, but I forgave him for that. The man could write, he was most discerning, and could turn his hand to anything. He had written one of the best histories of the Russian Revolution, for example, and he even knew what was going on in *Finnegans Wake*, a different kind of revolution, which had only made sense to me as *music*, when I heard an Irish voice perform it.

But was it really possible, I wondered, that one single painful experience at an early age, an emotional trauma, a humiliating hurt, could damage a person for life, and, for an especially sensitive person, be the source of—inform, as the critics say—an entire oeuvre? Charles Dickens, a veritable socialite compared with Marcel Proust, had been the subject of Wilson's major case study. He had suffered the Wound, according to Wilson, when, at the tender age of twelve, he had spent six months working in a blacking warehouse because his father, along with the rest of his family (a common practice at the time), was living in a debtors' prison.

It was a period of utter despair for the young man, said Wilson. He felt completely abandoned and unloved. His humiliating work, pasting labels on blacking bottles, was on conspicuous display for all to see in the window of the warehouse. And even though his father received an inheritance later that year and got out of prison, he let Charles go on working in the warehouse. After his father finally decided to take him out and send him back to school, his mother still wanted to keep him there. "I never shall forget, I never can forget," wrote Dickens, darkly, to his first biographer, John Forster.

Perhaps Kevin couldn't, or wouldn't, forget either. *His* blacking warehouse had been a funeral home. He passed it every day on his way to school. It had a big clock on the front, high up beneath the eaves, which reminded him that he was late for school. He was always late for school. Kevin would one day write a poem about that clock, which marked the slow, sad steps of his early years. It was the title poem of his first collection, in fact, *The Rags of Time*.

But Kevin didn't walk on past the funeral home on his way back home in the afternoon; he would always stop in, he told me, to get something to eat. He was always hungry—that's what he remembered most clearly about his childhood, he said—and he knew that there probably wouldn't be anything to eat at home, and no one to cook it even if there were. His foster parents would usually be out drinking in the afternoon, nursing their own wounds. If they were at home, they would be drunk, having started drinking earlier in the day, or asleep, or fighting with each other, or beating the other foster kids. Kevin was only ten, two years younger than Dickens, when he began serving his time in the blacking warehouse, and he had spent twice as much time in there as Dickens had.

The funeral home was a happier place than home, and always a crowded, busy place. No one noticed him come and go, and downstairs, in the reception room, there was always food and drink: coffee always on, though he didn't drink coffee; milk in the fridge, though he hated milk; large bottles of apple and orange juice, which he guzzled; and big platters of sandwiches, sliced fruit, vegetables and dips, pickles, crackers and cheese. Seeing this ubiquitous spread at book launches in later years, he said, would make him want to throw up, or drink toxic amounts of *plonk blanc*—all that was ever on hand at these things— after which he would feel so sickened by everything that he would want to punch out some unsuspecting Mr. Jones, who didn't know what was happening, i.e., didn't know who Kevin was, and couldn't tell real poetry from plonk.

Though there was always food and drink in the reception room, it was usually empty; the mourners and the visitors stayed upstairs with the dead. There were big comfortable chairs to sit in and tables to sit at, but, always on his guard, Kevin usually ate standing up. Once in a while someone came down to have a coffee and a cigarette and pick at the food. They never seemed hungry, but always looked sad, he said. On one occasion, a bald man in a black suit had spoken to him in an unusually cheerful tone, though he looked even sadder than all the rest.

"How ya doin', young fella? You're all by yourself," he said.

The ordinary youth's cool disdain for the obvious was even more strongly felt by the keenly intelligent and sensitive young Thomas Kevin Keough, but he also had a small measure of empathy, even at ten. Not wanting to make the sad-faced man feel any sadder—he may have had a dead wife or mother or child upstairs—he didn't tell him the lie, or half-truth, that he always told the others, but sat silently on the edge of one of the big sofa chairs playing with the promotional odds and ends on the coffee table in front of him. There were pens and notepads and mini stand-up calendars, all with the name and address and a fuzzy black picture of the funeral home printed on them. The calendar had a mini-thermometer attached to it, and he liked to put his thumb on the red bulb at the bottom and watch the temperature rise. In later years, when he felt himself getting angry, this image always came back to him, and he would try to control himself by releasing the pressure of his thumb on the red bulb.

Occasionally, he took some of these promo items away with him, not only for his own use, but as Christmas, Valentine's, and Easter gifts for his teacher, Mrs. Pendergast, a kind-hearted woman who had no control of her class whatsoever, but who, nonetheless, never, ever abused the children as the other teachers did—yelled at them constantly, strapped and smacked them at times, made them kneel on the hardwood floor for hours.

There was talk about Kevin among the teachers in the staff room, and not just because of the gifts. A teacher who lived near the funeral home had noticed his frequent visits, and on one occasion had seen him leaving with food.

The motherly Mrs. Pendergast had taken him aside one day after school and told him this, had asked him if there was anything he wanted to tell her, but he had just stared at the floor and shook his head. She didn't pursue the issue. The school was in a neighbourhood where not-so-obvious signs of neglect and abuse, the mere shadows of bruises, were frequently ignored in the constant presence of the real thing.

Kevin had become very good at telling lies, and the lie, or half-truth, or version of the truth, he was fond of telling people in the reception room at the funeral home was that his father had just died of cancer and was lying in his coffin upstairs. If they asked for names, he would pretend to cry. The whole truth was that he wished it had been his father, instead of his mother, who had died of cancer when he was eight. Having decided he couldn't look after the boy on his own, his father had gone off to the mainland, ostensibly to find work, and left Kevin with an uncle and aunt, an older couple whose own children had grown up and left home. But, after about a year, it became clear to them that the father was not coming back, that the son was on his way to becoming a juvenile delinquent, and they gave him up as well. He ended up in an abusive foster home, the first of many, though not the worst. After that, he had always expected the worst, and soon began to feel that the sad, bald-headed man's statement of the obvious, "You're all by yourself," was a naked truth, an inadvertently profound philosophical dictum that applied not only to him but to life in general.

Kevin had survived the worst, the trauma of lost parents and the terrors of foster homes, along with the tedious and demoralizing lows of junior and senior high. No more kind teacher-mothers like Mrs. Pendergast of grade 6. In the high school library, however, where he spent half his time—it also served as a student detention centre, the rationale being that it was a place where the only thing they could do was read, something they hated doing— he discovered other books besides textbooks, and, above all, he discovered poetry. There wasn't much in there besides the centuries-old stuff that was in the textbooks—it would be a while before he learned to appreciate that—but there were two more recent books that caught his attention: an anthology of

First World War poetry (he felt as if he were fighting some kind of war himself) and an anthology of contemporary poets who had chosen, from their own work, one of their favourite poems and tried to relate the feelings and events that had given birth to it. Some of these accounts were long, some quite short, and the one that struck Kevin most strongly—even more than the poem itself—was this: "A favourite poem of mine because it fills a central moment in the middle of the journey of my life when I came to myself in a dark wood." Kevin would not, of course, have noted the reference to Dante's *Inferno* till much later in life, when he came upon a new edition of this anthology and gave me a copy as a gift; but even as a sixteen-year-old, he said, he felt he was in a dark wood in the middle of a journey. Was it possible, he wondered, that poetry could lead him out?

Kevin had stolen these two books from his high school library, but lost them somewhere along the way. In the contemporary anthology, all the poets had signed their names, some of which were in very bad handwriting, almost illegible, Kevin noted with pleasure—like his own, for which he had been chastised many times. There were brief biographies of the poets at the back. They were mostly Americans—it was a Time-Life book—but there were a few English and Canadian poets in there, and even a Newfoundland poet, E. J. Pratt.

Kevin was surprised to learn that there was such a creature. Pratt had spent most of his life in Toronto, however, competing with the mainlanders in the poetry game. It must have been a game or a competition of some sort, he thought, for there were prizes for the best poets. Pratt had won the biggest, perhaps the only, prize for poetry at the time, the Governor-General's Award, three times. Right across the text of Pratt's poem, "Silences," Kevin said, someone had silently scrawled, "E. J. Pratt could eat no fat," which he would use as the title of one of his own poems in later years.

E. E. Cummings was in there (still inhabiting the upper case at that time, even in his signature), along with Frost, Patchen, Larkin, Cohen, and Ferlinghetti (of the dark wood). Kevin would make a pilgrimage to his City Lights Bookstore in San Francisco.

Many years later, in the new edition of the poetry book that probably had changed his life, Kevin noted, in hindsight, some auspicious things: It had been published in *Alexandria*, USA; the ancient Egyptian town of that name had been the home of the mythical Alexandrian library. The anthology opened with Robert Frost's exhortative poem, "Choose Something Like a Star." The opening lines of Pratt's poem sprang out at him: "There is no silence upon the earth or under the earth like the silence under the sea;/No cries announcing birth..."

Kevin loved these lines from Frost's opening poem: "Say something to us we can learn/By heart and when alone repeat," which he did learn by heart and repeated not only to himself but to many an aspiring poet in his poetry workshops in later years, a plea, an exhortation of his own. Many other lines he learned by heart and repeated to himself. From Pratt, another exhortation: "But let silent hate be put away/for it feeds upon the heart of the hater." From Larkin, consolation: "They fuck you up, your mum and dad./They may not mean to, but they do." And Leonard Cohen's entire poem, "For Anne."

"I want to write and read poems filled with terror and music that change laws and lives," said Cohen in his bio, and though he didn't think that this was one of them, he was wrong.

But it was the poem by the capital Cummings that affected him the most, a poem about his father. Though Kevin really didn't understand the poem at all, he knew it was about *his* father, too. He repeated the opening line to himself like a mantra—"my father moved through dooms of love"—alive, as it seemed to be, with the mystic mantra *om*, like the magic words *open sesame*, until the poem did open, and he finally did understand it.

"Choose something like a star," said Robert Frost to the sixteen-year-old Thomas Kevin Keough.

And he did.

He became an avid reader, managed to survive high school, became a voracious, obsessive reader as he worked, day and night for three years, at a dozen odd jobs, and then, at twenty-one, entered university by the back door, as he put it, as a mature student, where he thrived. He earned a B.A. and an M.A. within five years (a thesis on e. e. cummings, who else). And during that time, he also became a poet.

⁓⁓

I had met Kevin in our first semester at university in the Arts Building basement cafeteria. He was three years older than me, and many years wiser. He was sitting all by himself at a table at lunch hour. As there were no free tables and his had two extra chairs, I asked if I could join him, and he graciously agreed. He was still in his lying stage (perhaps he would never leave it)—playful, harmless lies, however, better characterized as fictions, perhaps, impersonations. That first day he told me he was the son of a "fascist farmer," up at six every day doing the chores before he came to class, and again when he went home at the end of the day; a farmer's son who always carried a book in his back pocket—philosophy, usually—to console him as he milked the cows, fed the hens and pigs, mowed the hay, and shovelled manure out of the barn.

This was a true story, but not his—the short life story of the young man, a new friend, Graham "Grim" McGillvray, who would join us for lunch, and who needed no introduction when he finally did. He removed the talismanic object from his back pocket—a copy of Nietzsche's *Ecce Homo*, "Behold the Man," an autobiography, of sorts—and placed it on top of the textbooks he'd laid on the table. Other books that sometimes filled the back pocket, I was to discover, were Camus' *The Myth of Sisyphus* and Boethius' *The Consolation of Philosophy*, their paperback covers crudely laminated, front and back, with Scotch tape to keep the slop and milk and cowshit from soiling them. But McGillvray would go on to become an actor, an impersonator himself, rather than a philosopher, after side trips into the seminary, music school, and social work.

"Behold the man, the philosopher-king," Kevin said, offering me a clever, bold confession. McGillvray offered his hand and we introduced ourselves. The book and the sour-sweet smell of sweat and manure, however, had already introduced him.

McGillvray went on up and joined the cafeteria lineup to get something to eat. He never had much to say in those early days, though the stage would make him much more garrulous. To avoid the subject of Kevin's fabricated, or displaced, story, I picked up and perused *Ecce Homo*, subtitled *How One Becomes What One Is* and containing amusing chapter titles such as "Why I Am So Clever," "Why I Am So Wise," and "Why I Write Such Excellent Books." On the cover, an image of the philosophical sublime: a bare-headed, black-suited Nietzschean figure holding a walking stick and standing on some high black rocks with his back to the viewer looking out over a mist-covered, mountainous landscape, though the tall black rocks might have been crags, and the mist, waves crashing upon them. It reminded me of the view, out over an invisible, fog-covered bay, toward St. John's and Signal Hill from the rough shoreline of Cape Spear, where I'd gone one cold September evening for a bonfire and weiner roast during Frosh Week.

Kevin and Graham had met in this same cafeteria during Frosh Week, avoiding all frosh shenanigans, and I had met them there a few weeks later, in late September. We'd grown up, three solitudes, in farming, fishing, and mining towns—small, dismal, suffocating towns—all within an hour's drive of St. John's: Graham, in the farming community of the Goulds; Kevin, in the fishing community of Torbay, though he had lived in foster homes in St. John's from the age of nine or ten; and myself, in the iron ore mining town of Red Island. But this was the real beginning of our lives, doubtless each of us secretly felt, though it was only a vague sense of something we couldn't—and didn't need to, wouldn't want to—put into words: freedom, hope, promise, escape, joy. All of these and more. Over the next few years, we would become close friends—friends for life.

4: ARRIVALS AND DEPARTURES

Dear Grim,

This is a very interesting part of town. Not at all the prissy old neighbourhood you described in your letter. I'm already excited by heady hints of material here. At this very moment, as I write, your next-door neighbour, Beulah, is sitting on her front step crying her heart out. I went over and introduced myself to her and her husband, as you suggested, when I moved in last week, but it looked as if I'd interrupted a fight.

About nine o'clock this morning, a generic moving van—no logo on the side—backed up to the garage door of their house as I was having a coffee and looking out over the city through the big bow window in your living room. (Quite a view from here—and I love the woods at the back!) I thought it might be a robbery at first, but her husband—Nelson, is it?—jumped out of the cab. I recognized his ponytail and ear stud, which was catching the morning sun. He was wearing a beret and dark green grease-monkey coveralls. He rolled up the garage door and the back door of the moving van and began to load up: a large flat-screen TV, a lawn mower, a power saw, and a snow blower. (Yes, yes, I recognized the snow blower. I know—the army does that kind of work where I live.) That's all he took. He closed the doors, got back in the truck, and turned on the engine. Then he jumped out again and ran back into the house.

When he came out, he looked like someone else entirely. He had cast off the dull coveralls and in the morning sun was gloriously aglow in a sequined suit. It must have been a stage outfit of some kind, for he was carrying an amp and a blue electric guitar. I recalled a character I'd seen last year in a film at the TIFF, an aging gas station attendant-cum-mechanic, crazy with lust and loneliness, manning some anonymous, rundown station in the mythical American Badlands. Every day on his lunch hour he would meticulously wash the grease off his hands, paying particular attention to his fingernails, and remove his grease-monkey suit to reveal a sequined shirt and black leather pants. Then he would roll up the garage door, plug in his amplifier and blue guitar, and wring wailing desperate music out of it as the camera panned the blank landscape and the empty sky. On days when he didn't feel like playing the guitar, he threw darts at the red-circled ass of a naked woman sprawled on the shining hood of a red pickup truck on the garage's pin-up calendar. Her face, turned towards him, looked as desperate and lustfully forlorn as his own.

Nelson put his amp and guitar in the cab and drove off. Around noon a car pulled into the driveway, and Beulah, in a lavender bandana and matching long print dress, got out and after poking around in her rock garden for a few minutes—it covers the entire lawn, as you know, though there's not much blooming there at present—she went inside the house. About five minutes later she came back out and sat on the front step and began to wail as loudly as that Badlands guitar. She's sitting there still—she's been there for an hour or more—with her face in her hands, though I think she's stopped bawling. If not, like Borges' squonk, she'll soon dissolve in her own tears. I should go over and speak to her.

Last week I received my honourary degree. They asked for my acceptance speech in advance. They wanted to vet it, I bet. But there was nothing to stop me from changing it once I was up there at the podium. Kevin, predictably, said it was as fine a piece of fiction as anything I've yet produced. I'm enclosing a copy for your reading pleasure.

I'll have to come out for a visit when the weather warms up— July maybe.

Don't worry about the house—I was a stay-at-home father! I'm going over now to check on Beulah.

Best,
James

✑✑

"Hello again," I said quietly, approaching Beulah's front step. She raised her red face out of her hands with a startled intake of breath. Her wet eyes widened.

"I'm your new neighbour," I said quickly. "James Nightingale…we met last week."

She put her face down in her hands again and began to sob, choking sobs that would get sympathy from a wolf.

"Can I do anything to help?" I said.

She shook her head, but was still hiding her face.

I heard shouts and squeals behind me and turned to see the chaotic tribe of teens that I'd noticed for the past few days straggling down the street on their daily lunch-hour trek between their school and a small park nearby, where they tied the children's chain-link swings in knots. Right down the middle of the street they came, some of the girls horsey-back riding on the boys, other boys throwing themselves with death groans down on the pavement in front of them, trying to trip them up. A we-three of boys in the rear was suspiciously crouched around a cauldron of mischief in the middle of the street. Just as they ran off, a car approached, as if on cue, and braked to a halt as a small geyser erupted in front of it from a big plastic bottle of pop. A boy in the empty driveway of the house across the street was throwing a basketball up on the roof, aiming for the large open-topped chimney.

In the wake of this teenage circus troupe, a man with a dome of copper-coloured hair was pushing a supermarket cart toward us, leaning well forward over the brimming basket. It was May but he was wearing a winter coat, what looked like an army surplus coat, a greyish green garment with a big fur hood at the back, and so low to the ground that I couldn't see his feet. Looking intently into driveways and gardens, he stopped in front of Beulah's Honda and looked straight at me. His cart was full of cans and bottles, and, on the lower level, a big piece of rusty metal—a wheel rim, perhaps—was resting on a hubcap.

"Good day, sir," I said, repeating a greeting I'd recently picked up from my father on my daily visits to the Veterans' Pavilion. He had taken to calling me sir.

He didn't speak or smile, just turned his head and walked on, the sun catching his fiery and wiry red hair—naturally dreadlocked, it looked—and as I stared at the oil-stained back of his coat, I recalled where I'd once seen racks of coats exactly like it.

Someone had once said to me that everyone in Newfoundland knew someone, or knew someone who knew someone, who had died on the *Ocean Ranger*, that "unsinkable" oil rig, the largest of its kind in the world when it was launched in 1976. But this was one of those meatless bones of exaggeration thrown empathetically about, I thought at the time, to disperse, to ease, to help share, the shock and pain that everyone felt, and that no one would tactlessly make a bone of contention. Only fifty-six of the eighty-four men who had died in the disaster were Newfoundlanders, however. But perhaps it was true, I thought later on. If I myself had known someone who perished when the drill rig capsized that freezing mid-February night in 1982—I who had been long gone from this place when the tragedy occurred—then perhaps every Newfoundlander did.

We had been students together at university, but not really friends. He seemed to be enrolled in every English course that I was taking, though he was studying business, so perhaps he was only auditing them. He didn't hang out in the cafeterias but spent all his free time between classes selling clothes in his father's army surplus store—coats like the one I was staring at now— and he was expected to take over the store when he graduated. He sold the coats—a very cool item of clothing, then—at a deep discount to me and my friends. He later quarrelled with his father over this tedious family business that he never really wanted to be a part of, and, in 1981, took a job on the *Ocean Ranger*. When I saw his name among the list of dead, in a St. John's newspaper in a Toronto library a week or so after the event, I imagined him floating in the freezing sea in that ghostly, greyish green army surplus coat, there being no survival suits on board, it was reported. His body was the first to be recovered and brought ashore—only twenty-two of them were.

When I turned around, Beulah had gone back into the house.

An hour later she was at my door with a plate of cookies covered with waxed paper, as if I were the one who needed consoling. Hermits, she called them. She was still wearing her lavender bandana—it was a long time since I'd seen anyone in a bandana. She asked me to excuse her embarrassing be-haviour earlier, and I of course replied, feeling a bit embarrassed myself, that there was absolutely no need to mention it. I invited her in for coffee but she selected a sachet of herbal tea—the Organic Passion herbal infusion—from a dust-covered assortment pack that the students who'd been renting Grim's house may have left behind. "A magical blend of hibiscus flowers, exotic herbs, and natural tropical flavours," I read on the open packet while it was brewing and Beulah was using the bathroom. I had another coffee, my fourth that day, having long ago, in the workaday aftermath of my heedless youth, grown wary of any herb described as *magical*.

Sitting at Grim's round, rustic, cherrywood kitchen table, waiting for Beulah to come out of the bathroom, I remembered, as I leaned a bit too heav-ily upon it, that its thick heavy leaves were held up underneath by fragile sup-ports in the shape of small Celtic harps. A leaf had dropped into my lap one morning, along with my laptop. The harps were visible only from a distance. The best view was from the sofa in the living room, through the framed glass panes of the single French door, like a borrowed view in a classical Chinese garden. I wondered if this were by accident or design.

Grim's house had been here even before this relatively old subdivision— early 1960s, perhaps—had been built. It was a partly renovated farmhouse-type dwelling full of old, heavy, real-wood furniture—massive tables, side-boards, desks, bookcases, beds, couches, chairs, rockers, furniture stereo and TV, an organ fit for a church—all antique, from the look of it, but much in need of refinishing and refurbishing. He had bought this fully furnished house, along with an old house around the bay, also fully furnished, in a package deal about five years ago, after he had made a lot of money playing some bit part in a locally made network TV show, some hugely popular CBC cops-and-robbers series, and, simultaneously, as "the voice" for several seasons of government tourist ads promoting a Newfoundland that didn't exist, perhaps had never existed. "Shit work," as he frankly and succinctly described it—the Scots name McGillvray didn't mean "son of the servant of judgment" for nothing. At that point in his life, though he was still struggling to make a living as an actor, he decided that he never wanted to do that kind of work again.

So, knowing that that much money in so short a time would probably never come his way again, he decided to invest it in something permanent: property, real estate, a place to live, a townhouse and a house to get away from town, and last year he had rented the townhouse and got away for good. The country house was on Random Island, a large island with about a dozen communities, and he had refused to tell anyone which community it was in. "Looks a bit like Woody Point, but without the tourists" was all he would say.

Stage work was all that interested Grim, Shakespeare in particular, but even the dreaded "collectives" if there was nothing else to be had. He had often regaled me with tales of the multiple miseries that ensued when creating plays with others, the creation itself a form of guerilla theatre. The collective was a hollering, collaring, clashing, clanging gang of others—actors, writers, and everyone a director. A collaborative nightmare of creation, it seemed to me,

but exhilarating, no doubt, for the right sort of temperament. He stopped doing collective theatre when he turned fifty-two, and began to devote himself to
the Bard, who had died at fifty-two. He created a one-man show of soliloquies,
sonnets, and songs, which he'd been touring, off and on, for about five years.
Shakespeare in Carbonear, he called it, based on the conceit that the Bard had
spent his so-called lost years, in the 1580s, in Newfoundland.

If a Hungarian poet who wrote in Latin could find his way onto an
English ship leaving Plymouth and bound for Newfoundland, he said, then
why not an English one? Stephanus Parmenius had come over in 1583 on
one of the five ships sent out by Elizabeth I in search of "remote heathen and
barbarous lands, countries, and territories," commanded by Sir Humphrey
Gilbert and manned by musicians, dancers, and actors as well as shipwrights,
masons, and carpenters. Parmenius had described the embarkation in three
hundred lines of Latin verse, and in a letter to his friend in England, Richard
Hakluyt, who had introduced him to Gilbert, had reported that the remote
lands were indeed "nothing but desolation." Both Parmenius and Gilbert had
drowned when their ships were lost on the return voyage. *Quid Non,* "Why
Not," was Gilbert's family motto, and perhaps McGillvray's inspiration for his
Shakespearian conceit. Parmenius became Shakespeare, whose biography is
notoriously sketchy, in any event.

And when there was nowhere for him to perform, Grim wrote things for
the stage himself, most of which had never been produced. But there had been
some successes, in particular a one-man show, a desultory dramatic mono-
logue, or monologues, called "I Never Knew the Island Was So Beautiful,"
set in a gravel pit around a campfire, with the sounds of TCH traffic buzzing
and roaring behind them as several fishermen discoursed on Newfoundland's
past and future after the cod moratorium in 1992. It had enjoyed a two-week
run at a theatre in Toronto about eight years ago, and Grim had practically
lived at our house during that time. The theatre company had provided him
with a place to stay, but he preferred ours.

Beulah finally came out of the bathroom. She must have used it at least
three times in the hour or so that she was in the house. Anxiety, I thought,

or illness, perhaps. We took our cups and the plate of hermits out to the living room and sat side by side on the sofa. She removed her bandana and shook her hair back over her shoulders—a dramatic and erotic gesture, but innocent and unaffected all the same. Her hair was long and black, with only a few streaks of grey. There was no makeup on her face, though it looked oiled or creamed, moisturized in some way, with just a few wrinkles, like quotation marks, above and below the outer corners of her eyes.

"I have to apologize again," she said, "for the way I acted out there. Speechless, I thought I'd never be, but I was. Nels left everything but his toys, but I don't think he'll be back. Did you see his truck?"

"I saw a small white moving van earlier this morning. No name on it, though."

"Yes, that's his. He works as a mover. Day job," she said. "A mover," she repeated.

She had a quietly intimidating self-assurance, even at this emotionally difficult time. I was surprised that there was no feeling of awkwardness between us, complete strangers that we were. We might have been old friends discussing what had happened to someone else. She dipped her little finger in her teacup and put it between her lips, displaying the pink tip of her tongue, then sniffed the tea before sipping it.

"Graham told me you're a writer," she said. "I guess you like peace and quiet. He's had university students here since last September—a lot wilder than the junior highs you saw out there today. Drinking parties almost every weekend, bonfires in the backyard that the fire department had to put out. It's not the kids I worry about, though. It's the adults. Some of the neighbours are crazy—you could put them in a book! Howard LeBlanc, God rest his soul—the house down at the corner with the Japanese hedge—put himself in his grave worrying about those kids. He hired a security guard to stand in his front garden lunchtimes when they walked by. He had spotlights and cameras up in the trees connected to a bank of computers in the house."

She shook her head, took a deep breath and sighed.

"What did he do, Howard? What kind of work, I mean?"

"That was his work—computer technology. He taught courses up at the vocational school and had nothing to do after he retired except get himself all worked up over those kids. Day and night scanning those computer screens. A pop can on his grass would drive his blood pressure off the scale. He had his wife so upset all the time she wouldn't leave the house, even to work in the garden. I only got to know her—Lillian—after he died. She found him at his computer post one morning, dead of a heart attack."

"When was that?" I asked.

"Just last year, around this time. Now look at me—same thing's happened to me, in a way. But every cloud has a silver lining, as they say. Perhaps for me, too."

She was looking straight at me, and strangely, as she said this.

"When Howard died, Lillian was re-born," she went on. "Though she'd hardly been out of the house, let alone the country, in years, she and her daughter went on a holiday to Hawaii—a childhood dream of hers—only a month after the funeral. She sent me a post card from Waikiki, and brought me back a CD by a blind, seven-hundred-pound man playing a ukulele and doing "Somewhere Over the Rainbow"—like a singing telegram from heaven, at least that's how Lillian described it. She said it was playing everywhere she went in Hawaii, and she was sure it was a message from Howie, as she called him. She said she felt she was in heaven herself. If you don't want to hear everything you never wanted to know about Hawaii, you'd better keep to the other side of the street. No…she's sweet, but I think she lies in wait behind the hedge. She gardens every day and goes shopping every night. She got her driver's licence at sixty-five, joined a women's choir, a Scottish dancing troupe, and the Slym-Gym. But she's a heavy smoker, and she likes a drop of wine. Always has a glass out there when she's gardening. Howard was a nonsmoking, churchgoing teetotaler. They had four kids—all girls—but it seems that kids, teenagers especially, were like aliens to him."

After a long pause, she added, again looking closely at me: "The strange thing is, I think she loved him, in spite of what he did to her. You can live in a peanut shell if you have to."

Though Beulah was talking about Howard and Lillian, I suspected she was thinking about herself and Nelson. She had drifted into a reflective gaze.

"I have a teenager of my own," I said, perhaps to distract her. "That's one of the reasons I'm here, actually—to spend some time with her. She just finished her first year of university. Her name's Cecilia, Celia for short."

"How long are you planning to stay?" she asked.

"Maybe till the end of the summer."

"That's nice. I'd hate to live next to an empty house. Here I am now, at forty-five, daughterless *and* husbandless, not to mention fatherless and motherless. My daughter Tansy's in BC with her father, my first husband, doing a degree at UBC. She'll be nineteen in November…coming home for Christmas, I hope. She came home last Christmas, after her first semester, with her head shaved, a snake around her neck, and then she tells me she's a lesbian. C'est la vie."

"Celia will be nineteen in November, too," I said, not knowing what else to say.

"Well…we have something in common besides the street, as Nels used to say about the neighbours." She smiled and reached for one of her hermits.

She was hard to read, Beulah. This unexpected, rather sharp remark, though perhaps directed more at Nelson than me, seemed to hang in the air, threatening to disrupt what had felt like a very cordial conversation. I put it down to emotional distress, though she looked cool enough. She sniffed her tea again and took another sip.

"I don't usually eat my own baking," she said, as she dunked the hermit in her herbal tea. It was not a delicate madeleine, no, but it stirred a Proustian yearning all the same. Perhaps in her as well.

"Graham used to love hermits," she said. "It was the name, I think."

"Why are they called hermits?" I asked. "It sounds like the cookie version of poor man's bread—flour, salt, and water. But they taste like Christmas cookies—cinnamon, nutmeg, and cloves…"

"You're just like Graham," she said. "He was always asking questions about food. What's in this? What's in that? He's got health issues, of course. Late-onset diabetes, and other things besides. He wouldn't eat anything unless he knew what was in it. Unlike Nels, who'd eat cardboard without asking any questions. Graham would actually poke his finger into things that I'd bring over to him, lift off a piece of crust and look in. Make no wonder he never got married."

Though I realized that we were complete strangers, that I knew nothing about her, really, that Graham and our same-age daughters—and the street— were all we had in common, it was beginning to sound as if Graham were the one she was attached to, not Nelson, as if he were the one who had left her behind. I wondered if he had had anything to with their breaking up, if perhaps that was why he had rented the house and moved away.

"What do you do, Beulah?" I asked.

"I'm a biologist," she said, smiling. It was her first really big smile, I realized, and it added a whole new dimension to her face.

"A biologist," I repeated. "I would have said the arts, not science."

"Yes…my speciality is fish, sub-specialty, cod and eelgrass. I work at the Marine Lab on Logy Bay Road."

Then she turned away from me with a sigh, as if she were suddenly tired of this conversation.

"What's eelgrass?" I asked, but she didn't answer. "Do you think the cod will come back?" I persisted. "Perhaps they could farm cod like salmon."

She seemed to be staring at a pool of sunlight on the hardwood floor, or perhaps at the Celtic harps under the kitchen table, which were also catching the midday sun. When she turned to look at me again, her eyes had filled with tears, as if I'd asked her if her husband or Graham or Tansy were ever coming back, perhaps an even more complicated question.

"I'll hang my harp on a willow tree," she said, and turned her face away. We sat in silence for a few moments.

"The short answer is: we don't know," she said, looking back at me, an admission of ignorance that had a ring of confidence and certainty, but I decided to leave the other questions for another time.

5: STILL LIFE WITH STRANGERS

I was on the phone with Alicia, my estranged wife; my strange estranged wife; my wife l'étranger. If our marriage were an artwork now, it would be *Still Life with Strangers*, that installation or piece of conceptual art I'd once seen in an otherwise empty gallery on Queen Street West in Toronto. I'd wandered in there one afternoon to get out of the rain. There was only one painting on the wall, a diptych of sorts. One half of what was inside the frame was a painting, at least, and the other half was a two-way mirror. Through the mirror you could see a person in another gallery, or the other half of the gallery, looking at an identical picture (the artist statement informed me), and looking at you looking at it. The purpose of this exchange, according to the artist, was to see if, through a process of "esthetic osmosis," an "esthetic empathy" might develop between the "viewing partners," as we were called, if we might incorporate the other's response to the painting into our own. Was I in a gallery, I thought, or a Skinner Box?

My partner that day was a beautiful red-haired woman in a revealing red tank top, and my erotic response overwhelmed my esthetic one. Whether she was a plant, a paid model, or just another gallery-goer, I couldn't say. Perhaps she was the artist, or a psychologist conducting an experiment. For the life of me, I can't remember the painting—forgettable flowers and fruit, perhaps. But maybe this was the real point of the exhibit, or experiment: to see if the erotic would trump the esthetic—all talk of "esthetic osmosis" and "esthetic empathy" as red a herring as my symbolically red "viewing partner."

But let's put Alicia and me in there, I thought, and let us long-time and now erotically neutral partners examine *Still Life with Strangers* and see what sort of empathy develops. The unexamined marriage is not worth living in, saith the philosophical marriage counsellor. But no…she would never consent to that…it's a bit too late for that. Still, life with Alicia has to go on. We share a daughter and material things, material culture, as the anthropologists would refer to our accumulation of household stuff, most of it, I admit, lovingly and tastefully accumulated by Alicia, but immaterial, nevertheless, to indiscriminate, tasteless old me.

And though there is still, at times, animated life—sometimes the old lively affectionate Ali, my ally, my friend, my confidante, mother of our daughter, will show herself—much more often now it is the cold, distant, lifeless Alicia, my mocking patron, my opponent, my landlady.

Today, Landlady Alicia was telling me that I was being evicted. She was going to sell the house. My house! Well…our house. This August. New Man Richard—his name is Richard Newman Loveys, would you believe?—has got a new job, a Composer's Chair, no less, at a small Southern college up to its chest in bequests. A bed o' roses, in the USA, land o' plenty, land o' money, land o' milk and honey. Capitalists with so much money they don't know what to do with it. From minding their business. "Mind Your Business" was the motto on the first American coin, I read somewhere, not *E Pluribus Unim*, "One Out of Many," or "In God We Trust," both of which are on there now. Trust in money came first.

Not that I begrudge *Dick* the Composer's Chair, and the money that comes with it. Modern-day composers of classical music make less money than writers, Alicia tells me, even less than poets. Kevin would be happy to hear that. He hates contemporary classical music, and now, on the airwaves late in the evening—every evening—his favourite time for listening to music, the Mother Corp. has taken to broadcasting *Two New Hours*, a program of avant-garde music that used to be on only on Sunday night. A few more pennies in composers' pockets, I guess, but if they really wanted to make their pockets jingle, a *Hockey Night in Canada* theme song, or some other jingle, is the way to go. And some of them, privately, do just that. The woman who composed *dumb-da-dumb-da-dumb, dumb-da-dumb-da-dumb*, the *Hockey Night in Canada* theme song, was a classical pianist, Alicia says, who has written more than five hundred *dumb-da-dumbs*.

"This August!" I shouted down the line—the land line, as they call it now. "I may not even be back by August," I said. "I can't deal with this from here."

"James...stop shouting, calm down," Alicia said. "You don't have to deal with it. I'll deal with it. I'm living in the house. I'm paying the mortgage. You're just the carefree tenant now, remember? You're not responsible. You don't have to worry. That's what you always wanted, isn't it? Freedom from worry. Freedom 35. So you could write your masterpieces."

"Don't be a cunt, Alicia."

"Don't you call me that!"

She hung up the phone.

I stayed where I was, standing with one hand flat against the wall. She would call back when she cooled down; five minutes, maybe. My other hand was still holding the heavy black receiver of the rotary phone, which felt at that moment like a weapon, but I laid it gently back in its cradle.

The phone looked like an alien, prehistoric thing. It was the only phone in the house. I suppose the university kids had kept it for a laugh, all having cells and Macs and iPods and everything else. It was an affectation of Grim's, but a genuine affectation, if I can call it that. I'm sure he liked the actual physical thing, its sculptural solidity, as well as the idea of it. An expression of what? A protest against the cellphone, no doubt, which he hated, and the modern, multi-gadgeted household in general. The most up-to-date thing in this house was a pop-up toaster that didn't pop, with a large pair of wooden tweezers for extracting the burnt toast.

Grim had an old cellphone that he used as a prop—and not just on stage. He'd found it on the street one day; it looked as if it had been run over by a car. He used it as a ploy, a defensive weapon. If he was in a café or some other public place, reading or writing, and someone began talking loudly on his cellphone nearby, Grim would put his phone to his ear and begin talking as well—even louder than his neighbour. He had even done it in our house when someone had answered his cellphone at our kitchen table.

But the rotary phone wasn't all that old. It was what my parents had used, what I had used as a child, one attached to the wall, with a so-called party line. As a tender innocent preteen, I had what I think of as my first sexual experience on a party line, shared with two of our neighbours, the Flemings and the Whites. As you can well imagine, the temptation to listen in to the other parties on a party line was just too great to resist. One fall evening when my father was working and my mother was out with my sister, Sheila, looking for a winter coat, I heard our other parties, the wives of the families, reviewing the latest CBC television cultural program—a ballet that had been on the previous evening. Yes, there was ballet, theatre, and music on TV in those days. Gone...like the land line and the rotary phone. But to my shock, embarrassment, and dismay, not to mention utter mystification, it was the sexual apparatus of the male ballet dancers that was under review.

"Did you see the gear on *him*," whispered Mrs. White. It wasn't a question. "Bulgin' right out of his tights. Wouldn't you like to get your hands on that." This wasn't a question either, but Mrs. Fleming, who had a lisp, drooled an answer.

"Yethhh," she breathed hoarsely.

The idea that Mrs. White, Mary to my mother, a churchgoing mother of three, thirty-five perhaps, but an older woman to me, would like to get her red chafed hands on that ballet dancer's private parts, hands that, like my mother's, I'd seen dutifully pulling her husband's long johns through the ringer of our washer—she used ours, not having one of her own—was more than a revelation to me. It was alarming, faith-shattering. It might have been just my imagination, but, as I got a bit older, I noticed that, when she was having a cup of tea with my mother, as she often did, her eyes would stray toward my own private parts, and my father's. Mother usually went out when she came over to use our washer, and I stayed away from Mrs. White, and especially from Mrs. White's. Mother could hardly get me to go over there to borrow a cup of sugar.

Alicia called back. I picked up the phone, but didn't speak. On the wall in front of me was Grim's sun-faded list of suggested responses to telephone solicitors.

"James?"

"I'm sorry," I said, "he passed away a few days ago. I'm just heading off to the funeral."

"James."

"No, I'm just here momentarily, robbing the place."

"James…listen…"

"A short survey? Of course. But could you join me in a short prayer before we begin?"

"For Chrissakes, James!"

"No, he's off having his willy lengthened," I said, lengthening the list. I was on a roll. "Would you like to join the Apostolic faith? I'm masturbating right now. Could you call back later? How many calls have you made today? How much work have you ruined? How many masterpieces have been still-born because of you?"

I liked that one. Real venom, real malice, as the English football league play-by-play announcers would describe a blistering shot at an astonished goal-keeper. The wordplay in the broadcasting booth was as good as the footwork on the field. I had switched allegiance from hockey to football—I couldn't watch the fighting and head-banging any more.

I guess I got carried away. There was silence on the land line. Alicia had hung up again. I called back this time. Fifteen rings before she picked up. Our answering machine had been disconnected.

"James, listen," she said, before I said a word. "I don't have much time. Sydney's here."

Sydney's here. Code words for trouble. To make me desist. Though there was, indeed, a real Sydney, Alicia's troublesome "baby" sister. I had other names for her, however—Stella, Vexilla.

"I can hear her getting up," Alicia said. "She's been asleep all day."

"What's wrong this time?"

"What's always wrong, James? *Her.* She's what's wrong. She won't seek help."

"*Seek?*" I said. "It's you this poor pilgrim *seeks* help from, Ali."

"I can't help her, James. She won't listen to anything I say. She needs *professional* help."

"She's just a baby, Ali. Don't be mean to her."

"Yeah…a baby who can drink five baby bottles of beer before noon, then take a nap for the rest of the day. That's how many empty bottles were on the coffee table when I came home for lunch. Then she'll get up and eat a whole pizza and go at it again."

Yes, I admit, I'd seen her do it. She was on the large size, with breasts so big she'd had them surgically reduced. By ten pounds, she told me, one night when she was loaded. Unlike other people I'd known who had a drinking problem, whose other desires were dampened by excessive drink, Sydney was a heavy, swollen, unfocused body of desire for everything—food, sex, love, *trouble*. Unlike sister Alicia, whose life was the epitome of focus. But I couldn't help liking Sydney. She was a naif, a lost fragile soul, albeit with a sort of demonic fragility. She could be as wilful as Lucifer or as passive as a stump. Twice divorced, and still only in her thirties. Two children from the first marriage, both in trouble with the law. Another child given up at sixteen before she was married at all.

Ironically, Sydney had first been married to a social worker, and then to an ex-brother turned heavy-equipment operator and filmmaker. He looked like Pope John XXIII, had changed his name to Sören (insisting on the umlaut), and wanted to talk about nothing but Kierkegaard. We'd had Sydney and Sören over for dinner—once—and tried our best to accommodate him, which wasn't hard, as he did all the talking. When he stopped talking, he showed us his latest film, on DVD: heavy equipment—massive front-end loaders, John Deere—looking as light and agile as real deer, and a lot lighter than Kierkegaard, performing a ballet set to music from the *Nutcracker Suite*. It might have made it onto CBC prime time in the old days. "Look at the nuts and bolts on that," as Mrs. White might say.

"Don't be too hard on her, Ali," I said. "She needs your help, your strength, your determination, your drive, your—"

"Cut it out, James. You helped her when you were here, didn't you. Going out and getting her Stella Artois for breakfast."

"She has discriminating tastes, Ali, like you. Anyway, it didn't seem to matter. She doesn't get drunk no matter what she drinks."

"No, she just passes out for six hours, then gets up and does it again. It's called alcoholism, James. I can't stand it. I don't want her in the house. But if I turn her out I don't know what she might do. Her children don't want to see her, either."

She was starting to cry.

"James...can we discuss the house...please?"

"Yes...I've been thinking...I think I'm going to buy it," I said.

"Thinking when? The last ten minutes? Buy it with what, James? You'll have to renegotiate the mortgage. They won't give you a mortgage on your income. What'd you make last year—ten thousand, maybe?"

"Only our accountant knows for sure, Ali. I asked Jackie not to tell me when I dropped off the shoebox with all our stuff this spring. Too depressing."

"James, this'll really complicate things. The house is worth about four hundred thousand—if we sell it soon, that is. This hot real estate market can't last, they're telling me. That means a big drop in prices. We still owe about a hundred thousand on the mortgage. The best thing to do is sell the house and divide up the money. After paying off the mortgage, we could end up with a hundred and fifty thousand each. That's equal to six Canada Council grants. You could rent an apartment and live on that for a long time with your life-style. The only things you buy are books and CDs. You haven't even bought anything to wear since your mother died."

"Or I could use my share to buy the house, rent it out to pay the mortgage, and stay where I am, in the apartment."

"What for? What's the point of that? Why not just rent another apartment?"

"If I move, I'll have to completely reorganize my life, Ali. I'm attached to that house. I'm used to the neighbourhood—the streets, the coffee shops, the bakery, the streetcars. I don't have to think about what I'm doing or where I'm going. When I leave there in the afternoon, my mind's not always with me."

"James, you're being totally ridiculous. You can find an apartment right here in this neighbourhood, right on this street. And as I said, the banks won't let you buy it. They won't give you a mortgage because your income is too low. It's not even minimum wage. They don't care if you're attached to the house. They'll detach you from it pretty quick if you can't pay back the money."

"I don't know. I'll have to talk to Jackie, see what she says."

I heard a long descending sigh, then a sound like wind whispering through wires, then silence. I imagined a long line of poles on windswept barrens with sections of the land line drooping between them, almost touching the ground.

Then Alicia said, as if she'd been preparing this: "I used to think you were a fox, James, that you knew a lot of things, a lot of tricks, but I think you're a hedgehog. You know only one thing, one trick. Resistance, stonewalling... stubbornness."

"You've been reading books, Alicia, instead of scores."

"I am reading a score, actually, a new piece Richard is working on. 'The Fox and the Hedgehog: a Theme and Variations,' based on an Aesop fable. 'The fox knows many tricks, the hedgehog only one.'"

"I don't think that's from Aesop, Alicia, but perhaps there could be a guitar part in it for me."

"I don't think so, James. It's an ensemble piece. You're strictly solo."

"Maybe I'll do a musical setting myself. My favourite Aesop fable is 'The Nightingale and the Swallow,' and there's a part in it for you and me. Here's how it goes: 'The swallow urged the nightingale to take up residence under the roofs of men, as she herself did. The nightingale replied: "No, thank you. I have no desire to revive the memories of my past misfortunes."' The Greeks ate nightingales, Alicia, but they never ate swallows. Maybe they still do. Maybe you'd like me to move down to the Danforth."

"Very funny, James."

"As I said, Alicia, I don't think that's authentic Aesopic material, but it is Greek, and you forgot the last line. 'The fox knows many tricks, the hedgehog only one. One good one.'"

"Yeah...I just told you what it is. And there's nothing good about it."

"Don't underestimate the hedgehog, Alicia. Those words of wisdom are from Archilochus, I think. Seventh century BC. Aesop came later, sixth century BC."

"Don't be pedantic, James."

"Archilochus was from Paros. We went there, remember? That was the place where we tripped over a turtle in the middle of the road while walking home late one night full of retzino. The good old days, eh? Good thing it wasn't a hedgehog. That would have been too small to see...and not a nice thing to trip over in our sandals."

"That was on Spetses, James, the first island we were on, the one close to the mainland."

"Pedantic, Alicia. 'Say goodbye to the island Paros, farewell to its figs and the seafaring life.' Archilochus again. Kevin also wrote a poem about Paros."

"I've got to go, James. Sydney's up and about."

"Be kind to her, Ali...You know what the hedgehog's trick is, don't you?"

"James, I really have to go."

"It's like a small porcupine, the hedgehog, with a hideful of quills. When cornered, it rolls itself up into a ball for protection. Works every time. Nonviolent resistance."

"Goodbye, James. Think about the house. What I'm saying makes sense."

"You were always the sensible one, Alicia."

"Goodbye, James. I'm calling you on Sunday."

"Everyone's calling me on Sunday. Van Loon, my editor...I'm booked up on Sunday."

"Goodbye, James."

She hung up the phone.

6: MISS KISS, HENRIETTA, MALCOLM AND ME

"You got to stop at this light right here."

"I can't, Dad. There's four lanes of traffic. I'm in the wrong lane."

"Call me *Malc*, will you? You're too old to be calling me *Dad*. You got to stop here…by the post office…and press that mileage thing-amajig. I got to get my bearings. The turnoff at Ocean Pond is 78.4 miles from this light."

Fierceness, I thought. *Ferocity*. That was it. That's what I should have mentioned to Dr. Payne (Dr. Pain!). Characteristic emotions will come to the fore, he'd told me, and might be even stronger than usual.

"I can't stop, Malc. The light is green. There's a mile-long line of cars behind me, all anxious to get out of town."

How could everyone be leaving so early? I wondered. It was just past two o'clock. Maybe we should have waited till Saturday.

"There…I set the odometer," I said. "Everything's all right. It's at mile zero. We know where we are."

"Where are we, then?"

"We're on Kenmount Road."

"I know that, b'y."

He shaded his eyes with his hand and leaned in over the wheel to try to see the odometer.

"It's kilometres now, don't forget," I said, and soon wished that I hadn't.

"What are you talkin' about, kilometres? I don't use kilometres."

Better let it go, I thought. I pretended to cough.

He wasn't wearing his seatbelt, had absolutely refused to buckle up. He wasn't wearing a cap or sunglasses, either, though we were heading west, into the bright afternoon sun. His white T-shirt, I noticed, was on backwards and inside out, with the Stanfield's label exposed. Probably the last article of clothing being made in Canada, I thought. Still as sturdy and comfortable as old Bob Stanfield himself had been. We might not have wanted him for prime minister, but we gladly wear his family's underwear.

The old man flopped back in his seat, looking warily reassured. He had taken off his tan jacket, complaining of the heat from the glaring sun and the car heater, so I'd turned the heater off. I had also closed the air vents to keep the exhaust from other vehicles out of ours, and the windows were steaming up. I opened the driver's-side window of the four-wheel-drive Jeep that I'd rented. We'd be going on gravel roads, he'd told me, and then on the rough railbed of the old railway line. The train tracks had been taken up, and it was now "the Trailway," used mainly by snowmobiles and ATVs.

He reached back and retrieved his jacket from on top of all the fishing paraphernalia in the back seat. As Sheila had sold the family house and everything in it, including all his fishing gear, we had to buy almost everything. There were two wicker fishing baskets that we'd spent half the morning trying to find, plastic having replaced the braided willow shoots that he favoured, as it had almost everything else, and he was having none of that. There was a fisher-friendly, closed-face spin-cast reel and rod for me and an open-face spinning reel and rod for him, the more complicated type that I'd never been able to master. There was a plastic bag full of assorted hooks, lines, leaders, spinners, lead weights, and bobbers that he'd very discriminately selected—lifting, feeling, stretching, biting, sniffing—from a mesmerizing array on display in the stores. Colour, size, weight, shape, length, strength, material—even smell—were all deciding factors, it seemed. He himself eschewed the bobber, he made quite clear, as he did the spin-cast reel and rod; they were for amateurs, i.e. me, he being a master caster and active troller, not one to sit and watch his bobber.

Beneath all this was a large, old, army-issue duffle bag that had felt practically empty when I put it in the car this morning. I'd taken a look inside it when he went back into the Veterans' Pavilion to use the bathroom. In the bag was a hammer, a small towel, a pocket knife, some knives, forks, and spoons that he must have lifted, a salt shaker with tape over the top, and a mickey of Old Sam. Alcohol wasn't permitted in the Pavilion and he wasn't allowed to drink because of his medications, so I wondered how he'd got his hands on that. I locked it in the glove compartment, hoping he wouldn't remember it.

In the trunk were two sleeping bags, rubber boots (hip waders for him and knee-highs for me), a tent, a Coleman stove for a boil-up, and some pots and pans I'd borrowed from Sheila, along with some old Melmac dishes she no longer used. There was a large cardboard box full of food: several tins of sardines (coals to Newcastle), Vienna sausages, Purity Jam Jams, Carnation milk, Mammy's bread, Good Luck margarine, and King Cole tea—all his favourite brands, found at Belbin's Grocery nearby. I'd bought some bottled water and fruit as well—apples, bananas, and oranges—though I knew he hated fruit and preferred pond water. We'd be catching lots of trout, he said, and he didn't see why we had to bring any food.

After putting his jacket back on again, he removed a paperback from the inside pocket, a Zane Grey Western, and began to read.

"Did you know that he and Mom had the same name?" I said, stupidly, I thought, but too late.

He looked across at me and I caught his eye, a fierce eye.

"Pearl," I said quickly. "His name was Pearl Zane Grey, from Zanesville, Ohio. He was a dentist before he turned to writing, and his wife was an English major. She used to edit all his books."

"Where are you getting all this stuff?" he said.

"I read it in the introduction to *Riders of the Purple Sage*," I said, "his most well known book."

"You're reading Westerns now, are you? That's something new."

"I came across it in a second-hand bookstore," I said. "I was surprised to find that it was set in a Mormon community."

"Oh, yeah. I don't recall."

Though I'd seen him almost every day in the first week after I arrived, I hadn't seen him at all last week. He made no mention of this when I came back yesterday. In the Blue Puttee Sunroom of the Royal Newfoundland Regiment Veterans' Pavilion, we'd sat for two sunless hours in the dead heart of the afternoon and planned our May 24th fishing trip. The Pavilion was a small private military wing of the McMurdo Geriatric Care Centre for civilians, who, for one reason or another—dementia, in some cases, like my father's—were now unable to look after themselves, or had no one to look after them. It was the first time I would be taking him out of the building, and I had to get special written permission from Dr. Payne, the Residential Care Coordinator. The friend who usually took him fishing, another vet, who'd been living on his own, had died two years ago.

"He needs adventures," Dr. Payne had said to me. "They would be good for him."

He didn't like being in his room at all. Though it was a private room, it was small and dim and airless. But the main reason, he said, was that "some woman" kept visiting him—or "appearing" to him.

"A big woman, so definitely not your mother," he'd said to me on one of those first visits in the Blue Puttee Sunroom. "She was so small when she was born they had to stuff her in a shoe box in cotton wool and put her behind the stove in the kitchen to keep her warm. But she grew to a good size, your mother. Five foot four."

He was no more than five foot six himself, but he was strong—quick and wiry, as many short, thin men like him have been described. He had worked as a security guard, or "watchman," as they were called in those days. I'd inherited the wiryness, and added another six inches to the height. A better diet, I suppose. Did diet trump genes? He'd drunk tea instead of milk out of his baby bottle, he claimed.

No, the visitor was not his dead wife, Pearl, my mother, but someone he knew, he said—or someone who knew him, he wasn't sure which. What he was sure of was that the woman didn't like him. It was her sister Irene, perhaps, who was deceased as well, but who would find a way to come back, he said, just to torment him.

"You taught me to read," I said, glancing at the cover of the Zane Grey novel, *Last of the Duanes*, which he was also using to shade his eyes from the sun. He would not wear sunglasses, and he had never needed eyeglasses, or so he claimed.

"Your mother taught you to read," he said. "You could read before you went to school. Miss Kiss told your mother you could read like a grade five. They put you a grade ahead."

Here was the elusive Miss Kiss again.

"Who's Miss Kiss?" I asked. At the McMurdo Centre, he'd said she was a nurse.

"Your grade one teacher, b'y. I met her on your first day of school."

"Mom dropped me off on my first day of school. She left me all alone in a big empty corridor and went on home. That's my earliest memory of school— my earliest memory, period, I think."

"Well, you forgot Miss Kiss. She was a lovely girl. From Spaniard's Bay. Used to come over on the *Kipawa* on Monday morning and go back home on Friday afternoon."

Dr. Payne had briefed me with a sort of bored and composed, but compassionate, air, distant but certainly not insincere. He said that though my father could recall minute details from "the long, long ago," as he called it, could tell you what he had for supper on a particular Good Friday the 13th in 1945, I shouldn't expect him to remember what he had for breakfast this morning, or even if he'd had breakfast, if he'd taken his pills, what day it was, or even my name or his own on very bad days. Maybe he'd met Miss Kiss on *his* first day of school, I thought, or on his first day in the Pavilion, or maybe he was reading so-called nurses' novels now as well as Westerns. He had always read more books than I did.

"You remember the *Kipawa*, I s'pose?" he said.

Here he was, checking my memory now.

"I guess I do," I said. "I got sick on it often enough."

"Not after you got your appendix out."

"What do you mean?"

"You never got seasick after you got your appendix out. Dr. Healey said it must be a cure. He saw the same thing happen with tonsils. Could be the chloroform, he said."

Dr. Healey! Dr. Payne! Was I in some kind of Dickensian time warp?

"They had to do an emergency trip that night. One o'clock in the morning, middle of February 1960, and the Tickle filled with ice. Calm as anything, though. No calmer sea than one covered with ice. But you could still see the waves, I remember, movin' through the ice—must have been a swell, an undertow—though you couldn't feel a thing, steady as she goes. It was a moonlit night, too…bright as day…and mild—must've been 40 degrees or more."

The old man was on Fahrenheit as well as miles.

"We were the only car on there—Cyril O'Neill's taxi. Do you remember how many cars that boat could take?"

"About a dozen, I'd say."

"Nooo…only six, seven in a squeeze. Took ages to load, too, over an hour sometimes. Fastest time Cyril ever came to the house, though he went to bed at ten o'clock to be up at five for the seven o'clock boat. He didn't usually take his car to the Cove—he was afraid of the water—but this time he took us right to the hospital. We stayed out on deck, standin' at the rail, lookin' out at the ice under the moon. I can still see it clear as day. Cyril said he didn't mind so much when he couldn't see the water. Dr. Healey stayed in the car with you. Cyril started talkin' about his time in the war. That was the reason he was afraid of the water. He had never been on the water, mind you. He wasn't in the navy, or the Merchant Marines, like me. He was stationed on Red Island during the war, part of what they called the 1st Coastal Defence Battery, mannin' those big guns that are still up there on the cliff above the beach. They were on twenty-four-hour watch for German subs comin' in the Tickle tryin' to blow up boats loadin' iron ore at the pier. Germany was a big customer for that ore, and now that the war was on, they weren't sellin' it to 'em any more. But the Germans knew where it was, and they didn't want anyone else to get it. They blew up three boats and the pier in the fall of 1942. The blast at the pier shook the whole island. We thought it was an earthquake.

"Cyril and the other gunners were given forty-eight-hour passes so they could go over to St. John's for the weekend, or around the bay, to see their girlfriends and families. One of Cyril's friends from St. John's—Cyril was a townie himself, but he was goin' out with a girl from the Island, married her after the war and moved over to stay—one of his friends wanted to go home that weekend to see his girlfriend, but he didn't have a pass. It was the second weekend in November 1940. Cyril had a pass that weekend and was plannin' to go home, too, but his friend was so desperate Cyril traded passes with him for the next weekend. Cyril's buddy drowned on his way back to the Island on Sunday night. November 10, 1940, it was.

"Almost twenty years had gone by, but Cyril said the whole thing was still fresh in his mind. Not a day went by when he didn't think about it. He even had nightmares about it sometimes. Someone was always accusin' him of a crime. A big crime. Not just one life, but a lot. Twenty-two people drowned that night. Two ferries collided in the Tickle—the *Garland* and the *Little Golden Dawn*. All of them were on the *Garland*. There were twenty-six on there altogether. It had no licence to carry passengers, no lifeboats, no life jackets, no flares, no nothin'. Her wood was rotten, too, they said, and she sank in five minutes. There were no passengers on the *Dawn*, just the captain and the engineer and some freight. They were only a quarter mile from shore when it happened. Cyril was on watch that night and said he heard the noise when the two boats hit. It was dark, with a bit of blustery snow, but pretty clear all round and hardly any wind. He said he saw a fire on one of the boats. The engineer on the *Dawn* lit a fire on top of the wheelhouse to get help. That boat sank right after they were towed to shore."

"I don't recall ever hearing anything about that."

"Sure, that was 1940, long years before you were born. You were born a Canadian, weren't you? And you didn't waste any time headin' off to your native land."

Well, there it was, I knew it was coming. Not exactly the proverbial bolt from the blue. I'd expected him to confront me with something like that on the very first day I'd gone to see him; but it had been what Dr. Payne had called "one of his bad days," and he thought I'd just come back from the corner store. "Did you get the cigarettes?" were the first words he spoke. And he hadn't said one unkind word to the prodigal son until now. Expect harsh, hurtful remarks, I was warned by Dr. Payne, any time at all, for no reason at all, let alone for being absent without cause for more than thirty years.

The bungalow on windswept Whiteway Street where my parents had lived after moving to St. John's, and in which my father had spent several years as a widower, had been shared by many live-in housekeepers, whom Sheila had hired to look after him. The last one was a woman from St. Mary's Bay whose husband had a salmon-fishing licence. She would bring my father fresh wild salmon, which he dearly loved, from the Salmonier River when she'd come back on Sunday evenings from a weekend off. Wild salmon was a rare delicacy these days, as there was no longer a commercial salmon fishery, and the only salmon available in the stores was farmed, what my father called *slub*. Mrs. Mulcahy, from Salmonier, had vacated the premises when my father, acting like a wild animal himself, had thrown a whole wild salmon out the window, and had threatened to do the same thing with her. After that incident, Sheila had found a place for him in the Veterans' Pavilion, the VP, as it was proudly called, as he'd refused to go and live with her.

"You might've come back for your mother's funeral," he said, getting closer to the heart of the matter.

"Celia was sick, Dad…with meningitis. I couldn't leave. I wrote you a long letter about that."

"Stop callin' me *Dad*. I didn't get any letters."

I wasn't ready for this right now. I was trying to concentrate on the road, which, after the long winter, had a lot of holes and cracks, ruts and channels, crumbling edges, and no lines to speak of.

"Is Cyril O'Neill still alive?" I asked him, trying to change the subject. Changing the subject is a good tactic, Dr. Payne, who was a clinical psychologist, had advised. Don't argue. Don't deny. Don't over-explain. Agree. Go along. Even with fantasies.

"I don't know," he said. "We left the Island a long time ago. Have you seen Sheila?"

"I saw her at the degree ceremony, remember? She brought you along."

"When was that?"

"About two weeks ago...when the university gave me an honourary degree."

"What'd you get that for? You flunked out o' university didn't you?"

"I gave them all my papers," I said. "My ten thousand drafts, a quarter mile of archives shelf. And I'm leaving them the fortune I made from writing in my will. They might name a tunnel extension after me."

I surprised myself with a bitter little laugh. Don't make jokes, I recalled Dr. Payne warning me.

"What are you talking about?" he said.

"Nothing, Malc. Don't mind me."

"You should talk to Sheila," he said, after a long pause. "Tell her to come and see me. She never shows her face. 'So that's what you look like,' I said to her the last time she came by."

"She told me she asked you to come and live with her and her husband."

"I couldn't live with him. I don't like his way. He don't want any kids, you know. He's a selfish man. Sheila wants kids, I can tell. She don't want to be workin' in a store."

"But she owns the store, doesn't she?"

"I don't know. What kind of life is that for a woman? A woman needs children, at least one or two. She don't need to have a brood."

"She's almost fifty years old, Dad."

He took his book from the dashboard and started reading again, and I decided to return to a safer subject, though no subject seemed safe with him now.

"What I meant when I said a while ago that you taught me to read," I said, "was that you taught me by example, without even being aware of it, without me even being aware of it, that reading was something that people did, something interesting, something important—and a lot of fun. I never saw anyone else doing it, not even the teachers. You'd jump up laughing in the middle of a book, shout sometimes, frighten us all, walk around shaking your head, looking amazed or amused. Sometimes you'd stay up reading all night long. Mom would find you in the morning on the daybed in the kitchen or in the smoker in the living room. You used to get mad at her for forgetting to put a book in your lunch pail."

He was looking uncomfortable. He never liked this soft-soaping kind of talk.

"What happened to that smoker, anyway?" he asked. "It's not in my room...Your mother loved the movie magazines and the *Star Weekly*. Along with the television."

"You never watched TV."

"I used to watch Jackie Gleason...*The Honeymooners*. That was a good show. Norton the plumber, Ralph the bus driver. '*Bang-zoom! Bang-zoom!*'"

"What?"

"'*Bang-zoom!* Alice. *Bang-zoom!*' He was always saying *bang-zoom* to his wife when he was fed up with her. But he didn't really mean it. He was a kind man at heart."

"They'd never get away with that stuff now—threats of wife-beating on prime time. But there's every other kind of beating you can name."

"I never once raised a hand to your mother," he said fiercely, looking hard at me.

"I can vouch for that," I said, with a certain emphasis, and he looked away, went back to his book.

"I read a book recently by Larry McMurtry," I said. "He said that the whole Western thing—cowboys driving cattle to market across the open plains (like in *Red River* with John Wayne; wasn't that your favourite movie?)—lasted less than a generation, but it spawned this great myth of the cowboy that's lived on to this day."

"So what?"

"Well, I thought it was interesting. It wasn't that long ago—the late 1800s. His grandfather was actually one of those open-range, wandering cowboys. Not some Roy Rogers or Hopalong Cassidy, but a real working cowboy who drove cattle across the lone prairie just over a hundred years ago. He wrote some Westerns you might like—Larry McMurtry, I mean. *Lonesome Dove*—ever heard of that? It was a bestseller, I think."

"'Take 'em to Missouri, Matt!'"

"What?"

"John Wayne...givin' the go-ahead to his son in *Red River*. To drive them cows to the railhead in Abilene."

"I thought Abilene was in Texas?"

"Kansas...wherever...You were a bit of a cowboy yourself, you know. You had a cowboy shirt, a set of guns and holsters, and a BB rifle. But what you always wanted for your birthday was cowboy boots. Other boys wanted boots and skates, but all you wanted was cowboy boots. They were too expensive, your mother said. You liked skating, though. You could skate like the wind. But you wouldn't go to the rink, you wouldn't play hockey. You only skated on Perry's Brook."

"I think I liked being up in the woods...and I didn't like having to fight all the time, getting beaten up."

"What do you mean? You could look after yourself. I taught you how to stand up for yourself."

"I wasn't that tough, Dad. The boys turned into thugs inside that rink. It was just a big parent-sanctioned bullying ground."

"A what? Stop here!" he shouted, pointing through the windshield at a service station just up ahead. "We got to get some worms."

In the service station store, while he went to the cooler to get the worms, I got two takeout coffees from one of a half-dozen Thermoses on a table near the counter. It was covered with a plastic tablecloth, which itself was covered with discarded plastic stir sticks, crumpled-up serviettes and sugar packets, small pools of milk, and scatterings of spilled sugar. I remembered that we had no sugar, so I took some extra packets to do us for the trip. We planned to stay overnight and come back the next day.

After I paid for the coffee, I walked to the back of the store and found the old man standing at an open door in front of the coolers. He had removed the plastic covers of about a half-dozen small Styrofoam tubs of worms on the bottom shelf, and was now poking around on the top shelf. He turned, somewhat startled, when I came up beside him.

"What was I lookin' for in here?" he said to me.

"We need some worms for the trout, Dad," I said, in a whisper.

"I know that, b'y," he hissed at me, then turned away and bent over with his hands on his knees. He began rooting around with his fingers in the black peaty soil in the worm containers on the bottom shelf of the cooler.

"Half dead," he said, looking at the damp soil on his fingers. "I want a few crawlers with a bit of life in 'em."

"How many tubs will we get, Dad?"

"Three…if I can find 'em. Go get me a Mars bar, will you."

"You're eating chocolate bars now? You always hated chocolate."

He looked at me as if I were the one who was losing my mind.

⮂⮀

We drove the 78.4 kilometres to the turnoff at Ocean Pond, followed a gravel road for 5.7 kilometres past a ramshackle of summer cabins, then turned right where the road crossed the Trailway and drove the final 4.4 kilometres to the pond. I was beginning to think that the old man had been misdiagnosed, that his mind was still as sharp as a hook, but it turned out that these precise distances were written on the inside cover of his book. Leo, his deceased fishing buddy, had written them down on their last trip, he said. He'd witnessed my father's gradual decline up close, I guess, and probably expected the worst. Perhaps his own health had been bad as well.

The old railbed was narrow and rough—the train tracks had been narrow gauge—with no room for another car or truck to pass. Fortunately, we encountered only a few ATVs, kids with even younger kids seated behind them, fathers with mere babies on their backs, not a helmet to be seen. They tackled the ditches as we drove past, not with any hostility or resentment toward us for forcing them off the trail, but with gusto and glee, with an increase rather than a slackening of speed. We passed several ponds before reaching the one the old man called Old Man's Pond, at the head of which was a space beside the track that, considering where we were, could legitimately be called a parking lot. There was room, perhaps, for four other vehicles.

We got out and stretched. The old man sniffed the air. We took off our shoes and put on our rubber boots. We strapped our fishing baskets to our belts and filled them with the tackle and the three tubs of worms. The old man managed to get all the food, the dishes, the pots and pans, and the tent, which was ingeniously packed in a long, thin nylon bag of its own, into his large duffle bag. So, loaded down with that, with two rods and reels, a Coleman stove, and two sleeping bags, we tramped the final two kilometres or so down the side of the pond. It was a fairly good path, though at certain points we actually had to wade in the pond before being able to get back up on the bank again. His fishing spot was at a rocky point where the pond opened up and we could see that Old Man's Pond was a very big pond indeed. (One man's pond is another man's lake—or another man's ocean.) Perhaps the old man had got it wrong, and *this* was Ocean Pond. It ran for a mile or more into the woods, as far as the eye could see.

We unloaded all our gear on a flat mossy bank about twenty feet above the water, what looked like a nice spot for the tent, and the old man went back down to the point and began to assemble his equipment right away. It was five o'clock and a perfect evening: cloudy, but no sign of rain—no rain in the forecast for the whole weekend, in fact—warm enough, maybe 12 degrees, and no wind to speak of. Ominous, in other words, for a May 24th weekend, which was notorious for bad weather. There were a few mosquitoes—we had forgotten the fly dope—but they didn't seem too eager for our blood, certainly not as eager as the old man seemed to be for fish blood. I sat on a sleeping bag and gazed out over the pond, its surface barely ruffled by what breeze there was. *Flat cam*, as the old man had described it when we'd reached the point. Only then, as I sat there in a sort of instant trance, did I become aware of how unearthly quiet it was—no bird or animal sounds; no boats; no cars, trucks, or ATVs; no roar of planes overhead; no trains now either, of course; and no other fishermen to be seen. How many cities are there left on earth, I thought, from which you can escape so easily, in a hour or two be out in the middle of the wilderness, completely alone?

No...not alone—*ay, there's the rub.* I was not alone at all but out in the middle of nowhere with a man who, as Dr. Payne had warned me, was not in complete command of his senses. But as long as he took his medication, he said, I had no need to worry. The medication was for high blood pressure, which was the root cause of his mental decline, his dementia. It had resulted in a series of small strokes, undetected over a period of who-knows-how-many years, which had damaged brain tissue. *Vascular dementia* was the medical term for it, the second most common type, after the dreaded Alzheimer's. The drugs would not reverse the impairment, he said, but would perhaps slow it down and prevent further damage.

I was worrying myself with these thoughts until I saw the old man, standing in water above his knees, *whip* his fishing line, and my fears along with it, far out across the pond. Mental deterioration, maybe, but lots of *physical* life, lots of zing and zest, left in him yet. Then I heard the call of what could only be a loon, so transparently, so lonesomely, so crazily *loon-like* as to be unmistakable, even to someone who had never heard one. The call of this iconic bird of the wild, now a domesticated fowl of the Royal Canadian Mint, was on the soundtrack, no doubt, of every Canadian wilderness nature show I'd ever seen on TV, and I'd seen a lot of them, they being one of the few peaceful things on there that I liked to watch.

But instead of filling me with peace, the sound of the loon only prompted more anxiety. As no actual bird was visible, and I was so intently focused on my father, it was as if the cry had come directly from him, as if it had been his loony voice that I'd heard. *Crazy as a loon*, I heard myself say.

Then a flash of white broke the surface of the pond—not a loon, however, but a fish, and it looked like a big one. I stood up and rushed down the bank to see it, just as he got it ashore.

"What a size!" I said, as he held the poor shocked creature in one of his red, chafed, oversized hands, hands that had always seemed much too big for his body, and was trying to remove the hook.

"Winnish," he said. "Hook's right down in his guts. I'll have to cut the leader."

He laid the fish down on the small strip of sandy beach and put his foot on it, rinsed his hands in the water and wiped them on a small blue towel that was hanging from his back pocket, then removed a pocket knife from his jacket and cut the line. He put the knife back in his pocket and the fish in the basket attached to his belt.

"Aren't you gonna fish?" he said, as he began to re-hook his line.

"What kind of trout is that?" I asked him.

"'Tis not a trout, b'y. Winnish…a landlocked salmon. A wannabe trout, Leo used to call 'em. They don't grow much bigger than that. Taste okay, though… but we're after the speckled. Get your line out there before it gets dark."

It took me a long time to get a line in the water: get the rod, reel, and line together; get a hook, leader, and bobber attached to the line; get a worm on the hook; then cast the line out without hooking into one of the trees or bushes that grew right to the edge of the water. My rubber boots were short and I couldn't wade out very far. By that time he had three more fish, all speckled trout this time. He was trolling his lead-weighted line along the bottom—they were bottom feeders, he said—and luring them in, not hooking them until they were almost to shore. I watched my bobber closely, but had nary a bite, though it sometimes seemed as if the bobber was being pulled along. I'd left my sunglasses in the Jeep, and the glare and ruffle on the water, even under a cloudy sky, tricked your eyes into seeing movement. I removed the bobber, attached some lead weights, and tried trolling; but the hook caught on rocks and weeds on the bottom, and I lost both hook and leader.

I gave up at that point and climbed back up the bank to set up the tent. I fired up the Coleman stove and boiled up some water in a pot for tea. By nine o'clock it was almost dark and he had caught his limit of twelve fish and begun to catch the dozen that he said I was entitled to. He'd stopped for only ten minutes to drink a cup of tea and eat a can of Vienna sausages and some Jam Jams. I'd eaten a can of sardines, some bread and butter, an apple, and a banana. I sat on the soft mossy bank drinking a second cup of tea and listening to the loons. There seemed to be a whole flock of them now, calling from various dark corners of the pond, but I still hadn't seen a single bird. On one of those TV nature shows I'd learned that the loon, scientifically speaking, was of an *order* all to itself, and its extremely reclusive nature made me think more of an order of monks rather than birds.

He caught four more fish before he gave up, but only because it was so dark he couldn't see what he was doing. In the tent, in our cozy new sleeping bags, we drifted off to sleep right away; but I woke up to hear him talking to me, or perhaps he was talking to himself. There was a faint light in the tent, enough to see my watch. I thought it might be early morning, but it was only two o'clock.

"Did you bring in the coal?" he said, having heard me stirring, I guess. "Did you bank the fire in the stove?"

"Yes, I did," I said, with only a slight hesitation.

"Don't forget to feed the hens in the morning. I won't have time before I go to work. And mow the hay down in that lower field. Don't forget to go get some water for your mother. Sheila's not strong enough to be carrying that."

"I won't," I said.

"What do you mean, you won't?"

"I mean I won't forget…Did you take your pill?"

"What pill?"

Dr. Payne had said that the confusion, the disorientation, the memory lapses might be worse at night.

"Your blood pressure pills. You take them twice a day."

There was a long silence.

"When I was gone you wouldn't do anything around the house. Sure, Sheila did your work for you—what your mother didn't do. You wouldn't bring in a bucket of coal, but you'd spend a whole night down in the hold of one of them coal boats for a measly fifteen dollars a shift."

"Remember what happened to me on one of those jobs? There were ten of us shovelling in a small space, and I got the edge of a coal shovel right in the face. I threw up all over Reg Tremblett's clothes. Then I passed out. I woke up in the surgery with you and Mom by the bed. I couldn't go near the coal shed after that. Just looking at the stuff made me want to throw up, let alone shovelling it, or digging it out with a pick when it was frozen in the winter."

"You were a devil for stealin' that copper wire, too. When we had that sleet storm and the power was gone for the winter, every light pole on the Island flattened, boys were gettin' electrocuted cuttin' that wire, some went to jail for stealin' it. Your mother was havin' fits every hour you were gone."

Did he know where we were? I wondered. I thought it better not to ask.

"I'm going outside to get your pills," I said. "I think they're in your duffle bag."

Outside, it was almost as if someone had turned on the lights, the stars were so bright. That tent must be almost opaque, I thought, though it felt like thin plastic when I was putting it up.

I found the pills in the duffle bag, poured some water from a plastic bottle into a paper cup, and went back inside. I tied the tent flaps open so he could see to take his pill, which, to my great relief, he made no objection to doing.

As I was zipping up the opening to the tent, he said, "Leave the door open, will you? This room is so hot."

When we were snug in our sleeping bags again, his mind flitted on to another story, one I vaguely remembered, but I thought it had involved a hen instead of a cat.

"You had a way of gettin' your face all cut up," he said, "and gettin' yourself in a mess. Rocks and shovels in the face, your hair burned off on bonfire night. That's why your mother worried so much. That old cat we had—Ruffin. Remember him? He scrobbed the face right off you on Confirmation Day. You picked him up to say goodbye in your new white suit—he probably didn't recognize you—and you got it all spattered with blood. We had to take you in to the surgery instead of the church. You never did get confirmed, as far as I know. You might still be a heathen to this day."

I knew I shouldn't be saying it even as I *was* saying it, shouldn't be contradicting him, but I did.

"I think it was a blue suit, Dad," I said, "and I think it was a hen that ruined it. Henrietta…the pet hen that I had, remember? She pecked me on the cheek when I went out to the henhouse to say goodbye. She was on the roost asleep. She used to sleep in the daytime, like an owl. The last of the brood. Then you tore the henhouse down. Remember the big beet we grew afterward on that ground?"

"Hens!" he scoffed. "What are you talkin' about, b'y? We never had any hens."

"Didn't you just remind me to feed the hens?"

Shut your mouth! I warned myself.

There was silence again, and as I gazed out through the screen of the tent, I could see the stars. I thought of distracting him with a little joke, though his sense of humor seemed all but absent now. Kevin had told me this one when we were out for a beer.

"You want to hear a joke?" I said, but I didn't wait for a reply. "It's about Sherlock Holmes, the detective, and his friend Dr. Watson, who used to help him with his cases. I gave you a Sherlock Holmes novel one time, remember?

"They're out in the country, in a tent—like us—and Holmes wakes up in the middle of the night—like we did—and says, 'Watson, wake up; wake up, Watson. Look up! Look up! What do you deduce?' 'Good golly, Holmes,' he says. 'There are millions of stars…and it follows that there are millions of planets circling these stars…and it follows as the day, the night that some of these planets must have intelligent life like ours. There must be extraterrestrial life!'

"'Watson, you idiot!' says Holmes. 'Someone's stolen our tent!'"

It must have worked like a soothing lullaby or a fairy tale, for I didn't hear a laugh but a gentle snore, so lulling and reassuring that snores of my own couldn't have been far behind.

The next morning he was up with the dawn and had caught and cleaned a half dozen fish before I awoke. I fired up the Coleman stove and we fried them up in the small cast-iron pan for breakfast—just trout with a sprinkle of salt, bread and butter, and tea. But they tasted like no fish I'd ever eaten before, even better than the capelin we used to cook on the beach, right out of the salt water. He caught another basket of trout before we left, cleaned the works on a sunker a few feet from shore, and though I made a few more hopeless, awkward casts, I caught nothing at all. I waited for him to remark on this, but he never did. He was too absorbed in the task himself, I suppose, but he didn't mention it on the way back in the car, either. We packed up and left not long after noon.

"What are you going to do with all those fish?" I asked him when we reached the highway.

"Thirty-seven fish," he said, "countin' the six we ate. Well…some of them are yours. Twelve a day is the bag limit, or five pounds plus one, so that's twenty-four for me, and seven left for you. We ate your other six," he said, with a flash of his old humour, infrequent though it had always been. "Nooo…you can have some of mine if you want. Take another five—an even dozen. That'll leave nineteen for me."

Sure, this man could be a mathematician, I thought. Dr. Payne had said that he had trouble with numbers, even basic arithmetic, but there was certainly no problem that I could see. Maybe he meant numbers in the abstract, not when there were things you could actually see and count, cook and eat.

"Seven is more than enough for me," I said.

Tapping out his thoughts on the dashboard, he said, "The boys will be happy with this, I can tell you. I think I'll ask Jim to fry 'em all up for tea."

About forty kilometres from town, as he was quietly gazing out the window taking in the view, he asked me to pull off into the next gravel pit so we could go for a short jaunt on the barrens. I thought that maybe he wanted to have a leak. We walked about a kilometre from the highway and stood on the crest of a low ridge looking out over a bleak, colourless, barren landscape of rock and bush and water: stunted trees, small ponds, peat bog, dense tangled ground cover, large erratic boulders white as bones. There was colour, of a kind, once you got up close to it, but it was pale, muted, *drained*, the sort of washed-out picture I always imagined a colour-blind person might see. The white rocks were the brightest thing of all. But looking out upon this alien vista, he exclaimed, in a muted, ecstatic sort of way:

"Jesus, it's beautiful. Bury me out here, will you, when I go…Now, I don't want to be—what do they call it?"

"Cremated?"

"Right…and *scattered*. I don't want to be burned and scattered all over the place. Plant me out here among these ponds and bushes. In the peat, pushin' up blueberries—boulder for a headstone, that's good enough. I don't want to be in some crowded old cemetery."

"I don't know if I could manage that. It might look a bit suspicious," I said, laughing. "They might think I'd done away with you or something. Anyway…don't you want to be near Mom?"

"Where is she?"

"In Mount Pleasant Cemetery."

"Where's that?"

"In the west end, just off Cornwall Avenue, I think. Sheila said it's a beautiful spot, high up on a hill. You can see right out through the Narrows."

"Yeah, me and Pearl can enjoy the view…She was never happy over here, your mother. I should've brought her back to the Island. I never should've listened to Sheila."

He strode off among the rocks and bushes along the side of the ridge—a small, stooped figure, hardly more than a hundred pounds plus one, I'd say, but steady on his legs, and still with a full head of hair. He walked down towards a little gulley surrounded by withered bushes and stunted spruce. I followed after him and he stopped by the edge of the water and stood giving the place a good sizing-up. I could hear the sound of a small brook running into the gully.

"This'd be a good spot for me," he said. "Remember to set that thingama-jig when you get back in the car."

7: THE GOLDEN HEIGHTS

I was climbing a steep hill, a real gravity grind, walking in the general direction of Honeygold Heights, and the mansion on the Heights, on a street called Primrose Haven. I'd had to comb the city map to find it. Of primrose path, lane, place, court, grove, close, and mews, I'd heard, but never *haven*. Even if the location had been clear to me from Sheila's directions, I still would have wanted to see that name on a map. I recalled that there was a place in Newfoundland named Bar Haven, but it was no longer on the provincial map. Resettled, perhaps, like so many other places. I'd always thought that it would be a great name for a bar—a bar to hide away in, to get away from the world.

I was more than a bit anxious about meeting Sheila's husband, Loyal—yes, Loyal. Even the name...but never mind. He was a corporate honeygold man, a money-maker, a money-protector, Sheila had informed me at the university reception, though of course she hadn't used those words. An investment *counsellor*, she called him, a man who made money for other people, mostly, but obviously had found the time, and the ways and means, to make a few dollars for himself. Was money-making such an anxiety-producing activity these days—with capitalist contrivances collapsing in public view, like controlled, but still startling, building demolitions, the so-called free market soliciting socialist intervention—that even savvy, venal investors needed counselling, psychological support to deal with the trauma, guilt, shock, and shame?

As a lifelong investor of time—and time is money, as they say—in the unlisted stock of "CanLitFic," as van Loon likes to call it, I can well understand the need for certain kinds of investment counselling; but I had an instinctive, almost philosophical, distrust of anyone whose profession was dedicated simply to making money. My own profession, in contrast, by a process of natural market selection, with minimal socialist intervention, was excluded from such odious activity. My apprehension about meeting Loyal was compounded by the old man's more personal negative feelings toward his son-in-law, who'd hied himself to Honeygold Heights from a more modest perch in downtown St. John's as soon as the honey-golden liquidities had come pouring in.

My first impression of Sheila and Loyal's house, however, was that it was nothing fancy, just a big, tacky, turreted box in a very ordinary, if newly constructed, subdivision, with the usual deforested lots and monocultural McLawns. A lone rhododendron had been planted on one side of the front steps; a cedar ball topiary, about the same height, sat in a ceramic urn on the other side. There was an abstract, sterile, prefabricated unreality about the houses, as if they had all been quickly and unthinkingly thrown together by some rich contractor's petulant, wayward, architecturally challenged son, who had been set loose in this big clear-cut sandbox of a new housing development with his toy jumbo geometry kit full of rectangles, triangles, cubes, squares, trapezoids, rhomboids, rhombohedrons, and what have you, and this was the result.

But it was certainly a well-appointed house, technologically speaking, right out of the slapstick celluloid suburb of Jacques Tati's Monsieur Hulot, who would have had a lot of fun up on Honeygold Heights. There were movement-sensitive security lights over the automatic doors of the two-car garage, both of which must not have been working properly, as the garage doors opened and the lights pointlessly spotlit me as I entered the driveway on foot in the bright light of early evening. The doorbell was connected to a sound system and an intercom. When I pressed the button, classical music came out of a small speaker grille above it, and then a male voice saying hello.

The solid-wood door had no sidelights, but you could still be spied through the glass peephole and admitted or not depending on your business here or how you looked. *What is your business here, brother?*

I wasn't sure.

As I stood on the front step identifying myself, communicating with Loyal, an Air Canada jumbo jet, coming in for a landing at the airport nearby, flew right over the house, no more than a few hundred feet above my head, drowning out our conversation. From the front step, I could see Signal Hill, Cabot Tower, and a strip of grey ocean. I seemed to be almost looking *down* on the Hill. Loyal opened the door dressed in a silvery blue, Hugh Heffner-type dressing gown that matched his pale blue eyes and greying hair. He was tall and his eyes were set very close together, but when he smiled and shook my hand, they seemed to move apart. His long frizzy hair was tied in a ponytail. This was not the investment-counselling brother-in-law I had envisaged.

He'd got home late from work and had just got out of the Jacuzzi, he said. He ushered me into the kitchen where Sheila, wearing one rubber glove and one oven mitt, was busy at an impressive oval kitchen island—something Alicia had always longed for but never got—operating three or four high-tech gadgets at the same time; but she abandoned them, let them whizz and whirr, as she presented me with both her hot flushed cheeks. She'd surprised me with this greeting at the university reception and seemed a bit self-conscious about it herself. She told me that she'd picked it up from the large number of French-Canadian friends and acquaintances who frequented her shop—Sheila's Brushes, Bonnets & Bows. The name sounded a bit flaky and frivolous, she admitted, but she specialized in "natural," "ethical" women's clothing and accessories, the haberdashery version of the gourmet, organic, shade-grown, fair-trade coffee phenomenon. She tracked her suppliers and their sources to be sure that nothing in her shop was produced in the notorious Third World sweatshops used by most North American clothing manufacturers. This was the balance, perhaps, for Loyal's unethical, or at least oblivious, pursuit of wealth, though she may have passed no judgment on this whatsoever.

Loyal opened the fridge and offered me a beer, or rather an impressive choice of European beers: a Czech Urquell Pilsner, a German Dab ale, or a Belgian Stella Artois lager. I chose the Stella. I'd once had one with Sydney after breakfast.

"A good choice," he said. "The champagne of beers." He carefully poured it into a tall glass, excused himself, and left me to converse with Sheila while he went upstairs to get dressed.

I was leaning against the stove, which felt unnaturally cold. On top of it, above the knobs and dials, was a long line of wishbones drying, a half dozen or more. Sheila looked very hot and flustered, and all the whirring and grinding noises were making it hard to talk.

"Have a seat in the living room and I'll join you in a minute," she shouted.

So I wandered off with my glass of beer and took the opportunity to see what I could see. What looked like a painting or print of a hockey goaltender—a Ken Danby, perhaps—over the mantel of the propane fireplace turned out to be an electronic image on a huge flat-screen TV. As I got up close to the screen, I expected to see a pixelated image—the new pointillism, perhaps— but the picture was as sharp and clear up close as it was from a distance.

Another jet seemed to be coming in for a landing on the roof, and the whole house vibrated.

In an adjoining room, an even larger TV was the centrepiece of a home-theatre system that faced a semicircular sectional chesterfield that could accommodate a fair-sized opening-night audience. There were book-case-sized towers filled with DVDs, videotapes, and CDs in all four corners of the room. No books, not even the dear brother's (sob), not even so-called coffee-table books—decor props, display books, adult picture books. I scanned the CD titles: *Timeless Classics, Pasta Classics, Silver Screen Classics, Romantic Wedding Classics, Going for Baroque, Vivaldi for Valentine's, Mozart for Meditation, Music for Daydreams, Adagios for After-hours,* etc., etc. A *Baroque for Bathtime* CD was open on top of the stereo, the music not going for broke, however, but gently bathing us in solemn, meditative rhythms.

What a grand time Alicia would have with those, I thought. What merci-
less scorn—I can hear her now—she would heap upon this desecration, this
desiccation, this travesty, this commercialization of the classics; this cannonad-
ing of the Great Western Musical Canon—atomizing it, trivializing it, dumb-
ing it down, making it palatable to the masses. A never-ending supply of music
in the free-for-all public domain, but which real human beings, composers now
long decomposed, had sweat blood, shed tears, and torn their long hair over.
Cheapo compilation CDs endlessly churned out like slices of processed meat—
ham duets, pepperoni preludes, mock-chicken mazurkas, bologna bagatelles—
and she would chomp it to pieces and spit it out every time she was served it.
Alicia didn't want music to relax you, to romance you, to calm you down, but to
rouse you, to agitate you, to stir you up. The Fires of London, based in London,
Ontario, one of three chamber orchestras she performed with, played only agi-
tating contemporary music, mostly Canadian. The orchestra had no conductor,
and played—churned, burned—standing up.

Scorn, yes. Alicia burned with scorn as well as music. It was her most
characteristic trait, and the one that I most disliked, that bothered me more
than anything else, not that I was entirely free of it myself. If Alicia ever develops dementia like the old man, I thought, her scorn, like his fierceness, will
intensify beyond endurance, will outdo his ferocity, and God help her New
Man, Richard, if he is still around, if he is the one caring for her. That will
test his famous empathy, for sure. But perhaps empathy is the best partner for
scorn. Perhaps they will make a happy couple.

Richard the Great Heart virtually *emanated* empathy, Alicia was always
telling me, and I myself lacked it, her favourite tactic these days during a fight.
It was a simple black-and-white thing, in her view, like lacking rhythm or being unable to sing in tune. Even the great Beethoven, she said, couldn't dance.
A defective gene, perhaps, if difficult to find. Even male pattern baldness has
now been connected to a particular gene, a "gene chip," it was reported recently.
Perhaps lack of empathy, like lack of hair, is caused by a gene chip as well, instead
of something like a chip on the shoulder, resulting in a certain baldness of the
emotions that simply reflects other people's pain rather than absorbing it.

"You're only empathetic as an author," she once declared, categorically and unempathetically.

"Do you mean the *real* author or the *implied* author?" I replied, being deliberately provocative, knowing how intellectually insecure she felt outside her chosen field. She was always affronted, as if someone had farted or burped, by the use of professional jargon in casual conversation, even though she sometimes used it herself.

"Fuck you *and* your authors," she implied.

∾ ℅

Over the course of the evening, I noted that there were TVs everywhere in Sheila and Loyal's house: another giant flat-screen on the wall in the master bedroom; a smaller one on a swivel arm—the Canadarm, Loyal called it— above the fridge in the kitchen; and another one on the long vanity facing the toilet in the main bathroom. This one was permanently turned on, with no control buttons or remote to turn it off, and no *Far Side* collection, no book of *New Yorker* cartoons, or, last resort, no graphic novel, to help tune it out. Science-fiction writer Ray Bradbury, I recalled, had described a house like this more than fifty years ago, when TVs were just starting to appear, in a novel called *Fahrenheit 451*, the title referring to the temperature at which book pages catch fire and burn. He had imagined a society where reading was forbidden—a book-burning society, in fact, one that feared the power and influence of books. The houses had TV walls: a "four-wall televisor" in everyone's dream home.

I was no longer a science-fiction fan, though I'd read some of the old classics in my youth. John Wyndham's *The Day of the Triffids* had been another favourite, but Bradbury's book had made the biggest impression on me. I had first read it as a teenager in the sixties, and when it turned up on one of Celia's high-school literature courses several years ago, I read it again. A small masterpiece! I thought. Small? No! I was beginning to sound like some mealy-mouthed critic, or like Alicia dismissing the so-called minor master Chopin.

She barely tolerated my romantic indulgence, made a dedicated attempt to cure me of it. Subtle music therapy sometimes, the more emotionally refined Mozart or Debussy, but at other times it was cruel shock treatment: Scriabin, Schoenberg, and the almost autistically atonal Webern, who was shot by mistake, Alicia tried hard to convince me, during the US occupation of Austria after the Second World War.

No, not small at all. Big. Huge. Awesome, as Celia would say. *Fahrenheit 451* was first published in a magazine in 1950 as "The Fireman," the introduction to her school edition had informed me, and published in book form, along with a special asbestos edition—seriously—in 1953. It had not appeared in Canada until 1963, when I came across it on the revolving wire rack of paperbacks at our local drugstore—almost an all-American cast in those days, and no Canadian books at all. There were other American sci-fi writers, such as Herbert, Heinlein, and Le Guin, and a few English ones, such as Clarke, Shute, and Wyndham. And there was James Baldwin, Ralph Ellison, James T. Farrell, and Jack Kerouac. Even Henry Miller a few years later, though he had been quickly and quietly removed.

But perhaps it was the cover of *Fahrenheit 451* that I remembered most of all: a young man (myself, of course), muscular, naked to the waist, a red sun at his back above the monotonous grey city walls, books strewn on the ground at his feet, but, in a heroic pose, holding one book in his hand at his side and triumphantly raising another high above his head. Not a trophy, a flag, a gold medal, or a prize, but a book! And it was all of these and more.

By 1950, the television set had not yet become the mesmerizing, ubiquitous part of our lives that it is today; but there were already a few million TV sets in use in Bradbury's U. S. of A., and I guess he'd seen the writing, or the screen, on the wall. He seems to have foreseen the entire late-twentieth-century electronic tsunami, in fact: Walkmans, iPods, cellphones, and all the rest. Not just multivarious monster screens for our eyes, but "both ears plugged with electronic bees."

Bradbury's book was steeped in a pervasive Chopin-like melancholy, an existential, end-of-things loneliness. Something had been, or would soon be, irretrievably lost. The same melancholy feeling pervaded the apocalyptic world-at-the-end-of-things of *The Day of the Triffids*, also first published in a magazine in 1950. (What was in the air in that year, I wonder?) The man and woman at the heart of Bradbury's story, a childless and loveless couple, were growing apart. Our rebellious narrator-hero had a secret life. "It was a pleasure to burn" was the novel's ironic opening line, and our hero, Guy, the "fireman" of the book's original title, burned with an inner fire. Perhaps as an antidote to his wife's and her friends' obsessive and oppressive infatuation with the "gibbering pack of tree-apes" ("That's my family," said his wife, Mildred) who lived in the television walls, who "said nothing, nothing, nothing and said it loud, loud, loud," Guy had begun hiding and reading books. This was doubly traitorous for a fireman, for his job was not to save houses, but to burn them down if they contained hidden caches of books.

∽ ∽

But lo and behold, when Loyal came downstairs after finishing his toilette, dressed in beige cargo shorts, white socks and black sandals, and a blindingly immaculate white golf shirt, he was—if not raising a book in victory above his head—at least carrying one in his hand, the reissued edition of my first book, *The Ropewalk*, it turned out, which he'd found in a Chapters bookstore at lunchtime. I didn't think it would be available until the launch. The book had the same cover design as before, but this time it looked like one of those cheap mass-market paperbacks that I'd perused on the drugstore racks all those years ago. He asked me to sign it and, on a whim, I treated money-maker Loyal to my favourite inscription: *il miglior fabbro*, "the better maker," famously used by T. S. Eliot in dedicating *The Waste Land* to Ezra Pound. How amazingly versatile and useful it is! The word *make* must be one of the foundation words of the English language.

The last time I had used this was for New Man Richard, who had turned up unexpectedly at the launch of my last book. I'm sure Richard, a classical musician, familiar with Latin and Italian words and phrases, knew what it meant, and, proud artist that he was, thought of course that I was referring to his musical artistry, his composing, never suspecting that it was his amorous artistry, his lovemaking, his lovingness, that I had in mind. His Lovingness! *Il miglior fabbro.* His very name was Loveys, for God's sake! And yes, Richard, I meant it, I meant it.

One Christmas I had watched Sydney's paper schnauzer, Snooper, descended from a vermin-catching terrier, shred every piece of gift wrapping under our tree. I had progressed—a moral progression, as I saw it—from having no qualms whatsoever about setting the little bugger loose among Richard's original music manuscripts, strewn all over our, her, their—Alicia and Richard's now—living and dining room, a mess she had never tolerated from me...I had progressed from planning and carrying out this unforgivable act—only a writer could know the harm, the pain, that this would cause—to at least an *ironic* gesture of gratitude. Why? Let's just say: this music, late one night, crept by me upon the troubled waters. "Famous Blue Raincoat," I think it was. "And thanks for the trouble you took from her eyes..." And I recalled the maniacal, melancholy mess of the shredded manuscripts. I wasn't quite capable of that kind of gratitude and honesty yet, but I was getting there. Irony is much harder to give up than cigarettes and coffee.

Now I ask you, fellow-writers and fellow-travellers: how many times have you tried to say something as simple, sincere, and direct—as unironic—as that, and failed? Failed completely and miserably. And do you know why? Because words as naked as that need music. *Where should this music be? i' th' air or th' earth?/It sounds no more: and, sure, it waits upon/Some god o' th' island.*

Leonard Cohen the lyric poet had abandoned poetry and Leonard Cohen the novelist had abandoned the novel—for music, for song. How can the poet and the novelist, whose only instrument is words, create music? *That is the question.*

Where did this man's music come from? I often ask myself. Surely not out of the earth and the air of this majestically banal wasteland of prairies, muskeg, mountains, barrens, bogs, great lakes, rock shield, boreal forest, and ice pack. Surely not "out of," as they say in the music business, Westmount.

No, he is surely out of no other place than the Bard's blessed isle, a *god o' th' island*. He could have gone into the clothing business with his father. Think about that for a moment. He could have been a haberdasher, selling suits and shirts and ties, silk with a slub.

∽ ∽

Yes, Richard must have known what that inscription meant, but Loyal clearly didn't, and he wasn't going to ask. He just smiled at it, gave me an uncertain thank you, and tucked the book under his arm again. We went into the living room and sat on the sofa with a straight-ahead view of the electronic Danby.

"Plasma, digital, high-definition," Loyal said. "I change the picture every few days. Sometimes, instead of watching a movie, Sheila and I look through the entire DVD, every print he ever made. I got a Robert Bateman collection, too, and a Fenwick Lansdowne. I love looking at birds, and his paintings are the best. He never used a camera, like everyone else. Painted from memory. I used to go out birdwatching, but I don't get time anymore. With all the market uncertainty these days, I'm in the office twelve hours a day, seven to seven. And I still get calls on my cell on the way to work and on my way home. It's a good thing Sheila has a business of her own."

"The chops are ready," Sheila sang out, and I followed Loyal into the kitchen, where he got a beer for himself and another for me, then laid his silver beer stein on a large silver tray that Sheila had prepared for him. On it was a stainless steel bowl full of pork chops in some kind of marinade, a long fork and a pair of tongs, a pair of oven mitts, some foot-long matches in a brass container, and a small bowl of olive oil and a brush.

I followed him out onto the deck, a broad three-tiered arrangement with scarlet geraniums in large ceramic pots. A glass table with an umbrella was set for three. The day had been surprisingly warm.

"Let's fire up the barbecue," Loyal said, softly and thoughtfully, more like a modern-day philosopher on his way to his study than a steelworker about to approach the fiery maw of a blast furnace.

The barbecue was not on the deck, but way off in the garden beside a picnic table. A red-faced sun was setting, but still glaring fiercely in over the tall wall of the back fence. There wasn't a shade tree to be seen in any direction, just acres of rooftops on the slope of a hill.

"I keep it back here because the last one blew up," Loyal said. "I lost both eyebrows." He gave me that close-eyed beam of a look, and I imagined him looking almost Cyclops-like without his eyebrows. "I had a microwave that exploded, too," he added, "and a modem that went up in smoke. These things only seem to happen to me. When I report it, they always say they've never heard of it happening before. You know it can't be true, but what can you do. Would you mind removing that cover?"

I lifted a heavy grey plastic cover off the barbecue, and he laid the tray on a wooden shelf on one side of it. Another large jet roared overhead, casting a luminous shadow across the garden. The tray and everything on it vibrated.

"The igniter switch usually works," Loyal shouted, "but sometimes I have to use these matches." He lifted the container of oversized matches off the tray and placed it on the shelf on the other side.

"Planes come in pretty low up here," I shouted back.

"Yeah, the airport's only about a half mile away. You get used to the noise—we hardly hear it any more. We're paying for the view. You can see the ocean from the bedroom window."

Loyal was gently feeling the heads of the matches. "Must be the humidity," he said. "The problem with the igniter switch, I mean. These matches are always soft when I have to use them."

"'Tell me, Watson, what do you deduce?'" I said softly.

"What's that?"

"Nothing, nothing...just thinking out loud."

He raised the cover of the barbecue and began to turn the valve on the white propane tank beneath it. He turned a dial on the front panel and pressed the igniter switch. Nothing happened. He pressed it again. Nothing. He turned off the dial and closed the valve on the tank.

"Matches again," he said, but cheerfully. He liked using those big sparkler-length matches, I could tell.

He blew on the barbecue and waved his hand over it, then rubbed his hands together for a few moments.

"Got to wait till the fumes clear," he said. "Just a minute or two."

He opened the tank valve again, then positioned himself on the side of the barbecue and removed one of the foot-long matches from the brass container. I stepped back several feet. He struck the match on a paper matchbook, but the top of it cracked off. He struck another more gently, several times, and it crumbled. There would have been a lot of hard swearing if I had been the one doing this, but Loyal never made a sound, showed no sign of impatience or irritation whatsoever. His third attempt was deservingly successful, and as he held the lighted match in his left hand, he turned the dial on the front of the barbecue with his right. Then he poked the long match into a small hole on the side and the gas ignited with a puffing flash. He turned on the other dial and the barbecue puffed and flashed again. He closed the cover and adjusted the dials.

I executed a downward adjustment, as the financiers say, of my hunched shoulders and reduced my distance from the scene of the anticipated explosion.

"We'll give it five minutes to heat up," he said, smiling victoriously.

There was...what was it about him? An innocence? Yes, a silver-haired and blue-eyed ingenuousness that was very off-putting, that only the guilty, perhaps, would find off-putting. But surely oblivious money-makers, money-marketeers, like venal politicians, pedophiliac priests, predatory pimps, and parasitic, vainglorious publishers, can only *dream* of innocence.

Loyal's performance at the barbecue might have drawn more briquets than bouquets, but the chops were delicious. Tender as a mother's pie crust. But perhaps it was Sheila's advance preparation that did it—the exotic marinade rather than the actual grilling. Not to mention the accompanying wine. The Château Latour à Pomerol, a 2000 Bordeaux, was rated *classic*, Loyal said, best vintage since 1961. This particular brand was also a "best buy," he added, and he'd bought two cases. Though it needed at least ten years of bottle-age to be at its best, preferably fifteen or twenty, he'd decided to break open a bottle for this special occasion.

"This is very generous of you, Loyal," I said, as I gently swirled the wine around in my glass and gave it a respectful sniff. "A reserved but complex nose," I said.

"Hey! That's good!" Loyal exclaimed. "That's exactly what one wine taster said about it. Let me read it to you."

"Really…I was just joking, Loyal," I protested, but he jumped up and rushed inside.

"What do you think, Sheila?" I asked. She'd hardly said a word all evening, had looked somewhat upset, in fact.

"It's a lovely wine," she said. "James …I'm worried about Dad. He called me today at work—he's never done that before—and said he was going to… 'break out of this place' was how he put it…break out if I didn't bring Mom—"

Another jet was coming in for a landing—at the airport, I hoped. There had been arrivals and departures throughout the meal, but neither Sheila nor Loyal made any mention of them. If they raised their voices, it was not in protest but simply to have them heard.

Loyal came back out with a big thick glossy magazine. "Listen to this," he said. "'Reserved yet complex nose'—how about that!—'of blackberries, raspberries, flowers. Full-bodied, with silky tannins and a soft, sweet fruit finish.' He gave it a ninety-five, a *classic* rating, as I mentioned. That's better than *outstanding*, the level below. An investment-quality wine, we call it. Something most investors don't even think about. Better than real estate. Do you have anyone handling your investments, James?"

I was swilling a rather large mouthful when he asked this, and, silky tannins and sweet fruit finish notwithstanding, I almost coughed it up.

"No…I've never had occasion to need that kind of counselling, Loyal. With all due respect to your noble profession—and I do appreciate your interest—I don't think you have any idea what kind of money most writers make."

"No, I guess not. I've never had any writer clients."

"Well, there's a good reason for that."

"In the six-figure range, though, I would guess."

"Guess again."

"High fives."

"No...we're not celebrating yet."

"Mid fives...no? Surely not low fives?"

"Very low fives, Loyal. Often down on all fours. I made $12,400 last year, before taxes. An outstanding year—not a classic, but outstanding. Could I buy a case of Château Latour with that? You remember that old battle cry from the history books: 54/40 or fight? The Yankees and the Canadians were fighting over where the border would be, I think. Recently, there was another border skirmish, with Borders, the American bookstore chain. Well, we might have kept Borders out, but we got Chapters...and Amazon...and Bertelsmann, the multinational publishing conglomerate. Writers lost the financial battle long ago, Loyal, if ever there was one. Fifty/forty/ten, you can't win, we were told, a decree from the oldest empire of all, the empire of *das kapital*: 50 percent for *das kapitalists*, the investors, the publishers; 40 percent for trade, as Her Majesty would say, the retailers, the booksellers; and 10 percent for us—if we're lucky. The bigger traders—the amazons—demand more—45 or 50 percent—and then the publishers reduce our miserable 10 percent."

I should stop, I thought. *Kapital* is his bread and butter. But Loyal looked genuinely dismayed by these figures.

"Who devised that scheme?" he asked.

"Who knows, Loyal? Lost in the mists of time."

"Perhaps you need an agent," he said.

"I have one, Loyal. He takes 15 percent of my 10 percent. But it's okay, I'm on wife-support." (Or *was*, I thought, but I didn't want to get into that.) "I've got a wife with tenure. Every writer needs a wife. Women too, of course—I'm speaking generically. But it's clear they've already found this out. The most successful writers in this country *are* women."

A wife of one's own, I thought, along with a room and a *partner*.

"How *is* your wife?" Sheila asked, interrupting my meditative fancy. *Your wife* sounded somewhat impersonal, but of course Sheila had never met Alicia, and neither had our parents. We hadn't had a family wedding, just a simple courthouse union that, in the beginning, we'd told no one about. I didn't tell my family until just before Celia was born, more than three years later. And I'd been home only once since I left, with Celia, but Alicia had not accompanied us. She didn't seem to have any interest in Newfoundland—indeed, in anywhere in Canada outside Ontario—though perhaps I was partly to blame for that. It must have seemed to her that I had little interest in Newfoundland myself.

∾ ∽

Celia certainly did, though. She was always asking me about it and always trying to draw its queer and difficult shape in her exercise books, fantasizing parts of it sometimes. She would put my sou'westered head on the Northern Peninsula neck and multicoloured waders on the Burin Peninsula boot. The Avalon and its narrow isthmus was sometimes a long-necked, double-winged bird; sometimes her own long-necked self in a ballooning red dress, arms and legs outstretched, dancing across the ocean. When she finally convinced me, when she was ten, to take her down (or *up*, if you prefer, north-northeast), I told her to pick any place on the map and I would take her there if there were a way to do it. Lushes Bight, Heart's Delight, Ladle Cove, Noggin Cove, and Leading Tickles—these were some of the places she'd marked in on the many maps she'd drawn, one of which I expected her to choose. But she decided to do a version of Pin the Tail on the Donkey. With a hatpin in her hand, she closed her eyes and walked toward an old road map that I pinned to the wall, one I'd brought with me when I came to Toronto over thirty years ago. Some places on this map probably no longer existed, I thought, had been resettled or had their names changed. There had been rumours before I left of an impending name change for all the Dildos—Dildo proper, South Dildo, Dildo Pond, Dildo Run, and Dildo Bight. And Gayside.

Celia pinpointed a park instead of a town, Windmill Bight Provincial Park, on the northeast coast, "the Straight Shore," as they call it—maybe they should change that as well—straight ashore from Funk Island, "the Funks," another place whose name delighted her. We flew to Gander at the end of July, rented a car, bought camping equipment and supplies, and drove to Windmill Bight, passing through Noggin Cove and Ladle Cove en route. We camped in the park just above a warm, natural freshwater swimming pool in Windmill Brook, and wandered the amazing sandy beaches in the park and at nearby Lumsden and Cape Freels. Every day for a week the temperature climbed to 25 degrees or more, though the ocean was still too cold to swim in. Celia was happy enough, however, just running through the surf in the sun and wind, like a cat with a gale of wind in her tail, collecting rocks and shells, building sandcastles, writing in the sand, chasing seabirds, hiding in the tall coastal grasses.

This was nothing like the Newfoundland that I'd known or remembered, but then all I'd ever seen, besides the old seaport of St. John's, were the highway towns: the mill, military, and airport towns. There was the existential, time-warp nowhere-land of Gander, where Celia and I had wandered among airport furniture dating from the 1950s; the dirty, smoky, sulphur-smelling paper-mill towns of Grand Falls and Corner Brook; and the former American military base at Stephenville. And then there were the dirty mining towns: the blinding red ore dust of my own hometown of Red Island, where every house eventually turned a shade of red, no matter what colour it had been painted; and Buchans, a company town in the dark heart of the Newfoundland wilderness where the ill-fated Beothucks had made their home. The old man had taken us to Buchans—for a holiday!—so he could go salmon fishing with a buddy of his who had once worked in the Red Island mines. He had promised us that there would be a circus—and there was. We had seen a sad-looking, single-tusked elephant dance.

Celia and I drove on to St. John's and spent a week with my family, then flew back to Toronto from there. But it was the week on the wild northeast coast of the Island that made its permanent mark on Celia, and which, eight years later, brought her back to Newfoundland.

∾∾

"Oh, Alicia's fine, she's fine," I said to Sheila. "Still teaching…and performing all the time." I didn't want to get into this—I knew what was coming. Loyal picked up the wine bottle and poured the silky dregs into my empty glass.

"I'm going to open another," he shouted. His voice seemed to have gotten louder over dinner. "'*Hold*,' they say. 'Built for longevity.' But I think I've held long enough."

"No, no, Loyal, not for me," I said.

"Yes, yes," he countered. "We're empty as well."

He went in through the patio doors with the empty bottle in his hand.

"Cecilia said you and Alicia are living apart," Sheila said quickly. "We had her over for supper at Easter."

"Well, yes…that's true. I was meaning to tell you about it. We're still sharing the house. I moved into the apartment at the back. Last fall, after Celia came here to go to school."

"I'm sorry to hear that, James. I don't mean to pry."

"No, no…it's okay."

"Cecilia could have stayed with us, you know. She's a lovely girl. She can still do that if she wants. She'd have the house to herself most days."

"Well, we didn't want to impose. Alicia hates *imposing* on anyone. Celia wanted to stay in residence, anyway, to be on campus. But now she's moved into a house downtown with another student. She's Polish, I believe, here studying geology. I'm having supper with them next Friday night. I don't know if Celia told you she's studying geology—or will be in September."

"No, I can't recall her mentioning that, though she did say a science degree, I think."

"I'm afraid she's rebelling against her mother, who always assumed she'd study music. I assumed that myself, to tell the truth. She's called after St. Cecilia, the patron saint of music. They were born the same month— November. Alicia thought it was auspicious. Do you know that you share the same name? I only recently discovered that. 'Sheila' is the Irish form of 'Cecilia.' Mother's people came from Waterford, I believe."

"Well, it sure didn't help me any. I can't sing or play a note."

"Celia's working with the Polish student down on the Southern Shore this summer, at Mistaken Point. Apparently, they've made some kind of extraordinary find down there—the geological equivalent of a new planet or something. She explained it to me, but don't ask me to explain it to you."

"Maybe she'll change her mind about the music," Sheila said. "Don't worry, she's so young."

Loyal came back with an open bottle of Château Latour and filled our glasses.

"This is really generous of you, Loyal," I said.

"No problem," he said. "Don't give it a thought."

I don't think I did think much, or talk much, about it or anything else for the rest of the evening. It very quickly became cool and damp out on the deck, and we went inside to the living room to eat our dessert, a delicious parfait. The wine flowed; *Adagios for After-hours* and *Music for Daydreams* poured out of the speakers built into the ceiling and walls.

Exactly at eleven, I thought I was being awakened by an alarm clock—the high-pitched electronic chimes of the Big Ben half-clock facade on the wall right beside me—and Loyal seemed to be shouting at me, telling me that someone—not me, I hoped—had to be at the airport at five in the morning to catch a six-thirty flight to Toronto. In my half-asleep, half-intoxicated state, the whole notion seemed like such a ridiculously nasty and unexpected piece of boilerplate reality—he might have been passing me a cheque for this wonderful meal—that I laughed out loud. But it turned out to be ridiculously true: Loyal said that he had a one-day investment counsellors' seminar on Bay Street starting at ten o'clock in the morning.

"Maybe you could catch it from the roof as it goes by," I said, Loyal's champagne beer and classic-vintage Bordeaux inspiring only a rather silly, inconsiderate, vinegar-vintage joke. Fine beers and wines, I've noticed, do little to improve the quality of an inebriate's humour. Chronic sour grapes, perhaps.

Loyal's Cyclops eye was gazing straight at me, and for a second I thought I had made him mad—ingrate, he was thinking—but he smiled kindly and his eyes drifted apart. He shook my hand warmly once again and said to be sure to come back to see him and Sheila before I left. Then he quickly made his way upstairs to bed.

Sheila made a pot of Japanese jasmine green tea that she'd bought from the Britannia Tea Shop next door to her own business on Water Street.

"Tell me about your shop, Sheila," I said, after the hot steaming tea had brought me around.

"Can we talk about Dad first?" she replied. "I'm getting more and more worried about him."

"Well, I had him out in the woods fishing last week and he seemed okay to me. He caught three dozen trout all by himself. I didn't catch a single one."

"That's not what I mean, James. Physically, he's fine, perhaps more fit than I am, but some days he doesn't know who's dead or alive."

"Yeah, he has his lapses, I guess, but I don't think he'll do any harm to himself. They keep a close eye on them down there. It's like a military post— a lot of hawk-eyed old soldiers always on the watch. You have to sign him in and out."

"Well, I hope you're right. I'm glad you're back, James. I'm glad you're home for a while. It's hard to know what to do sometimes. Loyal is great, but he's never around when I need him."

Not loyal enough, I thought, but more in fun than anything else. I liked him, I had to admit, though he had not found his way into the old man's heart.

Sheila stood up and came toward me and I stood up, too. I'd forgotten that she was as tall as I was. She put her arms around my neck and sobbed softly on my shoulder. It felt good having a woman's arms around me again, even a sister's.

8: THE FIRES OF LONDON

I decided to walk home instead of taking a cab. I do a lot of writing when I'm walking, especially late at night, when all is quiet. Around one o'clock, sidling back down the sidewalk of the same steep hill I'd climbed earlier in the evening, still half-drunk on the classic Château Latour à Pomerol, in spite of the hot tea, I encountered another lone soul going up, pushing a shopping cart piled high and wide with swollen garbage bags, like the mythical Sisyphean stone on wheels. He was groaning from the labour and urging his burden straight up the middle of the road.

Having been ideologically briefed by Kevin not long after I had arrived, I began to see these wagons and wagoners wherever I went, all over the boom-town range—the BMW of a new underclass, as he put it, the ubiquitous vehicle of a new visible minority. Some even slept in the king-size model under a tarpaulin, he claimed. This haphazardly mobile underclass was the most conspicuous evidence of the usual effect of sudden prosperity, economic booms, he said, which mainly benefit the chosen few, i.e., the rich, the investors, the exploiters, those who already have more than they need and make it even harder for those at the bottom to buy food, clothes, fuel, houses, and other necessities of life.

Kevin had attacked a cynical colleague of his with whom we were having coffee in one of the university cafés one afternoon when he deduced—crassly, perhaps—that the more stuff there was to be bought and sold, the more there was to throw out and the more there was to scavenge, and that this fleet of scavengers was performing a public service by collecting society's waste.

"They *are* society's waste," Kevin replied.

Plastic bags, with the necks of empty wine and liquor bottles protruding through the tops, were hanging from all sides of the shopping cart, and the man's thin body, head down and pushing flat out, was almost horizontal with the hill. Being full of wine myself, and a very expensive wine, at that, I felt a bit guilty looking at all the empty bottles as he shoved past. He raised his head as he did, however, and hailed me:

"Hey, brudder," he said. "I don't s'pose you got a smoke?"

"No, sorry...I don't," I said.

"You don't. You don't *what*?" he replied belligerently.

"I don't have any. I don't smoke," I said.

"No...*I'm sure you don't*," he said, in a very hostile tone.

"Good night, brudder," I said.

"Fuck you, too, brudder," he replied cheerfully, and put his head back down and pushed on up the hill, an aggrieved but stoic Sisyphus on the grave-yard shift.

His parting words, amplified by darkness, hung there in the foggy air in the empty street. Had I sounded like some evangelical ex-smoker? I wondered. (I had given up smoking the year Celia was born.) Did I, a smoker for twenty-five years, now sound like the sort of judgmental bourgeois who thought that smokers were a crossbreed of idiots and addicts? Or did I look and sound like the sort of person who wouldn't give a fellow creature a cigarette even if he had a pack in every pocket? Though his cart was full of discarded treasure, perhaps he hadn't found any of it in this neighbourhood of affluent and unsympathetic hoarders.

∽ ∽

Perhaps I did lack empathy for the poor, bare, forked animal, unaccommodated man, as Alicia claimed, as she did for poor, uninitiated, unsophisticated man, musically speaking. But if I did, it was not rooted in heartlessness or indifference, but in what I might simply and humbly call *dejection*, weariness of spirit—a chronic state, best described by Coleridge in his poems "Work Without Hope"—the title in no need of a poem at all; on good days I took it as wise counsel, an exhortation—and "Dejection: An Ode": "A grief without a pang, void, dark, and drear,/A stifled, drowsy, unimpassioned grief..." Not to be confused with depression, which is bad enough, or the less debilitating SAD, seasonal affective disorder; not a psychiatric condition, a clinical condition; not to be found in the *DSM*, the *Diagnostic and Statistical Manual of Mental Disorders*; but a spiritual condition, *the habit of my soul*, a malaise of the spirit rather than the mind, brought on by the slings and arrows, the slop, the sorrows, the daily grind of the workworkwork of art.

The ironic thing about Alicia's scorn for the musically illiterate was that she, an only child, had grown up in a home without music of any kind, not just classical music. Both her parents had full-time jobs and were avid bowlers, curlers, and golfers in their spare time, always on the go, and when at home watched bowling, curling, and golf on television. But her mother, Beatrice—or Beat, as her now deceased husband used to call her, and as she now wished to be called—had somehow got it into her head that classical music was an important thing in life; not intrinsically important, mind you—she didn't listen to it herself—but as a social stepping stone to better things.

Beatrice didn't read books, either, and certainly not the kind that I wrote. Not just literary fiction, however, but all fiction—mainstream, historical, romance, detective, whatever. She had no interest in any of it.

"I've never read a novel in my life," she had proclaimed proudly, the first time we met, when I told her what I did for a living. "Only fact-based material," she added.

Material, indeed; it might have been a swath of cloth she was talking about, but not whole cloth, of course. I had never seen a book in her house, in fact, not even a coffee-table book, only newspapers and so-called lifestyle magazines. In support of this anti-literary ideology—though I thought I had covered up my instinctive negative response—a few weeks after our introduction she had shown me, as if in her defence, a magazine article on Cary Grant (Beatrice's favourite actor, her "dreamboat"), who had also confessed to not being able to read novels.

"Why would anyone want to read something that isn't true," said the man who was described in the same article as being "the best actor in the history of the movies." It was not a question, I might add.

I wondered how this master of cinematic illusion saw his own work, how he could so easily dismiss his fellow workers, his fellow illusionists, in the literary field. Perhaps he was one of those actors who, as paradoxical as it may seem, saw the secret to acting as simply being yourself on screen or on stage, not playing a role or adopting a disguise at all, taking part in the fraudulent enterprise of art but not being taken in by it. Quite a high-wire act, to be sure, and adding a depressingly dull dimension to his kinsman's immortal lines, "To thine own self be true…"

I had once heard, while in the company of a hyper, post-performance Grim McGillvray, an old Stratfordian actor espouse this be-yourself view on a late-night TV talk show—the short-lived attempt to bring a version of Peter Gzowski's *Morningside* radio program to television, I think it was—and McGillvray had been talking back to the TV set as this actor rambled on, becoming particularly upset at his "demented" view of the acting process. Now, it must be said that at this time McGillvray was in Toronto doing his one-man show, "I Never Knew the Island Was So Beautiful," to which the reviewers had been very kind, and he had gone out to Stratford on his day off for an audition, but it had not gone well, so his hostility toward this Stratford stalwart might simply have been a reflection of that. Methinks he doth protest too much, I thought. Perhaps I knew him too well, and I was not the right one to judge, but McGillvray's Lear, for instance—or Falstaff, or Polonius—could at times be three parts McGillvray to two parts Lear.

But, in relation to Beatrice's reading habits, a most curious thing occurred years later, after Alicia's father died and her mother was living in a small condo on her own. It showed, if nothing else, that if dreamboat Cary Grant did not have the aptitude, the capacity, the stomach, the latitude for literature—"to read something that isn't true"—then Beatrice certainly did. But she had "lost her mind," she claimed, had lost three weeks of her life, at least, during which time she had read a novel—the world's first, perhaps, and greatest, and longest—

which I had never been able to get through myself: the exasperating, the enervating, the mentally dislocating, the anxiety-of-influence peddling, but gloriously all-embracing, *Adventures of Don Quixote de la Mancha*. She couldn't remember reading it, of course, but I bear witness to the fact that she did, and I watched the red-ribbon bookmark move from sheaf to sheaf in disbelief.

Beatrice had moved in with us, or we had moved her in, she being too sick with influenza, and then pneumonia, to look after herself. She spent all her days and nights in the spare room, venturing only to the bathroom, eating practically nothing, drinking only warm water and tea. She very slowly began to recover, and one night I was amazed to find her reading a book she had taken from one of the bookcases in the room. It was propped up on a pillow in front of her face, a heavier-than-thou, thousand-page hardcover edition of *Don Quixote* that I'd bought at a Trinity College library discards sale. I would have thought she wouldn't have the strength to lift it, let alone the inclination to read it. But lift it she did, and read it she did, all the way through, and a few days and nights into this marathon I myself was sitting in the living room reading, late in the evening, when I heard a loud thump on the ceiling.

Now, considering Beatrice's personal history—in particular, her antipathy to books—the only explanation for her peculiar behavior I could come up with was that the flu virus had broken through that mysterious firewall called the brain-blood barrier and entered the neural pathways of her book-barred brain. Only a security breach of this kind, I thought, could induce someone like Beatrice to read a *novel*, and especially one as outlandishly antic as this one. This was a serious consideration—I kid you not—and being alone that evening, and thinking off and on that such a biological breach could have fatal consequences, I rushed up the stairs thinking that I might find Beatrice's dead body on the floor. But there she was, sleeping peacefully. The book had simply slid off its supporting pillow to the hardwood floor, as it would again and again, and it appeared that she had closed it before she had closed her eyes, for the red-ribbon bookmark was in place between the yellowed pages.

But to get back to the daughter, my now estranged wife...In addition to the usual physical activities for little girls—dancing, figure skating, and gymnastics, along with camps of every conceivable kind—Alicia had taken lessons on piano and violin. And at the age of nine, after some probing and prodding on Beatrice's part, Alicia had been pronounced "gifted" by both her music teachers.

She had auditioned on the violin for music school, but at the end of her second year she switched to the viola, and went on to do a Ph.D. in viola performance. She was now the First Violist with the U of T faculty orchestra, along with performing in the Fires of London and the Corelli Consort. She had been personally consorting with the faculty orchestra's First Violinist, Richard Newman Loveys, for two years or more, and the Fires of London had been burning in more ways than one, before it had all been revealed to me. Simple human revelation, though, not divine. From Alicia herself, last August, the day after Celia had left to attend university here in St. John's. But we have laid the matter to rest, I believe. We are on coolishly friendly speaking terms, though living in different parts of the house, even after what she refers to as "the incident."

"We have outgrown one another," as Alicia had diplomatically put it during the revelation, the proffered verdict of a jury of one, a large heavy safe of a verdict, now on public display in our storefront window, and which no combination of words—arguments, pleas, other revelations, even words of love—could ever unlock. I have moved into the apartment at the back of the house; she has stayed in the house proper, and is paying the mortgage with her juicy U of T salary and generously not charging me any rent. Our contiguous embassies are always open. Richard will not be moving in, she said. She never wants to live with a man again. But he comes by often, sometimes stays overnight. On one of those nights, early on, the incident took place.

Now I have nothing against this man Richard. Dick. ("Please don't call him Dick," she says.) I bear him no hard feelings. No doubt he *is* an empathetic man, as Alicia has so often reminded me. It is an essential human quality, I agree. As I said, I am always working on my own. But when I first heard those erotically empathetic, those lovemaking, sounds coming through the bedroom wall of *our* house into my lonely bachelor apartment cell—or maybe I just imagined hearing them—I waited for Richard outside in the dark and jumped him from behind the overgrown hedge, sat upon his chest in the driveway with my hands around his throat.

"You're out of control!" I heard Alicia shout.

I remember, however, being careful not to squeeze too hard, for he was not really fighting back and his eyes were getting larger. I remember thinking how young and innocent he looked—a big sweet curl over his forehead, glistening under the streetlight—and I was the one feeling guilty, so I finally gave in to Alicia's frantic shouts and violent tugs on my clothes. Perhaps she was also pulling on my hair; perhaps she had *me* by the throat. Perhaps we were both out of control. Perhaps we were *all* out of control.

No, not Richard. He remained on the noble, higher ground, absolutely luxuriating in magnanimity. As I mentioned, he turned up unexpectedly at my last book launch. I had of course met him socially on several other occasions, as I'd often been dragged along by Alicia to various concerts, receptions, and parties, and we'd chatted about my books—he'd read them all!—and about his musical compositions, which the Fires of London had performed as world premieres. All of them had literary titles: "Sonnet for Violin and Chamber Orchestra," "Haiku Variations for Solo Violin" (fourteen miniature movements), "Intimations of Mortality for Violin and Piano," and the "Elegy at Evening for Viola and Orchestra" (written for Alicia, and performed by her at the premiere). In this piece, a theme and variations, he'd used an old technique called *scordatura*. The viola was tuned one whole tone higher than normal so that its part could be heard above the orchestra's viola section. He told me that I had used the theme and variations structure in one of my own books. An astute reader, a literary critic, no less, as well as a composer, a man so dedicated to music that he had sold the Rosedale mansion that his father had left him and used all the money to buy a rare Amati violin. He would have bought a Stradivarius, no doubt, if he had been able to find one.

I'd sometimes wondered if he'd been trying to compete with me for Alicia's affections, and to prove that music could do everything that literature could do, and more. (I for one would never argue with that.) If Eliot could write "Four Quartets," and Stevens, "Asides on the Oboe," well then, he could write sonnets and elegies and haiku and all the rest. But her affection for me had already cooled by the time she first met him, and she had probably made him aware of it.

Why had he come to the launch? I wondered. A display of his famous empathy? A simple gesture of goodwill? Did he see us as a triangle, some weird sort of artistic mélange? Did he want my blessing for taking Alicia? To see if I still cared?

⁓

The launch was at a Chapters bookstore. I had finished my reading and was sitting at a signing table and Richard was patiently waiting in line with the others. In the midst of distracting conversations, another part of my brain was trying to remember the names of the other people in the line whom I recognized but only half-knew; half-knew for a long, long time, however, and they would expect to be remembered. Some of them would kindly volunteer their names, but some would be finicky and withholding, oversensitive to my forgetting them. They would only reply (refusing to take the hint when I diplomatically inquired, "Whom shall I inscribe it to?" suggesting the very real possibility that the book might be for a spouse, a friend, a relative, or a lover)… stubbornly, like sulky children, they would only reply: "Me." Me me me. *I me mine, I me mine, I me mine.*

The tension was relieved, however, by my second-favourite songwriter in the Tower of Song, only one floor below the incomparable L. Cohen, Mr. Randy Newman. (He and Richard shared the same name! What was I to make of that?) He was singing "Lonely at the Top" at the top of his voice over the store's sound system, always in overdrive. It and the high-beam spotlights overhead must have been designed to irritate loitering browse-readers, notwithstanding the comfy chairs provided for them, who used the store as a library instead of what it was, a retail outlet, with units, product, on display; but for once I was glad that the music was loud. "Listen to the people paying just for me," Randy sang, as I smiled foolishly in the middle of a serious conversation with a customer, a book-buying stranger, and methodically and obligingly inscribed the books as requested and talked as cheerfully and sincerely as I could to strangers and near strangers and friends alike. Copyright was mainly for capitalists when all was said and done, Kevin had always argued, and he might be right. We made only pennies out of it.

Why had he come? What did he want? I wondered, as Richard neared the table. What would I write on his book? Go the fuck away, Richard, I thought; this is no place for a heart-to-heart. I could see his innocent curl over the shoulder of a man in a checked shirt in front of him.

"I loved the book," said this man when his turn came, laying no fewer than six of them on the table in front of me. "I read it last night—I couldn't wait. I'm giving copies to all my friends for Christmas. I just loved the scene at your wife's concert where you go to sleep behind the last row in the concert hall during the hour-long Schubert Quintet—'the Overdone,' as you call it. Yes! Two final movements, as you say, and then there's the Eighth Symphony, 'the Unfinished,' with no final movement at all."

The voice was familiar, though I had definitely never seen the face. For a moment, to delay my face-to-face with Richard, I considered initiating a tedious and tactless conversation regarding his naive identification of my narrator with me; but, thankfully, he diverted me by identifying himself.

"I'm Neville Behan, of CHRM," he said. "CHARM-FM," he added, in his sonorous radio voice, flashing a set of charming white teeth, a toothpaste-ad smile that was wasted on his faithful radio listeners.

"Charmed," I said, and shook his very uncharming—fat, hairy, and clammy—hand, the hand of the man Alicia called "the Bonbon Man," and his late-night, light-classical music program, "the Bonbon Show." I forget its real name, something like *Adagios for After-hours*," but it was on a local FM station that also played light jazz and light pop and everything light. The unbearable lightness of Behan, said the Punster, an impish, adolescent jack-in-the-box, the punning dummy on my left hand, the punning parrot on my shoulder.

∽∾

When I first met Alicia, she was a classical music evangelical, and I was an agnostic, at best; a very casual and indiscriminate listener all my life, though I had been an unconscious acolyte of the very discriminating Bob Kerr and his *Off the Record* classical music show. It came on in the early afternoon as my day's work was winding down, and I was ready for lunch and a break and some quiet background music. Then I might take a short nap or, more often, an hour's walk before going back at it again for an hour or two before supper. But for ten years or more—as undergrad, grad, and post-grad—I had painlessly, unconsciously acquired, perhaps through my pores as well as my ears, a superb classical music education from Herr Kerr, who had rigorous, authoritarian standards, excruciatingly discriminating tastes, and overflowing love for so-called serious music, without my taking it at all seriously. And though *he* certainly did, what came through most of all was this heartfelt, almost childlike, love for the stuff. He could fly into a rage, though, over "the notes"—not the musical notes but the liner notes—when they failed to offer any enlightened commentary on the composer, his music, and the performers. There were days when I thought he would chew an album cover to pieces on the air, or walk out of the studio in disgust. I understood. There were pages of manuscript about which I often felt the same way.

From the beginning, Alicia had insisted on my taking serious music seriously. Her self-appointed mission was to bring what had always been in the background of my life to the foreground. When music was being played in her apartment, which was practically all the time, I had to pay attention. No talking, no reading, and certainly no writing. I had to attend not only every recital and concert given by her friends and associates—and herself, of course—but, in the beginning, almost every bloody concert that was on in town. And though I usually got through them without a major incident (no attempted strangulations), really enjoyed some of them, in fact, there had been a few minor ones.

I had quietly rioted—a bit late, I grant you—at the inaugural performance (for my ears) of Stravinsky's "The Rite of Spring," as the opening-night audience had on first hearing it in 1913. I had acquired a bit of a reputation, in fact, without my being aware of it, as a routine killer of serial music, atonal music. I could not be trusted to attend any concert or recital with anything on the program by Schoenberg or that other Berg or Webern or Stockhausen or others of that stock without stepping on the toes of a whole twelve-tone row of people in order to get out in the middle of the performance. The ushers would not let you in once the music had begun, but they couldn't stop you from getting out.

And, yes, like my beleaguered narrator, I did lie down and nod off in the comforting dark behind the last row in the concert hall during the fourth movement of Schubert's hour-long quintet—not the famous "Trout," but the lesser-known String Quintet in C major, "the Overdone," "the Overstuffed." And this is melodic stuff, I must point out; not New Music but Old Music, full of *tunes*; no violent torque or atonal, twelve-tone *rows* (rhymes with *cows*). But quiet and slow, *very slow*. After the third movement, the (first) final movement, which I thought was the end but was just the end of my attention span, there was a tentative attempt to clap on the part of a scattered unsophisticated few, me included. I usually took my cue from Alicia in these matters, but she was not beside me that night; she was performing in the quintet—more shame, me—one of the five faculty artists. As the fourth movement, the (second) final movement, began, I made my move. I was sitting at the end of a row, a short side row, the second-last row—I was slowly learning new tactics—with a clear view of the enticing dark space at the back of the centre-hall seats, the carpeted floor, no ushers in sight. It was as easy as if I'd been sitting on the edge of a bed with the blankets rolled back.

I awoke to the sound of torrential applause, a standing ovation, and in the midst of it scravelled out the door.

∿ ∾

The Bonbon Man had left with his half-dozen signed books, which I had inscribed with the date and the old standby *Best wishes*, but this would not be good enough for the man standing in front of me now.

"Hello, Richard," I said, as warmly as I could, for he looked wary, as if he wouldn't put it past me to try and strangle him again, right here in the middle of this marketplace. But above all, he looked innocent, as brother-in-law Loyal had looked tonight. Loyal and innocent. They could have been declared preternaturally, *legally* innocent, both of them, their trust in others like a blind man's in a Seeing Eye dog. It must be that fucking curl, I thought. Did it turn Alicia on? Was it a fetish for her? Did she focus on it as she straddled him, bouncing aloft in her favourite position, moaning her little heart out?

"And what brings you out this fine evening?" I said. There were still quite a few people behind him, so I thought I should move the conversation along to whatever the point of it was going to be, if indeed there was going to be a point.

"To congratulate you, of course, on your new book. I know how difficult composition can be," he said pompously, "though of course I don't work with words. I'm sure it's much harder with the common currency of words."

Christ...the common currency of words, indeed. This sounded more like verbatim Minutes from the latest Craft and Sullen Art Consolation Society meeting at a Loblaws Community Meeting Room than an exchange between an estranged husband and his natural enemy, the new lover. But, on second thought, it might have been a clever elitist insult. No, not Richard.

"Please sign it for me," he said, removing his copy from a plastic bag, and also a pen from the inside pocket of his sleek black jacket. It looked like an old-fashioned fountain pen.

"Would you mind using my pen?" he asked. "I love the look of an author's name in ink. Squid ink, as my composition teacher used to call it. He would only use a quill pen and a bottle of ink on his staff paper—like the composers of old. Sometimes he worked by candlelight."

"My pleasure, Richard," I said, and, as if inspired by this ancient writing device, though sitting on a plastic chair at a plastic table under the glaring fluorescent lights of a modern, warehouse-sized agora whose units, whose product, could just as well be shoes or barbecues rather than books, I opened the cover of the book to the title page and wrote in my best Latin script my other old standby, though one usually reserved for my fellow writers: *il miglior fabbro.*

"Thank you," he said, as I handed the book to him. "I'm so looking forward to reading it."

And as he tucked the book under his arm and backed into the woman
standing behind him, I gave him my most magnanimous nod.

∞ ∽

"Oh, that's just like him to do something like that," Alicia said to me a few
days later, a remark she had often made about her mother, when I told her
that Richard had turned up at the launch. "He's so supportive, just naturally
empathetic."

She had come down in the basement with me as I tried to locate the
temperature gauge on what I still thought of as *our* hot water boiler, though
she reminded me that I had my own separate one now in the kitchen of the
apartment. This was real estrangement: not just separate beds but separate
boilers. She was convinced her temperature gauge was set too high, for her
water was extremely hot. Her friend Lesley, Ms. SuperGreen, had told her she
could cut down on energy use and CO_2 emissions, and of course save a bit of
money, by turning the gauge down ten degrees or so.

"What's empathy got to do with it?" I said.

"He sees you as a fellow artist. He respects you, he admires you—he
knows how hard it is. He wants to get beyond the personal."

"Well, that's going to be hard, too, don't you think?"

"It doesn't have to be, James. *Please*, James. We were killing each other.
I've told you so many times…Richard had nothing to do with our breaking
up."

"Did he say anything about the book?" I asked her, hoping she would tell
me if he had noticed the inscription.

"I don't think he's read it yet," she said. "He's really busy."

And that was the last I ever heard about it.

9: DUTCH NIGHTINGALE

Friday again, the end of another week—a whole week since I'd seen Sheila and Loyal, more than three weeks since I'd arrived—and I was way behind schedule. I got up early to get to work on the proofs, to read once again the terrible Parable of the Proofs—do we need this lesson again and again?—even worse than the Parable of the Talents, for I hadn't buried them, but used them, every last one of them, and look, just look, at the result. I also had an interview at four o'clock, and was expected for supper at Celia's at six. Commitments even as minor as these loomed large when I was trying to work.

I began the day with a bowl of Seven Motifs (what else), the auspicious or inauspicious French translation of Seven Reasons, an organic cereal that the students who'd been living here since September must have left in the cupboard. Or perhaps it was something that Grim, who was certainly not into organic food, had bought as a joke. Seven Motifs—The Best to You Each Morning—as the makers of that cornier brand of cereal used to say. But maybe Seven Brans was what we needed—The Best to All You Blocked Writers Each Morning.

Doubtless the day ahead would be an eventful one. I was feeling nobly, if dolefully, dutiful as I cleared off my desk—Grim's cherrywood (a bright and cheery wood) kitchen table—and set to work. A seductive view of the city from this perch, and I took that in for ten minutes or so. I have friends who prefer to work in windowless rooms, or rooms with views of bare brick walls, or rooms with blinds or curtains always drawn. I certainly can see the virtue of this, but I'm somewhat claustrophobic myself and have never been able to do it.

It was still only six forty-five, so I thought I'd check my e-mail, something I try not to do before starting work. (All the utilities were still in Grim's name, I had noticed yesterday, and May's bills were overdue.) There was no personal e-mail, but the sex spam, normally spasmodic, was spasming uncontrollably these days—thicker, larger, longer, and harder, so to speak—and was more amusingly, if sometimes poetically, illiterate than ever. *Put your lassie on fire of pleasement. Get ahold of your life, make your dig* [sic] *bigger. Six inches may be normal but...Make your dig a monster! Lengthen, thicken, enlarge, engorge... Baffle your friends, surprise your girls. Hello, I am pretty Russian girl. I can do for you is—what can not no girl! Free your willy with VPXL Herbal. Stun your friends, delight your girls. Hi, I'm from Russia, a dream to live abroad. My name is Mary, can we get started? Enlarge your brother with new pills. Get big dig or try dying* [sic]. *Ever wanted a giant rod? Click here. Women love if you have a 9-inch snake in your larder.* [In your larder?] *Hi from Brenna, do not ignore me please...* This visual white noise was distracting enough, but then I heard some real noise—outside the window, it seemed—a most peculiar, but, at the same time, very familiar, sound. *Caution,* I warned myself. I would not be fooled this time.

∽∾

The story is probably still making the rounds among Alicia's friends back home—*there,* I said it again. Kevin jumped on me the first time I said it. Where is *back home* now? I wonder. When I'm in Toronto, I call St. John's back home. Anyway, the story, the embarrassing story, is about my calling in a city maintenance crew to investigate a foghorn-like sound coming from the kitchen area of our house and the basement room below it, where the water pipes come into the basement from below ground. *No, he's not a complete Luddite,* I can hear Alicia saying. *Not General Ludd, in other words, just Private Ludd. He uses a computer, though he likes to say it's just a sophisticated typewriter. He even sends e-mails, though he doesn't surf the Net, as far as I can tell. But don't even say the word* cellphone *in his presence, or especially* my *cell.*

My cell, indeed. Her cell had embarrassed me all to hell, if only retro-spectively. Mr. Retro, as Celia is fond of calling me, though for her Mr. Young-at-Heart is what I've always tried to be.

While the other two members of the city maintenance crew poked around outside, the supervisor waited patiently beside me in the kitchen till we heard the foghorn-like sound again. Then we went down to the basement beneath the kitchen, where we heard it *again*, though not as loud as it was upstairs. He looked at the water pressure gauge and said the reading was a bit high. The other two men came down and said they'd found nothing un-usual outside. The verdict: airlock in the pipes, which would clear up by itself. They'd run the fire hydrant for a while to see if that would help. "Call us again if it doesn't clear up," the supervisor said. But I discovered Alicia's *cell*—she was on tour, performing with the Fires of London in Brazil—on the kitchen table, in the fruit basket, while eating my lunch not long after the maintenance crew left. It was set on *Vibrate*, my neighbour informed me—coming to your sex-spam e-mail inbox very soon—and I asked him to set it on *Silence*. It did help, however, to know that the ignorance was unanimous.

When the very promising young writer Cyril Connolly, who, all seemed to agree later on, never did live up to his early promise, famously identified the deadly "enemies of promise" back in the first half of the last century—yes, sex, for sure, along with drink, drugs, fame, journalism, politics, duty, family life, and perhaps one or two others that I can't recall (sleep and sloth, per-haps)—nowhere to be found among the notorious, insidious, enervating lot, the bushes and briars, the thistles and thorns, that get in a writer's way, that prevent him from doing what he has to do, was the one that I found the most distracting, the most inimical, of all: *noise*. Connolly was, to be sure, writing at a much quieter time, though the German philosopher Schopenhauer, a hun-dred years earlier, in the first half of the nineteenth century, had bitterly com-plained about this "daily torment"; in particular, whip-cracking, "this most abominable of all noises…the truly infernal cracking of whips" by cabmen and carters as they drove their horses and carts and carriages through the resounding cobblestone streets. "I would like to know," he said, in "On Din and Noise," "how many great and fine thoughts have already been cracked out of the world by these whips."

I myself was tormented by the daily din as well, and, in the week before I had left home—*home*—I began to feel that there was something new and unusual happening noisewise, as they say. On the Monday and Tuesday, from dawn to dark—and I was living in a so-called quiet neighbourhood—I'd been invaded by the usual suspects, now a twenty-first-century army of technologically sophisticated soldiers of noise production. Arrayed against me, against the writing life itself, against any kind of quiet work, were enemies of my solemn promise to deliver the proofs of the always hopeless, if sometimes deceptively promising, pudding before I left. Set against me, as if on a clockwork schedule someone had maliciously devised, were street sweepers, jackhammers, lawnmowers, Whippersnippers, hedge trimmers, tree trimmers, wood chippers, compressors, roof torches, and sewer suckers; trucks whose diesel engines were never turned off, ruffling the muscles in your chest, delivering fuel, cement, furniture, and empty waste-disposal units, and picking up garbage, discarded furniture, and full waste-disposal units; fire trucks, ambulances, motorcycles, and police cars; helicopters, hornet-like light planes, and jets; malfunctioning house and car alarms; barking dogs, cacophonous crows, and shrieking jays; and, of course, the ubiquitous telephone.

And in the early morning hours of a nondescript Wednesday, with no impending appointments or events on the day's calendar to distract me, a time and a type of day when I really like to work, even if I've been out drinking or have slept badly the night before—or at least to sit quietly at my post, keep vigil, dream, stare at the coal face, before everyone else is up and about and the hubbub really begins—I heard an unfamiliar, a most peculiar, sound. When I poked my head out the door, I sensed something new out there—a concentrated, high-intensity mezzo-soprano hum, as if all the electric and electronic devices in the world had reached some critical mass and were transmitting some unbearable overload of beams, currents, rays, signals, and waves, and the very air, every molecule, every atom, was alive and singing and the sound would never stop. I tried to tell what direction it was coming from, but it was impossible to say. It seemed to be coming from everywhere at once. Surround sound, with a vengeance. After an interminable half hour or so, though, it stopped. But the next day I think I heard it again.

∾ ᴄ∽

And now this, as the broadcasters say, as if they were flashers exposing their willies or breasts—deliberate, controlled wardrobe malfunction. What's that sound outside my window? The noise canary of the writing mine was again up early and at the coal face and was perhaps the first to hear it, surely a tipping-point signal, in the apocalyptic lexicon of the day. I heard it first, though I didn't really register it, as I hovered over the kitchen table, coffee in hand, looking out the open window, and then again, more distinctly this time, as I sat down and settled in for what I hoped was a final sortie on the proofs. Yes, clearly—it had come to this—from a still-bare bush in the garden outside, I saw, and heard, what could only be regarded as avian hostilities: a lone bird, not your common crow or jay or even seagull, nor your uncommon tickleace or waxwing or sooty shearwater—and certainly not your noble nightingale—but a vulgar, shameless, songless, copycat starling…imitating a cellphone!

At eight thirty I had a snack at my desk-cum-table, some comforting toast and marmalade and more coffee. I put on the Thomas Tallis CD that Celia had given me for my birthday—otherworldly Renaissance religious music—and was transported right away to a place where I did not hear the agnostic noise inside my head. This was sometimes worse than the noise outside—a compositional cacophony like an orchestra tuning, or the metronomic plink-plank-plunk of the piano tuner who used to show up with the regularity of a metronome himself, every six months to the day, to the hour of the day, and spend two hours tuning Celia's grand piano; a compositional buzz and crackle like the white noise between the unknown stations we are forever patiently tuning in. And there is no calibrated, brightly lit band for these frequencies,

Loyal Reader, no dial, no digital tuner. I imagined the fumbling digits of a half-deaf man fingering a Braille band for the blind.

Through the window I saw a straggling line of hooded, knapsack-laden, baggy-jeaned schoolboys trudging up the street, as if in procession with this solemn, ancient music. If it were not for the wires of their MP3 players running from inside their hoods to their jacket pockets, in which their hands were buried, you might think they were young monks out for their morning exercise. There was an existential weariness, a heaviness, to their walk, a pilgrim's progress, as if carrying some great burden at sixteen that was much heavier than the knapsacks on their backs, and they looked heavy enough. Perhaps the stresses and strains of the teenage life are much greater than they used to be, though Celia had seemed to move through it with ease. But she was so busy, so busy—she hardly had a childhood at all. She is *listening* to music now, she said; for the first time she is able to listen with pleasure to the music she only had time to practise before. Listening then would only have been more work. Was it right, I always wondered, for a young life to be filled with so much work? Was this why she had turned her back on it all?

The phone rang, the house phone, the land line, and it was my editor, Peter van Loon. He was "wondering" about the proofs. When is an editor ever *not* wondering, i.e., reminding you, harassing you, about the proofs? But I loved the man, our Dutch uncle. He was always on our side. You knew this for certain, no matter what he said, how much he disagreed with you, argued with you, about many things—a word, a sentence, a chapter, an outrageously bad pun, agent demands, dreary signings in commercial netherlands, changes to the proofs. He did not try to stifle the demiurge—that ur-creator and its urge to make changes to the proofs. He was always on the side of his writers, a bulwark against the marketers and costers and big-box profiteers. Nothing got past him: a book cover design with overtones of Stephen King; even mundane matters like typefaces, paper colour and weight. We might be a so-called *trade* publisher, he once said in an interview in our semi-official national trade mag, but we're not just *in trade*, as Her Majesty would say.

But I wish he wouldn't call so early in the morning. He was at his desk at 7 A.M. every workday, and usually stayed until seven in the evening. He did this so that he never had to work weekends. He had a big family—four girls perfectly spaced, five, seven, nine, and eleven, and a pediatrician wife who worked half-time and wrote articles for *Pediatrics Today* on the harmful effects of lawn pesticides, who had been on the front lines of the Ontario College of Family Physicians in their fight for a province-wide ban on cosmetic pesticide use.

I'd had dinner with them many times. Peter invited his writers over on long weekends, at Thanksgiving, Christmas, and Easter, and always had his girls, all Suzuki violin students, as Celia had been, entertain us with a mini-concert after dinner: from shaky solo performances of "Go Tell Aunt Rhody" and "Song of the Wind" to impressive ensemble performances of trio sonatas by Vivaldi and Bach.

Another reason he went to work early was that he always rode a bicycle and wanted to avoid the traffic. Cycling was in a Dutchman's genes, he said, though he never really considered himself a Dutchman. He was of Dutch descent, obviously, but he was a first-generation Canadian and spoke English better than I did. I was a first-generation Canadian myself; my parents had been born Newfoundlanders, and the old man still considered himself a captive Canadian. Peter's father had come to Canada after the war, found work on a farm in the middle of the Prairies—a twenty-year-old city boy who knew nothing about farming—married a Saskatchewan farm girl and moved with her to the city of Saskatoon. In his mid-forties now, Peter, christened Pieter, an only child, had graduated from the University of Toronto with an honours degree in English, then got a job as an editor with an educational publishing company. His parents were dead now, and he had never gone to see their homeland.

He was a mild-mannered, humorous, philosophical man, with no ethnicity hang-ups that I could see. Being very sensitive to language, however, he did carry on a sort of running joke about the English language being saturated with anti-Dutch sentiment, a hangover from the Anglo-Dutch wars of the seventeenth century, he said. After the children's concerts, over our coffee and liqueurs, he would sometimes engage us—there would always be at least two or three other writers in attendance—in a contest to come up with the meanings of all the derogatory Dutch phrases he pulled out of his Dutchman's breeches, a seemingly endless list of ethnic slurs that he laughed his way through, that were still in the language after 350 years. (And I had only a scattered Newfie joke to contend with.) There was Dutch treat, Dutch comfort…courage, defence, talent, auction…Dutch uncle, which I sometimes used myself; but my favourite, as you might expect, was Dutch nightingale—a frog—which could croak its way into his editing critiques at times.

On the phone, we had left the subject of the long-overdue proofs—I'd had them in my possession almost a month now—after my solemn promise not to rewrite the book this time round. (I was a difficult author in more ways than one.) He was sure this was what I was doing, as I was taking so long— the book was scheduled for September publication, he reminded me—and he dreaded another showdown with the costers. But I persuaded him that it was just family troubles that were delaying me. Then he brought up the thorny subject of publicity and promotion—PP, as he called it—something he himself never wanted anything to do with if he could manage it. I'd hinted in an e-mail that this time round I didn't want anything to do with it either.

"So what are you saying, James? You don't want to do any PP at all for this book?"

"Well, yes, in a manner of speaking…yes."

"You mean *no?*"

"Yes…no. No running around the country. I've done four books with you guys now, Peter. That new crowd is trying to market me as a mainstream writer. I'm not mainstream. I'll never be mainstream. I'm…sidestream…tributary."

"James…listen. You know that if you were just starting out and writing the kind of books you're writing now, you'd never get them published. We're not independent anymore, remember. Maybe no one's independent anymore. I'm just one of the editors here now, not the editor-publisher. We're with a multinational now.

We don't have the same control we used to have. They have different ideas about how things should work, a different agenda, a more commercial, a more international, approach. One of my colleagues was just told to turn down a manuscript because it was too firmly rooted in its Canadian *milieu*."

He pronounced this last word with the contemptuous flourish that this sort of rejection deserved.

"Can you imagine that happening to anyone among the previous generation of writers?" he said. "Dear Margaret...Dear Alice...Dear Robertson... about this Manawaka, this Jubilee, this Deptford. Anyway...they're not going to be too happy about this."

"They're never happy, Peter, no matter what I do. That's their job—to be unhappy for the firm, the team. To keep the firm unhappily buoyant. We're just product to them, and costs. They don't even read the books we write."

I realized I had said *we*. I meant *we*. Peter, more than any editor I'd ever known, knew how to help you finish a book. He had an uncannily intuitive way of knowing what you were trying to do in a book—things you might not even be aware of yourself—and helping you to bring it off.

"And how do you suggest I present this bit of news to the *team*, James?"

"Maybe they can think of it as reverse publicity—or *perverse* publicity. You know, the recluse effect—Salinger, Pynchon, even McCarthy and Roth. Seems to work for them down there. Maybe we can be the first to import it. Free trade, and all that."

"Yeah, they could issue a press release saying you no longer want to talk to the media; another to all the bookstores in the nation saying you're no longer available for signings; one to the Canada Council—you're no longer available for readings or tours; one to all the prize committees—you don't want to be considered for prizes anymore... *Perverse* would be the way they'd look at it, James."

"No, no...you could still submit my stuff for prizes, but if I win one of those lotteries I can refuse the prize. Look at all the attention Our Man Leonard got for rejecting the GG award. People still remember that. But can you tell me who won the GG last year?"

"Yes, as a matter of fact, I can."

"Well, you're not a good one to ask, Peter. You've got a vested interest in these things. I bet if you asked anyone on the street—"

"James…one more week. I want those proofs in a week. Then write a new book—don't rewrite this one. I'm going to call you a week from today."

"Cheerio, Mr. van Loon."

"Cheerio, yourself."

∾ ∽

Around ten o'clock, a colourful sweep of cleaners arrived at the house across the street, four young women in what looked like floral maternity tops, black slacks, and white sneakers. They looked tanned, though we hadn't had much sun, with short, streaked hair—green, orange, purple, red. They were standing with their bare arms folded while being spoken to by a silver-haired woman in a black raglan. She was standing in the street, leaning on the roof of a sleek silver car that looked like a lopped-off SUV, or a shrunken station wagon. The driver's door was wide open, swung out into the street, and the radio was on. The car was puffing exhaust fumes that were drifting back into the young women's faces. She must have been shouting to be heard, for I could hear a DJ on one of the local stations barking one of those commercials that stream so fast your brain always trails behind the sense of it. When she got back in the car, I could see a familiar company logo on the door: *Molly Maids*. (Alicia and I had used them once or twice a year ourselves, usually at Christmas and Easter.) She put her cellphone to her left ear, her right hand to the wheel, and drove off.

The maids stood around in the driveway for a while, amidst mops and brooms and buckets and plastic bags, talking, laughing, and smoking, gesticulating wildly at times and jumping up and down, then picked up their gear and went inside the house to begin their labours. Two of them, I noticed, had very familiar-looking blue-and-white clasps on their bare arms, their right arms, just below the elbows. I wondered where I had seen those before.

I stopped working around noon and had a bite of lunch. And a pathetic bite it was—Cheese Whiz on crackers with a cup of strangely reddish tea made from abandoned No Name tea bags. I really had to go out and buy some food—I was still eating most of my meals in restaurants and bars—but there was no supermarket, not even a corner store, within a convenient walking and lugging distance. The Ryvita cardboard rye crackers tasted as if they were already hosting that hallucinogenic ergot that grew on rye. O sweet lost days of my drug-dazed youth! What I was after these days was an hallucinogenic *argot*, but an inspired, universally comprehensible one.

While whizzing on ergot, my mind flashed back to an old black-and-white film on the CBC about the man with the golden voice and the famous blue raincoat—Our Man Leonard. The camera had followed him on a leisurely stroll from his house, on the trendy Plateau in Montreal, down the Boulevard Saint-Laurent, "the Main," as it's called, to his local depanneur, where we watched him gaze longingly at the not-so-trendy Cheese Whiz on the shelf, then pick up a jar and have a closer look at it before adding it to his basket. I had imagined the Kraft PP people—"good food and good food ideas," as their TV ads used to say, intoned by the man with the cheesy voice—sitting around and having a befuddled good look at this film that one of their younger, hipper employees had alerted them to, wondering how they could, or if they should, make use of it, if it would make the product whiz off the shelves or sink like a heavy wheel of Parmesan.

∼∽

I was beginning to feel a sense of unease about the impending interview, so I left the house early, just after lunch, and went for a walk along the hiking trail that began a short distance from my door. It led east, to a large pond, and then around the pond, in the general direction of the television studio. It was a dull grey misty day, but, not far along, a noonday star, a shining motif—one of the seven, surely—a book and a half, came burning through the mist: a teenage couple walking hand in hand, not intimately but abstractedly, the boy holding a cellphone to his left ear, and the girl holding one to her right. Already having a book and a half on the burner at present, however, I filed it a light-year or so away, hoping that its light would reach me when I really needed it.

Just beyond where the trail entered the woods, a creature in the huge root of a toppled spruce tree, almost at eye level, let out an alarming screech—an innocuous little squirrel, for God's sake. I was sure there hadn't been squirrels in St. John's when I lived here before. I'd always admired, on long walks through Toronto's parks and woodlands, not only Mister Lightfoot's pussy willows, cattails, and wild roses, but the wild squirrel's bright-eyed, electric alertness and alacrity, its workaday persistence, its aggressive curiosity. Like the squirrel, I myself was forever on browse-patrol—sometimes the tiniest acorn of inspiration led to pages, chapters, *entire books.*

Though this was not a motif I wished to pursue, not an acorn I wanted to tuck away, I'd read somewhere a while ago that a squirrel's testicles were exceptionally large for its size—more than 2 percent of its body weight. A testosterone-driven curiosity, perhaps. If extrapolated to an average human male—175 pounds, say, for argument's sake—this would mean almost four-pound gonads. While I certainly do admire an aggressive curiosity, all things considered, and speaking strictly for myself, this male is curious enough.

At the end of the pond, the gravelly trail led right to the public library, in a wing of the still-unnamed, Soviet-sounding Arts and Culture Centre, where the honourary degree ceremonies and convocation had taken place. It was an ugly, reddish brown building with pigeons roosting on its concrete ledges and in the eaves, pigeon shit creeping down the walls. While walking Celia to school one cold spring morning long ago—she must have been no more than six or seven—I'd noticed two baby pigeons on the sidewalk, still alive, but with their eyes closed and their small bodies featherless, absolutely naked. It looked as if they'd fallen out of a nest that had been built on top of a large air exchange vent or an exhaust fan above a dry-cleaning shop. I tried to walk quickly past, holding tightly to her hand, hoping she wouldn't notice this distressing sight—nature in the raw, if sans tooth and claw. But she did see it, and was distraught. I convinced her, however, that the mother, like the Holy Ghost, would descend and pick them up, as the mother in all the stories she had ever heard and read had always found, always saved, the lost duckling, puppy, bunny, or cygnet.

I went into the library to have a look around. A sign on the inside door said, "Be careful for the paint." The librarians seemed to be in a bad mood. Perhaps it was the dreary, sunless weather, or the windowless, airless, over-heated bunker they were working in, which smelled of drying paint. Or perhaps it was a permanent bad mood. As Kevin had pointed out, they had been all but forgotten, left behind. There was no room at The Rooms for them.

Being careful for the paint, I found a computer terminal and checked to see how many of my books were in circulation, then went to the shelves to have a closer look. Most of them were in rather than out, but there were some recent date stamps on the back covers, and, as I scanned the pages, I found some interesting marginalia as well—heartfelt mini-reviews, you might say, to be kind; spam, spit, scat, to be unkind. Some of them were very unkind, but pithy, as always, proverbial, even. Here's an enigmatic one, I thought: *Mediocrity is always at it's* [sic] *best*. O sweet dead apostrophe!

Mind the marginalia, be careful for the reviews, but *it is best* not to get upset by this kind of cowardly critical attack. That's my advice to you aspiring writers, emerging from your cozy cocoons. Like the sex-spammers I encountered this morning, the anonymous critic is a subspecies of pervert; not an outright pederast or pedophile, but a sort of penile-ecstatic with squirrel nuts for ballast, a fearful flasher in a grubby bulbous beige raincoat. He works in darkness, in secret, with rare startling visitations. "Look at the size of this critical insight," he says. *Make your dig a monster.* "Wouldn't you like to have this between the covers of your TLS, your Q & Q, your NYRB." *Mediocrity is always at it's best.* What a clever motif. A brain-burner. A proverb for illiterates. He should try expanding it into a book to see how clever he really is, to see how much he can endure. Lengthen, thicken, enlarge, brudder. *Get big dig or try dying.*

On my way out of the building, I noticed a sign on a door saying "Basement Theatre," Grim's usual performance venue in St. John's, Kevin had informed me, and I opened the door and descended a set of stairs to the lower level. Footprints painted on the floor, like a purposeful trail of crumbs, and arrow-signs at lengthy intervals on the walls directed me on a mazelike route to the theatre, but I must have taken a wrong turn at some point, for the footprints vanished and I found myself in a dimly lit passageway with arrow-signs on the walls saying "Arts and Letters." I must have gone astray again, however, for this path ended at a large, black double door on which one sign said "Costume Bank" and another, "Closed."

Was I dreaming? I wondered. Had I fallen down a rabbit hole into some Kafkaesque warren of an underworld where I was being made to understand my true place, along with Kevin's and Grim's, in the broader scheme of things? With the infernal fires of anxiety burning in my head, I finally found my way back up to the main floor, much tempted on the way by an emergency fire-exit door, a sign on which warned me not to exit unless there was a fire. Be careful for the door, I said to myself. But if there were fire and smoke down here, I thought, no one would ever get out alive.

It was only three o'clock when I left the Arts and Culture Centre. I still had an hour before the interview, so I strolled down to the liquor store in the shopping centre nearby, Churchill Square, named after Sir Winston Churchill, where I hoped to find a bottle of that New Zealand wine that Celia was fond of, a Sauvignon Blanc that tasted like flowers to me—fusillades of florality, as the wine tasters might say. This particular grape, and New Zealand wine in particular, had been all the rage among Celia and her friends. It was to be a vegetarian meal this evening, she'd warned me on the phone, which meant tofu, and a bottle of wine, even a flowery one, was always a good antidote for tofu.

With about fifteen thousand students attending the university nearby—though it was third semester, the thinnest one in terms of available courses and student numbers—you would think that this large central city square would be filled with students, but there seemed to be more seniors wandering around than young people. I was tired from walking and needed to sit down. There wasn't a bench anywhere in sight, however, so I leaned against an expired parking meter and surveyed the square. It looked more like a large parking lot—more than half of it lined with meters—than a great convivial public space where people might gather in indoor and outdoor cafés and bars, or take possession of the entire square in protest against some tyranny or other, local or international.

I had often wandered down here as a student myself, more than thirty years ago, and the atmosphere felt much the same now as it did then. It was a sad, impersonal, desolate, uninviting place, with no animating spirit except commerce. In the evenings, when the motley collection of shops was closed—except for a drugstore and a delicatessen and one solitary tavern—it looked even more cheerless and forlorn. Square, plaza, *place*, mall, *esplanada*, agora—from time immemorial it had been a social gathering place, and a site of protest, resistance, riot, and revolution; but as I leaned against the parking meter and looked across the square whose namesake had been a symbol of wartime resistance against tyranny, I thought that if there were a city square anywhere on earth that would never be the site of an insurrection, this was the one.

Revolution was simply not in our blood—though apparently there was in the historical record a sketchy account of a band of apolitical pseudo-guerrillas called the Masterless Men, who had gone off to live in the heart of the Avalon Peninsula wilderness to get away from any form of governance, women included. What had once been the independent nation of Newfoundland, a pine-clad constitutional entity, had been lost, irrevocably, in 1934, without any serious resistance whatsoever, and was now just a geographical appendage of the Canadian home and native land, a stem of the national Maple Leaf. Perhaps it was fitting that the British colonial administration who had controlled Newfoundland for fifteen years before Confederation, the Commission of Government, an unelected regime passively regarded as a tyranny by some, should have built this meek anonymous public square and the housing units surrounding it; but it was ironic that they had named it after their own iconic resister against tyranny.

A uniformed meter man was walking down the line of parking meters like a regimental sergeant major sizing up his troops. I gave him a smile as he walked past and put an obedient quarter in the expired meter I had been leaning against, a demonstrator of meekness and deference to authority whose iconic figure might have been cast in bronze and erected in the centre of this square, though I told myself I was just following the orders of my charitable self, doing a good deed for the forgetful driver—a poor pensioner, perhaps—whose car was parked there.

"Door closed…as precaution to the strong winds," said a sign on the entrance door to the liquor store. Was some sort of strange new idiom developing here? I wondered. Be careful for the winds, I said to myself, and pulled open the exit door, a sign on which said, "Enter here."

The liquor store had a "Mission Statement." I swear. Set in a large aluminum frame on the wall, it looked like some official diploma of merit, but I wasn't close enough to make out the smaller print. *To sell as much liquor as possible*, perhaps. No, fiction, or deceit, was their only recourse. I imagined the managers of this government-run corporation, with a monopoly on our legal recreational drug of choice, sitting around the board room table trying to come up with *les PP mots justes* for their mission without cracking up. Fiction, along with misery, acquaints a man with strange bedfellows. I threw back the bedcovers and went over to have a closer look.

Mission: *To be recognized as an exceptional organization known for its passion in customer service, strong business performance, and progressive corporate culture.* Passion, service, performance, progress, culture…Intoxicating stuff, to be sure. Mere Screech pedlars, legal drug dealers, they might be, but with the zeal, dedication, hubris, and cunning of missionaries, Olympians, statesmen, connoisseurs, and social workers.

I was not to be disappointed, and a good thing, too, for I would need this bottle of wine *before* dinner, as it turned out. Having declared my own mission to a young clerk—courteous and eager to serve, if perhaps a bit cool, passion-wise—and admitted my failure to carry it out, he led me to the very bottle I could not name by brand but whose label I could see with my mind's eye, an extra-tall, green bottle of New Zealand Sauvignon Blanc. He understood my confusion, he said, and apologized profusely for the fact that the few bottles of New Zealand wine they stocked were subsumed under "Wines of Australia," which took up three aisles or more.

"Oh, that's all right," I said, raising the bottle as if delivering a toast. "Mission accomplished."

10: THE ROPEWALK

The interview was in the studio of a private TV station that was even older than the local CBC, a taping for a half-hour arts show called *Profiles*. It was to be broadcast on the weekend, I was told, at the usual high-profile time for arts programming—three o'clock on Sunday afternoon, a rest time for most and a restless time for the rest, an asleep or afoot time, and I had always inclined toward the latter. Even eleven o'clock in the morning, worship time, would be better, when fidgety non-churchgoers, non-believers, could assuage their guilt by worshipping at the alternate altar of the arts.

Kevin had briefed me about the host of this show, a former jock, "a pugnacious little rink rat with literary pretensions," as he put it, whose name was *Dayv* Maddigan. (Had the parents just got it wrong? Were they afraid that some people would call him D*avvy*, or D*affy*? Had he changed the spelling himself? Why was I curious about this?) He had published a novel, a "non-fiction novel in the tradition of Truman Capote's *In Cold Blood*," as his publisher had described it, poaching for PP. Published when the Toronto Maple Leafs farm team was based in St. John's, it had been a local bestseller. The main character was based on a former Toronto Maple Leafs hockey player who had moved here in 1958 to work as a recreation director, player, and coach. He became much more well known as a TV sports broadcaster, however, and in 1968 was recruited by *Hockey Night in Canada* as a "studio analyst." He would introduce the "telestrator" to Canadian hockey fans, a video instant-replay device used between periods for incisive, and often highly critical, post-mortems.

Though perhaps for legal reasons novelist Dayv had not used the player's real name, everyone knew who he was—the not-so-meek Howie Meeker. The title of the book was *Inherit the Ice*. Maybe people with names like Meeker inherit some kind of curse, or chip on the shoulder, which makes them touchy and defiant—predeterminatedly pugnacious. The name "Meeker" is not so bad, I suppose; but what if your name is "Cherry"? What if you're a hockey player, a mediocre hockey player, at that, and your name is Cherry!? Just a rhetorical question, hockey fans. I used to be one myself—a player and a fan.

In fact, the Meeker character, Kevin said—Bobby Breen by name—was portrayed by Dayv as an unacclaimed precursor, a prototype, of Don Cherry, a hard-nosed minor-league player who, as we all know, went on to become a major-league TV celebrity-clown. The irony, of course, was that Meeker himself had been a star big-league player—an NHL rookie of the year with Toronto in 1947 and a member of four Stanley Cup-winning teams—but his TV star turn as a CBC hockey analyst had been eclipsed by the said minor-leaguer in the early 1980s.

In 1970, as coach of the St. John's Capitals, the senior hockey team that competed in the provincial league, Howie Meeker led the team to their first ever Herder Memorial Trophy, Newfoundland's Stanley Cup. In his playing days in the 1960s, though, Meeker's belligerent style of play, though belied by a "golly gee willickers" persona, had not gone over too well down here. And in the climactic chapter of *Inherit the Ice* (here's where the cold blood comes in), in the final game—the seventh, of course—for the 1971 Herder, played in a small town in central Newfoundland on the night of a bad snowstorm, with the roads blocked and the nearest hospital fifty miles away, our cocky, pugnacious Meeker-like protagonist, Bobby Breen—Dayv has made him the *player*-coach—is given his long-awaited comeuppance: a murderous, cross-ice, blind-side check into oblivion. Legal, of course. Inherit the ice, indeed. There was no stretcher in the building, so a door was removed from one of the dressing rooms to transport him from the ice and…

Kevin had left it there. "Maybe you'd like to read it yourself," he said. "A purloined round steak of a plot; sturdy, stocky characters; game-seven, overtime suspense; themes thick as figgy duff; prose like hardtack; police-blotter motives; foreshadowing, melodrama, donnybrooks—in short, everything you love in a novel. Anyway…Dayv could be trouble if he doesn't take a liking to you. A trip, an elbow, a hook, a high stick, a cross-check, a head shot–expect anything at all. But then you can be a bit of business yourself."

While rink-rats-turned-novelists were perhaps only a minor irritation, a step removed, if there was anything that Kevin couldn't tolerate, that he really resented, that really roused his territorial instincts and brought out the worst in him, it was rink-rats-turned-poets. Don't try to tell him that anything— even hockey—is a fit subject for poetry; don't bother to say things like, "If brain surgeons can be poets when they retire, why not hockey players?" He will not listen to you. He will not have you cast, in his presence, your gracious, egalitarian net.

These presumptive rats, of course, could also be in other rinks—journalism, business, science, politics, even the other arts, even his own avocational rink, academe, as well as the hockey rink. He especially ridiculed those of his own kind, who, having tired of selling only two hundred copies of books of poems they had taken ten years to write, had taken to "slumming in verse," trying to get on the poetry bestseller lists (five hundred copies) by writing entire books about legendary hockey players—garrulous goalies like "Gump" Worsley or fiery forwards like "Rocket" Richard.

Kevin had rigour. "Let the cobbler stick to his last" was his motto. He himself had peaked at three hundred copies, but what the hell. Poetry was a calling. If you'd spent your life answering other calls, got only irregularly called, or were called too late, then too bad for you. And one final word of caution: never use the words *hobby* and *poetry* in the same sentence, in the same breath, if you know what's good for you. You will inherit his icy scorn. And if he's had a drop to drink, perhaps something a lot worse than that.

On my walk I had decided not to give any thought at all to what I might say in the interview, to what Dayv Maddigan might ask. It has been my experience that things often work out best that way. It was the same as preparing for an exam. When you studied right up to the very last minute, you went in there with your head crammed so full of information that you couldn't think straight. It was best to think about something else entirely, or to listen to music, or go for a walk. And it was always best to assume the following, as unchanging as natural law: they haven't read the novel, they don't really know what a novel is, and they hardly know, or they've just found out, who *you* are. But, in the face of all that, the PP Golden Rule we were expected to follow was *not* the Law of Inverse Proportion: i.e., that x (graciousness, tact, and courtesy) should increase as y (naivety, discourtesy, stupidity, and ignorance) decreased. This was a natural response, it seemed to me, though it could be read as a clever behaviourist scheme of positive reinforcement to try to turn the interview around. No, the PP Golden Rule was what I thought of as the Law of Perverse Proportion: that x, courtesy, should increase as y, discourtesy, *increased*. For me, this set up an unbearable situation, to which my usual response was a harmless, fun-loving fiddling with the facts—not fiction, exactly, but fictiveness, fictioneering, unreality TV.

∽ ∽

Dayv Maddigan might have been a pugnacious little rink rat with literary pretensions, but he had a gruff charm, and he had done his homework. A saucy-looking, overgrown cherub or altar boy, I thought, or a pretty-boy enforcer who might sock you one just because it was, as they say, part of the game. He seemed to know more about my early life than I did myself. There was no preliminary chitchat; he just led me to one of the two beige wingback chairs on the set, a bookcase filled with fake books between them, a fake fireplace to one side, a clipboard on his knee, and said he preferred to "get right down to it." "It looks like they're gonna go," as *Hockey Night in Canada*'s Bob Cole would say, alerting us to the start of a staged punch-up.

They would just record everything and "whittle it down" later to half an hour, Dayv said. He began by asking me why I'd left Newfoundland, in an almost accusatory tone, if I read it right. It might have been a woman that I'd left and not a place—an ailing widowed mother or a pregnant girlfriend or a wife with five children at her apron strings. I'd committed some sort of offence, it seemed, and he wanted a confession.

"You left Newfoundland. You left in Come Home Year, 1966, when everyone else was coming back. Tell me why you did that. You were only seventeen. You went to Toronto. That was awful young to be leaving home. Tell me about that. Did you know it was Come Home Year? Were you making some kind of statement by doing that? That was the year I was born, 1966…"

Christ…was he taking it personally? I thought. Was he suggesting that I had left him, too? And was he ever going to stop and let me answer? I considered my opening gambit, my options, as, in a husky voice, Dayv whipped his dog team of questions onward. I was leaning toward the fugitive, the lyricized, facts, and by the time he paused, I had slipped into the once-upon-a-time zone.

"No, I think I was only sixteen when I left," I began. "I didn't turn seventeen till September. Three of us left home about a week after school ended in June. We spent a night at the Cochrane Hotel in St. John's, where Trotsky, Marconi, and Alcock and Brown were supposed to have stayed. They had framed photos of them on the wall in the lobby. Framed alongside them was an old yellowed page of illegible signatures from the hotel register, four of which, I assumed, were theirs.

"Early the next morning, with our grips in our hands, we walked all the way down Water Street to the train station, a mile or more, because we didn't want to waste the bit of money we had left on a taxi. We took the Bullet to Port aux Basques, the ferry to North Sydney—a rough crossing, I remember—then the train again to Union Station in Toronto. We arrived early on a Monday morning, and the Mamas and the Papas' 'Monday, Monday' was playing on a small transistor radio behind the counter in the station restaurant. The waitress, a beautiful young woman in what looked like a nurse's uniform, was making a fresh pot of coffee and singing along. We were drinking tea and sitting on stools at the counter, having had very little sleep during the three or four days and nights—in coach—on the train.

"It's funny the things that stick in your memory. I was staring at the last piece of apple pie in a three-tiered plastic display case on the counter—'deep-dish apple pie,' it said on the case—the thickest slice of pie I'd ever seen, with cinnamon-darkened chunks of apple like blocks of chocolate. My mother had made apple pies in the summer with sour crabapples sweetened with brown sugar and wild strawberries, but they were as thin as pizza compared to this. The Promised Land, I thought, staring at that pie in the display case, but not daring to ask how much it was."

"Let me stop you there for a minute," said Dayv.

"Sorry . . . I got carried away. What was the question you asked?"

"I was curious about you leaving Newfoundland in Come Home Year, if that was just a coincidence, or a deliberate thing."

"No…we were so young. I doubt if we even knew about that. It was just Leave Home Year for us."

"So…you're only sixteen years old, you arrive in Toronto. How did you get a job so young? Where did you live? Did you have any relatives or friends to stay with?"

"I probably looked nineteen or twenty—I might have lied about my age. I was almost six feet tall and had a whisker, as my mother used to call it. I'd been shaving for three years. My voice had changed early, too, I believe. Or perhaps it was the cigarettes that had changed it. Anyway, we all ended up down on Lake Shore Boulevard, where there was a small diaspora of Newfoundlanders ready to take us in or find us a place to stay till we found a job, which was pretty easy in those days—factory work mostly."

"But you didn't stay long?"

"No…neither on the Boulevard nor in Toronto itself. Living down on the Lake Shore was just like being at home, so we moved out of it, rented rooms up near High Park. But we didn't see much of Toronto that year, to tell the truth—Yonge Street, mainly—though we saw a lot of High Park, which was like being out in the woods. We were hardworking boys, had to be on the job by seven in the morning. We even worked overtime during the week and extra shifts on weekends—sent money home. We were exhausted by the time we got home in the evenings, completely beat out by factory work, and there were no meals on the table waiting for us."

"You only lasted a year, then," Dayv said.

"Yeah, I came back the following summer, but my two friends stayed. I drove down in a Pontiac Parisienne with a guy from Grand Falls. I forget his name. He got a great kick out of calling the car a *Parisheenie*, with a Southern drawl, imitating the salesman who'd sold it to him in Paris, Texas, the previous summer. He'd gone down there just to see the Alamo. The guy used to sing the Davy Crockett song as we cruised along at 120 K an hour. *Davyyy, Daaavy Crockett*...Remember that? He sometimes wore a coonskin cap to work. Norm—his name was Norman, if I recall. Are you out there, Norm?"

The other Dayv was frowning. I hoped he didn't think I was making fun of him.

"Norm was going home for his summer holidays that year, but I was going home for good—or so I thought. We were working in shipping and receiving at a washing-machine plant. At twenty-seven, he was a veteran of the factory wars and had worked in the same place for ten years. But factory work looked like a dead-end life to me, and I'd gotten wind of free tuition at the university back home.

"We left Toronto at the end of July. We drove straight down, stopping only for gas, coffee, and fast food, one of us sleeping in the back while the other was driving. I had some driving experience, but no licence, so Norm did most of the driving and I did most of the sleeping. He was one of those people who loved to drive. We made it back in about two days, if I recall, arriving in the middle of the night."

Dayv's round ruddy face had a holy-cow look of interest and enthusiasm, but perhaps it was just aglow with the studio lights, which were hot and bright. Sweat was running down my forehead into my eyes; my throat was as dry as a piece of hardtack. I hadn't been offered a coffee, or even a glass of water, before we began, though I'd noticed that there was a small kitchen nearby. Then I remembered the bottle of wine I'd bought for supper.

"Do you mind if I get a drink?" I said.

"No, go right ahead," Dayv said, making a cross-checking sign with his arms to the cameraman, who peered around from behind his equipment and gave us a rather surly look. "There's a kitchen just down the hall," Dayv added.

To hell with the kitchen, I thought. "I brought something along, " I said, and reached down into my knapsack, which I'd laid on the floor next to the wingback chair, and took out the bottle of wine. It was in a paper bag and had a screw-top cap, much despised by connoisseurs, I know, but most convenient at times like these. Dayv was not looking too pleased, but he didn't say anything as I removed the metal cap from the bottle. I left it in the bag, for what that was worth, for it had a conspicuous liquor store logo.

"From the French Alps," I said, grinning at him. "Best water on the planet. Can I offer you a drop?"

"No, not on the job," he said, exuding his soothing cherubic charm.

I took a couple of long swigs, between which I removed my glasses and wiped the sweat from my brow and eyelids with the back of my hand.

"It's hot in here," I said.

"It's the lights," he said. "You may have noticed my tan. We don't need a tanning salon."

When we got going again, I began to depart from even the fugitive facts. I was making things up as the cameras rolled.

"When we got to Grand Falls, around three in the morning, Norm pulled the Parisheenie up in front of a house he said was his uncle's. It was all lit up, even some Christmas lights that hadn't been taken down. We thought there might be a party on the go—it was a Friday night—but there was an eerie quiet. The only sounds we heard as we stood there on the porch steps were the buzz of the lights and Norm's gentle knock on the door. It opened slowly, with a Halloween creak, revealing a short, burly man whose face also lit up when he saw Norm, who introduced me to his Uncle Wils. In through the door we went, dazed and bleary-eyed from so much driving and so little sleep, and just not prepared to meet what was waiting for us—a corpse, Norm's Uncle Bill, laid out in a handmade wooden coffin on a table in the middle of the living room floor, surrounded by about a dozen men.

"'A heart attack…last night,' Uncle Wils said sadly.

"Norm looked as if he were about to have one himself. 'I was speakin' to him on the phone the day before we left,' he said, choking up. Then the corpse sat up and grinned and Norm recoiled, stepped back so fast he stamped on my foot, and the mock-mourners erupted in laughter."

"What a rush!" Dayv said. "You could use that in a novel."

"Yes, maybe I will."

"Now let's change the subject here," he said, with whistle-blowing authority. "We got to talk about your books. You published seven novels, and there's a new one coming out in the fall, I'm told, and your first one, *The Ropewalk*, is being reissued here this month by the Southside Press. That must be your most well known book, your most controversial. It wasn't very popular with the historians, though, was it? Tell me about that. What made them so mad? That was your only book about Newfoundland, wasn't it? All your other books are set in Toronto. Why is that? Did you forget all about Newfoundland once you left?"

"Well, there was another one…not so well known…*Bay Despair*…But no, not at all. I was always thinking about the place. I even dreamt about it sometimes. Yes, *The Ropewalk* struck a chord—or a nerve, I should say. Frederick Alderdice, our last prime minister—the undertaker, as I called him, the man who presided over Newfoundland's demise as a nation—was the novel's narrator. But I still don't know what made them so upset, the historians. Of course, they think that history is truth and fiction is lies, and never the twain shall meet. Their story, their version, is the cold hard facts, the unvarnished truth—the truth, the whole truth, and nothing but the truth, as they say in a court of law, but things are different in a court of letters."

"What do you mean—a court of letters?"

"In the court of letters, I am judge, jury, victim, accused, witness, prosecution, and defence. Not to mention court reporter and transcriber. It wouldn't work otherwise. I speak for everyone, including the so-called truth, the so-called facts. We like to say that the facts speak for themselves. But do they ever—or is someone always speaking for them? Whether it be authors or lawyers or politicians or historians—is it any different? Someone is always speaking for them. The facts have to be put into *words*."

"You called it an autobiographical novel, didn't you? What did you mean by that? You can't combine those two forms, can you?"

"Well, yes, offhandedly, when pressed by an interviewer soon after its publication. What I meant was that I let Alderdice tell his own story, and I said there was so little information about the man's life that I had to make most of it up. I was exaggerating, of course, but that was probably the remark that got me in trouble, or the fact that I used the prime minister's real name for my narrator, not a fictitious one. Perhaps that was what was most troubling for the historians. They might have forgiven me if I hadn't done that."

"We seem to have forgotten all about him now," Dayv said.

"Yes, I've been walking around the city a lot since I returned. I haven't seen any statues of Mr. Alderdice; in fact, I see we've put him in his place, so to speak. Hats off to the genius who thought of this. We've named a little street after him, a dead end, a cul-de-sac—Alderdice Place. I came upon it just by chance. It's right across from the Old Colony Club, believe it or not.

"Overall, though, I'd say *The Ropewalk* was a sympathetic portrait of Alderdice, the most pathetic figure in our history, the wrong man for the big moment, a turning point in our history—*the* turning point, some would say. Did he fight to hold on to our political independence in 1933 or did he sell the country down the drain? That's the question the book poses, to put it simply. I have him ask it himself, in fact, along with many other questions. We hear him wondering about all this on his deathbed: talking to doctors, nurses, political colleagues, family, friends, enemies, ghosts...talking to himself, talking in his sleep, stirring, as you might expect, a cauldron of emotions, from mere annoyance to bewilderment, arrogance, regret, shame, real grief..."

I was on a roll now, and swigging the Sauvignon Blanc as I barrelled along. And though Dayv was nodding and giving me his most indulgent angelic grin, I sensed that he had taken my number, as they say at the Rink, in the Room, and this baby-faced enforcer, with career stats probably at a thousand penalty minutes, plus a few goals and assists here and there, was lining me up for a cracking good headshot against a stanchion, or a clever, cross-ice, head-down (my head) check.

"Not many people think it was sympathetic," he said, almost smirking. "Here's what one reviewer said." He raised his clipboard and read: "'Enough information about rope and rope-making in there to fill an encyclopedia, and Mr. Alderdice has been unjustly hanged with a good length of it.'"

"Well…I tried to be. I began with his arrival in St. John's in 1886 as a fourteen-year-old Irish immigrant—this was just a generation or so after the Great Famine—to work in his uncle's rope-making plant in the west end, the Colonial Cordage Company, or 'the Ropewalk,' as everyone called it."

"Yeah, I'm quite familiar with it," Dayv said ominously, but I ignored it.

"The only voice in the novel, almost up to the very end, is that of the first-person narrator, Frederick Alderdice himself, pleading his case. Then the author intrudes. He wonders, first of all, whether Alderdice's psyche was at fault, whether the man had a tragic flaw, a psychic wound of some kind, whether the psychological effects of Ireland's eight-hundred-year colonial subjugation by England had something to do with his quickly caving in to his imperialistic British masters' rigid demands. Then again: though he was Irish, he was more of a conservative British loyalist at heart. But more to the point: the author wonders whether it is the Newfoundland nation itself that has the tragic flaw, a 'will to be ruled' as opposed to a 'will to power,' rooted in our own colonial history."

"You talk about the author as if he's somebody else," Dayv said.

"Well, he is, really, ideally—my second self, my better half. A difficult marriage, though; he's a lot smarter, a lot fairer, less judgmental, more morally neutral than me. I think of him as the director or choreographer. He might give me a cameo sometimes, let me say what I really think, what I really believe, or ask me to join him in a pas de deux."

"Can we get back to the Ropewalk itself, the rope factory?" Dayv said impatiently.

"Sure…by all means."

"As I said, I know a good bit about it. My grandfather used to work at that plant, and my father grew up on Ropewalk Range, the company housing. 'Fishermen use it, loggers have use of it, railroaders are not unfamiliar with its purposes, sealers are helpless without it,'" he intoned, looking really pleased with himself. "Rope, I mean. That was the company slogan. Grandad used to recite it to us.

"I had a look at *The Ropewalk*," he said, even more ominously. (Not *read*, I noted.) "Now your description of that plant is quite the thing—awesome, really. You said the six ropes that stretched the whole length of the plant looked like the strings of a guitar. I like that. I play the guitar myself. And I could really see the rope-spinning machines, the 'hecklers,' as they called them. But the plant was a lot more than one building. Why didn't you describe the place the way it really was?"

"I'm not sure I know what you mean," I said cautiously.

"I never saw it myself, of course. I was born in '66, as I mentioned, the year after it closed, but my father and grandfather used to talk about it all the time. The Ropewalk itself, the longest building, was definitely not a mile long—no more than a quarter mile, Dad said—and there was a dozen other buildings: six different storerooms for rope, tar, oakum, twine, hemp, and oil; a spinning room; a tarring room; an engine and boiler room, like on a boat; a finishing room; and a big smokestack towering over the whole thing. And it didn't burn down at the end when it closed. It burned down in 1885, but was rebuilt the next year. There was another, smaller fire in 1909. It was sold to Great Eastern Oil in the end. Ropewalk Range was torn down in 1957. A three-bedroom apartment there was only ten dollars a month, not a hundred."

"You sure know your facts, Mr. Maddigan," I said. "But I wasn't too concerned about how the Ropewalk actually looked. I sort of redesigned it, streamlined the look of it, compacted it into a single image. The ropewalk I was really writing about was the one Prime Minister Alderdice had to perform on—a political tightrope. He was the real rope-walker, or rope-dancer, a tightrope artist who had to perform a daring act to the music of that mile-long—

or quarter-mile-long—Ropewalk guitar, but he couldn't. He fell off, fell to his death, and took the country of Newfoundland down with him. The Ropewalk was a symbolic building in the book—though I realize it was a very real one for your family—and it was a symbolic conflagration when I burned it down. Just like in *your* novel, *Inherit the Ice*."

"You've read it?" he said, looking very surprised.

Could I do this, I thought—*should* I do this—dishonour myself and my noble craft in this shameless way? But an opportunity like this might never come round again: to exchange places with my interviewer, my interrogator, my everyday nemesis, my long-time tormentor, by pretending (as they often do) to have read his book?

Forget *should*, I thought. *Yes I could.*

"Yes, I have," I said. "Your main character is based on Howie Meeker, right? But you were smarter than me—you didn't use his real name. And if I read it right, the *ice* of the title is symbolic. It stands for the whole hockey world, hockey culture...and the *door* of the dressing room—the Room, as it's always reverentially referred to—which they tear off and use as a stretcher to carry the protagonist off the ice after he's knocked out...that's another important symbol, isn't it?"

"Yeah, I guess you're right. My publisher picked that title...but you're right. The door and all that—we come up with these things unconsciously, I guess."

"Yeah, writing's a funny business, isn't it? And the critics sure don't help. Using real people, living or dead, and inventing things about them, is, as you and I know, a thorny problem. It's not just an ethical issue, one critic said, but an artistic one. *It's a crutch*. It gives you a head start, a leg up. And it's better to use completely imaginary characters, he said, because you can know everything about them, but you can never know everything about real ones, historical ones. Maybe he's right, I thought, about the crutch. But not about the imaginary beings. They can be just as difficult, just as withholding."

"What do you mean?"

"Well, *nothing* in a novel, of course, is ever *totally* imaginary or *completely* real, and rarely, if ever, is it *fully* imagined. It's amazing how elusive, how resistant to imagining, imaginary beings can be. Like that exotic being, Mr. Borges' squonk, who can drown in its own tears when captured. They don't want to be taken captive, put on display in some literary zoo. I've had dozens of characters drown in their own tears—or maybe mine."

"I'm afraid I don't follow you there. You mean to say imaginary characters have some control over you and how you create them?"

"I mean to say...that the little buggers have more tricks than a squonk. It's a funny business, as I said."

He nodded his head ambiguously, but seemed to agree that it was, seemed pleased as well to be a part of such a wonderful fraternity—morally compromised liars and alcoholics on crutches though we might be.

"It was a privilege having you on the show," he said, not too convincingly, crunching my bony hand in his fisty cuff, then gave the cameraman the cross-checking sign once again.

It was almost six o'clock when the brawny, six-foot-plus Dayv Maddigan, one heavy hand on my right shoulder, his other hand firmly cupping my left elbow—writers-in-arms—guided me down the hallway and out through the side door of the TV studio. He might have been escorting an unruly, inebriated patron out of a bar. The fire-exit door, he called it, giving it a hearty push. I was at least half-inebriated, and feeling so hot I might have been escaping a fire. On the landing outside, with his third bone-crunching handshake of the day, Dayv bade me a fond farewell—so fond he didn't seem to want to let go.

11: FAREWELL TO MUSIC

I walked toward the campus of the university I had attended for five years over three decades ago, and left after a fraudulent year of graduate studies. I had used my fellowship money as a Canada Council grant—I'd tried and failed to write a novel. At least I didn't have to submit a final report.

I hadn't really seen the university since I'd been back. It was certainly not as I remembered it, but every building now had a billboard-size identification sign. I passed a massive, steeply terraced new library, next to which was a de Chirico-like triangular clock tower that reminded me I was late for supper—Celia had said to come over around six—but whose three clock faces told different times. There weren't many students on campus at this time of day, especially on a Friday, and the few I did see were siting on benches studying their cellphones instead of textbooks.

If you had a cellphone, ring-a-ling-a-ling-a-ling-a-ling-a-ling, you could call ahead and say you're on your way, sang that ludic elf of a self who was always tempted by the new technologies to the Luddite self who was determined to resist them. Some half-remembered tune from a high-school production of a Broadway musical—Celia's high school, not mine—had insinuated itself into my head. *I'll be there when I get there,* I sang back. *Not over till it's over,* it mimicked, in the same treacly tone. Celia had been enlisted to perform in this show against her will—*Fiddler on the Roof,* I think it was—or, more likely, against Alicia's will, for she looked down upon that particular brand of entertainment, even as a social lark for adolescents.

Celia had played a solo on the violin, or the fiddle, in the wings, and, to Alicia's even greater consternation, had discovered fiddle music: eastern European, klezmer music, to begin with; then Ontarian, Quebecois, Appalachian, Maritime (the treacly Don Messer), and Newfoundland (the far-from-treacly Émile Benoît). She played it for fun; she was always smiling when she played it. It seemed to provide a great relief from the stress of her classical playing, which was not because of the music itself, but from trying so hard to please her teacher-mother. A conscientious mentor and role model she certainly was, but also a perfectionist, a slave driver, a competitor, and an omniscient overseer. When Celia played the fiddle, she only had to please herself.

Next to the clock tower was a new student union building built right over a four-lane highway, with a glass facade like a traffic-control tower. Looking north, to the other side of this highway, I could see a spreading conglomeration of factory-like buildings with belching smokestacks and enormous empty parking lots. I turned in the opposite direction and walked past the old student union building, now redesigned as a corporate research facility, with a winding stairwell in an illuminated glass tower rising above the main entrance. Long, long ago, in a small windowless room in this building, one of several cramped spaces that made up the offices of the student newspaper, as literary editor I had read and chosen for publication many jejune submissions of poetry and prose—including my own—while in an identical room next door the political editor was grinding out yet another anti-Smallwood philippic. Mainly to amuse myself, I had also written and published many outrageous reviews—some of fictitious works of fiction—and fanciful pieces of reportage, à la Tom Wolfe.

But what had I actually learned at university? I wondered. What did I remember learning? What did one learn at seventeen, eighteen, or nineteen years of age that stayed with a person for life? There had been *classes*, the heart of the teaching-learning experience, supposedly, and I had gone to some of them, but the cafés, the common rooms, and the library—a social centre as much as a place for work—were where I spent most of my time.

My first year, I recall, was filled with more distasteful doses of the same high-school medicine—a curricular Brick's Tasteless Cod Liver Oil, though the English courses were an easy pleasure. But in my second year I branched out into anthropology, philosophy, and psychology, along with more English courses. I guess the first thing I learned was that I didn't know anything; or that there was something askew about everything I knew; or, as our anthropology professor had blithely informed us, "Everything you have ever learned is false." This momentous news he scrawled in chalk on the blackboard on the first day of class, his clever way of acquainting us with the first principle of his discipline, the cultural relativity of all values; but I think we took it as an insult, at best a joke, a ruse, to get our attention. It certainly did.

Our philosophy prof had got our attention as well. On entering our very first class, having loped down the sloped aisle of the large classroom with academic gown and long hair floating behind him—yes, profs still wore gowns in those days—he stopped to ask a student sitting in the front row, a stand-in, helpless husband, "Have you stopped beating your wife?" His big blue eyes blazed mischievously with the incriminating rhetorical question—our first lesson in philosophical interrogation—which I'm sure didn't seem so rhetorical when someone's face was two inches from yours.

A rumour had spread during the term that he always carried a copy of *Alice's Adventures in Wonderland* in the inside pocket of his lavender corduroy jacket, though Plato's *Republic* was the only official text for the course. And when he came down from the lectern, so to speak, as he often did, pulled back his gown and opened his jacket, put his hands on his hips, craned his neck, and gazed wide-eyed at us as if overcome by some ineffable question, some of the students at the front would crane their own necks to perhaps catch a glimpse of this unorthodox bible of philosophical thought. "Curiouser and curiouser!" was all he ever had to say on those occasions, when he said anything at all, though his quoting Alice's words had perhaps been at the root of the rumour that there might be an unofficial text for the course.

Toward the end of term, as a sort of lifelong philosophical assignment—no final report required—he invited us, challenged us, to "F" the Ineffable—the unutterable, the unspeakable, the inexpressible, the indefinable, the indescribable, he repeated synonymically, as if the very repetition could inspire us, mesmerize us, to take on the task—and if I took anything away from his course it was a desire to do just that. I entered into a lifelong relationship with the Ineffable, *ineffabilis*, to express, or to bring forth, what was beyond expression.

A pipe-smoking lesbian English prof dressed entirely in black (not a dress and academic gown, however, but a T-shirt and pants and knee-high boots) had also got our attention, at least initially; but she had spent half a term on Aristotle's *Poetics*—a Greek marathon of an exegesis, a pilgrim's progress, though one that would stand this pilgrim in as good stead as a Christian his Bible, as he progressed painfully along the literary *via dolorosa*.

And then, in my third year, came "the Whorl"—symbol of the Ineffable, perhaps. "To see a Whorl in a Grain of Sand,/And a Heaven in a Wild Flower..."; "The Whorl is too much with us...," we would intone to one another in the cafés, not parodying Blake or Wordsworth but in humorous, good-willed reference to our beloved twentieth-century comparative literature prof, the aforementioned Dr. Noel Eagleton, who saw the Whorl in everything he read, at least everything he had assigned to us: *Heart of Darkness*, *Riders in the Chariot*, *The Trial*, *Lolita*, *Catch-22*, *The Journal of Albion Moonlight*, *Finnegans Wake*. Modernist or postmodernist work, its pattern was always the Whorl. He mesmerized us with the Whorl. A dozen times a class he would break off from his line of thought and rush to the blackboard and draw this intricate, if primitive, little thumbprint of a figure, which we would all stare at to see if in some way it was any different from the last one, before he quickly erased it, as if the continuous sight of it might be too much for us to comprehend, too much to bear. Sometimes I still see the Whorl in dreams.

The Arts Building, in which I'd had most of my classes, had had a make-over as well: a glass extension with an atrium, and an elevator visible from outside rising to an extra floor on top. I walked past the old library, where I'd spent more time than in the classroom, but a lot less than in the cafés. It looked exactly the same, except it was no longer a library, but the home of a mathematics and computer science department.

I walked down the sloping lawn of the Arts Building to Elizabeth Avenue and stood on the sidewalk wondering whether I should go back to the liquor store in Churchill Square to get another bottle of wine. I decided against it, as I was already late for supper. I walked down Newtown Road, past the house where Kevin and I had rented a tiny, cold basement apartment in the middle of our first university year—less than five minutes from that house to a nine o'clock class anywhere on campus. A bit farther down the road I saw what looked like a giant igloo dwarfing the neighbouring houses. As I got closer, I could see that it was made of rubber or plastic and was being held down by heavy guy wires. A blue-and-white sign at the parking lot entrance identified it as a tennis club, and I immediately thought of the Molly Maids I had seen this morning, with the blue-and-white bands, or clasps, on their tanned arms. They were worn by tennis players, I remembered, afflicted with a common injury, so-called tennis elbow.

∽ ↄ

Celia used to play tennis, had been quite a good player, in fact. She had friends who played competitively, and she sometimes practised with them. Though she had never played hard enough or often enough to be afflicted with tennis elbow, she had been diagnosed—or misdiagnosed—with carpal tunnel syndrome, a painful disorder of the hand and wrist, as a result of her long hours practising on the piano and the violin, and she had started wearing a tennis clasp to give her hand and arm added strength and support.

As it turned out, however, it was a simple posture problem, a chronic misalignment of her head, neck, shoulders, and arms, causing problems in the nerves and muscles. Several sessions with a massage therapist who specialized in the Alexander Technique had sorted it out. But she had grown fond of the tennis clasp, and continued to wear it. Her therapist and her teachers had frowned on this quite severely, however, especially her violin-teacher mother, afraid that it would become a permanent crutch.

"I'll become a Molly Maid if you don't leave me alone. I'll quit school. I'll quit music. I'll leave home. You'll never see me again."

This was Celia's outburst—five threats, no less—one day after school in early December, in her last year of high school, not long after the Molly Maid contingent (sans armbands, this lot) had left the house and Alicia had begun her violin lesson. There had been much resistance, other outbursts, but none quite like this, in reaction to Alicia's rather severe and formal pedagogic approach, which she used with all her students, it seemed, young or old, related or unrelated. Alicia had never really taken these outbursts seriously, but I had.

"Mothers should never teach their daughters," a weary-looking music teacher-mother had said to me later that month, after a Christmas violin recital at our house by Alicia's students, including this woman's daughter, Kirsten, and ours, who were friends at school. She seemed to have deliberately sought me out to speak to me. "I mean formally, of course," she added, "music instruction or anything else. At least not after the periods start and the hormones kick in, which is pretty early these days." She was speaking from sad personal experience, she said, but she and her daughter got on fine now that Alicia had taken her on.

"*Ohhh*...that mediocre B. Music Ed. meddler!" alliterated Alicia, pronouncing her verdict on the person and her professional credentials simultaneously, after I had conveyed this wise counsel later in the evening.

"Maybe she has something there," I ventured.

Alicia quickly drained her glass of wine—always a signal that the case was closed, regardless of whether there was a witness waiting in the wings or not—and went off to her solitary bed. I was now sleeping in the spare bedroom, and in eight months would be outlawed to the in-law apartment.

Yes, five threats that day in December, and in February, in the bleak midwinter, an appropriately cold, cold winter, in the middle of the school year, about a month before she was to audition for music school, she followed through on one of them. One evening after supper, our dear and only child, Cecilia Catherine Coates-Nightingale—named by Alicia after the patron saint of music (a martyr, I might point out); daughter of mid-listing writer James Nightingale and first-desk violist Alicia Coates—took Alicia and me by the hand and led us into the living room and sat us down on the cold Italian-leather chesterfield, which her well-off grandparents had given us still-struggling-in-mid-career *artistes*, as her grandmother liked to refer to us, delicately *hee-hawing* each time she said it, as a tenth-anniversary present. We avoided it in the winter, however, because it was too cold to sit on, preferring instead the cheap but comfy cloth sofa in the Room of Many Names, as I liked to call it: the sun room; the music room; the family, TV, computer, even guest, room, for the sofa was actually a sofa bed. She led us in and sat us down in this cold, unlived-in living room—a parlour or front room, we would have called it back home—and clearly and confidently announced that she was *giving up music.*

She didn't actually say those words, however; they were Alicia's.

"You're *giving up music?*" she translated.

"I've decided I'm not going to music school" was what Celia said, I think, quietly but emphatically.

But Alicia's were the words that I remembered, the repetitive notes of a highly dissonant score, the foreground music of that very emotional evening.

"*Giving up music!* You can't *do* that, Cecilia. You can't *do* that to us."

Though I was no longer a committed part of the married *us,* I was, of course, still a very empathetic part of the parental duo, the *us* that Celia was briefing, as calmly as she could, in spite of Alicia's hysterics, briefing us for what lay ahead in that cool way she herself had been briefed so many times by her mother, professor of music and professed disciplinarian of the family.

Yes, she *was* giving up music, in a manner of speaking. She was not going to follow in her mother's footsteps, in any event, though she very thoughtfully didn't say that either; she was not going to music school after all, as everyone expected; she would not become a performer and a music teacher, like her mother. After taking piano and violin lessons since the age of four, "performing" Suzuki "Twinkles" on stage in front of a hundred dewy-eyed parents on a mock violin at that tender age, and after dozens of real performances thereafter—at recitals, concerts, festivals, competitions, examinations—she was not going to study music after all, but *rocks.* She was going to become a geologist.

"A *geologist?*" said Alicia, not laughing exactly, but looking as if she were trying to laugh and not laugh at the same time.

I had to admit that I was almost as surprised as she was, in spite of my premonitions. But as we were on the verge of *giving up marriage* by that point—and this may have had something to do with Celia's decision, though I don't know what—a small-minded, reckless, vengeful part of me was glad that she was not going to follow in her mother's footsteps. This would hurt Alicia a lot more than it would me, for music was her life. (Was I beginning to hate the woman I had once loved?) I was also glad, but I didn't know why, that she was going to study something as basic, neutral, unemotional, and non-threatening as *rocks*—at least that had been my relationship with rocks. It even occurred to me that perhaps I myself would have been happier having an occupational relationship with something like rocks. And my interior selfish elf was now applauding once again as Celia stated further that she was going to the Rock of rocks, Newfoundland, to do it, to where Alicia had never wished to go, to my home and native land, Rock of Ages, cleft from me, though I had left it long ago and had never felt any real desire to return.

Pressure was the word Celia kept repeating, in the rock-face of Alicia's incredulous response, the word Alicia didn't seem to hear, and, obviously, didn't want to hear. She was always under pressure; everything was pressure. Pressure to practice, to perform; pressure to excel. Expectations of her were too high; she was always being compared to her mother; she would never be as good as her mother.

"Your mother can't play the piano," I said, trying to lighten things up a bit, being the unmusical fool, the mere page-turner, of the family, and the wary fool of this unfolding tragedy.

"I'm not auditioning on piano, Dad," she said. "Anyway, you don't know anything about it."

That hurt, as it always did, but I let it go, as I usually did.

"Don't be disrespectful to your *father*," said Alicia, emphatically but unconvincingly.

"Well, he doesn't," Celia said, very convincingly.

"Your father has never missed one of your performances in his life," declared Alicia, and though I'd been relegated to a sort of musically incompetent third person, I felt warm, first-person stirrings of fatherly pride. I, *father*, had indeed been present, usually with video camera in hand, to Celia's great annoyance, for every note of her performing career.

"I'm not giving any more *performances*, Mother, so *Father's* going to miss them from now on," said Celia, defiantly upset now, and ready to run off to her room.

Alicia was silent. Celia's face had that brooding, smouldering, flushed complexion, as it always did when she was angry. She was small and fiery like her mother, though they both looked taller than they actually were—their erect posture and fine long necks, perhaps. They were olive-skinned and dark-eyed, and their dark eyes glowed, burned black, when they were mad. But Celia was still at an age when, no matter how sincere she was—and there was no doubt that on this day she was very sincere—she looked as if she were practising, learning the routines of genuine emotion rather than really experiencing the intensity of it. It was as if there were a gap, a time delay, between what she actually felt and what she could express, that she, still oh-so-very-young emotionally, even younger than her peers, was performing, putting on an act, but would eventually learn to bridge the gap.

The silence continued, and she finally did run off to her room, crying and slamming the door. Alicia looked calmer now, or perhaps I should say less distraught. It was a dark, serious, *pre-planning* calm. She was always pre-planning, as she put it. Not content just to make plans, she carefully planned those plans to make certain they were failure-proof. But the plan for Celia's life, the longest, most complex, and most thorough of her plans, now looked as if it were going to fall through.

"I knew this was coming," I said into the gloom.

She was literally biting, chewing, her bottom lip.

"I wonder where this geology thing came from?" I said, rambling on, trying to ease the tension in the room. "I know she's doing some amorphous course called Earth Studies—geology, geography, politics, agriculture, astronomy, climate…everything in there. I was looking at the textbook."

"It's got nothing to do with geology, James," she said coldly. Then, more abstractedly, as if she were talking to herself, she said, "Perhaps I should have let Isobel take her…Too late now…too late now."

"You mean that *is* the reason for this?" I said. "You're saying Kirsten's mother was right?"

"No…of course she isn't," she hissed. "I don't *know* what the reason is, but Cecilia's right about the pressure. You have to be a performer to understand that. But you learn to deal with it. You have to deal with it," she added, trailing these authoritative, if dampened, notes behind her as she left the room.

∿⌒

I didn't cry the day the music died, but I did not long thereafter. A terrible silence fell upon the house, deeper and closer and sadder than the one already there, the one between Alicia and me. It felt almost as if it were inside me now. No more piano, no more violin. Celia had usually practised violin in the evenings, while I was reading. Twice a week she had a formal lesson with her mother, or with Alicia's faculty colleague Isobel St. Clair when Alicia was away. In the afternoons, when I was working, I would hear her practising piano, or working with her piano teacher, the beautiful, if eccentric, Naomi Kitchener, who sang along, operatically, with every note that Celia played, and twirled and danced at times if the mood struck her. Celia had been entranced by this from the very beginning, though she had to learn not to be distracted by it. She loved the fragile, gay (in both senses of the word), hyper-allergic, seemingly always homeless and studio-less Naomi. She couldn't find a house fit to live in, or a studio fit to teach in, one that didn't make her break out in rashes, have hot flashes (though she was only in her thirties) and asthma-like attacks (though she was not asthmatic), sweat profusely, vomit unexpectedly, lose her appetite, have dizzy spells, lose consciousness, sleep interminably and miss her lessons, or not be able to sleep at all. Despite her unorthodox teaching style and erratic behaviour, however, Naomi got *results*—first place in festivals and other competitions; top marks in examinations; awards and scholarships—which were all-important to Alicia, though she could barely tolerate Naomi.

12: THE RESISTANCE

I was surprised that I still had the disorderly pattern of St. John's streets in my head, though I had to look at the signs to rediscover their names. Of all the things almost certain to confuse, distress, or seriously inconvenience the tourist, the traveller, the visitor to this city—the airport fogs, which might delay him for days or prevent him from getting here at all; our own time zone, which could make him late for his once-in-a-lifetime Canada Council reading; the dreaded screech-in, which might make him wish he had never come at all—the mesmerizing maze of city streets had to top the list. A stranger to this place might think he had entered the labyrinth of the inner ear.

Coming back home after being away for so long, I felt like a divided soul: sometimes a foreigner, a bewildered stranger; at other times, a comfortable native, someone who had never left the place and knew it intimately, and, in the formal but ironic voice of some Frommer's or Michelin guide, this confident, ludic leader would insist on showing the bewildered visitor around.

The hospitable and courteous atmosphere of the city is especially welcoming to the curious, if weary, traveller. Coming to a halt on the sidewalk of a busy street and just thinking about crossing, having spotted some interesting attraction on the other side, he will be surprised to see the traffic itself come to a halt to let him cross.

The intimate streets and laneways of the downtown offer their charms to the visitor. In the numerous downtown bars, the tourist will find all that is necessary for his intoxication. The many historic public buildings and intimate ecclesiastical edifices bid him welcome, astounding him with their architectural artistry and dazzling stained-glass displays. The architectural jewels that await the traveller's visit will leave him with unfading memories.

The visitor, after he has noted the earlier and expeditious mealtimes, and the different names for same—dinner for lunch, supper for dinner, a lunch or mug-up for a late-night snack—will be struck by the late hours at which musical entertainments begin...

It was as if one of my characters had taken narrative control and delighted in showing me how it felt to be led around by the nose, manipulated, shuffled here and there.

∞ ∞

From the tennis club igloo on Newtown Road, I tacked uphill to Merrymeeting Road, then paraded confidently down Parade Street to a huge, confusing, unfamiliar intersection where no fewer than six streets met. I retreated back up Parade to Merrymeeting, feeling a bit less confident and merry than when I had come down. I followed Merrymeeting Road down to Bonaventure Avenue, turned right and found myself face to face with The Rooms, the brutalist, library-less new arts and culture centre that Kevin had so brutally dismissed, and which I had yet to visit. At least it had a warm, inviting name. Bonaventure Avenue ended at a busy intersection without a light, then dropped over a precipice and became Garrison Hill on the other side.

On the west side of this hill (there were no houses on the east side), Celia and another student were sharing an old three-storey row house that looked from the outside to be in very bad repair. It had been completely renovated on the inside, however, and before supper Celia, very proudly, showed me around. The main floor bay window overlooked the sidewalk, had no blinds or curtains, just a lone spindly hanging plant, and throughout the evening curious pedestrians stopping to catch their breath on the way up the hill were not shy about taking advantage of the clear view of the house's domestic activities. The second-floor bay window and third-floor dormer had only shy views of the sea.

Celia and Hana Trela, a geology graduate student from Poland, were house-sitting for a geology professor until September, looking after a small animal kingdom of plants, cats, birds, and fish. I was reminded, as I looked around, of one of Chekhov's very short pieces, "What You Usually Find in Novels," a satirical three-page menagerie that included, if I recall, "a dog that can do everything but talk, a parrot, and a nightingale." No dog here, but a parrot who could talk, though it said nothing while I was there, and now two Nightingales. There were also two cats, a huge goldfish—a cichlid—which looked as if it wanted to talk, and a giant rubber plant, or tree, in a corner near the bay window. The owner must have decorated it at Christmas, for it still had a few forgotten dusty ornaments, along with various ornamental birds perched on the branches—an owl, a red oriole, and a dove—companions for the parrot perhaps, as it took refuge in the rubber tree when the cats looked longingly up at it on its perch for too long. It didn't seem to have a cage. And there were, as you might expect, lots of rocks as well, but those could presumably look after themselves. There was a piano in the living room—a good sign—though it was a dusty old upright with its keyboard cover drawn, and no music or music stool anywhere in sight.

I had seen Celia only briefly since I'd been back, before and after the convocation ceremony. As Hana's assistant—a summer job—she then had to rush off on a field trip down the Southern Shore, to Mistaken Point, where a world-renowned geologist was visiting and doing fieldwork. Mistaken Point had become a hotspot, geologically speaking, in recent years, she said, and Hana was writing her doctoral dissertation on the ancient fossils that had been discovered at the site.

Hana Trela was a formally courteous, svelte Pole who looked to be just a few years older than Celia (nineteen this November, I thought, incredulously), but Hana possessed that air of sophistication that I'd first noted among the European girls I'd met when I was about her age, travelling in England for the first time, dutifully visiting the museums and galleries and cultural shrines, but, like all horny young males, always thinking about sex.

There was Dorte from Denmark, who had been living in London for a year and working in a Danish delicatessen that I kept returning to for lunch until I dared to ask her out for a pint. She took me to a pub that served Tuborg on tap, and I proceeded to get so drunk that I was unable to have sex with her when we went back to her room. I threw up, in fact, and then passed out, while she, after drinking six pints or more, looked as if she hadn't drunk anything at all.

There was Evelyne from the Auvergne, a wild au pair girl also living in London, working as a nanny to learn English, whom I had met on her day off wandering through the Portobello Road Market looking for clothes. She was wild and daring enough to take me back to her employers' house in Hampstead in the middle of the afternoon, when they too were out shopping. When we entered the house, she removed her red sneakers (no socks, I noticed), hung up her leather jacket and pull-string bag in the porch, stepped barefoot into the foyer and began to take off her jeans and top right in front of me (no bra or panties), then ran naked, clothes in hand, up to her room on the third floor, laughing wildly and loudly, and assuming, quite rightly, of course, that I would run after her. She already spoke English serviceably well, said she was descended from a Celtic tribe called the Arverni, and told me about the extinct volcanoes near her home. She herself was an active volcano, sexually speaking, and I think she told me that I was her *dozenth* partner since she'd arrived. (It was an odd enough English word, and didn't sound like one at all when she said it.) It *doesn't* surprise me, I thought of saying, but I didn't want to insult her, and besides, a plum pun like that would have been wasted on her. But I thought later that perhaps she had said, or tried to say, that I could be her *dozent*, her teacher. Was she hoping to refine her English by a process of pedagogical-cum-sexual osmosis? She was trying hard enough, I can tell you—so loud and passionate that I was sure her employers would surprise us *in flagrante delicto*.

Finally, there was Irini from Greece, whom I remember most of all, a poet from Paros, who tried to teach me some Greek. I still have the yellowed sheet of paper on which she wrote out the Greek alphabet for me, along with one of her poems, in her tiny elegant handwriting. She played cassettes of anguished love songs on her tape player in front of the metered gas fire in her damp bedsit in Crouch End (and this was late spring), crouched under a low grey un-Grecian sky. The songs were all by a compatriot of hers from Paros—Parios by name. One song in particular, "Monos, Monos," which needed no translation, but which, she said, meant "All Alone," seemed to strike so deep into her heart—not broken by unrequited love but by exile from her native land, the blazing blue and white vistas of Greece—that she would take to her bed for an entire afternoon after hearing it, in retreat from exile's anguish and the rising damp, and take me with her for comfort. I didn't mind.

The feeling in those Greek songs was so intense, so full of longing, of an uplifting melancholy—though if I'd been able to read the lyrics I might have recoiled—that it struck deep into my heart as well, as did the music of an unknown (to me at least) Breton harper and traditional singer named Alan Stivell, whom we heard at a folk club later that summer. It moved me so much, in fact, that I wondered if I had been born in the wrong place. None of the Newfoundland traditional ballads that I'd heard in my youth, mainly derivatives of British and Irish tunes, had ever affected me like this. But I hadn't heard very many of them, for they'd been swept aside by a tide of American music—country, folk, pop, rock and roll—in the fifties and sixties.

But lest it should appear as if I were presenting my young self as some kind of Don Juan, when in reality a wan Don was more like it, this palely loitering and now middle-aged Don offers as excuse that at this moment he was looking across the table at a vision of his lost loves, his lost years, all of them lost, lost forever, at yet another manifestation of young sophisticated European beauty, but closer to my daughter's age now than my own, so I tried my best not to look too hard.

"Aren't you hungry, Dad?" Celia was saying. We *were* having tofu, as she said we might. Tofu tourtière, a vegetarian variation—desecration, torture-ière, some would say—on a traditional Quebecois dish, a double-crust spicy pork pie. A single-crust, peach-tofu cream pie, I noticed, was lying in wait on the kitchen counter for dessert. I had seen its peaches-and-cream complexion before.

"Oh, yes," I said, trying to impress her with a generous forkful of tofu. "I'm sorry about the wine," I added, and I certainly was. A good antidote for tofu, as I said. We were drinking a very sweet cider. "The interview went on a long time," I said, "and I didn't want to be late for supper."

"Sure, you were fifteen minutes early, Dad."

"Didn't you say six o'clock?"

"Yeah, you arrived at 6:45, fifteen minutes earlier than your usual hour late," she said, stretching her lips into a silly teasing smile.

Yes, I have lateness *issues*, as they say these days. It's true that I didn't want to be late for supper—or for meetings or appointments or concerts or readings or anything else. I never want to be late, I never intend to be late, I don't plan, as some do, to be *fashionably* late, but for some reason I always am. I don't mind Celia's teasing me about this, but Alicia has always insisted on analyzing it. Her pet psychological theory has to do with my aversion to beginnings, warm-ups, rehearsals, preambles, preplans, forewords, even foreplay (it got very personal in the end). I don't want to wait for things to get going. I don't want to arrive until things are getting underway. At bottom, she says, it has to do with my fear of the blank page.

"Look at all your books," she said one night—a bad night. "They all begin *in medias res*. Now, it might work for books, but it doesn't work for sex—at least not for the woman."

The woman in question, of course, was her. This was in our latter days, as I said, when the only time I touched her, she claimed, was for sex.

"This was never a problem for us early on," I said. "You yourself were always *in medias res*. As soon as it raised its head you were *hot* for it."

"Please don't use that word," she snapped. "You know I hate that word. I'm not some kind of household appliance—a clothes iron or a Crock-Pot."

How about crackpot? I thought. Just thought. Alicia was the only person I had ever known who used the term *clothes* iron, instead of simply *iron*, as if we were frequent wielders of other irons—branding irons, fire irons, tire irons—and she had to distinguish among them. The other iron we did use, and frequently these days, was heated in the cold fire of *irony*, and used not on cattle, fireplaces, or cars, but on each other.

"*Hot,*" Celia was saying, refocusing my thoughts. "Spicy, I mean. Too much cayenne, I think. But the pear cider goes good with it. Better than wine. It's from BC, the Okanagan. Mom said you were out there just before you came here, that you sent her a whole case of wine for her birthday. How sweet! What were you doing out there? How'd you get there, by the way? She said you won't fly anymore."

"I took the train. They gave me the grand tour of the Okanagan wineries after my reading in Kelowna. Let it be known far and wide that we have now reached the incredible point on the noble path of our literary history where the Canada Council reading fee will cover the cost of an entire case of wine, plus shipping home from the Okanagan, stomping ground of the Regressive Conservatives, by the way. On second thought, don't let it be known, or the Canada Council will get another cut and reading fees might be a thing of the past. Anyway, I hope your mother doesn't drink it all before I get back. I read at Penticton and Kamloops as well, did a couple of workshops, and some mentoring at Banff, where I started out. What a gig that was—transport to and from, great cuisine, your own apartment, six students at the stage where they could teach themselves—and me too—and a paycheque at the end. I had nothing at all to do. You know, I've got more readers out west than in Ontario or Newfoundland. I don't know why. A female motorcycle gang-slash-book club from Kamloops called the Hoodoos showed up last year at my door in Toronto looking to have books signed. Can you believe that?"

"Is that from your new book, Dad?" Celia said, with a mouth-wide-open grin this time, a glorious two-tiered orthodontic display whose cost for many years had eclipsed my royalty payments.

"Yeah…working title *The Hoodoos Ride Again*…and speaking of rides: what a ride I had coming down here. I found myself on a train with a VIA Rail engineer who must have been a pilot in a previous incarnation—AVIA, not VIA. Between Toronto and Montreal, not far from Cornwall, with a full load of passengers—a sold-out run—he was going so fast he missed a signal—one theory, at least—and we almost flew off the tracks. I was sitting with another writer, a poet who did skydiving in her spare time. She found writing poems much more terrifying, she said, so it didn't bother her at all when she was ejected from her seat and nearly ended up in my lap. The train came to a halt almost immediately, and all systems were shut down: engines, air conditioning, lights. By the time we got moving again, I must have learned everything there was to know about Siobhan Savard, the skydiving poet from the Gatineau Hills, in conversational free fall, it seemed. The only daughter of an Irish ballerina mother and a French-Canadian fiddler father, she was now betrothed to a Mexican matador. She got off the train in Montreal, where she was now living, but I was going on. The train line ends at Halifax now. Then you have to rent a car or take a bus. I took the bus from Halifax to North Sydney. From there, tired of the diesely bonds of earth—and the surly sea lay ahead—like St. Sebolt I crossed the Gulf, the dire Cabot Strait, on my cloak. I was glad I did, for I heard later on that the boat caught fire. At Port aux Basques, I slipped the surly bonds of earth altogether, caught the updraft through Wreckhouse, o'er the Gaff Topsails, a gale so strong it carried me all the way to St. John's."

"You're plagiarizing, Dad. I recognize that one—'High Flight,' the first poem you ever read to me. *Oh! I have slipped the surly bonds of earth*...You knew it by heart. But I thought you'd given up flying, Dad. You're in free fall yourself. I've never heard you talk so much. Have you been drinking?"

Perhaps I was still feeling the effects of the wine—I must have drunk most of the bottle I'd left at the station—and I'd had two bottles of cider since I arrived, but I was also feeling the effects of Hana. Truth was—though I could not say, of course—the embarrassing truth was that I was feeling shy, nervously shy, but gamely performing, over-compensating, in the quietly attentive gaze of this young Polish beauty who was my daughter's dozent.

"Sorry," I said. "I'm not writing these days...that's what it is. Just proofing...editing proofs...purveyor of fine proofs to His Majesty the Publisher... or *poofing*. Trying to make them disappear. Who wrote this? you ask yourself. You want to tear it up, rewrite the whole thing, but there's the implacable Ten-percent Rule, contractual obligations—change more than 10 percent and *you pay*."

"I thought you loved editing, Dad. Sure, you even used to edit my letters to Santa!"

"What!?"

"Yes, you did. I found some last fall in the trunk Mom sent down, in one of my books. My handwritten drafts, my typed drafts, *your* edited drafts. The Archives would like those. Your stuff's already in there, isn't it? Do they pay?"

"Ho ho ho. Don't you dare."

"I went along with you so I could use the computer. Now I can type ten times faster than you. Letters to Santa are just like novels, you used to say."

"Yeah, and I wasn't talking about editing, Celia. I was preparing you for life—the slings and arrows, the petty pace, the lump of coal, no prizes in your stocking. No replies, not even from the post office."

Hana had been exceptionally quiet while all this father-daughter banter was going on, popping back and forth to the kitchen to check on things. All she had said so far was a heavily accented *Hello, Yes, No. I'll get it. Do you like coffee or tea?* etc. Perhaps her English was not so good, though she smiled at all the appropriate times. Or perhaps she was just being courteous, thinking that she should stay out of the way, let the father and daughter re-bond, reacquaint themselves. On her black sweater, above her heart, was a small red pin that looked like an electronic device of some kind. After we had disposed of the tofu cream pie, I asked her what it was, trying to draw her out.

"That pin on your sweater, Hana," I said, "it looks like a microphone. You're not a spy, are you? The Cold War is over, you know."

Her ear for English was obviously good, for she gave me a big warm smile. "Oh, yes…Solidarność," she said, giving her sweater a small tug. "You have heard of Solidarność, Solidarity?"

"Yes, of course."

"Yes. I am from Gdansk, what the Germans called Danzig when they took it over, a port city like St. John's, about the same size. It was there Solidarność was born. It began the crack in the Iron Curtain. My father was a member, a *resister,*" she emphasized, pointing at the pin, "against the communist government. The Berlin Wall began to fall in Poland. This is the electrical resistor, the real one he wore—later there were badges—behind his lapel of his jacket, to prevent arrest, but to identify themselves for each other. In 1981, he was shot in a protest to martial law. I was only two at the time."

"He was killed?"

"Yes, he was killed by the police. Sunday is the anniversary when he died. That is why I wear it. To honour him."

"I'm sorry."

"Thank you. It was long ago. It does not pain me—I have no memory of him."

There was a silence. Celia got up and refilled our teacups. I thought then, despite what Hana had just said, that there was a note of regret in her voice, and that it was not a stranger's politeness or shyness that had underlain her reticence earlier, but a natural sadness at witnessing the intimate bantering between Celia and me.

"You're studying geology, Hana?" I said. "Why here in Newfoundland?"

"I am not studying rocks exactly, but fossils. I started as a geologist, but now I am in evolutionary paleontology, doing fieldwork. Do you know that the word *Pole* means "field"? The *Polanie* were field dwellers, so it must be my fate. But my field is made of rock. It is at Mistaken Point, where a lot of ship-wrecks happened, I am told, on the southern tip of Newfoundland. The land was one time connected to Africa. The oldest animal fossils in the world are there—the diamonds of the fossil world, we call them—our oldest ancestors, half a billion years old, preserved in volcanic ash. A big eruption happened beneath the ocean. There are thirty different types of soft-bodied fossils, right on the surface of the rock. When you visit, you must take off your boots and walk around in your stockings. It is proof of life in the Precambrian period. Darwin knew there was life then, but there was no proof. This established a new geological period—the Ediacaran, we call it—like discovering a new planet for an astronomer. There are now twelve instead of eleven. The earliest fossils found before were in the Paleozoic era, and they have hard shells."

"But what does this all mean, Hana? Why is this so interesting for you—for us?"

"My friends call me the philosophical paleontologist. We all know of course why animals have hard shells, why people wear hard shells. The survival of the fittest, as Darwin called it. But did it have to be that way? Did we have to evolve that way? The soft-bodied organisms lived peaceably, in the Garden of Ediacaran, as I think of it. What would have happened if they had gone on living, if they had not been destroyed by a volcano? Would our evolution have been different? When did we change course, and why?"

"Those are very big questions, Hana. And it all happened so long ago. Do you think they can ever be answered?"

"No, perhaps not, but it is interesting to ask."

Celia had now become the quiet one, the soft-bodied creature, slumped peaceably in her chair with her head resting in her hand, her eyelids looking very heavy, like the child I had sung to sleep not that long ago. I had never seen her as soft, however, though certainly not hard, not aggressive, not belligerent, not the fittest to survive, but a passive resister, a non-violent civil disobeyer. I felt a certain solidarity with her, a fatherly pride in that strong spirit of hers, even if it hadn't come from a soft-body like me. Celia was wearing a black sweater like Hana's, and I mentally pinned a red resistor to it, too, above her high-spirited, good-natured heart. Hana looked more like the Ediacaran type as well. She had stood up and was standing in the doorway leading to the stairs. "I will say my good night," she said. "I am very happy to meet you. You can come down with us sometime if you wish to see the fossils. You will be very interested in that."

"Thank you, Hana," I said. "Yes, maybe I will. Good night."

Celia's head was resting on her arms on the table now, but her eyes were open, if barely, looking up at me. Not the time to discuss her resistance, I thought—her new career or her abandoned one—or to ask her to play something for me, some dreamy Chopin nocturne that might stay in my head and accompany me home.

"I'll let myself out," I said. "You go on to bed. Thanks for a lovely meal."

But she followed me to the door, and as we stood there close to each other in the porch, she held my lapels and bumped her head sleepily against my chest, like an old familiar lover. Alicia, to be more specific. Doubtless Celia had witnessed this display of tenderness many times.

"We'll talk," she said, and I kissed her damp hair where it met her forehead. It was pinned back with clips and bobby pins and tied with an elastic in a ponytail, in what seemed a very old-fashioned way.

Earlier in the week, in a bar downtown, Kevin and I were sitting on a long brocade wall-seat at a table at the back. At the adjoining table, three young women, one of whom I had been slyly glancing at because she looked so much like Celia, were knocking back pints, much faster than we were, and laughing uproariously at times. Serious drinkers they seemed to be, though perhaps only in their early twenties. Though we were sitting very close, they were paying no attention to us whatsoever, or to the young men at the table on the other side of them. One of them, a pale young man with long hair, was slumped drunkenly in his chair, not talking to his friends at all, but with his gaze directed at the young women's table.

I had forgotten all about him until he was standing right at my side between me and the young woman who looked like my daughter, and, reaching out his hand to touch her hair, pinned and clipped and tied up just like Celia's, he said, in a weak lilting voice that didn't really seem to be coming out of him but out of the smoky air, "Ah, colleen, take those clips from your hair and let it fall."

It was an apparition right out of Joyce's "The Dead," a reincarnation of the young Michael Furey, the delicate, dark-eyed young man who had died for love. He had left his sickbed to sing to his sweetheart in her walled garden in the rain after she had written to him and told him that she was going away, going to join the convent. "Locked in her heart…that image of her lover's eyes when he had told her that he did not wish to live."

Not so for this longed-for lover, however.

"You might call 'em clips in Killarney, Paddy, but we call 'em barrettes where I come from," she said coldly, and turned her head and heart away.

He withdrew his hand, said nothing, and went back to his table.

"Yes, let's have a good chat soon," I said to Celia, clasping her small but strong musician's hands as they held my lapels, and looking into a sleepy but clear-eyed face that, in less than a year, seemed no longer the face of an innocent little girl, but, like her lookalike in the bar, that of a beguiling young woman, capable of breaking hearts and extinguishing hopes and dreams. She would do it gently and kindly, though, I hoped, and would not have her own heart bruised and broken too badly. I knew full well, of course, that the mysterious tides of the heart's affections and rejections were beyond our control.

Closing the storm door on the step, I turned to see the cold white face of the moon, grounded like a spring iceberg upon the Southside Hills.

13: THE GAME

Beyond all this, the wish to be alone/However the sky grows dark with invitation-cards…as the unsociable, the unlovable, Larkin had put it. But the sky had cleared—nearly a week with no invitations whatsoever. All the institutional formalities and obligations—the ceremonies, the luncheons and dinners, the readings, the interviews—were behind me. There was nothing left but the launch, which I was not looking forward to. The summer, or something like it, stretched ahead. It was the tenth of June, and the first heady, if anxious, month of my stay was over. I wasn't sure that I wished to be alone, but I was.

The tenth of June…and the thought quietly occurred to me as I took the long walk down to the shops in Churchill Square on a cold Saturday afternoon, wearing a pair of chequered black-and-white wool mitts that I'd found in the pine deacon's bench in the porch, mitts that I thought of as sealers' or mummers' wear, the ubiquitous mitts of David Blackwood's stark, near fantastical prints…the thought occurred to me that, according to the calendar at least, we were now two and a half months into spring. It's a modest season here, I know, one that did an admirable job of not displaying itself; but the mummers had long since discarded their veils; the sealers, their gaffs. The populace at large, however, had hung onto their mitts and caps and scarves and boots. As Kevin liked to say, "You've been away too long."

I went into the supermarket to buy some groceries, a lot of groceries, enough for a month. I had to bring them back to the house in a taxi.

They filled the entire trunk, and I gave the driver, who helped me carry the bags into the house, a five-dollar tip, which I could ill afford. A lot of processed food, I noted guiltily, as I put it away, not the nutritious *whole food*, preferably local and organic, that Alicia bought, cooking most meals from scratch. Sensible and politically correct, I know, and Celia was now following her mother's example (at least unconsciously), but even more rigorously. She avoided all meat and certain species of fish, all genetically modified vegetables, fruit, and grains, anything treated with pesticides, and pasteurized milk and cheese.

Had I not felt chastened at all by Alicia's after-supper lectures about whole food? Not that I was indifferent to her pleas and concerns, which for Celia had ballooned into one great ecological, apocalyptic, fate-of-the-earth issue involving sustainable agriculture, genetic engineering, biodiversity, deforestation, recycling, endangered species, animal rights, globalization, climate change, overpopulation, and world hunger; but it was such a complex web (and of conspiratorial design, some believed) that it paralyzed the mind when you thought about it. Thinking about your next meal—not to mention your next page—was hard enough, especially when you had to cook it yourself. There were restaurants, of course, and the blessed house-spouse, if you had one, who actually liked to cook; but your next page you always had to cook yourself—and always from scratch.

Yes, buying and eating food was now a soul-searching, complex, ethical act. Innumerable nuanced, nitty-gritty nuisance thoughts and feelings stood between you and your grub, involving not only what you bought and ate but how it was packaged, what you carried it home in, how many miles it had been transported to get to your store, what the people who had harvested it had been paid, and even what you cooked it in—if, indeed, it should be cooked at all, instead of eaten raw; if, indeed, you should be eating at all, instead of going on a hunger strike, for a billion people were starving or malnourished and every day several thousand of them died a slow and agonizing death while you feasted on fast food, which I happened to be eating on this Saturday evening while I was contemplating all this.

Frozen pizza. It had come in a big, cheerful but perhaps totally unnecessary box, the fine print on which said, "Assembled in Canada from imported ingredients," as if it were a washing machine or a TV set. I could have assembled it myself, of course, after I had made the dough from organic whole grain flour, spun it in traditional fashion over my head, puréed organic local tomatoes for the sauce, chopped organic garlic, onions and green pepper, grated the organic unpasteurized mozzarella, and snuck in some organic bacon, Italian sausage, or pepperoni, perhaps. But it would take *hours* of preparation, *days* in the search for ingredients, not to mention enormous patience and culinary skill, none of which I had in any great amount.

But Celia's young and ardent heart was into it, and, thankfully, without the hectoring and lecturing I usually heard at home. I didn't know what my heart was into any more. Too many performing selves; too many shows; too many characters, impersonations, imitations. My True Self, if there was such a thing—perhaps I was still fashioning it—was always watching from the wings. A heart like a deck of cards, and when I shuffled it these days it was usually the Joker that turned up—a wild card, not really a part of the deck at all. Rarely the Jack, the earnest Everyman Jack, lumberjack Jack; baker, soldier, tinker, tailor, candlestick maker. I got myself in trouble last year impersonating an earnest soldier Jack, whose name actually was Ernest—my neighbour Ernie Cronquist. It was reality fiction, a true-life story, not unlike reality TV. And even then I was accused of being the Joker.

The tenth of June, and the last round of the Playoffs was under way. *Oh, do not ask, "What is it?"/Let us go and make our visit.* The Playoffs, the Game, *our* game; the big spring bullfight, the big spring teat of the Mother Cow, the CBC: *Hockey Night Every Night in Canada*; "Hello, Canada, and hockey fans in the United States and Newfoundland." Though it looked like it might snow, appropriately enough, here in Newfoundland (a less than refulgent spring evening in St. John's), tonight's game was taking place in some hot, bright spot in the USA—Carolina or California, Florida or Texas.

Grim's ancient, floor-model television had no sound, no remote control. I was lucky, I suppose, that it had a picture, and not a black-and-white picture, either, but living colour, as they say, ideal for what the CBC crew called "the colour commentary," which included the colourful intermission diatribe delivered by the most colourful commentator of them all, You Know Who, in full peacock regalia.

I didn't want to hear You Know Who, and I didn't need sound. I'd heard the ancient Foster Hewitt cattle call, along with that familiar, bumpity, benign music—*dumb-da-dumb-da-dumb, dumb-da-dumb-da-dumb, dumb-da-dumb-da-dummmb*—since I was a child. Milk-fed, middle-of-the-road jazz of some generic lounge, but as anthemic as "O Canada." *Daa-dumb, daa-dumb, da-da-da, daa-dumb, daa-dumb, da-da-da, daa-dumb, daa-dumb*...it would roll on and on and on at the end, like a soundtrack to some endless dumb-show or dummy run of despair.

The pre-game show had begun with shots of our gladiators, dressed in business suits, entering the Rink earlier in the day, after leaving their BMWs and Lamborghinis in the parking garage, and being watched by admiring fans dressed in sports clothes—not sports coats and khakis but hockey sweaters and shorts, jogging suits, baseball caps, and sneakers. Soon the players would hit the ice for period number one, and we'd hear—if I could hear—the low-key, unexcitable voice of play-by-play announcer and hometown boy Bob Cole, whose cheerleading moan, *Oh, Baby*, always sounded so restrained, artificially icy, like an old man's post-coital lament. But he did his best to arouse us, to create suspense, even when there was no hope of any, only *daa-dumb, daa-dumb, da-da-da, daa-dumb, daa-dumb*, all the way through the Game.

At intermission, a *very fortunate* player from the home side would be interviewed. It didn't matter which one; he would be *very fortunate* to have done whatever it was he had done. He and his team had overcome *adversity*, and they were now playing with more *intensity*. With sweat running down his face, having ignored the sissy towel he'd been given, he would profess to being *so* fortunate that only one cheekbone had been shattered when his face was smashed into a steel stanchion only two weeks ago, and was even *more* fortunate in avoiding that fifth concussion that his doctor said might have put an end to his career. And tonight, fortunate to be still wearing a cage to protect his cheek, as he was standing in front of the net when his teammate's one-hundred-mile-an-hour slapshot had deflected in off his caged face and he had been credited with the go-ahead goal. But hey, you had to take your knocks to earn your million loonies a season; and didn't the fans in their $125 seats and matching $125 hockey jerseys deserve as much? It's *part of the game*.

After that, You Know Who, the Don, would appear with the show's host on *Coach's Corner*, dressed in one of those outrageously florid suits that only he and a macaw would feel at home in—he himself looking like a macaw in a straightjacket. He would threaten to ring his timid host's bell if diverted from his agenda, which involved replaying footage of all the punches thrown and landed in the first round—sorry, period—perhaps during the past week, saving his particular disdain for anyone who "turtled," who, when knocked to the ice, covered up his head to avoid taking a punch. Then he'd show pictures of young Canadian soldiers killed on other battlefields in other wars. The Don, it was clear, saw life itself as a war, whether fought on turf or surf, desert sands or ice—the frozen ponds and lakes of the True North strong and free or the artificial ice of the Forum and the Gardens, our playing fields of Eton.

After the second period, we would gather around the Hot Stove—no longer the Hot Stove *League*, with stirring tales of the Rocket, Boom Boom, the Golden Jet, the Gumper, and the Greatest of Them All, but the *Satellite Hot Stove*, with rumours and inside news of union-management negotiations, boardroom decisions, salary caps, team sales, arena financing...*daa-dumb, daa-dumb, da-da-da, daa-dumb, daa-dumb*. Beam me up, Maurice, Bernie, Bobby, Gumper, and Gordie.

Before the game began, I heaved myself up off the chesterfield before I sank permanently down into it—the chesterfield and the boredom, the *da-dumb* despair. *It's the Real Thing*, as the Coke ads used to say. But just when I had made up my mind to skip the game and work on the proofs, the phone rang. It was Beulah next door, wondering if I was going to watch the Game. Nelson had gone off with their TV set, she said. "A brand-new, fifty-inch, flat-screen, plasma model," she added, underlining her disappointment with her thief of a husband. I was on the verge of revealing that I'd seen him do it.

"By all means," I said. "Come on over. I'm a big fan." Anything to avoid working on the proofs, I thought. I told her that Grim's TV wasn't working too well, but she said she knew. "Then come on over," I said again, like some over-enthusiastic game-show host.

∾ ∽

The Big Fan had lost touch with the Game over the years, and though we'd already had two full months of playoff games so far this spring, I hadn't seen a single one of them. Last year, however, I'd reluctantly got myself back in touch with the Game after agreeing to write a Father's Day piece—the Playoffs had finished up just before Father's Day—for one of the Toronto newspapers. It ran a guest column called First Person Singular ("real-life stories"), but the content of my piece, the Lifestyles editor had discovered, wasn't really "true." The day after the column had appeared, someone apparently had phoned the paper and told him "the truth." A hockey parent who knew me, I guess, some literal-minded, non-fiction do-gooder of a hockey parent who had recognized my name and decided to blow the whistle, to report on my paternity status.

People—editors, critics, and reviewers above all—will get upset about the smallest details. Anachronisms seem to be a big bugaboo. Take houses, for example. A piece of plywood on the windows of a boarded-up old saltbox in an outport resettled before plywood was invented, gyprock on the walls instead of plaster, the wrong kind of insulation, or any kind, between the walls can send them into a frothing feeding frenzy. Are we contractors or artists? I ask you. All any writer wants to know—though we live in fear and trembling about this—all any writer wants from the dribbling fountain of a *critick's* fountain pen is the answer to a simple question (well, maybe two...maybe three): Is it dead or is it alive, and will it be alive one hundred years from now? Put another way: is the workworkwork of art a work of art or isn't it?

I told the newspaper editor that the piece was emotionally true, philosophically true, spiritually true, i.e., truer than true, realer than real, and that the narrator believed every word he was saying.

Well…you'd think there was something scatologically provocative about that poor innocent word *narrator*.

"The narrator!" he screamed at me. "The fucking narrator! There wasn't supposed to *be* a fucking narrator. I didn't ask for a short story. It was supposed to be non-fiction, i.e., fact, written by you, a non-fictional father, a real father with a real son—true, honest, from the heart, up front, first person singular."

"It was in the first person," I said, "and it was from the heart, from someone else's heart. It was my neighbour's story, and a bit of mine, and there were plenty of facts in there."

"Facts in there!" he shouted. "Facts in there?! Like the fact that your son was born on September 11? Well, I'm told that you don't even have a son. You have a daughter…and she wasn't born on September 11 either…and she doesn't play hockey…Facts in there? Like salt and pepper? Herbs and spices? Leavening? A bit of jam filling? Icing on top?"

"You're mixing your metaphors," I said, trying to lighten things up, but it was obvious that it would be useless to continue this conversation. When pushed to the philosophical limit, I would assert that all is fiction, even non-fiction. So I added, charitably, I thought, though not really expecting to be taken up on it, "Give my fee to your favourite charity, then."

"I will," he said, uncharitably. And that was that. My one and only engagement with the Fourth Estate.

All is fiction, as I said. Here's a line from an article in the same issue of that paper, on the same page as First Person Singular. "Six just back from the most recent tour, and four in theatre right now on the present tour," said a theatre troop spokesman—yes, that's *troop* not *troupe*—to a representative of the Fourth Estate. Not a National Theatre tour, not the Cirque de Soleil, but the Canadian military on another Taliban-routing mission. "Pacification," as it was called where Ernie Cronquist came from, dropping napalm and Agent Orange on an insurgent population daring to protest their country's occupation. When only a teenager, Ernie had done a tour of duty in the theatre of Vietnam, and was perhaps suffering from what later came to be called post-traumatic stress disorder—he'd seen the effects of pacification first-hand.

He was an American immigrant, an army deserter, a born-again Christian, and an anti-war folk singer. As a disaffected hockey fan, I had taken up his cause, a bad career move on my part, I had to admit, however brief. Ernie's son, an angry young man, having rejected his father's Christian and pacifist ideals, had become involved in another war. He had found another way to fight, to legally beat up people with impunity: he had joined a hockey team.

After his first and only tour of duty in 'Nam, as he called it, on a sunny Saturday afternoon in July 1971, while home in Detroit on leave, Ernie Cronquist was watching a baseball game at Tiger Stadium with his family— his mother, father, brother, and two sisters. During the seventh-inning stretch, when the fans were singing "God Bless America," he left his seat in the stands on the pretext of going to the washroom, and never came back. He left the stadium, walked to a used-car lot a few blocks away, bought an old Chevrolet and drove across the border to Windsor, Ontario, then on to Toronto, where he'd made a life for himself as a taxi driver and musician. His family had disowned him, except for his younger sister, Judy, who sometimes came to visit.

I had met him at a house party in the late 1970s, where I'd heard him sing "Crow on the Cradle," surely the greatest anti-war song ever written, a national anthem for pacifists if ever there was one. He'd sung a raucous partying crowd, though filled with sympathetic American draft dodgers and Canadian war protesters, into a sad silence. *Somebody's baby is not coming back, sang the crow on the cradle,* sang Ernie Cronquist, and the line had a double meaning for him, as it did for all the other expatriate Americans present. They'd helped bring an end to the Vietnam War, but the next generation would be led into other foreign wars, in Iraq and Afghanistan.

Later on, Ernie became a landed immigrant, then a Canadian citizen, and then a husband and father. His son, unfortunately, got involved in the Great Canadian Game—the national sport in everything but name, causing his father untold grief. The kid was angry, for whatever reason, and liked to fight.

For Ernie I had shed my satirical silks and put on the earnest cable-knit cardigan, though he knew nothing about it, of course. (I don't think he ever read the newspapers.) It is, if not important to be earnest, at least a good exercise; even us civilian types need *exercises* before our tours of duty in the actual theatre—the fiction wars. So here is what I had to say: *The poor Production of that Refuse of Time which has lain heavy upon my Hands, during a long Prorogation of Parliament, a great Dearth of Forein News, and a tedious Fit of rainy Weather...*

First Person Singular
"Looks Like They're Gonna Go":
Thoughts on Fatherhood, Hockey, and War.

I GREW UP IN A HOCKEY TOWN— A *HOCKEY-MAD* TOWN, I SHOULD say. I even played a bit of hockey myself, though I learned to skate much later than my friends and never did catch up. I played pickup games on the brooks and ponds, sometimes at the arena, but in a town where every boy played hockey, I was just not good enough to make the high-school team, the centre of attention of all the teenage girls, and therefore of all the teenage boys. We had minor-league, high-school, junior, and senior teams that competed in provincial leagues and tournaments. After movie stars—there were two theatres in town—hockey players, from the local level to the NHL, were our heroes, perhaps even ahead of movie stars.

The best hockey player in my hometown was a small, frail asthmatic named Garry Gosse, who, both on and off the ice, always wore a black scarf wound neatly around his neck and tucked inside his jacket or jersey, which made his long, pale face look even paler. He could stickhandle through a whole hockey team and back again, leaving opposing players frozen to the ice. And after deking the goaltender out of his hockey pants and having him completely at his mercy, he would not oblige his loving fans by simply scoring, flipping the puck into the open net. He would circle the net and skate back up the ice to the blue line, then stickhandle in a wide arc back in again. While the goalie was now back on his feet and had a fair chance, Garry would slip the puck under his arm or through the so-called five-hole.

He was *playing* hockey. For him, it was a sport, really a game. After scoring a goal, he would never raise his arms and whoop, smack the glass, or pummel the air (perhaps he didn't have enough air left in his lungs to do it). He would simply drift, half bent over, toward the bench, eyes ablaze and blinking fiercely, an expression of complete amazement on his pale face, as if he had just come out of a trance and had no idea what he had just done, or, if he did, how he had done it.

I had a first cousin named Patrick, who was a year older than me. He was bigger, stronger, and healthier than Garry Gosse, though they were about the same age, and he was arguably, as they say, an even faster skater. The argument was about whether he could be faster carrying a hockey stick and in full battle gear and uniform. But Patrick had no interest at all in hockey, either in playing it or watching it, except for a scattered pickup game on the brook. He was interested only in drinking, smoking, and sex.

Perhaps if he had gone to school beyond grade 6, he would have been forced into joining the high-school hockey team, and we would have found out just how fast and tough he really was. For on the team there were bigger and stronger hockey players, if much slower and much less skillful: slugs of players, toothless turtles, though they certainly would never, ever turtle; players who lived by brawn alone, who were more than willing to put him to the test. Their job, as they saw it, though there were no "role players" back then, no designated "policemen" or "enforcers" for protecting the finesse players on the team, was to slow down the other team's skillful speedsters. This was done by hooking and holding, plastering them on the boards, or, best of all, taking a mid-ice run at them if they were taking a pass at top speed with their heads down.

As I recall, though, the asthmatic, black-scarfed Garry had never been the object of these kinds of assaults, perhaps because he was so small and so fast that he was able to avoid them, or perhaps because they saw him almost as an invalid, though one capable of scoring at least a hat trick a game, and took pity on him. But they would have had no pity at all on a gentle giant like Patrick.

So, hockey being in my blood, a blood sport in more ways than one, I still watch it on television, still go to the odd live game, still read about it in the sports pages, though I have a complicated love/hate relationship with it. Esthetically, it can be *the* most beautiful sport to watch, and I still regret that I never learned to play it well. But the violence, the fighting—often staged as a gratuitous set piece—which is such an accepted part of the sport, disturbs me.

Fighting in basketball, soccer, even football, where the players are armor-clad, results in immediate ejection from the game; but in hockey, so the conventional wisdom goes, it's "part of the game." So apologists for, and promoters of, the violent aspect of the game keep telling us, the most prominent being Don Cherry of *Hockey Night in Canada*, watched by millions of Canadians every Saturday night. Hockey is the only organized professional sport that I know of in which, along with goals and assists, a player's penalty minutes are recorded and reported as a significant part of his performance statistics; a game in which a player can beat an opponent's face to mush—the enforcer's job is to do just that—be assessed a major (read: five-minute) penalty, and then be given the opportunity to go back out on the ice and do it again. When the play-by-play announcer of *Hockey Night in Canada* says, "Looks like they're gonna go, looks like they're gonna dance," they're not headed to the penalty box or to a dance party; they have dropped their gloves and are about to fight. The referees usually leave them alone until they wear themselves out, until one or both of them fall to the ice, or until one player gets such an advantage that the other might be beaten to death. This, dear readers, is our national sport.

My son was born on September 11—not *the* September 11, but in 1990. On January 17, 1991, the first Gulf War began, a US-led invasion of Iraq under Commander-in-Chief Father George Bush, and one cold night around that time I vividly recall holding the baby bunting in my arms around four in the morning after he had woken up in our cold house. My wife had been desperate for sleep. I walked him around the living room to try to stop him from crying, turned on the TV to see if the world had gone up in smoke, and then settled down on the chesterfield to give him his "espresso," as we called it—expressed breast milk kept in a plastic bottle in the refrigerator—and we watched the military fireworks. Those images of the war were the first TV pictures he saw.

More than a decade later, as we were getting ready for my son's eleventh birthday party on September 11, 2001, his godfather phoned to tell us the tragic and incredible news. This event, of course, led to the invasion and occupation of Afghanistan less than a month later, an occupation that still continues. On January 17, 2003, I noted in my journal: "A second Gulf War is perhaps only weeks away. 'It looks like they're gonna go,' as Bob Cole would say." And they did: on the 20th of March, another US-led invasion of Iraq, this time under Commander-in-Chief Son George Bush. They're still there.

But it is a mistake, of course, to identify the US government with the American people. Millions of Americans are opposed, and have always been opposed, to the policies of their government. The US is, no doubt, a militaristic nation, but I do not wish to single it out. It is just that, at the beginning of the twenty-first century, the American Empire, with the most powerful military force on earth, is in the limelight. But as George Steiner says in his book *Errata*, in a judgment that includes all nations, "It is plausible to suppose that the period since August 1914 has been the most bestial in recorded history."

Are we plainly and simply, then, *beasts*, *savages*, unable to stop the carnage among the warring factions of our species even if we wanted to? Arthur Koestler has, indeed, proposed such a theory in his book *The Ghost in the Machine*. "When one contemplates the streak of insanity running through human history," he writes, "it appears highly probable that *Homo sapiens* is a biological freak, the result of some remarkable mistake in the evolutionary process." The human brain developed too fast, he says, and the newer and older parts of the brain are in constant conflict (empathetic self-consciousness vs. the survival instinct and the will to power).

This is a seductive, and perhaps neat and simplistic, theory; but if one considers merely the astronomical twentieth-century death tolls from numerous political, religious, and ethnic conflicts referred to by Steiner, the notion of an evolutionary error in the brain-building process is nonetheless, for a layman, at least, reasonable and convincing. You can witness the result at your local hockey rink any day of the week.

I have actively discouraged my son from playing hockey. But though he is not athletic, he has been playing organized soccer, a much more civilized sport, for six years, and I like to think that he remains blissfully beyond the violent "sporting" ethos that Don Cherry espouses and actively promotes. I like to think that he is safe from all that, that both he and I are not a part of all that, but I know that I am only fooling myself. September 11 is his birthday, after all, and that is reminder enough.

✦✦

There you have it, Loyal Reader—earnest and sincere, if nothing else. I know, I know—the odour of smug virtue as strong as an armpit after a good old hockey game, some might say; perhaps even worthy of the Goody Gumshoes Trophy, "the Puker," an NHL award I had established in honour of Don Cherry. Mixing his metaphors as he often does, and unintentionally insulting the civil law-enforcement division of his holy trinity of heroes—cops, soldiers, and hockey enforcers—he once referred to a high-profile sportswriter, who had suggested that the NHL ban fighting, as "a goody gumshoes who makes me puke."

But Ernest Cronquist was an earnest man, a virtuous man, a real Little Goody Two-shoes. Ernie had deserved an earnest advocate, if, even in my own eyes, a morally toothless one.

⁓⁓

At exactly eight thirty, game time, the doorbell rang, and there was Beulah. She was dressed all in black—mourning clothes?—but with a beautifully simple, contrasting, red-and-white necklace: an opalescent disk attached to numerous strands of waxed red string. Hanging from her hand was a six-pack of Quidi Vidi Honey Brown Ale. I welcomed her in and opened two right away—they were ice-cold—and like an old married couple moving from the kitchen to the living room after an ordinary evening meal, we sat down on the chesterfield and turned our faces to the TV. The absence of sound, however, the play-by-play and colour commentary, exposed our unfamiliarity and slight discomfort, but it gave Beulah the opportunity to provide some colourful commentary of her own. It was a tearful tirade, during the entire first period, against her not-so-dear-departed husband, culminating in the hurtful revelation that the *cruel bastard*—her words—had actually taken the time while abandoning her to grace his exit with a soundtrack, to select a painful goodbye song for her—one they used to dance to, the one she had first heard him play on his guitar. He had put a Three Dog Night CD in the stereo and programmed it to repeat the song "One" over and over. "One is the loneliest number that you'll ever do."

While in a nightclub with a girlfriend one evening, she said, the band that had been advertised to start at ten finally came on around midnight, when she was well on her way to being drunk, and she heard her future husband play the rhythm guitar part of this tune with such desperate passion—but off to the side, out of the spotlight—that it had actually made her sexually aroused. Nelson had never made it into the spotlight, though he had made it into Beulah's bed that very evening. Fame had eluded him, though he had written songs for several self-released CDs. He had remained a part-time musician all his life—a "benefit boy," she called him, performing more often at charity events for free than at paying gigs—with a day job as a furniture mover, and the odd humiliating night job moving and setting up other, more popular, bands' equipment.

"Do you know that song?" she asked.

"Yeah, I think I do."

She began to sing it, in a low sad voice, but not an untuneful one. "One is the loneliest number that you'll ever do/Two can be as bad as one/It's the loneliest number since the number one, yeah."

"Yeah, yeah, yeah," I repeated, trying, unrealistically, to load this common packhorse of an affirmative not just with a recognition of the song and its tragic theme, but with an appreciation of Beulah's singing.

"Reminds me of that old nursery rhyme," I added, and I half-sang, half-recited, "'I'll sing you one, O./Green grow the rushes, O./What is your one, O?/One is one and all alone/And evermore shall be so.' My mother used to sing it to me at bedtime. She knew dozens of songs."

"Sad song for a lullaby," Beulah said.

"Yeah...perhaps it was some sad old ballad, but she sang it to a happy tune, clapping my hands with hers. I'm sure she never gave any thought to the words, and neither did I."

The thought struck me that I still hadn't visited my mother's grave. Perhaps I would take the old man out there next week—if his wife was going to be dead next week. One week she was dead and the next week she wasn't. One week the old man read the numbers in his bankbook as representing the money he had in the bank, and the next week the numbers were his blood pressure readings or the times he had to take his pills or the dates he had to see his doctor.

After the second period, about the time of the seventh-inning stretch in baseball, I thought, though unlike Ernie or Nelson I wasn't planning on abandoning anyone, I went out to the kitchen to get more chips and salsa and our third Honey Brown Ale of the evening, and when I came back Beulah had pulled out the fold-down sofa bed and was lying under the patchwork-quilt cover with her head against the cushions. Her eyes were closed, and I could see that her shoulders were bare. Had she removed her clothes? When I sat down on the edge of the bed, she opened her eyes, reached out her arm, and put her hand around my wrist. She held it there as if she were taking my pulse. The sports commentators on TV were gesticulating aggressively around the Satellite Hot Stove. Beulah's hand was surprisingly hot. Time for beddy-byes, it seemed. Lullabies first, perhaps.

"'I'll sing you one, O./ Green grow the rushes, O,'" I recited again, but more singsongy this time. Having taken my pulse, Beulah must have decided that I was more than ready for beddy-byes. She moved closer, laid her head against my leg and put her arms around my waist.

"Take me into the rushes," she said. Her eyes were closed again, and she was smiling.

"It might be a bit marshy," I said, "especially if I don't put down these beers."

She removed her arms and rolled over to the other side of the bed, shifting the quilt as she did so and revealing, in the warm orange lamplight, a puce-coloured nipple and her long, honey-brown back and black panties. I felt my blood rush as I stood up and laid the beer aside, turned off the TV and the lamp, and removed my clothes. I slid in under the sofa cover alongside her—into the green rushes, two *ones* who knew as well as anyone that *one is one and all alone* and that *two could be as bad as one*; but for this night at least, this cold night in June, just a few degrees above zero outside, we were grateful for the warm breath of summer inside, for the comfort and tenderness of *two*.

14: WOOD AND ASH

An unconscious desire to reclaim my lost identity, Kevin said of my decision to get a Newfoundland driver's licence, and added for good measure that it was highly symbolic that my Ontario licence had expired while I was here. Kevin had an official poetic licence, of course, and his sensitivity as an augur had proved itself in the past; but today, at his house for lunch, as he sat across from me at the kitchen table and our root soup simmered on the stove, his credibility was in question, his distinguished-poet aura, professorial aspect, and raggedly dignified demeanor undermined completely—and this was somewhat disconcerting to contemplate—by a broken tooth. Yes, something as simple as a broken tooth. Yesterday he had met his match: an unpitted olive, a miniature Trojan Horse, in a Greek salad. He could be a simple vagrant now, a wino, a panhandler. How easily ruined a piece of work is man!

He had offered to drive me out to Motor Vehicle Registration after lunch. The licence office was way out in Mount Pearl—politics, he said—and as the Mount Pleasant Cemetery, where my mother was buried, was about halfway between St. John's and Mount Pearl, we could drop in, as he put it, on our way back. I had tried and failed to take my father out there; he didn't always agree that she was out there, or even that she was dead at all. But perhaps today I would be able to make my visit, to see where she was laid to rest.

Though I had finally settled in and was feeling more at home, I was still dreaming restless dreams, as I always do when sleeping in strange houses, even for long periods of time. Dreams of subway blackouts, house fires, sleet storms, schoolyard beatings, graveyards, funerals—a recurring dream about my mother's funeral.

In the dream, I am at my mother's funeral after all, but I seem to be a mere observer, watching another mourner, a stranger—myself, perhaps—from a distance, wondering who he is. He is standing at the graveside with the other mourners watching the urn in its small casket being placed in the ground. It is a cold, wet, windy day, and when one of the funeral home attendants removes a small vial of ashes from the inside pocket of his jacket and traces a cross on top of the casket, the ashes are blown into our faces.

After the brief burial service, I look for the mourner I had been observing, but he is nowhere to be seen. I trail after the priest to ask him if the ash that burned our eyes, that I'd tasted, literally tasted, was merely ceremonial ash or…I continue to follow him, but I'm unable to catch up. I want to shout but I cannot. Then the priest turns and looks around, stops to wait for me, and I see a spot of ash on the priest's forehead, like the mark imprinted on my own forehead by all the priests of my childhood on Ash Wednesday, the first day of Lent. I open my mouth to speak, but I've forgotten what it is I want to ask. But as if in answer to my unspoken question, the priest raises his hand, raises his black thumb, and, as he comes toward me it seems to grow in size, to fill all the space between us, and I can see white, dense contour lines, the fingerprint of some fearful topography, but before it actually reaches my forehead, I wake up.

∾ ∾

Not long after I had arrived in St John's, Kevin showed me his house and introduced me to his neighbourhood.

"As you may have noticed, James," he said, as we set out for a leisurely stroll, "St. John's has changed. There is O-I-L, and oil money." Pointing at Porsches and BMWs and the "monster houses" of the nouveau pétrole riche like a bright-eyed, fledgling birdwatcher, he gave me his Marxist analysis of oil money, which he saw as the ruination of not just his neighbourhood but all of St. John's—of Newfoundland itself.

"This neighbourhood is a microcosm of what's going on," he said. "Look at that monstrosity across the street. The garage is bigger than the house I grew up in.

"Let me give you a bit of history, James. A few years after you left, about 1979 or thereabouts, up through the sea came a-bubblin' crude—Hibernia oil, the first big discovery, though it was almost twenty years before that well began producing. Black gold, Texas tea, light sweet crude, as they call it, as opposed to that heavy dirty stuff we import from Siberia and refine out in Come By Chance to pollute the countryside. All the sweet stuff is shipped out for refining in the USA, where they need the jobs and the money a lot more than we do—to buy houses and property here that we can no longer afford, safe from the imminent climate-change apocalypse, houses overlooking defunct fish plants around the Bay, bought from someone in Famish Gut who's moved to Alberta to work in the oil sands, and converted into summer mini-mansions, mock saltboxes with Jacuzzis."

He took a deep breath, and I took the opportunity to slip in a few questions: "Why are they going to the oil sands to work? What about the oil waters? Why aren't there oil jobs here?"

"Well, there are, but the good ones are all filled by people from somewhere else, though the oil companies and the government spend a lot of money on TV ads trying to convince us otherwise. Most of the jobs are for servants—*in service*, as they used to say—in the so-called service industry; but they're still servants all the same and, as you might expect, most of the people in those jobs are women.

"And as for oil royalties, we're getting writers' rates or worse. They decided that the book-publishing profiteering scheme was ideally suited to the oil industry here—50 percent for the publishers, i.e., the oil companies, the investors; 40 percent or more for the bookstores—the oil companies again, retail division; and 10 percent or less for the writers—the owners, the government, us, we the poets, we the people."

Kevin owned what he called "half a house," half a duplex, a semi-detached dwelling with an identical twin, which he'd bought cheap in the mid-seventies when he got a sessional job teaching English at the university. Nothing had been done to the house since he bought it, except for the construction of a narrow deck all around the perimeter so that he could sit out and read all day and avoid the sun. He hated the hot sun, and St. John's, he said, was now getting its share of summer days when the temperature hit 30 degrees or more (though I had yet to see any of those).

And it will only get worse, Kevin said. He has joined the cult of Gaia, led by James "the-end-is-nigh" Lovelock, the high priest of global warming for true believers. Not fanatics, mind you, simply those who've stopped acting as if it's business as usual. The entire earth, the theory goes, all animate and inanimate matter, personified by the goddess Gaia, is a totally self-regulating system whose goal is to make the planet habitable for all living things, and She has done this for over three billion years, about a quarter of the time that the earth has been in existence. But, ignorant, greedy, and uncaring creatures that we are, we have been actively undermining Her purpose since the Industrial Revolution. Our burning of fossil fuels is rapidly making the earth uninhabitable. We must stop producing and burning them immediately, says Mr. Lovelock, or that will be the end of life as we know it.

Ironically, Kevin said, this edict came at a time when Newfoundlanders, perennial denizens of Canada's Third World, were charting a new economic course based almost entirely on fossil-fuel extraction from the ocean floor. Though the cod and salmon fisheries had collapsed, the price of oil had more than doubled in recent years. So what were we to do? Were we to obey Mr. Lovelock and stop oil production immediately? Yes, said Kevin. Oil money was ruining the place, in any event, and the oil companies were getting most of it.

"I've been looking at the Budget Estimates these past few years," Kevin said, "the Gospel According to Treasury Board, the god of material things. It would blow your mind what's in those—but no one reads them. Not even the media. They just take dictée at the budget lockup and then scuttle off with the breaking news. Well, here's news for you: We're still taking in more revenue from gambling and liquor and tobacco than we are from oil, and we've been producing oil for a decade. The most recent Budget Estimates showed revenues from oil royalties would be just over $200 million, while revenues from gambling, liquor, and tobacco would be $300 million. How come that didn't make front-page headlines? If we stop drinkin', smokin', and gamblin', we're going to be in trouble."

Kevin must be the only living Parnassian I know, I thought, who reads government Budget Estimates and still listens to Donovan Leitch, perhaps at the same time.

His house was in an old neighbourhood, the first housing subdivision built after the war, beyond the slums of the Old Town, north of the Old Track, the railway line, now Empire Avenue, whose terminus was the Newfoundland Hotel, as Newfoundland itself might have been the terminus of Empire. It was now the terminus of what Kevin called the "Empire of Capital." But his house, this old neighbourhood, the Old Town, and all the rest of the city were now, one and all, part of the New St. John's, the New Newfoundland. The Newfoundland beyond St. John's, however—"beyond the Overpass," as townies jokingly referred to it—was a sad joke indeed, Kevin said. It was the Old Newfoundland cheapened and undermined—culturally, socially, economically, and architecturally debased and demoralized; communities depopulated, resettled; the remaining inhabitants physically and spiritually unsettled, a revolving-door diaspora of domestic migrants or hangashores trapped in a government tourism TV-ad, a closed-circuit cultural fantasy, or a tourist theatre pageant of their own creation. And the boom town of St. John's had not fared much better.

But though Kevin's half of a house was not worth much more than what he had paid for it thirty years ago—it had not been maintained properly, had not been renovated, and was a mere thousand square feet, just an apartment, really—the entire duplex was sitting on a ten-thousand-square-foot lot that was worth a fortune, a sweet overripe plum for real estate agents, for developers, for speculators, who knew real-estate carrion, even fruit flesh, when they smelled it. For the past ten years, Kevin had been trying to ward them off; they wanted to buy and raze the duplex. They had even threatened to buy and tear down half of it—a Mrs. Houlihan owned the other half—and had lied to each of them that they had made a deal with the other, but Kevin had held out, and had convinced Mrs. Houlihan not to sell as well.

She was now eighty-two years old, her husband had passed away, but she could still look after herself; she even did some of her own shopping. Though bent over with osteoporosis, in the summer she crept back and forth to the supermarket nearby, pulling a small wheeled cart behind her, and to a distant downtown cathedral on Sundays, a pilgrimage equal to that of a healthy pilgrim's trek over the famous Spanish Camino to the Cathedral of Santiago de Compostela. Kevin was attached to her in more ways than one. He mowed her lawn in the summer and raked her leaves in the fall; in the winter, he shovelled her walkway, raked snow off her roof, and drove her to church. Belbin's, an old family grocery, delivered her meagre groceries every two weeks.

∾ ∽

Kevin had been ranting on about all this since the day I arrived, but today he seemed to be in a more introspective, more conciliatory, mood. No talk of oil or Budget Estimates, but we had been listening to Donovan Leitch, along with Arthur Brown, Percy Sledge, John White, and Omar Blondahl, four other favourites. But to balance these off, and you needed a lot of weight, also in his retro collection of records, 8-tracks, and cassettes were Dinu Lipatti, Kathleen Ferrier, and Kirsten Flagstad, playing Bach and singing Bach, all found at the Sally Ann Big Box, as he called it. (They had moved into a huge building vacated by a car dealership.) He also owned such bizarre, multi-record box sets as the *Reader's Digest* "Background Music for Your Every Mood," which came with a cardboard "Pleasure Programmer" capable of devising over 2 million Pleasure Programs from the 10 LPs. There was "Listen While You Work," "Light-hearted Concert," "Music to Lift Your Spirits," "Serenade for You Alone," and many, many more.

The smallest thing could set him off, however. I was browsing through Kevin's music collection as he stirred the root soup—Grim's recipe, he said, a creamed blend of carrot, turnip, parsnip, potato, garlic, and onion—and I was just about to put on "Listen While You Work," when Kevin's word-sensitive ears pricked up as he picked up the *p*-word from the radio, the volume so low I could barely hear it. No, not *prick*, but *pancake*.

"Pancake-fucking-breakfasts for the homeless!" he shouted. "Can you believe that? And in June now—not just on Pancake Day. It's pancake-fucking-fundraising year round. No one questions it. Should we be doing this? Why are we doing this? First principles. Number one: equality. Don't look for it in the Charter of Rights and Freedoms. That's right. It's not in there. We're free to pursue equality, but we don't have a right to it. That's my reading of it. Nowhere does it say we have a right to an equal share of the basic material necessities of life. There's something wrong there. Is equality such a difficult thing to grasp? I ask you. Get rid of every stopgap patchwork rag of the social welfare quilt—tax credits, EI, welfare payments, baby bonuses, disability allowances, etcetera—and the outrageous bureaucratic cost that goes with administrating it, and bring in Guaranteed Annual Income Access, another GAIA, a new goddess, to redistribute the wealth, make the country economically livable for all human beings. The simplest way to create social equality. And people are not going to stop working as soon as they have a house to live in, enough food to eat, and clothes to wear. It's not Einstein's physics or Heidegger's metaphysics, not dark matter or the Immaculate Conception. Share the wealth—we all own it, don't we? It can be done.

"Oil is not going to change anything, I can tell you, unless we redistribute the wealth. There'll just be more rich people at the top and more poor people at the bottom. You can see it already since the so-called *Boom*. Boom-Boom Man is on the loose downtown, an omadhaun, a mad Pied Piper. 'Everyone owns the Boom,' he says. 'Seize the Boom...be the Boom...marvel in your little Boom moments.' *Marvel in your little Boom moments*...I think he heads the Board of Trade. Jesus, I'm so bored with trade. This used to be a place for artists. Now it's just a capitalist game preserve, a rich cruiser's port of call.

Boom's the word. An explosion of homeless people begging on the streets, an explosion of food banks, more manned grocery carts than taxi cabs—there's a guy renting them out in Bowring Park—Sally Ann franchises, hard drugs, drive-by shootings in the suburbs, sixteen-year-olds whoring downtown, addicts robbing corner stores every week. St. John's has changed, James. It's not the place you left thirty years ago. And St. John's *is* Newfoundland now—the rest of it has been abandoned, forgotten, by the government and residents alike. Foreigners are buying up every piece of real estate they can get their hands on. Oil money is going to be the nail in the coffin. Nothing good will ever come of it, I tell you. I'm startin' to hate the place already, to tell the truth. I should get the fuck out of it. Should have left long ago, not stay till the bitter end like I usually do."

I just listened up and didn't say a word—there wasn't much chance to say a word. No doubt it wasn't as simple as all that: society being transformed by GAIA, social equality brought about virtually overnight; but who was I to argue with someone who had been a homeless and hungry person himself, who had used a funeral home as a food bank and the Sally Ann as a haberdasher.

Arguing with Kevin about whether or not GAIA could produce social equality would be much like arguing with the old man about whether or not a bucket of cured navel beef could restore his physical equilibrium, cure all his gastrointestinal ills within the week.

∾ ∾

We set out for Motor Vehicle Registration in Mount Pearl. Kevin's house was five minutes from the Churchill Square shopping centre, ten minutes from the university, and fifteen minutes from downtown, so he rarely needed a car, though he owned a twenty-year-old, fire-engine-red Toyota Corolla, whose odometer was registering almost four hundred thousand kilometres. This car probably should not have its licence renewed any longer, I thought, but there were no renewal inspections anymore, he said, unless a car was sold, which was unlikely for this piece of junk. Kevin advised me to lock the door on my side to make sure it stayed closed; the windshield wiper on my side didn't work; neither did the defroster—the windows were all steamed up—nor the seat-belts; there was just a hole where the handbrake used to be, and fumes were coming up through the floor, so I rolled the window down. My door popped open after we had driven a few kilometres, even though I had locked it, and I had to keep the door closed by putting my hand out the window and clutching the outside handle.

As well as being ready for the junk heap itself, the car was also full of junk, stuffed to the gunnels, front and rear. It looked as if he might have been living in it, and perhaps that was why his house looked so bare. On the dash-board, the floor, and the backseat were piles of books and magazines; stacks of files and decks of government documents; caps, gloves, scarves, and coats; plastic bags full of dirty laundry; black banana skins and desiccated orange peels; a bicycle wheel and a spare car tire (the trunk was probably full of junk as well); a baseball bat, a tennis racket, and a hockey stick (though as far as I knew, he played none of those sports); beer bottles, newspapers, and other re-cyclables; a rusted car radiator and a rusted muffler; and other, less identifiable mechanical remains, engine parts probably. A toaster, a mop, and a bucksaw were on display on the back-window shelf. Nothing less than a combined ga-rage, basement, and attic sale on wheels.

We were driving out what he still called the Arterial Road, perhaps not wanting to acknowledge any official name for a road whose construction he had protested against more than thirty years ago—a scar across the Southside Hills, as he called it. He said the sign at the beginning, "Pitts Memorial Drive," was both a warning about the condition of the road, which was pretty rough indeed, and a belated acknowledgment that it had ruined the landscape. There were many such scars on the landscape now, he said, and he had pointed them all out to me out on a new map on the kitchen wall of his house. Besides arterial roads and memorial drives, there were bypass highways and outer ring roads—the latter going straight through "the last real forest" left in St. John's—ringing and bypassing and connecting dozens of other old roads and lines and secondary highways to bedroom communities such as Logy Bay,

Outer Cove, Torbay, Portugal Cove, St. Philip's, Paradise, Topsail, the Goulds, Kilbride, and Petty Harbour. Pictured on a map, the whole thing looked like the haphazard and fantastic outcome of a big multicoloured ball of yarn being set upon and torn apart and dragged across the landscape by an old tomcat galin' for a storm.

Kevin was hunched over the steering wheel, his chin almost touching it. He had 20/20 vision, he assured me; it was just a bit cloudy. He had never worn glasses or contact lenses.

"Waiting for my cataracts to ripen," he said, "so I can have them removed."

He began to urge out a mimicky version of Donovan's organ-grinding "Hurdy Gurdy Man," which was playing on the car's cassette deck, shaking his head and jowls for additional vibrato.

"Hurdygurdyhurdyhurdygurdy..."

"Where are we, Kevin?" I said.

"We're in Mount Pearl, b'y. Don't you recognize Mount Pearl?"

"Well, I used to come out this way on the yellow bus with McGillvray, out to his home in the Goulds, but that was a long time ago. It seemed like we'd be driving around for hours before we got there. He used to practise his arias on the way out, to a captive audience. The bus driver would tell him to be quiet or get off. The bus had great acoustics, he said, but, on the minus side, bad air. We were half-poisoned with diesel fumes by the time we got out there. This doesn't look like anything I remember."

"You probably went through old Mount Pearl. It was sort of a community then, a real place, full of baymen. They wanted to be townies, they wanted to live *in town*, but not in St. John's. It was a bit like Rabbittown, but without the hills. You remember that hutch we lived in for a few months on Sunny Goodge Street, right close to the university? It crossed a platoon of hilly streets commemorating our involvement in the wars—Aldershot, Malta, Cairo, Suez..."

"You mean Goodridge Street? There was a pizza place we used to go to at the bottom of one of those hills, on Empire Avenue."

"That's right—Pizza Empire. We used to spend more time in there than in the hutch. We won an OPE, remember? An Order of the Pizza Empire, for the most orders in a single month. Sometimes they used baloney instead of pepperoni. And up the hill from Sunny Goodge, on Merrymeeting, was a convenience store with a magazine rack full of plastic-wrapped skinbooks, high up on the rack, but there was always one with the plastic removed—sort of a sampler, I guess. There were unwrapped homemade apricot squares on the counter, and I think the owner was more afraid of you fondling the squares than the magazines.

"Anyway, this is the new Mount Pearl we're in now—suburbia, any-wheresville, strip malls, big-box stores, traffic jams—just like the so-called Greater Metropolitan Area of St. John's. Motor Registration got moved out here because this is where the Minister of Motor Cars, or whatever he's called, got elected. I know it's out here somewhere, just bear with me."

He pulled into a service station, got out of the car, and went into the at-tached convenience store.

"Straight down that road, he tells me," he said when he came back. He had bought a bunch of bananas. He tore off two and handed me one, then crammed the others between the dash and the windshield. He thumped his chest with his banana and let out his Tarzan call before peeling it. When he finished eating it, he gave me a broken-toothed grin, and then threw the peel over his shoulder into the compost at the back.

Motor Vehicle Registration, a place whose purpose was to register vehicles and drivers so that they were clearly identifiable, unmistakably distinguished from each other by photos and licence plates and serial numbers half a mile long, whose practical purpose was distinction, was, ironically, located in a building distinguished only by an almost existential anonymity, as architec-turally plain and dull as it gets. It didn't even have the distinction of being ugly. If it were a hospital, it might be described as a placebo or a bromide.

Kevin said he would wait in the car and read. I was given a number at a desk just inside the door and sat down in a long room that did remind me of a hospital waiting room, full of patients looking impatient, anxious, tired, and bored. Some were slumped in their chairs, arms folded, with their chins on their chests; some were bent forward with their arms on their legs, tapping their feet; some were gazing intently at cellphones or at the electronic counter on the wall that told us when our number was up. After about half an hour, my turn came.

I proceeded to the counter with the registration form I'd been sent and found myself behind a short, leprechaun-like man who turned and looked up at me with an impish grin and very active bushy eyebrows. When the young female clerk asked him whether any of the information on his registration form had changed since last time, he said, simply, without a moment's hesitation, "Sex." Then he turned and looked up at me again, winked at me this time, while waiting for the clerk to consider this. After giving her a few seconds, he said, "Not getting half as much." She pressed her lips tightly together and narrowed her eyes as if exhibiting an uncontrollable hormone-sequestering physiological response at the mere thought of anyone having sex with this ugly creature standing before her. But she kept her eyes on the paper in front of her, then said, very formally, "Please come this way, sir," and led him toward the cubicle where the photographs were taken. He made a kissing sound at her back as he followed along behind.

After I had been similarly processed, I was given a plastic holographic card—my new driver's licence—which, when held at certain angles, showed vertical bands of light like those apocalyptic sunbeams signifying conversion in old religious paintings. Embedded in these beams, however, was the name *Newfoundland* and the four quadrants of the red shield of our Coat of Arms, its lions and unicorns *passant,* as they say; but where the silver cross, which formed the quadrants, should be, there was only empty illuminated space. This hi-tech red shield was planted directly upon the photograph of my unshaven face—accidentally, I presumed—and it looked as if I were wearing the helmeted mask of the chivalrous knights of old. My chin was resting on the word *Newfoundland.* Was Sir James being recruited, I wondered, for some brave, bold, if quixotic, deed? If so, he didn't look all that happy about it.

My face had the sullen and shut expression of one whose picture is being taken against his will, or at least with only mute consent, by an impersonal automaton of the bureaucratic estate.

∾ ∽

On our way back to town, Kevin took me to Bowring Park, but to show me something other than the park. As we weren't allowed to drive inside, Kevin left the car across the road in the parking lot of the Waterford Hospital, "the Mental," as we used to call it when we were young and foolish—Boys o' Bedlam ourselves—and prone to making cruel and gratuitous adolescent jokes about the place. We walked across the road and in through the main gate. Just inside was the duck pond and the swannery and a statue of Peter Pan, dedicated to "a dear little girl who loved the park."

"One of the Bowring children," Kevin said, as we sized up the statue. "A sad story. She was only three years old when she and her father, along with maybe a hundred other passengers, were lost at sea in a winter storm on the way to New York to visit her sick mother. This was not long after the sinking of the *Titanic*. The ship was called the *Florizel*, the flagship of the so-called Shakespeare fleet. The Bowrings named all their ships after Shakespearean characters. Who knows why. They were English, of course, the Bowrings. There was a *Titania* as well, a *Prospero*, a *Romeo*, a *Cordelia*, even a *Hamlet*. Florizel was in *The Winter's Tale*; he was in love with the king's daughter, Perdita, which means 'the lost' in Latin."

He shook his head wonderingly. "I'm going to that washroom over there," he said, pointing to a small concrete structure.

"Yes, I need to go, too," I said.

When we came out of the washroom, he led me up a clay embankment to a trail that followed the old railway line, the tracks long since removed.

"Not once upon a time," he intoned as we walked along, "but in your time and my time, a prosperous time, a boomer's boom time, there lived a man named Jack, beneath a bridge."

A few hundred yards farther on we came to the bridge, or a huge overpass sweeping across the park, motor vehicles roaring over it like low-flying aircraft, and beneath it, parked haphazardly, was a large fleet of motorless vehicles—supermarket carts. It was being guarded by a man in a ragged black overcoat and circular, black-framed glasses that magnified his eyes to an enormous size—an I-swearable likeness of our supreme being, James Joyce (my namesake, I like to think, though my parents had never heard of him), in his latter, near-blind days, after a dozen eye operations, several leech interventions, even a sphincterectomy, an unpleasant invasion that he must have put to great use somewhere, probably in the *Wake*, but I have never come across any obvious reference to it.

"I always have the impression that it is evening," Joyce once said, referring to his failing sight. Condemned to a sort of "roamin' in the gloamin'" he was, for more than half his life, in the words of that old Irish song by the McNulty family my mother used to sing.

Perhaps it was evening now for all of us; we were all merely roamin' in the gloamin'. It was past sunset for my father, for Alicia and me, and approaching sunset perhaps for Kevin, Grim, and me—for our sputtering careers, at least, not that the sun had ever shone brightly on either one of us. But, as Kevin is wont to say, we did what we had to do, what we wanted to do, in a tone of voice that was sometimes convincing and at other times sounded like a great regret, though one kept in a heart-shaped locket in his pocket instead of on a chain around his neck.

And as for our home and native land, well, it was certainly Kevin's impression that here the sun was going down as well, though the opposite might appear to be the case—booming prosperity the likes of which we'd never known. But at the heart of it was a ticking time bomb, the production and consumption of fossil fuels—a double-barrelled irony, so to speak. We were quickly becoming economically dependent on oil at a time when it would be best for the future of the planet if it were left in the ground, if the view of an overwhelming consensus of the world's scientists was anything to go by, at least. We were on the eve of destruction once again, as we had been a generation or two ago, when a nuclear holocaust seemed inevitable, and this time *we*, our obscure little race, we Newfoundlanders ourselves, also had the bomb, or one of the bombs. A slower, less dramatic fireball this time, perhaps, but relentlessly approaching. The burning of fossil fuels was causing the earth to heat up at an alarming rate.

It was ironic as well that oil, a non-renewable resource, had almost immediately replaced a renewable one, cod, which the European and Russian deep-sea draggers and factory-freezer trawlers had fished almost to extinction. Our own draggers, too, of course; we shouldn't forget that.

His Likeness was standing with his back against a concrete wall, reading a folded-up newspaper, and, sure enough, Kevin introduced him as J. J. He barely nodded.

"How's business?" Kevin asked him.

"Booming," he said. "Buy or rent?"

"Just browsing," Kevin said, and he mock-kicked the small rubber wheels of a couple of supermarket carts.

Though Kevin said he'd been here before, J. J.'s huge bug eyes watched him suspiciously.

"Well, we'll be seeing you," Kevin said, and J. J. half-nodded once again.

"Just wanted to introduce you to the penurious glories of oil wealth," Kevin said, on our way back down the trail. "A place for everyone, and everyone in his place."

He walked on ahead of me, not wanting or even expecting a reply, a man with the bitter taste of funeral-home food still in his mouth, and the dark conscience of a modern-day Dickens weighing heavily upon him.

∾ ∾

Kevin parked the car on the street outside the Mount Pleasant Cemetery, and we entered through the main gate. Sheila, a businesswoman with a gift for figures, had given me very clear directions as to where the family plot was—the actual number of steps up the roadway from the main gate, then the number of steps up the second paved walkway to our right. But opposite this walkway our attention was diverted by an enormous marble slab memorial, almost in the middle of the road, in the middle of the cemetery, as if it were the pivot of the entire cemetery plane, gravesites sweeping uphill to the north and falling away downhill to the south. "Smallwood" was all it said. Not the more affectionate "Joey Smallwood," as he was usually known, or the more formal "J. R. Smallwood" or "Joseph Roberts Smallwood, Father of Confederation." No titles, no dates, no epitaph, nothing. Just the name Smallwood, and not in small letters carved in wood, but in tall grey letters carved on a black granite tomb larger than life, as he had been, the presumption being perhaps that no other information, no context, no explanatory detail whatsoever, was necessary.

I remembered a picture of him that I'd seen a year or so after he'd had a stroke that left him speechless. *Speechless*—the man for whom speech, rhetoric, volubility, the gift of the gab, was the very air that he breathed. I will never forget the look on his face—shock, disbelief, bewilderment, fear, resentment, death-in-life—as if he'd been mistakenly transported to the afterlife, or to a planet where the gas essential to effortless and incessant speech, i.e., to life itself, did not exist.

Kevin himself was speechless—most unusual for him as well. Surely he had strong feelings (negative, most likely, I thought) about Joey Smallwood, as everyone did one way or the other. He was staring hard at the black marble tomb, his arms folded against his chest, his head slightly bowed. I couldn't really see the expression on his face, but his eyes seemed to be filling up and he sounded all choked up and he said, "As Randy Newman sang about someone or other, 'He might have been a fool but he was our fool...' Put that on his tombstone. Free tuition and salaries—remember that? I was living in a rathole when he announced that. Senile socialist regrets, perhaps, but I never would have got to university without him..."

His voice trailed off, and we turned and walked up the path to my mother's grave. Perhaps because I had experienced a disturbing rehearsal of this visit in my dream just a few nights ago, the actual visit was not the anxious occasion of grief that I had expected. Too many years had passed since my mother's death, I guess, and today I was affected more by fearful reminders of the failing health of the person who wasn't there, but might soon be, than by any painful memories of the person who was. I stared at the empty space on the mauve granite headstone that awaited my father's name, and the empty patch of barren ground reserved for him. I didn't want to stay very long, and I think Kevin sensed as much. But he said he would like to show me the gravesite of the man he regarded as his mentor, an obscure poet named Raymond Carey.

Obscurity, of course, is every poet's middle name; the writers of sermons have larger audiences, not to mention larger paycheques, even in these days of empty pews. It was Carey, in Kevin's view, not the former sermonwriter E. J. Pratt, despite his armful of GGs, who had paved the way for contemporary Newfoundland poets. And though more than one critic had noted Kevin's indebtedness to Pratt, it might have been more emotional and patriotic than esthetic. Carey's was "the first modern voice I heard," he said, though perhaps he meant postmodern. Pratt's relationship with Newfoundland poetry—not to mention Canadian poetry and modernism itself—was somewhat problematic, in any event. He had spent almost his entire writing life in Toronto (though who was I to talk). Though Pratt's first book of poems, *Newfoundland Verse*, had appeared at about the same time as *The Waste Land*, it had not been embraced as a modernist classic. Indeed, the poetry had been described as archaic, precious, and pietistic by the Canadian *Oxford Companion*. Kevin had written a limerick about his alleged debt to Pratt. "E. J. Pratt Could Eat No Fat" was much called for at public readings.

> *E. J. Pratt could eat no fat,*
> *Keough could eat no lean.*
> *And so between them both, you see,*
> *they licked the canon clean.*

Kevin had never met Raymond Carey in person. In contrast to Pratt, Carey had never left Newfoundland, and had lived most of his adult life in the woods, according to Kevin, in a cabin he had built himself at the end of a gravel road just beyond a community called Jamestown, in Goose Bay, at the foot of Bonavista Bay. It had no amenities whatsoever—no electricity, running water, or indoor toilet—just an outhouse, a natural spring for washing and drinking, and cod-lamps for light. A few hens running around the yard. But though he lived in the woods, he was definitely not a nature poet, Kevin said, at least not of the Romantic variety.

Kevin had written a poem for his mentor, which he read at Carey's funeral service about ten years ago. It had been organized by the Newfoundland Writers' Association, for though there was an executor, an old school friend of Carey's, for the so-called estate, there didn't seem to be any relatives, Kevin said. At least none had come forward after his death, and none had appeared at the funeral service. The military had paid his funeral expenses, as he had served in the navy, the Medical Corps, during the war. But no veteran colleagues had turned up either.

Carey's grave was marked only by a plain military gravestone, with his name and rank and dates of birth and death beneath a simple engraved cross. It stood among rows and rows of identical markers, though Kevin had no trouble locating it. I guessed that he was a regular visitor here.

"Only four books," he said, "but at least a dozen outstanding poems. Not a lot, you might think, but remember what Randall Jarrell said, in reference to Wallace Stevens, I think, 'A good poet is someone who manages to get struck by lightning maybe a half dozen times; a dozen times and he is great.' Can we ask any more than that? For you, one book maybe, one novel would do it. Which one would you pick? Which of my poems would you pick? Never mind. It's best to think that they haven't been written yet. Stevens wrote his best poems early on; Yeats wrote his very late. You never can tell."

Kevin stood in front of the simple marker and recited the poem he had written for Raymond Carey, "For Ray," an autobiographical poem, he called it.

Hi, Ray,
Thanks for the wood.
I'll square up later.
Saw you on the road on my way up,
but I don't think you saw me.
I also wasn't sure
if I was to take the door.
I did—
but I'll return it
if you want it.
Love, Kev.

Kevin said he had gone out to Jamestown to find Carey. He had parked his car about a mile away from Carey's cabin and started walking down the dusty gravel road. They passed each other walking on opposite sides of the road, clouds of dust drifting up between them from a car that had just passed by. In the end, he was glad that their meeting had happened this way; he would have been too shy to introduce himself, in any event, he said. But he had walked on into the woods to find the house, had even taken a look inside.

"Just like the place I imagined Thoreau built," Kevin said, "but, as I said before, Carey was no nature poet. He was a poet of the wilderness. He was not afraid of lightning, or getting bushed, or being alone in a dory out on Windemere."

Standing with his arms folded, he stared silently at the grey granite marker. Then he said, "You see that building over there—the big grey one, corrugated steel, no windows?"

"I do."

"That's Grandy's warehouse. Appropriate location, eh? Next to the grave-yard. He stores all of his backlist books in there. He has a warehouse sale twice a year, like garage sales, yard sales. All books at half price. He never re-mainders anything—that's one thing I can say for him. Grandy turned down one of Ray's books, I was told. Lucky for him. One evening last fall I was out here and I looked across the street at that building and I had the strongest urge to go over there and burn it down. I even went over and walked around it, but it was steel from top to bottom, from the roof to the ground, and no windows, as you can see. I might do it yet if I can find a way."

"Thomas Kevin Keough, the book-burning poet. You don't want that on your tombstone, do you?"

He let out a crazy laugh. "Maybe I'll just drive a poisoned picket through his heart. I'll get an opportunity at your launch. When is it, by the way?"

"It was supposed to be this month, but it's been moved to July. No date yet."

"Don't hold your breath. I guess you expect me to attend."

"Don't be funny, Kevin. What I expect from you is to stay as far away from that fucking launch as possible. You'll just make trouble. You'll get into it with Grandy."

"Sure, I haven't spoken to that old fucker in years. He may not even be at the launch. I think his brother is looking after the business now. At least that's what I hear. He's a magazine distributer, and runs a craft shop-bookstore— mostly Grandy's books—downtown. I think Grandy's moved out to the Bay, to his house in Brigus or Trinity or King's Cove. The King of NewfLit returns to his cove, his country seat. He has seasonal residences, like the Royal family."

"You're still keeping tabs on him, are you?"

"Well, you know, it's a small place. People are always telling me things I don't want to know."

15: RANDOM HOUSE

Meanwhile, out on Random Island, Grim McGillvray was living on mackerel, root soup, and ginseng tea, and rehearsing for another tour of *Shakespeare in Carbonear*. The special diet, he'd explained in his last letter, was his way of "reinvigorating" himself, getting "primed up" for the rigours of the road and the stage.

Grim was still fond of the old ways. He wrote real letters, handwritten letters, some of them six and seven pages long—and no snail mail these, but delivered by a mailman in blazing black Postal Oxfords right to my door. (I had inquired about the shoes, as I needed a new pair of walkers, and who better to ask than a postman.) I couldn't remember the last time I'd received letters in the mail, and Grim had sent me a half-dozen or more in the short time I'd been home. One had been waiting for me at his house when I arrived, an informal introduction to the neighbourhood. I'd replied only to the first letter and the last—the mailman had kindly taken the letters, there being no mailbox nearby—in which I told him that I was coming out for a visit. I thought it might be a peaceful place for one final go at the proofs.

Grim had been awarded an Arts Council grant in the spring and was using it for his upcoming tour. He had received the grant money for something else, however; a parody of a project that he'd called "ArtHoles." Sick and tired of having his more conventional applications—usually for traditional theatre productions—rejected in favour of other, "less worthy" ones, projects that were not just superfluous, even ridiculous, as theatre, but were barely on the fringes of art itself, he had devised a similar project, simply as a joke. Not in theatre, however, but in the visual arts, and, to complete the disguise, he submitted the application under a pseudonym (including a CV with a full page of fake exhibitions). It might have been a joke, but only he was laughing. He laughed even harder when he received the news that his project had been funded—a grant of five thousand dollars. He thought of returning it and revealing the hoax (he thought that the name of the project alone would have given it away), but scrapped that idea. He deserved the money, he decided, and felt no moral qualms whatsoever about using it for his tour. He had worked his arse off all his life for Newfoundland culture, he said, while the politicians had merely patronized artists. They talked the talk while cutting the funding, handing the real money over to "pulp mills, salmon farms, and cucumber plantations." His one-man-jury judgment of the less worthy ones had been fair, he thought; he had kept a close eye on the results of the competitions, in all disciplines. They might be considered the cutting edge, he said—especially if you were on the right side of it, the cutter rather than the cut—but his own applications had been cut one time too many.

For the ArtHoles project, Grim had proposed the use of a "Newfoundland cultural icon," the root cellar, as a "creative crucible" for the artist (him), and as a "found gallery" for the arseholes—sorry, the visitors; tourists, most likely—looking to savour our old, authentic culture. In the nineteenth century, archeologists had discovered cave paintings that had been done about fifteen thousand years ago, during the last ice age, at Altamira, in Spain, and Lascaux, in France, images of animals that had been hunted or worshipped—the bison, the wooly mammoth, the reindeer, the bull. We were not entering a new ice age, however, but a fire age, due to global warming. We were going to be consumed by heat; baked, not frozen. In another fifteen thousand years, or much sooner, our planet would look like Mars or Venus. So, on the walls of the root cellars, on the pork barrel and molasses puncheon staves, in a half-dozen Random Island communities, Grim would document our fast-disappearing way of life. He would paint images of the animals we had hunted and fished—cod, capelin, salmon, mackerel, squid, moose, caribou, turr—

and visitors would enter these eight-by-ten-foot "caves" with miners' hats with lights on top and imagine themselves discovering these "cave paintings" fifteen thousand years in the future.

∾ ℅

In early July I rented a car and drove out to "Random House," as Grim called his country seat, the house that had been "thrown in" as part of a two-for-one deal when he'd purchased his St. John's house about five years ago. He hadn't expected much, he said, when he first went out to see the place, but he'd been pleasantly surprised. So last year he decided to rent his town house and live out there year round.

Just before I left, he called to say that he had just got a telephone installed temporarily, for arranging his tour, so I was able to call him from a restaurant on the highway to get directions to his house. I was glad I did. Random was the second-largest inhabited island on the Island, just a few square miles smaller than Fogo, he said, though more than half of it was totally uninhabited. I had to cross a causeway, drive down one side of the Island, then all the way across it and down the other side, almost to the end of the road. As promised, to identify the house a straw broom with a red scarf tied around the business end of it was sticking up out of an old oil-drum garbage can at the beginning of a long rutted driveway. At the end was a rusting Chevy van, blocking the entrance to an asphalt path leading to an old saltbox overlooking the ocean. It had a clear view, as he said, all the way to Ireland's Eye, another island, where he had once performed in a play in which the dead inhabitants rise from their graves and speak about their former lives in their now resettled home.

"Well, you got yourself tucked away," I said when he answered the doorbell, an actual bell with a black shoelace tied to the clapper.

"No tourists or creditors going to find me here," he said.

Grim had never been one for formalities, even conventional informalities. It was two o'clock, I was hardly in the door, standing with my knapsack at my

feet in the kitchen, and I hadn't seen him for five years or more, but he immediately left me to my own devices. He said he had to go down to the beach to
rehearse; his tour began next week, and he was on a tight schedule.

"Where are you going, exactly?" I asked.

"There's a lovely shale beach about a mile's walk from here," he said, "totally deserted, with a big cliff overhang like a proscenium arch."

"Sounds great. I was thinking about the tour," I said.

"Oh yes, the tour. Starts in Bonavista a week from Saturday, at the
Garrick. You should come along. On second thought, you should wait and
see the show in St. John's. I'll be in top form by then."

"Whatever you think."

"After Bonavista, I'm back to Trinity the next day, then on to Eastport,
Woody Point, and Cow Head, back here for a few days, then on to Brigus, St.
John's, and I finish up in Carbonear, as you might expect. Then I'll go back in
for your launch. Kevin says he's really looking forward to that."

"Oh yeah...I wonder why."

"He wants to *reintroduce* himself to Grandy, I'd say."

"I can do without that."

"Should be a bit of fun, a bit of *drama*."

"You wouldn't be planning something with him, would you?"

"Listen...I got to go. Make yourself at home. The bedrooms are upstairs
if you want a rest. I'll be back in a few hours."

Though the house was old and rundown—it had been used only as a
summer place and had been vacant for two years before he moved in—it was a
spacious two-storey, completely furnished, and with all modern conveniences,
including a dishwasher, a microwave oven, and a television, but Grim probably
didn't use any of them. Except for the basics—electricity, water, and sewer—
he was not a big fan of modern conveniences, especially "time-wasters" like
the Internet and cable TV. He didn't use a computer, didn't watch television,
and used a telephone only when he had to. "I still read books," said a button
he sometimes displayed on the lapel of his decades-old tweed jacket, while
on the other lapel there was one that said, "Buttons won't change the world."

The technician who had climbed the pole to connect his telephone, he said, had thought he was doing him a big favour by illegally connecting his TV cable (another company's, a competitor's) at the same time—he warned Grim to be quiet about it—but he had been quite taken aback when Grim sent him back up the pole to disconnect it.

As I said, the stage was all that mattered to him, but of course, like poetry and LitFic, there was no money to be made from that, and he was very sensitive about the fact that most of the money he had made came from TV ads and TV shows. The juvenile, drugs-and-sex, cops-and-robbers show he had appeared in for three years was still on the air, and, as Grim put it, looked as if it might last longer than its mental age, thirteen by his estimation. "But what's thirteen years," he said. "Trash is short, but art is long," he added, but unconvincingly. Earnings from these gigs, however, had enabled him to buy his two houses and perhaps live rent- and mortgage-free for the rest of his days.

I looked in the fridge for something to drink, but there was only a loaf of white bread, a large bottle of what looked like root soup, a tub of margarine, a jar of marmalade, a giant jar of mustard, and an open tin of milk. The freezer was jam-packed with whole mackerel, and two more were defrosting on a plate on the counter, looking right at me. Next to them was a box of ginseng tea. I made a cup and went outside and sat on a small wood and cast-iron bench beneath two tall trembling aspens—the biggest ones I'd ever seen. In front of me was a large birch, and for an hour or more, in a sort of lethargic daze, my usual state after driving for several hours, I looked through its low-hanging branches at the blue waters of the bay.

It was a sunny and windy summer's day: a meadow of swaying grass and wildflowers—daisies, buttercups, fireweed, clover—sweeping down to the ocean; the incessant sound of rustling leaves and the sweep of waves on the beach; the distant, haunting cries of gulls, Pratt's "wild orchids of the sea"; whitecaps, wilder orchids, on the blue water; cumulus clouds cascading across the sky, their shadows darkening the meadows and the ocean. A summer's day from my childhood, stored in amber.

"*Die Erde hat mich wieder,*" said Goethe's Faust. "The Earth has me back again." I felt at peace, but as always, it was a sad peace. O mortal life! You could easily imagine all this gone, and you along with it. Or worse: all of it still here, but without you. Or perhaps worst of all: you still here, but without someone dear…

In the summer of 1908, a year after he had lost his eldest daughter and suffered a heart attack soon after, the composer Gustav Mahler retired to a "composition hut" in the mountains of northern Italy and wrote *Das Lied von der Erde*, "The Song of the Earth," a work—especially the last part, "The Farewell"—filled with a deep resignation, a painful awareness of the transience of life. "Can this be endured at all?" he asked a friend who was to conduct the piece. Was he talking about the music or the death of his daughter? Perhaps both. The performance did not take place until three years later, in 1911, after the composer's death that same year.

∾ ∾

Yes, a summer's day from my childhood, on another island, one most of us had abandoned. In June of 1966—Come Home Year, as Dayv Maddigan had pointed out to me—I finished high school and took off for Toronto, as so many of my compatriots had done before me, domestic migrants for the mines, mills, farms, and factories of Ontario and points west. At the end of June, the mines on Red Island closed for good, putting hundreds of people out of work, including my father. Most of the unemployed workers and their families left for the mainland, but my father stayed on. His job as watchman lasted for another year, but by the time I returned in August of the following year he had boarded up the house and moved the family—my mother and sister Sheila— to St. John's. He found another job as watchman with the Newfoundland Railway and bought a small house on Whiteway Street, a long, bare wind tunnel of a street with hardly a tree in sight, though this house was surrounded by tall, straggly pines.

It was also the only house on the street with its "front" door on the side—a house "with the wrong attitude," as Kevin had described it the first time he saw it. This door led right into the living room, so we never used it; we always entered through the porch at the back. But Kevin had the right attitude as far as my mother was concerned. She took to him right away—he made her laugh—and she fed him large quantities of fish and brewis or roast beef or Jiggs' dinner every time I brought him over for a meal. He might have been a returning prodigal son; a long-lost younger brother just released by a cult; a baby given up at birth, taken from her arms—she an unwed teenage mother; or she might have known about his former life as a foster child forced to live on funeral-home food.

I had moved into this house—just for a couple of weeks, I thought—when I returned home in the summer of '67, but I decided to stay there when I started university in September, as the house was on the doorstep of the campus. Before the next semester began in January, however, I moved into a basement apartment with Kevin. As he had reminded me, there was free tuition and salaries [sic] for students in those glorious days. The next September, Kevin and I shared a three-bedroom apartment with Grim, who had moved into town from the Goulds. That fall our house on the Island burned to the ground—arson, most likely. The old man had refused to sell it for the pittance the government had offered residents looking to move away to find work.

∽∽

"Did you say the *Garrick* in Bonavista?" I asked McGillvray after supper that evening—an appetizer of root soup followed by fried mackerel and boiled potatoes, with a bottle of locally made dogberry wine, perfectly chilled, straight from his root cellar-cum-wine cellar.

"Yes, that's right," he said.

"Is it named after that actor in Shakespeare's company, the one who first did all the great roles at the Globe?"

"Well, you're half right. Garrick did all the great tragic roles, but not at the Globe. You're thinking of Burbage, Richard Burbage, and the King's Men. David Garrick was perhaps even better than Burbage, but he came later, eighteenth century, Drury Lane. There are Garrick theatres all over England, and the Garrick in Bonavista was built in 1945, when we were still a part of jolly old England. Garrick was the first actor to be buried in Westminster Abbey, in the Poets' Corner, right beside Shakespeare, in fact, or at his feet. Only two others—two more great Shakespeareans—have been given that honour: Sir Henry Irving in the nineteenth century and Sir Laurence Olivier in the twentieth. The twenty-first is still open. Why do you think I'm doing this?"

"To Sir Graham McGillvray," I said, offering a toast. "You got my vote."

"Well, thank you, sir…arrrgh…a bit doggish," he said, grimacing and planking his earthenware beer-stein wineglass down on the table. "A Garrick vintage," he added. "Garrick was a wine merchant before he became an actor, though acting was his consuming passion and it was said that all he had in his *wine* cellar was *vinegar*. Audiences—even critics and other actors—were enraptured by him from the beginning. They were saying things like: 'I never knew what acting was till he appeared.' 'If this young fellow is right, then we've all been wrong.' 'The blind can see him in his voice.' 'He will never have a rival,' etcetera. Garrick is my man. I'd be happy to be buried at *his* feet. You could say he single-handedly created modern acting. He rejected the old, stilted, bombastic style. This was Burbage, doing *Richard III*: 'Now is the winter of our discontent…'"

He switched to Garrick, doing the same soliloquy, but in a much more natural-sounding voice.

"You see what I mean? Garrick's *Richard* was the talk of London. He had trouble getting work before that, but he was breakin' a leg before long. 'Break a leg' originated with him, in fact. He was so wrapped up in a performance of *Richard* he wasn't even aware that his leg was broken."

"Now *lookit*, Grim," I said, in my best Toronto idiom, "everyone knows that expression originated with Bobby Clobber and the Stanley Cup-winning '67 Leafs."

"Yeah, right…hockey being the main form of theatre in TO."

He rattled on, fueled by pre-pre-performance anxiety, perhaps, which always culminated, he said, with his purging himself backstage, just before he went on on opening night—and every night after that.

"Garrick and Sam Johnson were good friends. They went down to London together to seek their fortunes. Johnson wrote his obituary. 'Death has eclipsed the gaiety of nations,' he said, 'and impoverished the public stock of harmless pleasure.'"

"'Harmless pleasure'?" I repeated. "Not 'the axe for the frozen sea inside us,' as Kafka claimed? He was talking about the book, of course, not the theatre; but it's all the same, isn't it?"

"Yes and no. First of all, don't forget that our greatest writer was a playwright. But no…that's a writer's rigorous notion, James, or a rigorous writer's notion—the quintessential Mr. Rigour, in fact, Kafka—not a reader's, not a playgoer's, not an actor's. 'The drama's law the drama's patrons give,/For we that live to please must please to live.' Johnson again. There's that intermediary between the play and the audience, i.e., me, the actor. It doesn't exist between the writer and the reader. There *is* the critic—Lord save us—but forget about him. He's expendable. There is the writer himself, of course, but we all know that writers can't read their stuff. Listen to Eliot; listen to Yeats. They'd put you to sleep.

"Acting has always been a kind of religion for me; the theatre, my church. But the work is most human, not divine, and leaves this poor player most vulnerable in the doing of it. Yet this is exactly what audiences come to see, whether they realize it or not. They come to see humans playing at being more human than we otherwise allow ourselves to be in everyday life. And as Hazlitt said, 'The genius of a great actor perishes with him.'"

"What about film?"

"Forget about *movies*—that's something else entirely. And I don't think Franz 'the Axe' Kafka could ever have written for the stage. Give me rigour, but give me warmth, give me tenderness. Give me Chekhov, for instance. There's something icy and unfeeling about Kafka. End of sermon."

Later that evening, he became immersed in a book, and seemed to want to avoid further conversation—or sermonizing. He had always been an obsessive book reader—never newspapers or magazines, except for reviews of his plays. He used to carry a book with him wherever he went. The next morning he was pounding out something on the typewriter, furiously typing away on a clattering old manual at seven o'clock. In the afternoon, he went off again by himself to the beach to rehearse.

He was at the typewriter at seven every morning, in fact. A voracious reader, yes, but I had never seen him *write* like this—so intensely, so obsessively, with such dedication to the task. He seemed inspired, typing in tongues, beside himself. He was always happiest, he said, when he was beside himself, which was how he perceived his transformation into a character on stage, when he was no longer "play-actin'." "Beside Himself" had been the name of one of his one-man shows.

We were usually in bed by ten o'clock, which was easy to do, for it was pitch black and totally quiet except for the sound of the waves on the shore, like Arnold's "eternal note of sadness" in "Dover Beach." But at seven in the morning the infernal sound of the typewriter would be rattling through the house once again.

Noisily at his task, yes, but secretively. He would not discuss whatever it was he was writing, though it was as if he wanted me to know and not know at the same time. I was tempted several times when he was out on the beach rehearsing to go up to his bedroom and have a closer look—I *had* taken a peek—at the stack of typed pages on his desk, next to which was a handwritten stack, but I had a writer's block against doing what I myself would have regarded as a serious breach of trust had someone done it to me.

Well…one afternoon I did take a closer look—at the title page, "The Art of Theatre; or, A Scourge of Reviewers," and the first page…the second page… but I felt guilty and quickly left the room.

I went outside with a cup of ginseng tea and sat on the same hard bench under the aspens and thought hard about rigour—artistic rigour. I had been thinking about it even before I left St. John's, about *Banville*—a writer and a place, as I thought of it, a place even John Banville himself, a writer I admired greatly, wanted to escape from periodically. He had admitted this in a recent interview I'd read. For him, escape from Banville meant release from the suffocating and paralyzing rigour of composition—a "constant torment"—and from the "nonhuman pursuit" of beauty. He was still "diligently practising," he said, after about a dozen books; he might turn out a few words a day and change those the next.

So, under a pseudonym, Benjamin Black, he had turned his hand to more formulaic, less rigorous, less tormenting work—the detective story, the murder mystery. Most readers, as he well knew, cared only about *plot*, though the critics could be very dismissive of the murder-mystery genre. "Who cares who killed Roger Ackroyd?" wrote Edmund Wilson in *The New Yorker* in 1945 in reference to what is now generally considered to be Agatha Christie's masterpiece, *The Murder of Roger Ackroyd*. And Wilson had conscientiously taken it upon himself to read a second batch of detective stories because readers were so upset that he had completely dismissed the first, but his experience was even more disillusioning the second time round. "A true connoisseur of this fiction," he concluded resoundingly, "must be able to suspend the demands of his imagination and literary taste." But, on the lighter side, he said it was simply a minor vice that ranked somewhere between smoking and crossword puzzles.

An acquaintance of mine in Toronto makes a good living as a writer of "papular" fiction, as he calls it—mysteries, Westerns, romances, soft porn, anything at all. But he is also a vigorous, omnivorous, discriminating reader of literary work—an amateur Beckett scholar, as he sees himself—who says that the whole of Beckett's oeuvre can be read as a parody (a serious one, of course) of the Romantic notion of the agonizing labour of composition.

"'I can't go on. I'll go on,'" he quoted, apropos, when he first told me this.

"Go on," I said, and he did.

"Not to mention the futility of realistic representation," he added, "along with…" But I'll spare you the rest.

In any event, along with the Banville interview, my earlier deliberations on the subject had been prompted by a book of photographs I found in one of the second-hand bookstores in St. John's of the rigorously eccentric residents of the Chelsea Hotel in New York, mostly artists of one kind or another. There was one terrifying picture in particular: of a writer and his family, a wife and two young children—a boy and a girl who had actually been born in the Chelsea—victims of rigour. With over *thirty* unpublished books to his credit—he drove a limousine for a living—the haughty expression on his face, his unwelcoming eyes and downturned mouth, testified before one and all that he would not give a fucking inch. We denizens of Banville recognize the pose. O come, all ye faithful, bitter and defeated, O come ye, O come ye, to the Chelsea Hotel, to Banville, to Kafka's hunger artist's cage, to Beckett's dustbin...Rigorous or not, I thought, in the end we will all be consigned to Beckett's dustbin. And, as if to remind me of this sad fact, I found myself in one, literally, if willingly, when I gave a reading at the university last month.

A small lecture theatre had been booked for the event, but I was informed ten minutes before it began, as people were filing in, that we would have to move to a different venue, a *larger* theatre, and my heart swelled at the thought of a large appreciative crowd, my whole cult following, Newfoundland division, together in one place. Alas, the reason for moving was not to accommodate the anticipated mob, but because the smaller theatre had been double-booked, and thirty or so people in a four-hundred-seat theatre looked even more dispiriting than in a hundred-seat one. I managed to cheer myself up, however, and the audience as well, I think, by installing myself in one of the large, almost chest-high, papier mâché garbage cans that were part of a set on stage, using the rim and one of the bulbous handles as a makeshift podium. (They had forgotten to bring along the podium from the other room.) A theatre troupe had just finished rehearsing, and there was a perfectly placed spotlight overhead. The set, coincidentally, was for a production of Beckett's *Endgame*, opening the next night, and was quite appropriate for the piece I was reading.

∾ ᔕ

Sitting on the bench sipping my tea, I watched an *emmet* (as we used to call a smaller specimen of ant) carrying a piece of straw out the cracked-asphalt walkway, which Grim said was composed of salvaged pieces of pavement that had broken off from the edges of the road, boiled up and reconstituted in the old oil drum at the end of the driveway. (The whole process had a familiar ring.) Not by him, of course—he was as useless with his hands as I was—but by a previous owner of the house, years ago. Over small sticks and stones, cracks, bits of clay and other debris, through a forest of grass shoots and weeds growing up through the cracks, the tiny insect was carrying a straw ten times longer than it was. Couldn't it simply have crawled to the end of the walkway without the straw and picked up a piece at the end of its trek? I wondered. But perhaps there was something special about this piece of straw that a non-emmet could never know, like that tantalizing *mot juste* I sometimes hoped to recover from the deepest recesses of my brain after a long meditative trek through the woods.

And not far behind the emmet was a coal-black beetle—Kafka's Gregor Samsa, perhaps—back on the wrack. Perhaps Kafka had not suffered enough in writing "The Metamorphosis," "a self-portrait and a self-punishment," one critic had called it. It was rolling a perfect ball of dung with its back legs, in a very straight line, though facing in the opposite direction from wherever it was going, its head pointing toward the ground. (Cows sometimes wandered through Grim's meadow, so there were many fresh dung-patties lying about.) While it is probably safe to conclude that a beetle rolling a ball of dung is a dung beetle, and not some other kind of beetle—there are more beetles on earth than any other insect, I once read, and I've helped a few back on their feet in my time—we cannot be certain, of course, that the insect into which Kafka's character had been transformed was indeed a beetle. In translations of the story that I have read, it is merely referred to as a "gigantic insect" or a "monstrous insect," though its having a "hard, armor-plated back" has led most readers to that conclusion. There are academic papers devoted to this subject, of course, and not just whether or not it is a beetle, but what sort of beetle.

When this dung beetle encountered one of the many obstacles that the ant had previously met, which prevented the dung-ball from rolling forward, it would do a most peculiar thing: it would climb on top of the ball of dung and do an elegant, pirouetting little dance. What was it doing? I wondered. Scanning the terrain and taking a compass bearing? Taking a well-deserved break and expressing its sheer joy at being alive and on top of the world, i.e., a perfect ball of shit, on this fine summer's day? Then it would climb down and proceed around the obstacle and get back on its straight track once again.

Alas, this dung beetle's thwarted pilgrim's progress—not to mention the nature of its artistic material and its pathetic little joyful dance—along with the emmet's mysterious, dedicated trek, both performed on the symbolic stage of salvaged and reconstituted asphalt debris, had all-too-familiar occupational intimations and reverberations. Is this what working on page proofs can do to your mind? "Die Merde hat mich wieder," said Sam Beckett, taking a comic kick at Goethe. "The shit has me back again."

After that, I just didn't feel at all like working, and after three more disconsolate days I stopped pretending that I was, though I was way past my deadline for the proofs. The proofs themselves had become dead lines. What usually took two weeks had stretched into two months. Luckily, van Loon couldn't reach me out here. Fuck the proofs, I thought—I was rewriting the book, no doubt. Next year, maybe.

Just before I left St. John's, I had made the mistake of digging out my first draft—the whole thing, I discovered, handwritten on the back of Celia's discarded mimeographed music sheets, which she used to pile up on my desk. She was scrupulous about recycling, but her teachers were obviously not about copying. I was looking for a particular passage in this first draft that seemed to have disappeared from later drafts. I couldn't find it, but in the process kept finding other passages, whole pages, in fact, that seemed much better, more inspired, than later versions. That discovery had just about immobilized me for several days. And it wasn't just the writing that did it, but the silent music on the other side.

There it was again: all the violin and piano music Celia had once performed and had now left behind; years of it, scores of it, scores of scores. Music for sonatas, duets, trios, quartets, quintets, suites, concertos, and symphonies; by Bach, Vivaldi, Mozart, Kreisler, Bruch, Brahms, Chopin, and Schubert; scores for playing in school musicals, with church choirs and school choirs, at benefits and memorial services. Now just silent notes upon the page, in stark black and white, and I could hear the silence as clearly as I had once heard the music. And there was something alarmingly inauspicious, in hindsight, in having my own words inscribed on the back of these pages, these discarded pages.

I took to reading instead of writing, but not Grim's manuscript. I managed to restrain my curiosity a little longer. But I had come face to face with the realization that I was more interested in what Grim was writing than in what I was writing myself. I fetched a large box of books I had deliberately left in the trunk of the car, in the vain hope of keeping my mind focused on the proofs.

There is a tune in the Suzuki repertoire that Celia played on the violin in her early years—"The Happy Farmer"—and one time when she was playing it, and I was sitting in a chair listening and reading, she stopped playing and looked over at me and said that I was "The Happy Reader," that I never looked so happy as when I was reading, and she was probably right. Ah, Happy Reader, Loyal Reader, you don't know how happy, how lucky, you are, Kafka's axe hanging over your head like a Sword of Damocles notwithstanding. In my homing heart of hearts—Heart's Content, Heart's Delight, Heart's Desire—I simply want to be one of you, at Little Heart's Ease.

The box of books was the harvest of my obsessive browsing in the many second-hand bookstores in St. John's. (The Happy Reader starts a library wherever he goes, even on a two-week vacation.) The bookstores all had a small section called Classics, usually tucked away in a back corner, as if it were a small patch of porn protected by large scarecrow stacks of Bestsellers, Romances, Westerns, Mysteries, Comic Books, and Textbooks.

I stuck my hand down into my treasure trove and selected Wordsworth's *Selected Poems*. I read "Michael," a very unromantic pastoral, several times. *If from the public way you turn your steps…*Ah, that voice! On one of my walks, on an old abandoned farm nearby, I had seen several rock walls that reminded me of sheepfolds and shepherds, and I felt as if I were, mentally and physically, in the very place where the old shepherd's heart had been broken. I thought that Celia could just as easily do the job on me if she so desired, or without even being aware of it, as Michael's wayward son, who had gone off to the city never to return, had probably been totally unaware of the suffering he had caused.

I closed my eyes this time and put my hand in again. *Oblomov*, by the much-neglected Ivan Goncharov, though he became a censor toward the end of his long life. I read my favourite part, "Oblomov's Dream": "Where are we? In what blessed little corner of the earth has Oblomov's dream transferred us?" In the heart of the heart of the country, as it turns out, far away from the sea. "Let it stay where it is! It merely makes you melancholy: looking at it, you feel like crying." I was looking at it—I could hear it, in fact—and I did feel like crying. But perhaps it wasn't the sea, just a sea of troubles.

I read Kafka's "Country Doctor," Chaucer's "Wife of Bath's Tale," all of Keats' odes (could this man have been only twenty-six when he died?), Dante's *Inferno*, Chekhov's *Cherry Orchard*, Gogol's "Overcoat," about half of Shakespeare's sonnets, coming to grief on the astounding closing couplet of No. 72: *For I am shamed by that which I bring forth,/And so should you, to love things nothing worth.* What hope for the rest of us? I thought.

Then *Heart of Darkness*, finally cleft for me. I saw the light—Heart of Light! This book is about writing! I thought. Listen to this. Marlow is talking about Kurtz, thinking about Kurtz. He is always thinking or talking about Kurtz, of course. "I made the strange discovery," he says, "that I had never imagined him as doing...but as discoursing...The man presented himself as *a voice*...The point was in his being *a gifted creature*, and that *of all his gifts the one that stood out pre-eminently*, that carried with it a sense of real presence, was his ability to talk, *his words—the gift of expression*, the bewildering, the illuminating, the most exalted and the most contemptible, *the pulsating stream of light*, or *the deceitful flow from the heart of an impenetrable darkness*." All italics mine, as they say. Ambiguity? Paradox? The ineffable? What else. *I made the strange discovery*, indeed. Passing strange.

"Words have been my only love, not many," said the gifted creature in Beckett's "From an Abandoned Work."

Abandoned? They're all abandoned, the published ones as orphaned as all the rest.

I can't go on. I'll go on.

Go on.

I found myself in Grim's bedroom-office once again. Not my fault, I thought, I have nothing left to read. But look! Look there! I heard a voice say, and I noticed a stack of magazines and newspapers in a corner of the room. Yellowing, acidic, wood-pulp papers going back decades, all opened and folded to a highlighted review—in ink of an acidic lemon hue. I picked up a batch and carried them to the desk. The reviews themselves ranged from the acidic to the adulatory, and everywhere on the spectrum in between, including the ignorant, the soporific, and the damned-with-faint-praise. After an hour's reading, I dropped the newspapers on the floor and sat staring at the manuscript on Grim's desk: "The Art of Theatre; or, A Scourge of Reviewers." A great title, I thought—a scourge being both a person who causes suffering and a whip used to make him suffer in return—but titular praise would be my only praise, for I knew instinctively the noxious nature of this document without having to suffer a word of it; but suffer it I did, or at least half of it.

The shit has me back again.

Now, I have friends who claim they don't read reviews of their work, but I have never believed a word of it. I have told the same lie myself. But if there is anything worse than reading negative reviews, it's reading pathetically defensive replies. And here was—what?—an almost two-hundred-page pathetic philippic, so unworthy of this man, my lifelong friend, my brother in art, this gifted creature, whose sterling career as an actor I had witnessed from the proverbial Day One. Under the humble proscenium arch between the kitchen and the living room in our apartment, he had cracked us up (though cannabis had certainly prepared the ground) with an imitation of Pope John XXIII having a morning crap as if he were performing a sacramental rite. (One of the more progressive popes, John XXIII, but Grim had issues, as they say, with the

Catholic faith, which he had been brought up in, and long before it had been revealed that the "Christian buggers," as he called them, had sexually abused the defenseless orphans in their care.)

And much later in his career, in *King Kean*, Grim's stage adaptation of Cassie Brown's *Death on the Ice* for Toronto's Theatre Passe Muraille, his portrayal of Captain Abram Kean as a veritable Newfoundland King Lear was one of the most moving performances I'd ever seen. But it was a very unsympathetic portrait of the old sealing captain (seal killer extraordinaire—over a million pelts to his credit) and his coming to the gradual realization, if not acceptance, of his guilt—not for killing seals but for killing sealers. The tragic and horrific deaths on the ice floes, in March 1914, of seventy-eight sealers from the SS *Newfoundland*, some of them found frozen in each other's arms, would haunt the Newfoundland psyche for generations.

Indeed, *King Kean* was a very unsympathetic picture of the seal hunt itself; in particular, the ruthless profiteering merchants and ships' captains who had prosecuted the hunt and persecuted the sealers. Greenpeace had abandoned their wrong-headed protest of the play after only a one-night stand. Grim's two-week stand, a one-hander, as he called it, had been held over for two more weeks.

I put Grim's handwritten manuscript, on yellow paper, and the manually typewritten manuscript, on white paper, together in a plastic bag and carried them downstairs and out the door, down the cracked asphalt walkway, down the muddy, rutted driveway, to the oil-barrel garbage can at the end, with the red-scarfed broomstick still sticking out of it. And it was a good thing, too, that red flag, for it made me stop. I knew I couldn't burn them, anyway; but I would convince him to do it, I said to myself, not very convincingly, as I took the same sad steps back to the house with a burden of bile and bitterness hanging from my arm.

16: GIFT HORSE

After another Friday night dinner at Sheila and Loyal's, after we'd finished off a few more bottles of Grand vin Château Latour à Pomerol, we nonchalantly concocted a late-night notion, logistically complicated though it seemed to be, of taking a trip down the Southern Shore the very next day to see the famous fossils at Mistaken Point, and, on the way, take Sheila's Little Sister, Roseanna, horseback riding on a Newfoundland pony at a farm between Bay Bulls and Witless Bay, where Sheila and Roseanna had gone riding last summer. After our third bottle of wine, fossils and horses seemed a lot more interesting to Loyal than markets, and he confessed that he sometimes wished he had a more down-to-earth job—as he himself put it, though he seemed oblivious to puns—as an archeologist or carpenter or fisherman, or even a jockey, where he would actually, physically, have his hands on things. Though he had to "huddle" with his business associates, his "fund managers," in the morning for a couple of hours, he would be free by noon, he said. Then he would treat us to lunch downtown, and we would head off down the coast in his new BMW SUV, which he had yet to try out on the highway. Sheila had her own car—a tiny grey-and-blue Mercedes-Benz Smart Car, which reminded me of a 1970s platform shoe. It was ideal for skipping around the congested streets of St. John's at rush hour, she said, but she would never take it out on the highway.

Mistaken Point was at the southernmost tip of the Southern Shore, just below Cape Race. It was about a hundred miles from town, at least a two-hour drive on a winding, narrow highway, and we would need about two hours for the trail ride as well; so the plan was to stay overnight in Trepassey, a town close to Mistaken Point, look at the fossils on Sunday, and then drive back later in the day.

"Tell me about Roseanna," I said to Sheila. Loyal had gone off to bed, as he had to be up by seven, he said, for his nine o'clock huddle. As I had noted last time, Loyal seemed to require much more than the ordinary amount of time for his toilette.

"Well…she's eight years old," Sheila said, "an exceptional child, and I don't mean just in the general sense. She's been clinically tested, I was told. Her mother's an alcoholic, in detox, banned from the home…where lives her workaholic father. I pick her up on Saturdays at eleven, after her dance class. She loves books, you'll be happy to hear. She's reading *Black Beauty*—she's in love with horses. I'm reading it again myself. Do you remember it was written from the point of view of a horse?"

"Really? That's appropriation of voice."

"If you say so, James…And *Peter Pan*—we just finished that. His family had a Newfoundland dog for a nurse…a nanny. Do you remember that?"

"No."

"Yes. A Newfoundland dog named Nana. The woman who wrote *Black Beauty* had an accident as a child—fell and broke both her ankles on her way to school. It crippled her, and she spent her life dependent on horses to get around—in a carriage. This was the late 1800s, in England. She must have developed a great empathy for them. It was her only book, published when she was almost sixty, just a few months before she died. But it was a great success."

"Here's to Prince Posterity," I said, raising my wine glass off the carpet. I was stretched out on Sheila's plush beige carpet, and I sat up and laid the glass carefully on the glass-topped coffee table beside me.

"What matter if you don't live to taste the fruit of your vines," I added. "And, as Kevin says, one good book is all you need. Maybe I could write one from the point of view of that Newfoundland dog-nurse—a sequel to *Peter Pan*. Should be a big market for that—a variant of the British upstairs-downstairs social-class thing. Or a historical novel of some sort—Newfoundland his-tory from the point of view of the Newfoundland dog. Nana gets stolen and taken aboard a fishing boat going off to the Grand Banks of Newfoundland. People used to use Newfoundland dogs to get around on sleds, and for haul-ing wood. I could spend the winter doing research out at Grim's house on Random Island: get a sled and a dog and ride around on the snow, go ice fish-ing, bring home wood for the wood stove, get a feel for the animal and how he thinks, how he behaves. At one point in my illustrious career I thought of writing a book from the point of view of a bird—a nightingale, of course. Lots of mythical material there, but trouble locating, observing one in the field. None of them in these parts, as you know."

"I think you should get some sleep, James," Sheila said. "It'll be a long day tomorrow. It's late—do you want to stay here for the night?"

"No, I'd better go back, but I think I'll take a cab."

∽ ∽

On Saturday morning, Sheila and Roseanna came by around eleven fifteen. Roseanna brought along her hardcover copy of *Black Beauty* and a big white sheet of bristol board inside a translucent blue garbage bag. Pasted on the board was a display for her unfinished science project: pictures of a small, cuddly, dark-eyed mammal that looked like a cross between a chipmunk and a bat. It was a sugar glider, she said, an Australian marsupial, pictured chewing on eucalyptus flowers, flying through the air like a kite, and carrying its young in a pouch like a kangaroo. There was also a picture of its enemies, the usual suspects—a cat, owl, and lizard—but they had been cut and pasted together to form an unlikely predatory trio. They looked like three hens roosting on the branch of a tree.

Roseanna herself was as tiny and dark-eyed as a sugar glider. The photos of this sad and secretive nocturnal creature—eating, nesting, sleeping, and flying—were from a magazine her father had brought back from Australia. Roseanna had cut them out, glued them to the bristol board, and pencilled captions below them in an eight-year-old's rudimentary cursive hand: "The sugar glider lives in eucalyptus trees in the woodlands of Australia…Their nests are made of eucalyptus leaves…They sleep in the day, they fly at night, gliding through the forest searching for food…They love sweet-tasting nectar sap from eucalyptus flowers."

These lulling words brought to mind the Lotus-Eaters of the *Odyssey* and, by further association, my brilliant, if unhinged, classics professor, Dr. Whittick, who used to recite in class, in a strangely ironic, incantatory way: "They eat the fruit of the lotus; they mean you no harm; they give you lotus fruit to eat; and then you want to stay with them forever." In recalling the many eccentric profs I'd had at my old alma mater, in the lotus groves of academe, I'd completely forgotten about him, appropriately enough; the fruit of the lotus, the fruit of forgetfulness, had been an obsession of his.

Dr. Whittick was from England, home of Nana and Black Beauty, a late-middle-aged, mild-mannered man whose ascots matched the colour of his shoes, always black or white, neutralizing, perhaps, what might have been the mesmerizing effects of his striped and chequered shirts, jackets, and trousers. Unlike the other professors, he wore no gown. Though his recitation had first occurred in context, during a lecture on the *Odyssey* at the beginning of term, as the weeks wore on it became a recurring motif. He began to throw it in arbitrarily during his lectures on other books. He would sometimes incant at the beginning of class, like grace before a meal, before he began to talk about anything at all; or sometimes abruptly in the middle of a lecture; or at the end, just before the bell, when he would make the sign of the cross over us as he spoke, or raise his hand with two fingers in the peace sign.

"They eat the fruit of the lotus; they mean you no harm…"

"They sleep in the day, they fly at night…They love sweet-tasting nectar sap…"

I had two theories about this, both perhaps far-fetched. One was that he was not referring to the Lotus-Eaters at all but to us, sitting there in what he perceived to be a passive, dreamlike state—with the lotus attitude if not in the actual position—after yet another long night of drugs and sex.

(This *was* circa 1969.) But I think he was advising himself not to take our indifference personally. Also, he may have had a perverse fascination with what he saw as our carefree, promiscuous lives, and was warning himself away. My other theory was just the opposite: he was referring to himself and all his sedentary, academic tribe, to his imprisonment in the ivory tower, his seduction by its soulless, compromising comforts and consolations, and he was warning us away.

"They give you lotus fruit to eat; and then you want to stay with them forever." Dr. Whittick had not stayed, however. One fall he was there, and the next, he was gone. As improbable a creature as a talking horse or a nurse-maid-dog, just a figment of my hazy recollections, perhaps, of those long-gone, dreamlike student days. And the existence of the sugar gliders seemed as much a fiction to me as the existence of Homer's Lotus-Eaters. One seemed just as fanciful as the other; someone could just as easily have invented either. Their enemies, the threats to their existence, were simply of a different kind. Lizards, cats, and owls, on the one hand; the unwilling suspension of disbelief, on the other.

Sometimes I am innocently asked, after a reading or wherever: was that really true or did you make it up? And, to tell the truth (to tell the truth!—as if we are usually lying and depart from this fictive narrative only by an act of will), to tell the truth, the truth to tell, after seven or eight books, it's sometimes hard to remember if I made it up or not.

Roseanna stared down at the floor as if the bright sunlight in the white kitchen hurt her eyes, as if she were an elusive and vulnerable nocturnal creature herself, now among her enemies; or as if she were a creature of the imagination, and eye contact with unbelievers, unwilling suspenders of disbelief, would make her disappear, but if she didn't look at them, they could not do her any harm. Sometimes she peeked at us beneath her bangs and her raised eyebrows, but her face stayed almost parallel with the floor.

I imagined Roseanna eating lotus fruit or eucalyptus flowers and living happily ever after among the sugar gliders or the Lotus-Eaters, or among the fairies, like Yeats' sad-eyed stolen child; away from the unhappiness of her home and family, safe from her enemies—the unusual suspects, father and mother. The silent father, the absent mother.

> Come away, O human child!
> To the waters and the wild
> With a faery, hand in hand,
> For the world's more full of weeping
> than you can understand.

Sheila set her up at the coffee table to finish her project while we sat at the kitchen table drinking coffee. With her coloured pencils and bristol board in front of her, Roseanna now looked determined and purposeful, and a lot more at ease; her disabling shyness seemed to have fallen away.

Sheila said that she had agreed to look after a child from the Ukraine next summer, a young girl the same age as Roseanna, who would benefit greatly by being removed from the Chernobyl radiation zone.

"You're slowly accumulating a family," I said to her.

"Not too late, I suppose," she said, rather sadly I thought. Perhaps the old man had been privy to things that I had not. As Kevin was wont to say: you've been away too long.

Roseanna was standing in the doorway, addressing her ballet slippers. She had taken ballet lessons since the age of five, Sheila said, and was already a veteran performer on the big Arts and Culture Centre stage. At one of those concerts, Sheila herself had performed: a daring on-stage rescue, a one-woman show, a one-hander, literally.

Roseanna had fallen over, Sheila said, and was flat on her back inside a large alphabet-block box—the letter *R*, coincidentally—her small arms and legs flailing in the air like an upturned beetle on the sidewalk. *The Uprighting of Rosanna*, as we might title the playlet, had involved Sheila's leaping up onto the stage from her seat in the front row after watching Roseanna struggling helplessly for a full minute or more, and, with one hand, pulling her to her feet. She'd received enthusiastic applause, she said, from the full house of empathetic parents, but a collective frown from a full house of ushers on her way back to her seat.

I knelt down to Rosanna's height to hear what she was saying, but she wouldn't look at me.

"What would you like, sweetheart?" I said to her.

"A glass of water, please."

"Would you like some juice or milk?"

She shook her head.

"Some sweet nectar sap?" I said, trying to tease her.

She shook her head again, but I could see a smile.

Loyal phoned from his office, exactly at noon, to say that his meeting was over and suggested we meet him at his favourite restaurant downtown, Hamme's Chop Suey House on Water Street. The restaurant was full, but he had arrived early and was holding a window table to which four menus had already been brought. On offer was the usual Canadian-Chinese fare, but also dishes in a variety of authentic "styles": Szechuan, Canton, Hong Kong, Taiwan, Peking, Singapore, and Shanghai.

"Leady to oda?" said a harried-looking waitress holding a pen and pad.

"I think this plant would like to order first," Sheila said, lifting a flowerless and dusty specimen from the windowsill. She smiled at the waitress, who smiled nervously and uncomprehendingly back.

"I'd like some water, please," Sheila said in a tiny voice, doing a ventriloquist shtick with the dummy-like plant. She smiled maternally at Roseanna, who was almost grinning.

"Hoy yah," said the waitress, and took it away.

When she came back, but without the plant, we ordered spring rolls for everyone, along with a family bowl of egg drop soup. Sheila ordered milk and sweet and sour chicken in a bird's nest for Roseanna, and for herself, a tofu hotpot, Szechuan Style. Loyal ordered sweet and sour ribs, Cantonese Style, and I stuck to the style-less lemon chicken I'd had in many Chinese restaurants over the years.

"You want lice," said the waitress, and we reluctantly agreed. She began collecting the menus, but, under Vegetarian Dishes, Sheila, the haberdasher, spotted *chic* peas, and said she just had to order some of those as well. Then she and Loyal began acting like doting parents, performing a little *habiliment* routine to amuse Roseanna. They tried to come up with the *chicest* outfits for the peas, alternately ushering their models down the catwalk in a fashion show.

"Miss Polly Pea is wearing a see-through polka dot raincoat over a gossamer chiffon gown," Sheila began.

"Miss Priscilla Pea, a fairy gown of Chantilly lace," said Loyal.

"Miss Peggy Pea, a gown of angel hair and satin."

"Miss Pansy Pea, a pink cotton-candy gown."

I was impressed. But these lines came out so easily and spontaneously that I was sure they must have put on this show before. They were certainly a different couple here today than they were during my visits to their house. Loyal did a rough sketch of Miss Pansy Pea, with a purple pansy face, on the back of his placemat, and Roseanna's big brown eyes lit up like a sugar glider's.

The spring rolls arrived, and the egg drop soup soon after. Roseanna squeezed a package of plum sauce onto her plate, dipped her roll into it, and took a bite. Loyal and I followed suit, and Sheila poured the soup.

The rest of the food arrived before we had finished our soup. The not-so-chic peas were disappointingly dressed in a dull brown sauce, completely outshone, in fact, by the sweet and sour's glamorous neon-red viscous coating and the lemon chicken's lambent yellow glow. Afterward, Sheila inquired about desserts for Roseanna, as there weren't any on the menu.

"Only we have deep-fly coconut pudding," the waitress told her.

Roseanna didn't like the sound of that, and who could blame her, but it turned out that they did have ice cream. We also ordered a large pot of green tea, which came with fortune cookies for us all. Both mine and Loyal's said, appropriately enough, "You are going on a long trip."

"On a short horse, a Newfoundland pony," Sheila joked.

Sheila's fortune said, enigmatically, though she seemed pleased, "Your boundless energy will come home to you." Roseanna put her fortune cookie, unopened, in the zip-pocket of her jacket.

"There are no fortune cookies in China," Loyal informed us. "They laughed at me in Wuhu when I tried to describe them. I was there with some friends on a business trip one time."

"Where do they come from?" I asked.

"From the States, where else. A man by the name of Jung invented them. 'Jung' as in 'Carl Jung,' but his name was George. He was Chinese, though, not German."

"Swiss, I think—Carl Jung, I mean. You're a Jungian, Loyal?"

"I used to read him long ago. I think he helped me understand my father, who was a tyrant at home but a coward out in the world. I was always afraid I would turn out like him."

∽ ∽

Sheila left her Smart Car at the parking meter, parking being free on Saturdays and Sundays, and we headed off down the Southern Shore, which is really the eastern shore, longitudinally speaking, but the road down the coast runs due south from St. John's. About twenty miles down this road, just past the town of Bay Bulls, we saw a sign saying "Trail Rides Ahead," and a few miles farther on we came upon the same sign, with "Ahead" covered with a piece of wood. About a dozen horses were hitched to a rail in a gravel pit beside the road. We pulled off the road and stopped alongside a large, black pickup truck, and, as we did, the doors flew open and an entire family, two adults and four children, got out of the cab to greet us. Roseanna ran right past them, straight for the horses, who were eating hay that was spread upon the gravel. Sheila and Loyal, like cautious parents, followed quickly behind.

"I'm Mike," said a big, suede-jacketed man, dark as a gypsy, whom I assumed to be the father of the family. "Nice day for the ride."

"I don't think we booked," I said, interpreting his use of the definite article and their quick exit from the truck as indications that they'd been expecting us.

"Oh, no matter," he said, "lots of horses to go round."

"Sheila," I called out, trying not to shout, and the whole family turned and looked in her direction. I began to walk toward the hitching post, and they followed along behind. Sheila and Loyal and Roseanna were all crouching down in front of the horses, watching them eat. Roseanna seemed to be trying to look right inside their mouths as they chomped on the hay. They were not small and short, however, like Newfoundland ponies, but big, solid-looking creatures, workhorses probably, farm animals used to pulling plows and carts, sleighs and catamarans loaded down with logs, if anyone still used horses for farming or logging these days. Probably not, and this was the reason they had been freed up to stand around all day in the sun, eating hay, being called on only every few hours or so to carry some anxious city dwellers on their backs for a trail ride.

"What happened to the ponies?" Sheila asked, sounding very disappointed. "There were Newfoundland ponies here last summer."

"They're off on another farm this year, ma'am. But we'll have 'em back next year," said Mike.

Roseanna herself didn't look disappointed. She was hand-feeding the horses now. One of them raised his head to look at us, or perhaps just to look at me, as he'd already sized up the other strangers. He had what I thought was one blind eye—milky white, like a large, cloudy marble—but when I inquired, I was told that his sight was normal. Champ, as he was called, had been born walleyed, with an unpigmented iris. His other eye was brown, as was his entire coat. Though he was about the same height as the others, he was leaner and more fine-boned; his legs seemed to be longer—a racehorse's legs, perhaps, not a workhorse's. He looked a bit high-strung, more nervous than the others, but overly alert, very intelligent, very aware of what was going on around him, and, at least this was the way it struck me, not completely happy with his lot.

Indeed, the look on his face, perhaps intensified, or given focus, by that one blank eye, immediately stirred in me feelings for a fellow creature, other than a human being, that I couldn't remember ever having felt before. I had fallen under his spell as suddenly as gravity can bring you to the ground—slipping on ice or falling off a roof; one second you're on your feet, and the next, very humbly, on your face or back.

I would not have been at all surprised, in fact, if, at that moment, Champ had opened his mouth and spoken—*sung* even—perhaps those moving, mandamning lines uttered by the catamaran driver in "Tickle Cove Pond," regretting his lack of empathy with his own horse, Kit, having ignored, to his misfortune, the wise creature's hesitation in crossing thin ice:

> *All this I ignored with a whip-handle blow,*
> *For man is too stupid dumb creatures to know.*

"About suffering they were never wrong,/The Old masters…," as Auden wrote, the masters of folk song as well as painting. And so, when Mike said, "Let's get on the go," and we all wandered back to the small landing of weathered wood at the other end of the gravel lot, which looked like a small wharf with the tide gone out but was used to get inexperienced riders up into the saddle, I knew without a doubt that I would be paired with Champ.

Mike, Sheila, Roseanna, and Loyal were all mounted and waiting up ahead as one of the daughters held Champ by the bridle and I got up into the saddle from the top of the platform. I was having trouble getting my blundering Blundstones into the stirrups. Mike, who was to be our guide, came trotting back, dispensing advice. I guess I looked like the one who needed it most, and I was also riding the most headstrong horse.

"You got to keep a firm grip on this one," he said. "Let him know who's boss, keep his head up, and don't let him eat. He loves the var, this one— moose food. He'd eat it all day if you let him. Hold the reins this way, with your thumbs stickin' up. Pull on the left rein to go left and the right rein to go right, just like the steerin' wheel on your car. Dig your heels into him to make him move. He don't like water so you may have to give him a little kick now and then when we go through the puddles. Use the whip if you have to—right there on your saddle horn. They may stop to have a piss—you can let 'em do that—but they shit on the run. They know where they're goin', so you don't have to worry. They been up this trail a thousand times. If you start to feel a little sore, you know where"—he grinned out of one corner of his mouth as he said this—"stand up in your stirrups and take the pressure off. It takes a little while to get used to the gait. And don't worry—these are sure-footed, four-legged creatures. Not like you and me. They don't fall down."

Famous last words, I thought, as he left with a laugh and rode on up to the head of the pack. Mike's wife and children waved goodbye to us as we left the lot and set out on a small, paved side road with Loyal close behind Mike, followed by Roseanna and Sheila, and me holding up the rear. Roseanna's feet dangled above her stirrups, but she looked safely settled in the saddle, and every few minutes or so turned around and beamed a smile of sheer delight. The horses stayed on the sandy shoulder, avoiding the pavement. As we rounded a bend, a steep ravine appeared to our left, with a river running far below. Sure-footed, four-legged creatures, I reminded myself. We crossed a small bridge, then clopped to the other side of the road and entered a broad path into the woods. It quickly became a narrow, winding path with muddy pools, rocks, and thick brush and trees, mostly alders and young balsam fir, or "var," as Mike called them, on either side.

I was surprised and pleased that I still knew my trees, having been privately tutored by Sheila way back in the day when a science course had been a requirement for all degrees at the university. I had gratefully taken General Physics for Arts Students, which didn't require a weekly three-hour lab, but Sheila had taken Dendrology, the scientific study of trees. Though she herself was a commerce student, one of her closest friends was doing forestry and had persuaded her to take the course.

Champ kept his head inclined to the left. I could see his white eye, and it seemed as if it could see me. He avoided the mud, rocks, and water wherever possible, staying on a narrow edge of mossy bank close to the trees, and nipping at a few fir twigs every now and then.

The path began to wind uphill, and soon we were out of the woods and at the top of a ridge between two hills. To our right, on the side of the lowest hill, was the appalling vista of a garbage dump; to our left, at the base of the other hill, was an expanse of green grass geometrically subdivided like a patch of idyllic English countryside, but with rail fences instead of rock walls.

We rode on. The trail made a wide circle around an area of moss and scrub, but Champ turned left instead of right, and we stood facing the others as they came around.

"Turn him around, dig your heels into him," Mike shouted. "Give him a crack with the whip."

The whip was a short piece of knotted rope attached to the saddle horn. I wouldn't have been able to use it on a woodhorse, let alone a horse made of flesh; but I gave him a nudge with the heels of my shoes, and he obediently crossed the mossy median to the other side. We trotted around the circle and came up behind Sheila's horse, who, at that moment, as if in chastisement, let out the loudest fart I had ever heard. Roseanna turned around and giggled with her chin tucked into her shoulder.

We set off down the hill, back the way we had come, with Mike now holding up the rear. It seemed harder for the horses going down. Champ was now even more particular about where he trod, trying to negotiate the mossy edges of the trail so delicately that branches grazed my leg, arm, and face. Perhaps he was getting really hungry, for he nipped at fir twigs every chance he got. At one point he just stopped dead in his tracks on a mossy bank. I prodded him with my heels, but he wouldn't move.

"You can let him do that," Mike said.

He was a quiet urinator, to be sure.

When the trail left the woods and joined the narrow paved road again, I felt my body release the mild but constant feeling of unease that had been with me since the ride began. I stood up in the stirrups, as Mike had suggested, to relieve the pressure on those parts of the male body that he said were most prone to saddle sores. But the unease returned as Mike rode to the front, turned his horse around, waved his hat, and shouted that we were going back by a different route.

We turned off the road onto a trail that ran alongside a quiet stream—not that quiet, for I could hear the proverbial bubbling and babbling, and perhaps it was trying to tell us something. Then we skirted a gently rolling meadow with a few large erratics and scattered stunted spruce. The meadow dipped down into a small valley that led to a perfectly flat stretch of land covered by clusters of tall, elegant juniper, whose whispery, feathery branches, like arms and fingers, seemed to be beckoning us into their midst. The grassy trail wound through this dreamlike forest, which seemed to go on forever, a fairy-wood landscape that might have been the home of Lotus-Eaters or sugar gliders.

I had lapsed into an almost somnolent state when I heard a whinny and a shout and saw Mike's horse rear up on its hind legs, but he quickly brought it under control. The other horses seemed to tense up and draw back, but kept all four sure feet securely on the ground. Champ turned his white eye right around, as if looking directly at me, the world's most inexperienced horseman, for direction, for protection; but after Mike got his horse settled down and came riding back to see if everyone was all right, the other horses, and their riders, seemed to relax as well.

"Fuckin' ferrets—beggin' your pardon, darlin'," Mike said, smiling and nodding at Roseanna. "They're everywhere this year."

All of a sudden, Loyal's horse whinnied and reared, then bolted, and disappeared into the trees.

"Jeeesus," Mike rasped and took off after him, leaving Sheila, Roseanna, and me behind, anxiously mounted on a bunch of very jittery horses. Within a minute, however, they all had their heads down, nonchalantly grazing.

At first, Roseanna seemed relatively unperturbed by all this, as did her big, grey, docile-looking horse, which looked incapable of rearing up and running off, even if it wanted to; but then she burst out all at once with an anxious flurry of questions: "What's a ferret? What are these trees? Are we lost? When are we going home?"

"Ah, 'tis a wee, sleekit, cow'rin, tim'rous beastie, darlin'," I said, smiling at Roseanna, but Sheila wasn't amused, and perhaps neither was Roseanna.

"We don't have ferrets in Newfoundland," Sheila said calmly. "It must have been a weasel, a furry little creature about a half foot long. But you wouldn't go near it—it's not tame. Not like a chipmunk or a squirrel. A ferret is twice as big as a weasel, and not friendly either. 'You little ferret!' our mother used to say to us. Remember that, James? It was the worst thing she ever said about anyone. 'That little ferret!' I can hear her now. About anyone sly or conniving or gossiping or just causing trouble."

Sheila must have learned about a lot more than trees in that forestry course, I thought. She was intent on distracting Roseanna, and perhaps herself as well.

"These trees," she said, reaching for a soft, wispy branch and pulling it through her fingers, "are called larch, but everyone in Newfoundland calls them juniper, same as they call weasels, ferrets. But a juniper is a tuckamore—a stunted little tree, just a bush, really—and a larch is...*largch*. That's a way to remember it. A larch is *largch*. It's a type of pine tree, though it's not an evergreen, like spruce and fir, which are also pine trees, by the way. Confusing, eh? And though they look like evergreens, larch are deciduous trees, like maples and birch and weeping willows, which means they lose their leaves every fall. Other things can be deciduous, too, not just trees. Most people think *deciduous* just refers to trees. But moose lose their antlers, ants lose their wings..."

"Daddy is deciduous," Roseanna deduced. "He lost his hair. Mommy called him a bald-headed bastard." She looked at both of us, as if expecting chastisement. Big Sister and her big brother looked at each other.

"Well...your mom and dad had a lot of fights," Sheila said kindly, "but they still love you very much. No, your dad is not deciduous, because his hair is not going to grow back."

"Yes, it is," piped Roseanna. "He's going to a place where they're growing it back."

"Really! Well...I guess he's sort of half-deciduous," Sheila said, and gave her a big compromising smile.

We heard hoof beats, and turned to see Mike's horse approaching.

"Where's Loyal?" Sheila asked anxiously.

"Well…he fell off his horse," Mike replied. "May have hurt his shoulder, but he looks okay. He's out of the woods, waitin' for us back at the road."

Within ten minutes we were out of the woods, too. We had made some kind of great circle, and the trees ended just a few hundred feet from the gravel lot.

We found Loyal sitting alone on the small wharf-platform, holding his left shoulder and swinging his legs as if he were paddling in a pond. He turned and grimaced at us as we approached. His face was white, but he spoke calmly and matter-of-factly, saying he didn't think he'd be able to go on to Mistaken Point. He thought he should go to the hospital to get his shoulder checked out. Sheila very solicitously agreed. She sat beside him on the platform and held his free hand.

⌒ ⌒

Sheila took over the driving, and on our way back Loyal told us that this hadn't been his first encounter with ferrets—or whatever it was that had startled his horse. (Sheila was still insisting that it was a weasel.) Last year, on a business trip to Manchester, England, he recounted, one of his business associates had taken a party of them to a "real ale" festival in a small village outside the city, and after several pints—an incendiary, mind-bending brew, he had to admit—and a hearty lunch of bangers and mash, they'd stumbled out of a pub into the stunning sunshine of an early afternoon right into the middle of a local "ferret-legging" competition. And while it might have been a small-scale local event, he was told it was for the world championship, as the world record-holder lived right there in the village.

The object of the competition, believe it or not, was to keep a ferret down your pants in front of the judges for as long as you could stand it. Twenty-five years ago, the world record had been, understandably, less than a minute, but it now stood at over five *hours*. The competitor's trousers are tied at the ankles,

Loyal told us, and his belt is pulled tight after the ferret is dropped in. The vicious, red-eyed little creature is, as you might imagine, quite upset about all this. It is, of course, a carnivore, and would not be out of place in the company of a piranha, a shark, or a pit bull terrier. It lives only to kill, and when it sinks its teeth into something, it never lets go. When Loyal and his friends came out of the pub, the event had been in progress for almost an hour: six contestants, all men, in various stages of agony and distress. No protection—absolutely no jockstraps, not even underpants—was allowed.

Sheila had been shaken by seismic sniggers throughout Loyal's account of this incredible event, cleverly censored because of Roseanna. It nevertheless led one to the burning question, the unthinkable but inevitable question, which, of course, again because of Roseanna, one had to postpone posing till a more appropriate time.

17: CAPTAIN OF THE COURSE

A ugust month, as the old man calls it—by *his* calendar, at least. It was only July 31, however—a Wednesday. If it were Wednesday, August 1, the first Wednesday in August, the Royal St. John's Regatta, the Races, would be going ahead, and there would already be hundreds of people down at Quidi Vidi Lake—*lakeside*, as the radio announcer had referred to it early this morning, infusing the word with all the pastoral longing of a man locked away in midsummer in a small, hot, windowless studio. "Only a week to go, folks, and of course our own crew will be down at lakeside [*sigh*] next Wednesday to bring you all the race results live as the big day unfolds."

O, ye cruel Fates. How did a wall calendar with only thirty days in July end up in the room of a man who is losing his mind?

"This is the big day," said the old man, who doesn't listen to the radio, watch TV, or read the papers, when I turned up at the Veterans' Pavilion at seven this morning.

Every morning for the past week at this ungodly hour we have walked down the steep hill from the Veterans' Pavilion to look at the lake. It is only about ten minutes away, and the hill is so steep we almost roll down it, making me even more aware, on this particular morning, of the secret work of unseen forces.

The old man was getting more anxious by the day. The self-appointed "Captain of the Course," as he calls himself, had to decide if the Races were going ahead. Wind, not temperature or precipitation, is the crucial factor, he says. A call to the weather office won't do. "*Useless,*" he says contemptuously, "utterly *useless.*" His favourite word these days. He squeezes it like a lemon, getting every ounce of juicy contempt out of its bitter flesh and over everything that displeases him. "Useless as philosophers," he added this morning, giving me a brazen, knowing look. Last week, on a whim, instead of the steady stream of Westerns I've been getting him from the Afterwords second-hand bookstore, I gave him a copy of Bertrand Russell's *The Conquest of Happiness,* thinking the warlike title might appeal to him, that he might get something out of it. He did find some use for it. When I came back two days later, I found it on the floor of his room. He had used it to conquer a huge housefly, which was plastered on the cover.

I wondered if there was such an official as the Captain of the Course. It recalled lines from some late-Victorian doggerel by one of "the Hearties," as I believe that school was called: *I am the master of my fate;/I am the captain of my soul.* By Henley, or Newbolt (Henley Newbolt?)—perhaps even Kipling—imperialistic, cheerleaders' philosophy disguised as verse, which was still being inflicted on our school in *the sixties.* I am the master of my fate; I am the captain of the course. Strange that the old man should be asserting mastery in his declining years, but perhaps not. Perhaps that's just the way it goes.

Surrounded by ducks, gulls, and pigeons anticipating food, he stood at the edge of the water at the head of the lake and sniffed the air. Sitting on a bench behind him, I thought of the legendary Lauchie McDougall, whom the old man claimed to have met one time on our legendary locomotive, "the Bullet." Human wind gauge, Gale Sniffer Extraordinary to the Newfoundland Railway, Lauchie McDougall had been hired to sniff the wind and inform the engineers in Port aux Basques by telephone if it was too strong to allow the Bullet safe passage through Wreckhouse, about ten miles inland, a community of fifteen souls living on an exposed and barren coastal plain in the windiest valley in the western world. Ferocious winds funnelled down through this valley from the nearby Table Mountains, right down to the world's windiest port,

Port aux Basques, and a twenty-two-car train had once been blown off the tracks when the engineers had not heeded the warning of the most sensitive son-of-a bitch in the valley.

Even today, house trailers and tractor trailers get blown off the highway, and thirty-thousand-ton, sixty-thousand-horsepower passenger ferries get blown ashore just trying to leave the dock in Port aux Basques. After Lauchie died, his house, to no one's great surprise, also blew down. Only a plaque now marks the spot where it once stood.

"Not today," said the Captain of the Course. "I checked the glass—there's wind on the way. Forty knots by mid-morning, I'd say, maybe sixty in the afternoon." He held on to his peak cap as if expecting a sudden breeze at any moment, but there was barely a ripple on the lake.

"Might blow them right off the tracks," I said, my thoughts still off on the Wreckhouse siding.

"Goddamn right," said the old railwayman, surprising me by catching my drift. *Only connect*, I thought, and he can surprise the hell out of me at times. These leaps seem easier than lockstep logic for him. For some reason, our thoughts connect better this way.

A calendar right there on the wall, however, right in front of his face, was like something carved in stone. How could they be wrong, those big numbers there in black and white? There was no way I could convince him that they were, that today was Wednesday, July 31, not August 1. I admit, I had never seen a misprinted calendar before, and this was the last place I wanted to see one. Computers, those supposedly infallible number crunchers, are no doubt making calendars these days, but of course these machines don't know the old rhymes.

"Thirty days hath September, April, June, and November. All the rest have thirty-one," I had recited, innocently enough, in his room this morning, but that was definitely the wrong approach.

"Cut the nursery rhymes, will you," he said. "You think I'm a baby? You're telling me the calendar is wrong?" he added, rapping Wednesday, August 1, with a big red arthritic knuckle.

"Yes," I said emphatically, turning back the page to July, which ended at Tuesday, July 30. "There's a day missing. There are 31 days in July. So today is Wednesday, July 31, and tomorrow is Thursday, August 1."

But he couldn't, or wouldn't, connect this series of dots. I suppose I could have gone in search of another calendar, but he just would have insisted that it was wrong and his was right.

We sat on a bench next to a bronze sculpture called *The Rower*. He didn't seem to know what to make of it, the rower's suspended movement, the frozen stroke—as if it suspended his thought patterns as well, erected a barrier along his neural pathways, with no detour sign for an alternate route. He continued to stare at it with a puzzled look, then averted his eyes, looked out across the lake. I noticed that he was wearing a new cap that said "North Carolina Tar Heels"—black, as you would expect, with a white logo that gave no hint as to whether it was for roofers or football players or race-car drivers or whoever.

"Where'd you get the new cap?" I asked him.

He took it off and looked at it, raised his eyebrows as if to ask himself the same question, but put it back on and shifted it several times to make it secure, still thinking about the impending change in the weather perhaps. Then he took it off again and laid it on the bench between us with the peak beneath his thigh.

"Must be Eric's," he said. "He's from Catalina. Used to work with the highways department driving one of them steamrollers on the asphalt."

It was such a good guess that I didn't want to spoil it by telling him he'd read the name wrong. I noticed that he still had all his hair, with no thin patches anywhere to be seen, but he was as grey as a badger, as they say, and so was I.

The sun came out from behind a cloud, or perhaps it had just crested the eastern hills, and a wasp came out of the concrete garbage bin between the benches and began to circle us. The old man grabbed his cap and made a few vicious swipes at it.

"*Git*," he said, but it wasn't gitting anywhere. "It wants to get inside our heads," he said, flailing his arms again. Another wasp had entered the fray.

"What do you mean?" I said.

"Haven't you ever seen a hornet's nest, b'y?"

"Don't think I have, no."

"Yes, you have. They were in the shed in the back garden every summer. Course you were too scared to go in there. Grey and round. See anything grey and round around here?"

I looked at him and he pointed two index fingers at his grey head, then at mine. I let out a laugh, and he grinned, too.

"If Mom were here with her beehive, we'd really be in trouble," I said.

His grin was replaced by a dark look. He seemed to be thinking seriously about that.

"I think her hair was like that when I saw her last," he said, and his smile came back. "We'd better not take her to the Races."

Unlike the wasps that were trying to get inside our heads, I fought the urge to sting the old man back to so-called real time. *Mom is gone, Dad. Mom is dead.* What was real time, anyway, the elusive present, the so-called here and now, and who of us lived there instead of in the future and the past, deep in regret, nostalgia, desire, hope? *The thing with feathers/That perches in the soul,* hopeless Emily Dickinson called hope. Which poem was that? I can't recall. Was it a turkey or a skylark, her hope?

And the young live in another dimension altogether, a virtual world, a wired world. Does the teen on the park bench with an iPod in her ears, texting or e-mailing on her cellphone or laptop, inhabit real time, real space? Or, for that matter, the old man on the bench next to her reading Louis Lamour or Zane Grey? The mind is intent on not doing any real time, on not being in the place it's actually in, and has innumerable tricks and tactics and diversions— illusion, delusion, daydream, drugs—for evasion and escape, for release from the existential bonds of ordinary, everyday weariness and dreariness. Perhaps dementia itself is just one strategy among many.

I awoke from my own reverie and said, "Dad, I'm going to be leaving soon. Is there anything you want to do before I go?"

"You'll be here for the Races, won't you?"

"Yeah, I should be here till the end of August, but you know how I feel about crowds."

"Oh, don't be so foolish. Claustrophobic, are you?"

"Well...yes...I don't like small spaces, airplanes, for example...and agoraphobic, too. I don't like big spaces with a lot of people milling about."

"They're not going to hurt you, b'y," he said. "No matter," he added, sounding a bit hurt himself. "All the boys will be going down. I'll go with them...Look at them out there, will you," he said, pointing to a racing shell passing by. A few crews were out practising, observed by a scattering of onlookers. "Good they don't have to fish for a living. No wonder that record held for eighty years. That Outer Cove crew were out in boats from morning till night, and when their time was finally beaten—but only because of those new fibreglass boats—they came back and set it again."

"When did you get interested in the Regatta, Dad? We never went over there when I was young."

"What are you talking about? You're losing your memory, b'y. I used to take you over every year. I couldn't get you away from the Wheel of Fortune, the hard cash. You won the very first time we played it—twenty-five dollars—and that was the only game you'd play after that. No cryin' for teddy bears for you. Every year you'd head right for it. You'd remember exactly where it was among the hundreds of booths. Nothing wrong with your memory then. But I don't think you ever won again. Funny, isn't it? That's the Wheel of Fortune for you.

"Your mother would never go," he added. "She must've had what you got now. What'd you call it?"

"Agoraphobia."

"Yeah, and she didn't know. It must be passed down."

There was no point in countering or denying any of this, of course. During the first week of August, if I recall, we would go over to St. John's, but only to take the train across the Island to Port aux Basques and back. The old man had always loved trains and was overjoyed to get a job at the railway when he moved to St. John's.

Changing the subject, I said, "Did you say you wanted to go picking blueberries? Or partridgeberries?"

"No blueberries for at least a couple of weeks yet, and the worms won't be out of the partridgeberries till October, or after we have a frost."

"I always thought that was a myth, about those worms."

"No. Go pick a few and boil them up in a pot and you'll see. They'll float right up to the top and you'll get a good look at them."

"We'll go pick some blueberries, then. Do you know a good spot?"

"A good spot! I know *the* spot. I'll take you out there, but you got to promise not to tell a soul where it is."

"I'll wear a blindfold."

"You can't do that, you fool. You got to drive."

"Just kidding, Dad. Sure, who would I tell? I hardly know a soul around here. And I'll be gone in a few weeks."

"Gone gone gone…you're always gone…Not even your sister, mind. She won't pick berries, but that husband of hers—what's his name?"

"Loyal."

"Loyal," he repeated, with a sort of bemused disgust. "What kind of a name for a man is that? He'd start a blueberry business with mechanical harvesters if he found that motherlode out there. It's out towards Cape St. Francis. That's all I'm going to say."

"When was the last time you were out there?"

"The last time? Your mother and me must have been out there last summer. We filled four beef buckets to the brim and it was awful hard luggin' them out, I can tell you. She wasn't too well, and I was feeling a bit out of sorts myself. The path in to the berry grounds goes straight up a rocky ridge about a mile, and when you get back down with your buckets full it's another mile or more back out that cart track of a gravel road to the car. You can't drive right in there unless you have a Jeep or an ATV. Your mother would never get on one of those, of course. I'd never get the Dodge in there without tearing the bottom out of her."

"I'll rent a Jeep again," I said. "We had one for our camping trip, remember?"

"Your mother won't be able to go this year. Her hands are all crippled up, and her knees are gone. You'll have to get the beef buckets, though. I don't have any. Try one of the butcher shops, that's your best bet."

"I'll see what I can do. What if I can't get those? What else can we use?"

He ran both hands through his hair several times, then held them there and contorted his face as if he had banged his head and was in severe pain. The thought of picking blueberries without beef buckets, being in the midst of that bountiful wild harvest without the largest containers that a person could carry without warping his spine, was perhaps too much to bear, and a thought not worthy even of a modern-day, sedentary hunter-gatherer. But I had been forced to carry them as a child, if only for short distances, to give my mother's arthritic limbs a rest, knew very well the dead weight of them, and was already secretly and disloyally making plans to find some more humane receptacles for the blueberries.

"You'll find them, b'y, don't worry," he said. "There's no moratorium on salt beef, is there? Or riblets? Crosbie hasn't taken them away from us, too, has he? Come to think of it, I haven't had a bit of salt beef since your mother died. How long ago was that?

"Murphy's," he shouted, "at the Cross," remembering the old family grocery at Rawlins Cross, long closed, where we used to shop. "That's the place to get them."

"I'll find them, Dad. Don't worry. There's lots of time."

"I'm not worrying—you're the one who's worrying."

The wasps were still tormenting us so we got up and began strolling down the side of the lake toward the boathouse, which was at the foot of the hill we had come down. When we got there, he said he wanted to go home—the first time he'd ever referred to the Veterans' Pavilion as home—but when he turned and looked up the steep hill he said he wanted to go back by the cemetery route, one we had taken a few times before. The cemetery was also on the hillside overlooking the lake, but the route was more scenic and shadier, so to speak, and it also allowed him to tack along the numerous paths among the plots. It was situated alongside Her Majesty's Penitentiary, but no penitents were visible for they were securely locked away inside high stone walls with barbed wire on top—like something out of the Middle Ages.

When we reached the cemetery gate, a work crew with a front-end loader was blocking the entrance, which was strewn with piles of broken asphalt. The workers were all wearing "John Deere" caps—not a "Tar Heels" logo among them. Snarling and roaring like a dinosaur, the huge machine, its articulated arm raising its steel-toothed, gaping maw above our heads, articulated threat. Its bared teeth bit down into the asphalt like some wild hungry beast or ferocious watchdog at the entrance to a gated community—though, like the penitentiary next door, not one I wanted to be a resident of.

This unexpected sight stopped the old man in his tracks. For a few moments he stood transfixed with his hands on his hips as if he were about to confront this monster head on, but he quickly turned tail and said, "Come on," heading back toward the hill. I followed after him, still thinking about what we had just seen—an angry beast blocking the entrance to Death's kingdom. Did the old man see it as an omen, I wondered, and if so, good or bad? A warning that he was not prepared for the other side? A message that his time had not yet come? That he had promises to keep—but to whom? Miles to go before he slept—but to where? For the moment, at least, straight up this hill toward his earthly home. It was obvious that the beast had stirred something in him, for he took the grade at so fast a clip I had trouble keeping up with him.

18: A LIFE UNLIVED

Can one really talk about unlived lives? I don't mean a life that was cut short before it really began, like Keats's, for instance, at twenty-six, though what he achieved in that short span of time was greater than what most of us accomplish in the three lives of that duration we are now statistically allotted. I mean the notion that our life could have been different, completely different, if only…As if our life were a fiction we were inventing as we went along, but at some point lost the artistic will to continue. It happens.

Is the unlived life a mere fantasy, then, a feeling rooted in regret, loss, bitterness, a sense of failure? We made the wrong choices, we had no choice; we were forced to do things against our will, we had no will; we were too lazy or too fearful, too weak or too ill; we were too poor, too rich; too prone to temptation, too disciplined in resisting it. There was someone or something else we could have been, should have been; something we should have done, but we didn't do it.

Consider Lillian LeBlanc, for instance. (Appropriate name, in any event.) Today, when starting out on my afternoon walk, I met Lillian for the first time, though Beulah had mentioned her and her deceased husband, Howard, several times. Her house was on a corner lot, with a beautiful burgundy hedge, at the far end of the street, and she said hello from behind the hedge as I walked past. The hedge was thick and glossy—might be called luxurious if it were hair—but not tall, so I guessed that Lillian was relatively short.

Only the top of her head was visible: grey hair tied back with a blue bandana. (The returning native has noted that cotton bandanas and plastic rain bonnets are still very popular in these parts, wearing apparel that my poor mother was fond of.)

Beulah must have told Lillian about me as well. "I hear you're a writer" were the first words she spoke when she opened the wooden garden gate, a faded plum-red with a rounded top. The house was the same colour, trim and all. The roof was green with moss, the walls covered with vines. Lillian's face was smoke-grey. She was wearing a muddy gardening smock, gardening gloves, and black rubber boots up to her knees.

"Yes, ma'am, I am," I replied, Dr. Suess-like.

"Come in," she said. "I want to have a word with you."

That sounded ominous. She walked back into the yard and picked up a cigarette lying in an aluminum pie-plate ashtray on an old tree stump. An empty wine glass was perched on the stump as well. She took a long drag on the cigarette as she sized me up, then put it back in the ashtray. Looking up, I noticed that the cameras Beulah had mentioned were still sitting like small black owls on the lower branches of the trees.

"I'm Lillian LeBlanc," she said, "and you're James Nightingale," as if she were assigning us our roles for a play, a two-hander. "Beulah has told me all about you," she continued. "I'm writing a book myself. Well…I want to write one. It's sort of an autobiography, or a memoir. It might be a novel, but I'd have to change some names. I'm going to call it *A Life Unlived*.

"I'm not *un*educated, but that was a long time ago. English, actually. I was majoring in English at the old Memorial University College, but I didn't finish. That's where I met Howard, my husband for forty years. He was in one of my English classes—a course on the Victorian Age. Howard looked Victorian. We were studying George Meredith, *The Egoist*. He was very anti-Victorian, of course. Do you know the book?"

"Yes, I have read it, but, as you said, a long time ago."

"Well, what a coincidence it seemed—no, something much more than that. There I was, sitting on a bench on the campus grounds under an apple tree, its blossoms in full glory, reading the chapter entitled 'The Double-Blossom Wild Cherry-Tree,' about Clara Middleton and Vernon Whitfield, the earnest young scholar—do you remember? She falls in love with him after finding him asleep over a book beneath the beautiful branches of cherry blossom, for she thinks, 'He must be good who loves to lie and sleep beneath the branches of this tree!' Then I heard a snoring sound and looked behind the apple tree to find Howard lying asleep against the trunk with *The Egoist* open on his lap... Yes, that was a long time ago...

"I just finished reading the novel again. These books are lost on us in our youth, don't you think? 'Wonder lived in her,' says Meredith, as Clara stared at the clusters of blossoms on the cherry tree, but it was quickly displaced by the more mundane thought, 'He must be good...' And why? Because of her 'longing for happiness'—a 'disease,' he called it. That made no sense to me then, but I understand it now. I had that disease, too, like all young girls—to be married to a good man was all we wanted—and it took my life away."

She reached for her cigarette in the ashtray on the bleached tree stump, but it had gone out and she poked it down into the small mound of butts.

"I think I might need some help with my book," she said. "I need a... What do you call it? What's the word?"

"An editor?" I said.

"No, more than that."

"A ghostwriter," I said, smiling.

"Yes. I sometimes feel like I am a ghost...that I died a long time ago...Do you think you could do that? I'll pay you, of course."

"I don't know, Lillian. How do you see it taking shape?"

"Come in and have a cup of tea," she said.

We went in the back door and passed a small open pantry whose shelves were three-deep with jars of pickles and jams. There was a white plastic bucket of honey on the floor. We removed our footwear and went up some steps to the kitchen, which was dark and smoky, yellowed blinds half-drawn, half-full ashtrays on the stove, the counter, and the table. Lillian put the kettle on and led me into the living room, also dark and smoky. Flowery wallpaper covered the walls, and fluffy, diaphanous curtains, the windows. A swarm of doilies and tasselled cushions hovered over an enormous sofa and two wingback chairs; ceramic figurines, balls of wool and knitting needles, board games, books, and magazines covered the long coffee table and end tables; on the walls were photographs, watercolours, plaques, diplomas, thermometers, and barometers. It was a small private universe of dusty claustrophobic clutter, as if nothing had ever been touched, moved, changed, rearranged, or thrown out during Lillian and Howard's long married life, even after her husband's death.

Lillian lit another cigarette, took a long drag on it as she gave me a thoughtful look, then laid it in a brass and ceramic stand-up ashtray.

"Please sit down," she said, making no mention whatsoever of the congested state of things. From beneath a large book on the coffee table, she pulled out a dark-green file folder, from which she removed some pale blue sheets of paper.

"Listen to this," she ordered. Though Lillian had a certain charm, she was all business, much like her neighbour Beulah, I thought.

"*A Life Unlived*," she began emphatically, staring hard at the page. "I like Chaucer, *The Canterbury Tales*, especially 'The Wife of Bath's Tale,' which begins: 'If there were no authority on earth/Except experience, mine, for what it's worth,/And that's enough for me, all goes to show/That marriage is a misery and a woe.'"

She paused and looked up at me, then read on.

"I married Vernon Whitford in the spring of the year, in 1955, when I was twenty-one years old. We got married beneath the cherry blossoms in Bannerman Park. It was the happiest day of my life, May month, the 31st of May. My favourite month, and the blossoms were early that year. The cherry tree is long gone, split open in a glitter storm in 1962, and now Vernon is gone as well. He was an atheist and didn't want to get married in a church. He grew up in the orphanage with the Christian Brothers. That's why he was no longer a Christian, he always said."

The kettle began to whistle and Lillian laid her manuscript on the coffee table and ran off to the kitchen. She came back carrying a large silver tray.

I moved some books and magazines and she laid the tray in front of me on the coffee table. On it was a silver teapot as big as a samovar, two bone china cups with hand-painted pictures of English thatched cottages, matching milk and sugar containers, and tarnished silver spoons. Her cigarette had burned out, and she lit another. She picked up her manuscript and read some more.

"So, what do you think so far?" she said when she finished.

"I think…you don't really need me, Lillian," I said. "A great beginning…the hardest part. Well…maybe the ending is the hardest…maybe the middle. Maybe the whole damn thing! I love those cherry blossoms and the split cherry tree…so evocative…ominously so, of course. And you changed your husband's name?"

She smiled mischievously and poured our tea. I put milk and sugar in mine, but she drank hers straight, and in silence. It was getting hard to breathe. I felt as if I'd smoked a few cigarettes myself. Fresh air had not penetrated this house in years.

"Yes, I think I will," she said. "And maybe the author will be Clara Middleton. Who knows who might read this book? And it was apple blossoms, really," she added. "We couldn't find a cherry tree."

"Ah…well then…you've got a novel there, Lillian. You're well on your way. How much do you have written?" I asked.

"Oh, I've just begun, but I must have about twenty-five pages. I began just after Howard died. He was an unusual man, even I could see that, a perfectionist. I'm trying to keep the garden the way he wanted it. There are more than two dozen types of trees out there—shade trees, flowering trees, a dozen fruit trees and bushes. I'll give you some quince jam before you go. Howard would get so upset when those schoolboys—and girls, too—walked through our garden, picking berries and flowers, climbing trees and breaking branches, eating apples, leaving pop cans and bar wrappers behind. Sometimes they would just throw them in over the hedge, and up onto the roof. He even got into a fight one time and had to go to court. What a bother. What was the point of it all."

It was not a question. She trailed off, sighed, douted her cigarette in the stand-up ashtray.

"I was thinking you could take it from there," she said. "I could tape-record my story and you could write it down."

"What are you hoping to do with it, Lillian?" I asked. "Do you want to have it published?"

"It's for my children," she said, "and my brothers and sisters…maybe my friends. For me, too, of course. It's a confession. It will be good for my soul."

"Maybe it's something the world would like to read as well," I said.

She lit another cigarette as she pondered this, then took a sip of tea.

"I think you should continue on," I said. "You've made a great start. I'll have a look at it when you're done."

She was silent. She inhaled, exhaled, smiled like a weak sun through cloud.

"You're the professional," she said. "I'll take your advice. Do you like quince jam?"

"I've never eaten it," I said.

"It's the best," she said. "Let's go outside."

I had started to cough, and was very glad to hear that directive. Lillian's house was like a small planet with an atmosphere inhospitable to life.

On our way out the back door, she went into her pantry and brought out a wide-mouth Mason jar of quince jam. The label said "Garden Grove Quinze," with a *z* instead of a *c*, and I recalled the sly and wry Mordecai Richler's cruel cursory assessment of one of his literary precursors, one Frederick Philip Grove. (I had once done a paper on him for a CanLit course.) The proverbial nail in the coffin, it was, an epitaph of sorts, worthy of Swift, for the literary life unlived (at least according to Richler): "He was a good speller," he said.

Ironically, the only literary work of Grove's to be honoured by the state, the country he had chosen—he had faked his suicide and come to Canada from Germany in the early 1900s—was the fictitious story of *his* unlived life, *In Search of Myself.* It won a Governor General's Award for *non-fiction* in 1947.

He died the next year; perhaps fame had been too much for him. A prodigy of sorts, he had published his first two books in Germany at the tender age of twenty-three. Literary detectives, it seems, have been in search of the real life lived by Frederick Philip Grove, born Felix Paul Greve in Prussia, ever since, though the rest of his fiction was canonized by the New Canadian Library in the fifties and sixties.

Out in the garden grove, Lillian pointed out the flowering quince, the crabapple, cherry, gooseberry, blackcurrant, redcurrant, forsythia, dogwood, wisteria, mountain laurel, and other bushes and trees, all of which looked faithfully pruned. The flowers were nodding in their well-made beds.

"Well, I'd better get going on my walk," I said. "I'll be in touch to see how the book's coming along."

Lillian seemed to have forgotten about the book. She was staring up at the eave of the house.

"Look at that creeper," she said, "and that moss. Oh, my."

"It was nice meeting you, Lillian," I said, opening the gate.

"And you," she said. "I'm going to read one of your books."

"Why, thank you," I said. "It'd be an honour."

"Do you have a favourite? Is there one you'd recommend?"

"Well, they're like children, Lillian. I'd better not play favourites. I have to love them all. Not to say they were easy to raise."

"I have four daughters," she said. "I *understand*. Do you have any children—real ones, I mean?"

"Yes, I have a daughter, too."

I started to close the gate, thinking I was free to go, when she added, resignedly, as if this were something she certainly didn't understand: "Howard disowned them all. He changed the will. I must have signed it, but I didn't know. He looked after all our papers, and he was always asking me to sign things. I don't think they believe me, except my oldest, Myrna. She's more like a sister to me. She took me to Hawaii last winter."

"Why did he do that, Lillian? I'm sorry...I know it's not my business to ask."

She looked at the gate. She moved her hand affectionately over its rounded top. Its faded paint was peeling, and she removed a few flakes.

"Howard didn't know how to love," she said slowly. "That's what I'm going to write about. Did you ever know anyone like that? It wasn't his fault. He had no parents, no brothers and sisters. He was an orphan. He didn't know how to *be* loved, either. You have a daughter—you know that careless, carefree way that young girls have... It confounded him, I think. They had to earn his love...Oh, I'm sorry, I'm sorry. Here I am telling you about someone you never even knew. I'll explain it all in the book, though it's really about me, not Howard. My thoughts come out much better on paper."

"Mine, too, Lillian," I said. "Mine, too."

"That's how I keep in touch with my daughters...letters...instead of the phone. But off with you on your walk," she said. "It's such a beautiful day for a walk, but my poor knees wouldn't get me very far. And bunions...on both feet. Bye-bye."

And with that, she closed the gate, turned her back, and waved me on my way.

And wouldn't you know it, Loyal Reader: on the way she waved me on, though dubious I certainly was about the whole idea, I was to encounter, that same day–within the hour–one of my own unlived lives. When I left Lillian, I gave no thought to the fact–and even if I had, it would have seemed to me a mere coincidence–that the route I was about to take, had thought of taking even before running into her, would lead me through Bannerman Park, where Lillian and Howard had been married under the apple blossoms. But it would seem much more than mere coincidence by the end of the day.

∽ ⌒

As the traveller approaches Bannerman Park from the northwest, having walked through the woods of Pippy Park, across two busy four-lane streets, across the plain of Churchill Park, where only goalposts grew, down Elizabeth Avenue and along the Rennie's River trail; as he leaves the trail and climbs

Rennie's Mill Road, the Church of Scientology bids him welcome. No dreaming spires or even sleeping steeples to inspire the pilgrim, just an uninspired, beige stucco box, but he crosses the road nevertheless and reads the sign, which says: "L. Ron Hubbard's Thought for the Day—Two Tests of a Life Well Lived: Did one do as one intended? Were people glad one lived?" And beneath the thought, a commandment: "Go Clear." Enigmatic, to be sure, morally obscure, but at least there is only one, as opposed to the clearly burdensome ten of the Judaeo-Christian tradition.

Go clear he does, and wonders as he wanders on up the hill, about intentions, the so-called intentional fallacy, in particular, the notion that an author's expressed (or *express*, as the lawyers say) intentions do not matter, are totally irrelevant with regard to the meaning or artistic success of a literary work. Might this apply to life as well as literature, to moral work—good works—as well as literary work? Whatever the case: of what worth, a life of good intentions? But perhaps better to leave that question to the theologians and the philosophers—for one of somewhat lesser dimensions. Of what worth, a literature of good intentions, then? For that may be all she wrote, Loyal Reader, endangered species. She may be intentionally conceived and lovingly wrought, but the gap between what is intended, what is imagined, and what is finally—painstakingly, agonizingly, pathetically, resignedly—realized—no, abandoned—in the wrought-iron agony of words is usually so great as to render the intentional fallacy moot—no, mute.

But onward and upward. There are architectural, if not literary, jewels that await the traveller, and as he ascends the hill, on his right he sees the broad, turreted, dozing dome, and above it the widow's walk, of the fairy-tale, castle-like Winterholme, and on his left, at last, Bannerman Park, which bids welcome to the visitor with a pleasing circle of pines surrounding a small knoll. A Peace Grove, the plaque informs him, dedicated by a Governor General in 1992, but for what purpose it does not say. (Peace is an end in itself, of course, intrinsically valuable—like literature, as we all know.)

He is hot and tired from the long walk, and the Peace Grove is a very secluded shady place, with park benches for the weary traveller. He is even tempted to have a pee in there, but is a cautious person by nature and does not take the chance. He sits on a bench on top of the knoll and gazes through the pines across the park, and he sees, coming down a path in the distance, a very large pram being pushed along under the hot sun by a woman in a wide-brimmed straw hat. She is in his direct line of vision, coming straight toward him, it seems, perhaps heading toward this shady grove for a rest. As the pram gets closer, he prepares to say a few kind and cuddly words to or about the beautiful baby bunting, but is shocked to see looking out of the oversized covered carriage an aged and wrinkled face, and in a bandana-bonnet at that, and he is glad that he is protected from this startling sight behind the circle of tall pines.

Out of the cradle endlessly rocking...From the cradle to the cradle, the pram to the pram, and then to the grave, he thinks, and in an instant, knocked on the head by the Zen master's begging bowl, the proverbial flash of enlightenment: not her lifetime, or his, but time itself has telescoped, shifted, imploded, has revealed itself, its deep mystery, and to him alone, something neither the physicists nor the philosophers have been able to figure out. And then, of course, like time's chariot itself, the revelation is gone. *Gone, gone, gone. You're always gone...Well, they are gone, and here must I remain,/This lime-tree bower my prison!* This pine-tree bower his prison, time his prison.

But a large postpartum space in his head remains, and three things rush into it all at once. One: a pine tree with over five thousand growth rings had been found, he read somewhere, and was thought to be the oldest living organism on earth. Two: a renowned physicist at an American Ivy League university, who had consulted a philosopher about Time, confessed that upon leaving the philosopher's office he had checked to make sure the way was clear, as if he were leaving a porn shop or a whorehouse or an astrologer's den, and didn't want any of his colleagues to notice. Three: he recalls his bewilderment, as a child, about so-called daylight savings time, time springing ahead in the spring and falling back in the fall, as his mother would describe it to help him remember, if not understand, what was happening.

And in a sort of mindful trance he sees, sitting on a branch up in the large pine tree directly in front of him, a togaed philosopher holding something like the Scales of Justice, but with two large, transparent globes instead of scales, perfectly balancing one another. Inside them are black and white balls, black in one and white in the other, and he is looking up at them and thinking that here are not only all the daylight savings time hours he has lost and gained in his life, but all the daylight and all the dark; all his hours and all his days; a life elsewhere and a life here in his native land; a life lived and a life unlived; a lifetime account book perfectly balanced. And here, in the Peace Grove, he feels a great sense of equilibrium and, yes, peace.

But this is not to last for long; time is not done with our time-traveller yet. After a sort of time-gap, time-nap, time-lap, he bestirs himself and walks on across the park.

19: THE LADY WITH THE LITTLE DOG

Now consider this, picture this. Look, zoom in from afar, telescope from above, from the heights of speculation, if you will; look down upon this city park on Mother Earth. You see two diagonal paths crossing this old park in the centre of town with its one-hundred-year-old shade trees, and a man out for a late-afternoon walk after a hard day's work. He is crossing the park on one of these paths, heading for a coffee shop downtown, perhaps, to relax and read the paper; no desire to meet or talk to anyone, least of all a desire for an intimate meeting, a tryst; all desire sucked out of him, in fact, after plastering five or six hundred words to the page since early morning.

And down the other path comes a woman with a little dog (seriously), and not just any woman, but a woman with a much younger woman inside her (don't they all, you say), a girl he once knew, when he was young, too (it must be all of thirty-five years ago). And they meet exactly where these paths cross and recognize each other immediately after all these years. Would you not assume that something was up? Not mere coincidence, but synchronicity? What Jung called the "acausal connecting principle"—the most difficult connection to put your finger on. There had been a strong connection between them—call it love, if you wish—and perhaps on some level it was still operating, if unexplainable, beyond scientific explanation, at least, the old peer-reviewed, reliable, reproducible cause and effect.

"Sandy," I said. "Sandy Carroll. Is that you?"

"James...James Nightingale."

"Alexandra Carroll."

I think we wanted to hug, but something held us back. The little dog—well, not that little—was between us as well, looking straight at me, as if it were thinking something like, "Stay clear." It was a spaniel, I think, a scruffy-looking creature with long, drooping, scraggly ears. It was black with a white chest, but it had a greying face, and perhaps the chest was grey. A very wise old face, I might add, not a dog to be patronized, or treated like a dog. Its expression was almost human, in fact, and it looked at me as if it knew me, and was not very happy about it.

There had been a domestic animal in our brief life together—a cat, and it had suffered a tragic fate. Thinking about it even now sends an icy shiver down my spine. A horrible, senseless death, it seemed, the result of a ridiculous chain of events, though a logical cause-and-effect chain, I suppose.

But of course you want to know about the woman, not the cat, not the dog. Sandy began to gather in a long leather leash while trying to hold two black hardcover books under her arm.

"Let me take those books," I said.

"Thank you."

I glanced at the spines: Eliot's *The Waste Land: A Facsimile and Transcript* and *The Annotated Waste Land*.

"Try teaching *The Waste Land* on a summer's day like this," she said, "even out in the *grass land* under the trees."

"You haven't changed a bit," I said. "Except for the glasses—or the absence thereof."

"Laser surgery," she said, "twenty years ago. One of the first in line. Cost a fortune, but worth every cent of it."

I handed back the books.

"Have you been teaching here all these years?"

"No, I came back, about two years ago now, when my mother was ill. I came home to look after her. She died last year. I was only on leave from my job in Saskatoon, but I decided to stay. I'd been out there twelve years. It's *cold* out there. No permanent jobs in the English department here, though. I'm just contractual. Half of us are sessionals and contractuals. Maybe half the entire university faculty. It's run like a department store these days."

"Sorry to hear about your mother," I said. "I guess you did finish that master's degree we started."

"And the Ph.D....at the other end of the country...U. Vic. I started teaching in BC when I finished, in the Okanagan."

"I was out there in the spring," I said, "doing some readings."

"Yes, your fame has reached Saskatoon," she said.

This was sincere. Sandy had never been anything but sincere.

"Well, you must have lots more news," I said, famous last words I was to recall later that day. "Listen, I was just going downtown to have a coffee. Would you like to join me?"

She hesitated, but agreed.

"I won't be able to leave Burton outside too long," she said. "He gets lonely. Then he starts to whimper. *Poor baby.*"

"How old is he?" I asked.

"Oh, he's only ten. Just a pup."

I looked at Burton, and he looked at me. Loneliness didn't seem to be something that would ever bother this old pup.

∾ ᧁ

But I must tell you about the cat. As I said, when I first met Sandy she had a cat, a large, neurotic, inbred, male Persian named Snowball. White, as you would expect, but usually off-white, because he was an unneutered outdoor cat and, unlike most cats I'd known, didn't seem too concerned about personal grooming. Or perhaps it was just the huge amount of fur he had to deal with. He spent half his grooming time trying to remove it from his mouth, and after a certain point of frustration was reached, he would utter a two-syllable *me-ow* that sounded for all the world like *fuck it,* and give it up for a bad job.

Sandy was living rent-free in a summer house on the ocean in Flatrock. It was owned by her uncle, her father's brother, who was a contractor. Her father had died young, and the uncle seemed to have taken on the role. Her parents had been separated, and Sandy was not on good terms with her mother, a very fussy, interfering, and domineering woman. She was English, a war bride who had come to Newfoundland with Sandy's father after the Second World War, and the reason Sandy's English, though with only a hint of an English accent, contained words like *cooker, boot, tarmac, pavement,* and *washing-up.* We did the washing-up after supper, prepared on the cooker, groceries brought home in the boot of the car, which was driven on the tarmac, carefully avoiding the pavement, i.e., the sidewalk.

The house was the only dwelling on ten acres of land on which her uncle was planning to build a new subdivision. Close by was a mile-long, steeply sloped promontory called the Beamer, as it resembled a long ship resting on its side, on its beam ends. Its barren and windy and rocky deck beamed straight out into the wild North Atlantic. On weekends, in the fall, Sandy and I would walk right out to the end of it, stopping to pick cranberries and partridgeberries along the way. The end of this headland was a bleak bulwark of reddish rock high above the foaming and crashing waves. Standing on top of it and staring out to sea, with the wind and salt spray in our faces and our arms around each other for security and weight, we did indeed feel as if we were on the prow of some huge, listing bulk-carrier, scanning the horizon for signs of rescue.

Sandy was driving back and forth to the university in some dysfunctional European car that her uncle had given her as a birthday gift. A Skoda or Lada or Simca, an import that had unsuccessfully predated the Honda and Toyota dynasties, it was a former test-drive vehicle. The uncle had owned a failed dealership. The thing was a diesel, and it was hard to find diesel fuel in those days; it was not at every gas station, as it is now. The car also had tubes in its tires—a tragic flaw, as it turned out for poor old Snowball—and one day in late November as we were driving out to Sandy's house, we got a flat tire. There was no spare tire to be found in the *boot,* nor jack nor tire-changing tools of any kind, even if there were one. Luckily, there was a service station en route (though not one that sold diesel), and the mechanic was able to patch the tube.

So on we drove. Snowball was in his cathouse when we arrived. It was like a doghouse—the cat was almost as big as a dog—serving as a shelter and a place where Sandy left food and water, as she was in town a lot of the time. Snowball made no move to greet us. Usually, he would wait until after dark to come inside, unless it was wet or freezing or he smelled something cooking, preferring anything we ate to the bowl of hard, dry stuff Sandy always left for him. It was very cool that evening, though there still hadn't been any snow. Less than an hour later, over supper—leftover pizza heated up in the oven of an old-fashioned wood stove, the only source of heat and the only *cooker* in the place—we heard a loud bang. When we rushed outside, Snowball was crawling away from the car, dragging the rear half of his body over the gravel, mewling in agony. The car tire was flat again. The tube had burst, we found out later; the patch had not held. After we had arrived and gone into the house, Snowball, as he sometimes did, had climbed up on top of the warm tire, in the shelter of the wheel well. When the tube burst, the body of the car collapsed on top of him, breaking his back.

Sandy screamed and ran toward him, reached down to pick him up, but he snarled like a wild animal and tore at the air with one of his front paws. His white fur was turning red. We couldn't get anywhere near him. I thought of grabbing one of the birch junks in the pile beside the house and slamming it down on his head, putting him out of his pain, but I knew I couldn't do it, and neither would Sandy let me if I tried. Her hands were covering her eyes now, and she was mewling like the cat.

I ran into the house to get a pair of gloves. I dumped the birch junks that were in the cardboard box by the stove out onto the floor. I grabbed a garbage bag from under the sink. I was surprised that my impractical and usually abstracted self was thinking so clearly and acting so calmly and quickly. Perhaps I was drifting toward the wrong profession, I thought; perhaps the academic life was not for me. Medicine—veterinarian, paramedic, doctor, nurse—might be where my aptitudes and sympathies lay, though I could hardly bear the sight of blood, even a cat's.

Back outside, I managed to approach Snowball from behind, grab his front paws—though he bit into my leather wood-chopping gloves—lift him up, and nestle him gently in the plastic bag that Sandy was holding open inside the cardboard box. He was hissing and spitting and snarling and mewling in a most pitiful way, though he made no attempt to get out of the box, and Sandy was still crying pitifully herself.

"We'll call the SPCA," I said, "to see what we should do. Let's bring him inside, so he doesn't try to escape."

That sounded foolish. I knew that cat wasn't going anywhere. He had quieted down, in fact, and his eyelids were drooping as I picked up the box and carried it into the house. I feared the worst, though it was probably, as they say, all for the best. Snowball expired, in fact, right in the middle of my conversation with a woman at the SPCA, Eileen by name. Sandy had been gently rubbing his head, and Eileen herself may have heard the news.

"His eyes are closed! I think he's dead!" Sandy screeched. Her face was a red mask streaked with tears. I had never seen her so upset before.

After I explained what had happened and the predicament we were in—that we were far from any neighbours and without transport—Eileen said she was not that far away, at the SPCA's animal shelter at the old airport on Torbay Road, and very kindly offered to come and "collect the remains," as she put it, that very evening. She would take them to "Humane Services" in St. John's, she said. That was humane in more ways than one, for Sandy couldn't bear to look at the remains any more. After I got off the phone, I suggested putting them in the car. Sandy wasn't too fond of this idea, I could tell, and she followed me out to the car with some warm milk in a small bowl, which she placed, "just in case," in the box in front of Snowball's face. I closed the trunk, very gently, and we went back into the house.

∿ᘯ

As I said, I had never seen Sandy so upset. She was a cool person, generally speaking, rational, not emotional; somewhat elusive, but not mysterious, not distant; kind, easygoing, giving, and forgiving was how I remembered her. If I recalled anything unusual about her, it was the fact that she was the only person I'd ever known—up to that point in my life, at least—who never listened to music. This had seemed very strange to me because I was always listening to it; but Sandy would never turn on the radio, at home or in the car, put a record or tape on my stereo, or go to a concert. She liked silence, needed silence. She didn't really hear music, it seemed to me, though that may sound strange; she heard it only as a distraction, to be more precise, so it was noise she was hearing, not music. If it were playing in the background while she was reading or working, she would often ask me to turn it down, and I would usually turn it off.

Alicia, violist extraordinaire, with superb musical taste, along with perfect pitch, she claimed, had posited four categories of relationship between people and music. She meant, of course, so-called serious music, classical music, *real* music, and the implication embodied in the whole proposition was a sort of categorical imperative, an unconditional obligation, as applied to listening to music instead of your conscience. Yes, the tone in which she expressed it verged on the moralistic. No point in saying *I don't, I can't, I won't.* You must!

Let me see if I can remember all four categories:

1. People who never listened to music—the Damned, lost souls, headed for Hell. They couldn't be saved, but, fortunately, they were few in number. Music was a totally unnecessary part of their lives. Alicia professed to not being able to understand these people. Alas, Alexandra may have been one of them.

2. People who always had music on, a goodly number, but they weren't listening to it. It was just wallpaper, white noise. It was not that they either liked or disliked music; it was just that

they hated, or feared, silence. They were destined for Limbo, an indeterminate state. There might be some hope for them— Alicia wasn't sure.

3. People who merely used (or should I say *abused?*) music as a sort of personal lubricant, like K-Y Jelly, for sex, dancing, soundtracks, marches, rituals, *relaxation.* (Italics can not express the depth of Alicia's disdain for the latter.) They were going to Purgatory, where they would suffer for their sins, and after spiritual cleansing would be admitted to Paradise.

4. People who loved music, also few in number, and they were already in a paradise on earth. She and New Man Richard, of course, as both rigorously attentive listeners and consummate musicians—and he also a *creator,* as he liked to call himself— occupied a special music room in one of the Lord's earthly mansions.

❧ ❧

The year we first met, Sandy and I had been part of a small, happy-go-lucky group of students working at a spring-and-summer job in the English department and socializing almost every day after work and sometimes late into the evening. We had just finished our undergraduate degrees and were waiting to begin graduate work in the fall, working for a professor *emeritus* in the department who was compiling entries for a proposed *Dictionary of Newfoundland English.* Clerical emmet-drones we were, about fifteen of us, filling out file cards and filing file cards, lugging cartons of new file cards from the storeroom in the basement of the Arts Building up to the third floor, then conveying cartons of file cards that had served their lexical purpose—semantic, phonological, or morphological—back down to the storeroom, working a three-storey anthill eight to ten hours a day. We had been encouraged to do our own research, to consult members of our extended families about peculiar dialect words from the Old World still in their vocabularies, from Poole or Waterford or Galway Bay. My mother had suggested a dozen or more, but the old man had expressed utter disdain for the whole idea of a Newfoundland lexicon.

Once a week, at the end of the day, a few of us would be invited to supper at the home of the professor *emeritus*, a bachelor and a notorious lush, a man so distracted by painless abstraction that on at least two occasions he announced our arrival—to his housekeeper-cook—by crashing his car into his house. And during what he called the after-dinner "symposium," which was more in the spirit of the original Greek custom, i.e., a drinking party, than the modern-day one, when we proffered for discussion dialect words we had solicited from our families, he would, after several glasses of port or brandy, inevitably fall asleep in his recliner. Then we would drift off, sleepily intoxicated ourselves, into the summer night.

Ah, the academic life, the scholar's life—I had almost fallen for it. I could easily have become a somnolent scholar myself. But alas, my prized symposium contributions—*emmet, oxter,* and *whitlow*—cleverly documented in triplicate on file cards, to be sure they didn't get overlooked, had never made it into the *DNE*, published in 1982, more than a decade later. Kevin had brought me a copy as a gift on one of his trips to Toronto.

There had been pairings among our little student group all summer long, of course, sexual couplings, but Sandy and I had not made love until the summer was almost over and our first term of graduate work was about to begin. I didn't even know where she lived. Then one day after work, a cool, windy, late-August day, a Friday, the last day of our last week of work, we had ended up as the last two drinkers at our usual pub table—perhaps most of the others were going out of town, going home, before the term began—and Sandy surprised me by inviting me out to her house for supper. And that evening our more intimate relationship began, in a one-bedroom summer house made entirely of sheets of corrugated steel, on a hill only a few hundred feet from the ocean. In the fall and winter, the wood stove did more than an adequate job of heating that small house, though it had no insulation whatsoever. We slept together that late-August night with the window open, and long after Sandy had closed her eyes, I lay awake listening to the sea crashing against the cliffs.

We shared many more nights like that during the fall, and by chance a night in more opulent surroundings, on New Year's Eve in a room in the old Newfoundland Hotel. Our relationship had remained carefree and casual, however, though there were no competitors that I knew of, certainly not on my part. At the time, I put this down to the fact that Sandy was very focused, very studious. She loved reading, loved literature—studying was not a chore for her—and could spend a whole weekend with a hefty Henry James or Thomas Hardy, and often did. She had very poor eyesight, probably from all the secret, late-night, low-light reading she'd done growing up, sometimes just by the light of the street lamp or the moon shining into her room, she said, when she was meant to be sleeping. She wore large, oval, peach-brown plastic frames with bookworm-thick lenses.

If Sandy had ever seemed detached, self-conscious, uncomfortable, even displeased, when we were making love—a question I was to seriously ponder when I left her place late that evening after our fortuitous meeting in the park—what impetuous, self-propelled, heat-seeking missile of youthful ardour would have noticed, or paid any attention to it? Was I simply recalling the way she looked when I removed her glasses before we made love—shy, vulnerable, exposed, naked almost? I was always the one to remove her glasses, and it was as if I had removed her clothes. Taking off her clothes after that seemed like just an afterthought, an impersonal, secondary, unnecessary thing that she did with ease.

I gladly would have moved in with her had she asked—I was living in a tiny bed-sitter at the time, close to the university—but, feeling that she didn't want to become too involved, I kept my distance. In the new year, as if our special night together in the Newfoundland Hotel had been some kind of prearranged, celebratory farewell, we began to drift apart, as I drifted further and further away from academic work and began to get more and more serious about writing and Sandy became more intent on an academic career. In March, my first short story, "Houseflies," was accepted by a mainland literary periodical—

one with a top-notch reputation, but perhaps not for proofreading. When that plain, earthbound, realist bungalow of a story was finally published, it was given a castle-in-the-air, magical-realist title. "Houseflies" was changed to "House Flies." Well, the titles did have *wings* in common. In April of the following year, I left Newfoundland again for Toronto, on wings myself this time. I might have been older and a bit wiser, but, when all is said and done, I have come to believe that nothing beats pure innocence and wonder as a shield against the slings and arrows, the doubts and fears, and, finally, "the seal, despair," as Dickinson called it.

I had never forgotten those days with Sandy. The smell of woodsmoke, especially, would take me right back to that house by the sea. A bad omen was not a black cat crossing my path but a white one. And one night on *The National* there was a "story" (as they call news reports these days) about the construction of a new Newfoundland Hotel, and I watched a wrecking ball smashing into the old one, into the side of the building with the best view of St. John's Harbour, perhaps into the very room that Sandy and I had shared that New Year's Eve so long ago.

We'd had drinks and a light supper, and then more drinks, in the hotel bar. A storm had come up and we'd been unable to go home. (No one gave any thought to drinking and driving in those days, or toking and driving, for that matter.) The storm had also prevented some couples from getting into town for dinner in the ballroom, followed by the fancy-dress New Year's Eve ball and an overnight stay, a popular New Year's Eve treat, so we were lucky that a room was available. We had even gone down to the ballroom for a dance when the celebrations were well underway, but after the climactic midnight hurrah. Though Sandy was wearing a pleated skirt—she always wore dresses or skirts, with tights of many colours, never pants or jeans—in our casual clothes, we felt very self-conscious among the suits and gowns; but no one seemed to be paying us any attention.

∾ ᴄ

Yes, I had often thought of Sandy and wondered what had become of her, and the sight that evening of a wrecking ball smashing into the old Newfoundland Hotel as if into the facade of my past life, scattering bricks and dust and debris in all directions, had stirred the dust of old memories. And now here she was right in front of me, and here we were looking out the window of a coffee shop right across the street from the new Newfoundland Hotel, and she looked as astonished as I felt.

We talked about all of this for an hour or more. We could have shared a life together, I was thinking as we talked—marriage, children, work, a civilized, peaceable, if painful, divorce after perhaps twenty years—instead of just casual, romantic, carefree sex in a house by the ocean for a few months, and then painlessly drifting apart. But how wrong I was. I should have taken better notice of the fact that Sandy was being less than forthcoming about her personal life—relationships, marriages, children—and seemed to be deflecting any questions about it by focusing intently on mine. She apologized for not having read any of my books; she was hopelessly lost in the seventeenth century, she explained, though as a non-tenured teacher she had been forced to enter the twentieth. Some of her friends had read them, she said, and had said good things about them, and she had noted their inclusion in some CanLit courses in her department in Saskatoon, though, strangely enough, not in Newfoundland.

Sandy seemed to have forgotten about Burton—he hadn't made a sound—tethered to a parking meter outside the coffee shop, though she had cast motherly glances in his direction a few times. And then, déjà vu, she invited me back to her place for supper, this time to a condominium at the very top of a converted church on Queen's Road—she even owned the belfry—from which great views of the Harbour, the Narrows, the Battery, Signal Hill, Fort Amherst, and the Southside Hills offered their charms to the visitor, I was told. She could see right out to the ocean, she said, though when we arrived everything was beneath a bank of fog and you couldn't even see the docks.

After our meal and a bottle of wine and more warm, nostalgic talk, the young couple, the young lovers inside us, were nostalgically coupling as easily and naturally as we had done all of thirty-five years ago...But not the old lovers, the old couple, though both the afternoon and the evening had been filled with such warm memories, such fortuitous promise.

"James, there's something you need to know," Sandy said suddenly, after we had moved from the dining room table to the loveseat—yes, the loveseat—in the adjoining living room, wineglasses in hand, into which I had poured the last drop of Chilean Merlot, ensuring that the levels were perfectly equal, though there had been some left in Sandy's glass, so I guess I got the better of the bargain. Considering what I was about to hear, I would need the extra drop. Burton was stretched out on his side on the rug in front of the unlit propane fireplace, a paw under his jowls like a human, looking comfortably melancholy.

"I know we were intimate back then," Sandy continued, "but I didn't know myself then, and the times were different, and our circle was so small... and not really open-minded at all. James, I'm not heterosexual, is what I'm trying to say."

"You mean you're..." I stammered, as if I needed a translation, or further explanation, a birds-and-bees refresher for an innocent of a certain age, of a prehistoric time.

"Didn't you...enjoy our time together?" was all I could say. *Enjoy.* What a tasteless watery Popsicle of a word, I thought. A waiter's tip, his grace, his bland routine parting blessing. If words were birds, *enjoy* was a flightless one, or at best a sidewalk pigeon. *Pleasure, delight, rapture, ecstasy* were what I remembered, what I still had in mind.

"Of course I did," she said. "You were so easy to be with. We would spend hours just reading together in front of the wood stove."

I guess I was the Happy Reader even then, I thought, but that wasn't the sort of distinction I had in mind.

"I remember having *sex* on the rug in front of the wood stove," I said.

"You were the only man I ever had sex with, James. How could I not remember. But it was such a long time ago."

Another dubious distinction, I thought.

We both smiled, wanly it seemed. We were silent. Our glasses were empty. This was not the way I wanted the evening to end.

"When did you know you were...?"

"A *lesbian*, James. Is that word so hard to say?"

"No. I'm sorry. A lesbian," I said, as if trying out a word in a foreign language. "I think I was in love with you back then," I added, with more emotion than I expected.

The loveseat was small. We were close together. She turned and put her arms around my head and kissed my brow.

"Oh, James, you're such a sweet, innocent man," she said. "As sweet and innocent now as you were then."

"Will you be a witness at my divorce proceedings?" I said. I had mentioned our separation and perhaps imminent divorce, had told her a lot about Alicia and me.

My not-so-innocent arms were around her body, and I gave her a gentle inviting squeeze.

"At least no one can accuse me of being sexist," I said, inappropriately appropriating that much overused word.

"And just as funny," she added, removing her arms from around my head, and I reluctantly removed mine as well. We were still holding our empty wineglasses, and they accidentally clinked as we disengaged, as if we were making an unintended farewell toast. The unintentional fallacy. Burton's ears had caught the sound, and he raised his head and looked at us with the sad but wise expression of an old judge who'd had much experience in annulments, legal separations, the cut and thrust of custodial wranglings, the cut-and-paste of divorce settlements, and had just settled a somewhat unusual case.

20: WATER MUSIC

The music crept by us upon the waters. We were sitting on a bench on a riverbank, Celia and me, under a weeping willow, by the Rennie's River, close to the site of the old Rennie's Mill. Grind on, good miller; run softly, sweet Rennie's, till I end my song. Where could this music be? In the air or the earth? Or just in my head? The music that had once been such a big part of our lives.

I had persuaded Celia to take a walk along the river trail. Walking was not something she had ever liked to do, so we sat on every inviting bench, under every shade tree, along the way. A small commemorative brass plaque on the back of this bench said, "Frances Harding, Flying Free." In a couple of weeks, I would be flying free myself, though *fleeing* rather than flying might be a better way of putting it. Eight miles high and then two thousand miles away, but I knew I would be far from free, just as bound to earthly cares as ever.

We were gazing silently at the old mill stream. There was no wind, not even the slightest breeze. In the silence and the stillness I heard myself say, somewhat formally and elegiacally, trying to keep my distance from this subject, perhaps, it having caused so much family distress in the past: "If I had to do it all again, it would be music."

"Do what again, Dad?" Celia said, innocently enough, though trying to keep her distance as well, no doubt.

"Life, my sweet—the artistic life. *Ars longa, vita brevis*; the life so short, the craft so long to learn."

She laughed, a sound as sweet as any murmuring rill to a father's ears. "Why do you think music would be easier?" she said. "You mean composing?"

"No…just playing. Not having to make it up. No blank pages in front of me every morning."

"Not much written for the 12-string, Dad. Even worse than the bassoon."

"Very funny. The piano, of course. I would have it all there before me, the whole piece—nocturne, étude, prelude, waltz, gymnopédie, song without words—all the notes, and I would just play, even if only for myself. Composing would be just as agonizing as writing, I would say."

"Playing piano is not as simple as you think, Dad. You never really know if you got it right, even with all the composer's markings. You have a lot of freedom in the way you play any piece—tempos, dynamics, phrasing. That's the hardest part—the interpretation, stylistic liberties, the balance. But, like, if there are particular things you want to say, to express—original things— you'd have to compose the music yourself, wouldn't you? You'd never be happy with what someone else wrote—it'd be like reading another writer's book. You'd probably be a stylistic freak, music-wise. Another Glenn Gould. You'd take too many liberties with the composer's work."

"It's not the same thing. Playing someone else's music would let me express my feelings much better than reading someone else's book, I think."

"Maybe. Like, why are you bringing all this up? It's not like you to talk about your work."

"No reason."

"Come on, Dad."

"Well, you're not going to bring it up, are you?"

"Bring what up?"

"Music…You never want to talk about music…playing music."

"What's the point of bringing that up?"

"No point, I guess. Are you talking to your mother these days? E-mailing her or anything?"

"Not for a while."

"A while?"

"Couple of months, I guess."

"The whole summer!"

"Come on, Dad. I've been working all summer. There's no Internet at Mistaken Point. And no cellphone service."

"Land lines? Anyway…"

"Let's not talk about this, okay? There's no point in talking about it."

"I was never one to talk about it, as you know. It was your mother's issue, not mine. I'm just interested, that's all. You've been away a long time."

"Yeah, less than a year, Dad."

"Well, it seems like a long time."

"Is Mom putting you up to this?"

"No, Celie, we're not even talking. Well…she's been calling about the house. She wants to sell the house."

"Sell the house? Why?"

"I guess you know about Richard, do you?"

"Yes, she told me."

"They're moving away. Richard's been offered a position in the States, a composing chair at some rich private college in the South, the Land o' Cotton, Dixieland. Look away, look away…"

"She's giving up her job at the university?"

"Leave of absence, I think. Sabbatical, maybe. Till they see how it all pans out."

"Hmmm," she murmured.

"You should keep in touch more, as I said. So you know what's going on."

"It doesn't matter. I'll find out sooner or later."

There was an uncomfortable silence, during which I decided to change the subject.

"I'm sorry for not taking you over to the Island," I said. "I want to remember it as it was. The land, the garden, is still there. The house may be gone, burned to the ground, but I can still see every room in it, every stick of furniture—my old iron bed, my grandfather's old black leather smoker that I used to curl up in and read. I can see the view from every window, from the rickety front gallery, every tree in that old overgrown garden—the lilacs, the gooseberry bushes, the trembling aspens, the crabapple, the old cherry trees. It's like being trapped inside a Chekhov play."

"Dad, it's okay…there's no need. I understand. I've been over there twice with Hana to look at the rocks. Listen…I've got something to tell you. I know you've been thinking about this and it means a lot to me that you haven't bugged me about it, like Mom's still doing, e-mailing me all the time…but I don't answer. I haven't stopped playing, Dad…the piano or the violin…and I've joined a band."

"A band? What kind of band?"

"It's what we call post-trad. You might like it. You grew up with rock music and folk music, and you never liked traditional music, you always said, at least not the kind that was popular in Toronto—the Newfoundland-Irish stuff, Harry Hibbs. Didn't you tell me you got thrown out of the Newfoundland Club?"

"Well…I left peaceably. That was before you were born, even before I met your mother. I'd only been in Toronto about a year. I was sitting at the bar by myself, cryin' in my beer, probably, shaking my head at some maudlin song the band was playing—I may have made an offhand remark—and I heard the bartender, who must have been a sensitive sort, all of a sudden say, 'You can leave if you don't like it.' That famous Newfoundland hospitality—the hybridized Toronto kind. When I looked up, I realized he was talking to me, and he nodded toward the door to make his point. So I raised my glass to him and left."

"We're not doing Irish-Newfoundland, Dad. There's two Irish musicians in the band—Sean and Liam—and they hate that stuff. Wait'll you hear 'The Trinity Cake'…and 'The Kelligrews Soiree.' We're rocking it up. We're deconstructing it, Sean says. He's our lead singer and guitarist. He studied classical guitar at the music school here, and he's a composer as well. I'm doing fiddle and keyboards. There's another guitarist, a drummer, a bass player, a mandolin player, a piper, Liam, and a button accordion player. We're rearranging traditional tunes, and composing new tunes as well—twelve-tone traditional, if you can imagine that."

"Punk McNultys is what I'm hearing."

"Is that a band? Like Dropkick Murphys?"

"No, it's a joke. Like who?"

"Dropkick Murphys. They're a trad-punk band. They were here for the George Street Festival."

"Trad-punk, post-trad...You know, I hardly heard any traditional music growing up. The McNulty Family is all I can recall. Not for purists—'Molly Malone' and all that stuff. They sounded Irish, but they were from New York. They were always on the radio, and they even toured Newfoundland in the 1950s. My mother heard them perform in the CLB Armoury on the Island. She mentioned it to me more than once. It must have been a once-in-a-lifetime event for her and the town. I used to imagine her standing among an ecstatic crowd in that packed hall, used mainly for Christian paramilitary drills, swaying to the music with her arms in the air—perhaps with her silver Zippo lighter in one hand—like a fan at a modern-day rock extravaganza. But most likely it was a sit-down-on-a-hard-chair, no-dancing affair.

"I even missed what you might call traditional rock and roll—Chuck Berry, Bo Diddley, Carl Perkins, Li'l Richard, Jerry Lee Lewis. I didn't listen to that stuff until the late '70s and '80s, when there was nothing else to listen to. There was Elvis in the '50s, of course. But music really began with the Beatles for me. Elvis was all washed up by then. It was their versions of 'Matchbox' and 'Roll Over Beethoven' that I first heard, and then all the other '60s stuff, and then your mother began to deprogram me not long after we met, and reprogram with 'Western art music,' 'serious music,' as she likes to call it.

"I don't think I ever told you that when I first met your mother—at a poetry reading I think it was, but there were folksingers there as well—and I found out that she played an instrument, I suggested that we play together sometime. Just my way of getting to know her—she was still an undergraduate then. She was reluctant, as you would expect, but she eventually agreed to do it."

"That must have been a barrel of fun, Dad—the 12-string and the viola," Celia said, imagining the sound this dissonant duo might produce.

"I didn't even know what the viola was, to tell the truth, and I certainly didn't want to ask. Perhaps she thought I played the classical guitar. I was still on the 6-string then, by the way, but it didn't matter. Your mother tried to play along, but she couldn't. Couldn't play by air, couldn't *jam*. I think she was as surprised as I was, and a bit embarrassed, too. The straitjacket of strict notation, as someone once called it. She needed a score, needed the notes in front of her or she couldn't play at all."

Irreconcilable musicalities, so to speak. I should have seen it as a sign, I thought—very quietly to myself. I fear children can hear traitorous thoughts like these.

"That's the way it is with most classical musicians, Dad," Celia said. "They're not really into improvisation, *jamming*, but don't forget that they can play a whole sonata or concerto from memory."

"I know…but still…that was a revelation to me. So…you should know that I am responsible for at least one aspect of your amazing musical versatility—the fact that you can play by air, as well as by *rote*. We started you out on violin in the Suzuki program, so you learned to play by air before you learned to read music, which you did when you started on the piano, about a year later. Anyway…she'll be glad to hear that you're playing again. By hook or by crook, as they say. By bow or by hoe. Just be sure never to use the words 'fiddle' and 'keyboards' in her presence. I'd stick to 'violin' and 'piano' if I were you."

"Okay, Dad…listen…will you come and hear us? We're doing a show downtown this month."

"Better than that. I'll do a solo spot on the 12-string—with the band, I mean, a lead spot."

"Yeah, sure. 'Walk Right In,' punk New Christy Minstrels. Wasn't that your signature song?"

"Used to be. I've moved on. You don't know 'All Along the Watchtower' do you?"

"Is that some kind of religious song? Wasn't there a magazine…?"

"Yes, *The Watchtower*. They used to bring it to our house. Largest circulation in the world: over 40 million copies a month, someone once told me, more than double the *Reader's Digest*. Imagine if you had a book that sold 40 million copies! Or a CD. In a lifetime, even—I'm not greedy. Forget per month. Sorry, just fantasizing there. But no, nothing to do with the song. *You*, my darling, have had a sheltered upbringing, musically speaking. It's a Bob Dylan song, famously covered by Jimi Hendrix—the version everyone knows. Most people probably think he wrote it as well. Now you'll never guess what happened at the spring Writers' Union conference. I joined a band myself. I was discovered! At a late-night jam, the lead guitarist for the band playing at the Saturday night dance—the Mudlarks, a three-piece band doing sixties covers, just guitar, bass, and drums—asked if we knew 'All Along the Watchtower,' and I rattled off those four big 12-string beats—*chuk chuk chuk chuk*—that start off the Jimi Hendrix version, like the four that begin Beethoven's *Fifth*, and I passed the audition. Did you know that the Beatles failed their first audition?"

"You take your guitar to writers' meetings now?"

"No, just to the last one. It was almost next door and I could take it on the subway. I wouldn't want to take that monster on a plane. Sure, that's the best part of the meetings—the late-night jams. 'Who talks about books at those things!' as Alonzo Grandy would say."

"Who?"

"My first publisher…long story…Anyway, as I was saying, the much pooh-poohed 12-string is just as important as the lead guitar in that song, but who's ever noticed because of Hendrix's pyrotechnics. It was my first audition, and my big break. I got to play at the dance. Just that one song, but it was such a hit that we played it again with the encores."

"So that's where and when you decided on music? For your next life, I guess."

"Yeah…my 'moment of elimination.'" I started to laugh at my own private joke. Ain't it funny how your mind stores and retrieves these things.

Celia was laughing, too. She was as overly aware of words as I was myself. As a writer-father, I had perhaps been a bit of a lexical superego, and she was now always alert and ready to pounce, to get her own back. She turned and looked down her nose at me.

"You must mean *illumination*, Dad," she said.

"Yeah…something funny just came back to me. When I was out in the country at my friend Graham's house on Random Island, I read some Chekhov stories, some I've read a dozen times. Have you read any Chekhov yet? What are you reading these days?"

"No, I haven't. I'm reading a Polish novel Hana gave me—called *Ferdydurke*, about a man who sort of becomes a child again."

"Try some Chekhov when you finish that. I think you're ready for him now."

"What do you mean, *ready*?"

"Well, he's so subtle and indirect, so *nuanced*, as they say now, that I'm sure I didn't get much from him when I was your age, or from any of the others for that matter—Woolf, Conrad, Joyce, James—but as a reader you must be ten years ahead of where I was then. You're almost thirty, I'd say, *reading-wise*."

"A lot more mature in every way, Dad."

"Yes, indeed, my sweet," I said, to her sweetly smiling face, and as I did I remembered what it was I was going to tell her, but quickly realized that I couldn't after all.

One of the Chekhov stories I had read out at Graham's house was "The Lady with the Little Dog," his most well known one, I suppose, in a book I picked up at a second-hand bookstore. It was a student's copy, no doubt, sold at the end of term, the margins filled in with notes, one of which said, at the story's climactic point, "moment of elimination." This note, as pathetically funny as it was, had been written next to these memorable lines: "Now it was plain to him that no one in the whole world was closer, dearer and more important to him than she was." The man and the young woman whom Chekhov was talking about, of course, were lovers, not a young woman and her father, but yes, it was just as plain to me. And of course I was even more unable to tell her than he was.

So I left the Chekhov and returned to the music.

"But seriously," I said. "I was serious about the music, and I know exactly when my moment of illumination was—when I heard you play that Mozetich piece at a recital long ago. You were no more than thirteen. Isn't he Polish, Mozetich?"

"Canadian, I think. Maybe Polish ancestry, I don't know."

"He has Chopin in his blood, wherever he's from. If I could play that, I thought—and if I could play like that—when I first heard you play it, I would be the happiest of men. The Happy Pianist. But perhaps I was already the happiest of men hearing you play it."

"You're not so *nuanced* yourself, Dad. You're making me feel guilty now, just like Mom."

"I'm sorry, I didn't mean to."

We were silent for several minutes, but it didn't feel like a cold silence, a resentful silence, in spite of what she had said. There was music all around us—water music, birdsong, whispering leaves. A breeze had come up, stirring the willow branches above our heads. I could hear the melancholy Mozetich in my head.

"Will you come down to hear us?" she asked. "It's at the Kil—the Kilowatt Club on Water Street.

"What's the name of the band?" I asked.

"The Slew," she said. "Because there's so many of us—eight altogether, a whole *slew*. But we use the Irish spelling: S-L-U-A-G-H. Because of Sean and Liam. The Sluagh."

"I'd cross a slough to get there," I said. "Of course I will. Will I need earplugs?"

"I wear them myself. They're specially designed, basically a sophisticated hearing aid, so I can hear what the rest of the band are playing—and what I'm playing myself. But you won't need them. It's a big club, and you can stand or sit at the back. Unless you want to enter the mosh pit."

"What's that?"

"Haven't you been to a club lately?"

"Not that kind of club."

"Well, in the clubs where we play most of the crowd are out on what you probably still call the dance floor, a big knot of hardcore fans, not dancing exactly but all doing their own thing. It looks like chaos, but there is such a thing as mosh-pit etiquette."

"Well, there's no need to brief me on that," I said. "I'll take your advice and stay at the back. If my friend Kevin comes along, though, he might join in."

"Is that the man I met in Bannerman Park?"

"That's him."

"Oh, please, bring him along. He's so fun."

Famous last words, I thought.

We walked on down the river trail, past the white bones of old willows lying in broken heaps on the riverbank. We passed a young man being pushed along in a wheelchair, wringing two thin white hands in front of his face as if they were moulded together and he was trying to pull them apart. We'd had a lot of rain in the past two days, and farther down the valley, where the land was flatter and the river wider, a low retaining wall of pinkish plastic sandbags that looked like butterball turkeys lined the riverbank; but the wall had been breached, and we weaved our way through sky-blue pools of water at our feet.

21: THE MOSH PIT

There was such a thing as mosh-pit etiquette, as Celia said. If a liquor store can have a mission statement, I thought—as I stood reading a sign above a stopped-up urinal in which a round white deodorizer as big as a hockey puck, and smelling worse than urine, wobbled on the foam—then I suppose a mosh pit can have rules of etiquette. Celia's "post-trad" band, the Sluagh, was now on stage, and the music was beating its way in through the open washroom door.

I was at the Kilowatt Klub (or the Kil, as the kids liked to call it). Though I didn't make it down to see the fossils at Mistaken Point, *mistakes were made*, as the passive-voiced passenger politicians, darkening the skies in ever-increasing numbers, as once did the now-extinct passenger pigeons, are wont to voice the sentiment. We do our due diligence but...*mistakes are made*.

No, I do not wish to hide the fact that I was responsible for this mistake, though it did have a somewhat happy ending. I had responded warmly to Celia's invitation to go hear her band, had foolishly extended the invitation to Kevin, at her request, and he had responded even more enthusiastically to the active voice on the old land line requesting his presence, and ignoring a lifetime of interpersonal provocation, individual insurgency, and adolescent risk-taking on Kevin's part. In any event, I needed the company. This was not a John White or Harry Hibbs or Omar Blondahl soiree, and I did not want to be the only grey head in a club full of obstreperous teens and twenty-somethings. Even the bouncers—rosy-cheeked, clean-cut kids with Security stencilled unconvincingly in bold black letters on the front and back of their white T-shirts—looked to be barely out of their teens.

Hana Trela, who had invited me to go see the fossils, had come along as well, and though I felt a bit like a fossil myself in her presence, she was dressed very conservatively in a homespun cotton smock and matching beige cardigan, on which, however, she still wore her father's Solidarity resistor, though the beige background wash seemed to diminish its symbolic charge. Hana, Celia had confided to me, had turned out to be a bit of a disappointment as a housemate. She was devoted to her work, had a boyfriend back home and so rarely went out, and even went to church on Sundays—at the Kirk, which was almost in their back garden, though she said it was only to hear the one-hundred-year-old English-style organ. Her mother was the organist at her church back home, and Hana had sung in the choir. Not at all like those wild and wayward European girls I had known in my youth.

The Mosh Pit Etiquette sign, a list of behavioural no-no's scripted in commandment black—and there were ten of them—was screwed to the wall behind a rectangle of quarter-inch plastic. There were three of them above the ten or more urinals in this hangar-sized club.

MOSH PIT ETIQUETTE

1. No punching, kicking, stomping, scratching, poking, or elbowing.
2. No headbanging.
3. No groping.
4. No throwing objects.
5. No stage-diving or crowd-surfing.
6. No bottles or glasses in the pit.
7. No sandals, slippers, or pajamas.
8. No spiked bracelets, necklaces, or large rings.
9. No helmets, heavy belt buckles, or chains.
10. No nudity.

Please Respect The Band And Your Fellow Moshers
Mosh At Your Own Risk

Just getting past the mosh pit on my way to the washroom had been a risk. We had found a table of sorts, a wide ledge or overhang toward the back of the club, on a second level a few steps up from the main floor, at which we sat perched on high stools. The undecorated walls, as well as the concrete floor, were painted entirely in black. On the main floor there was a large stage in front, a dance floor (or mosh pit) in the middle, and two identical bars at opposite sides selling "only Molson product," as a bartender had informed me earlier, with men's and women's washrooms at opposite ends of the bars. One side of the club, in fact, looked like a mirror image of the other.

Celia's band, which was supposed to start at eleven, had finally got underway around midnight. The first thing they gave us to tackle, as the song says, was a slice of "The Trinity Cake," and then they straightened our eyeballs and scoured our eardrums with "The Kelligrews Soiree." An intense, relentless version of "Feller from Fortune," with an endlessly repeated chorus—"Oh, catch a-hold this one, catch a-hold that one,/Swing around this one, swing around she;/Dance around this one, dance around that one,/Diddle-dum this one, diddle-dum-dee"—sent the moshers into hysterical overdrive, chanting "diddle-dum, diddle-dum, diddle-dum-dee" when the song was over till the band had to take it up again.

The musical tide was still at full bore. From our ledge-table at the back, I'd had to work my way to the front, between the bar and the expanding and contracting mini-universe of the mosh pit, the air thick with the metallic smell of deodorant and belched booze. I tried to keep close to the solid-wood security of the bar, though both the floor and the ceiling, and the very air between, seemed in vibrant motion, and through my straightened eyeballs I thought I could see atoms dancing. I stayed as far away as possible from the barely contained fury, the unstable energy, the dark matter, of the pit, where a unique form of dancing—I use the term loosely, as Kevin is fond of saying—was in progress. It was an attempt by the dancers, Kevin had speculated, "to get back in touch"—a desperate attempt, it might be said—after '50s jiving had changed to free-form dancing, alone or with a partner, in the '60s and '70s, and then, in the '80s and '90s, after punk, metal, and grunge had appeared, to what looked like a form of mixed martial arts. In this desperate attempt to get back in touch, the dancers ran around wildly and recklessly in a closed circle—a ring of onlookers standing shoulder-to-shoulder, hemming them in—flailing their arms, pogoing, leaping and thrashing about, pushing and shoving, slamming their bodies against each other. In a word, moshing, all the while, in this frenzied state, practising mosh-pit etiquette.

I had made it to the washroom without incident, but on my way back, as I worked my way through the crush of onlookers, non-moshers, between the pit and the bar, a wet and shirtless young man wearing huge, chequered, belted shorts, elbow pads, knee pads, and a neck brace, came reeling through the circular wall of the mosh pit and tumbled to the floor. He was quickly picked up and thrown back into the fray.

I imagined a mosh-pit marathon of the literary arts: a Mockey Night in Canada sponsored by the CBC (who else?), an offshoot of their book battles, bashes, faceoffs, and slams, an annual catharsis for writers, editors, agents, publishers, distributors, booksellers, critics, academics, prize juries—the works—all thrown into the mosh pit to get back in touch, with a post-lit band called the Remainders, perhaps, in a club called the Slough. Or maybe the Kil would be more appropriate.

As I squeezed through the crowd close to the bar to get some more Molson product for Kevin and me, and another Perrier for Hana, I was surprised to see a row of knitters at the far end of the bar: three women-of-a-certain-age, with long, woolly-looking hair, knitting and purling away—and not sheepishly—each with a bottle of water in front of her. Band-parents like myself, perhaps—*we're with the band*—they looked as if they were sitting comfortably at a kitchen table at home instead of at a bar in the midst of this hurly-burly.

When I returned with the drinks to our perch on the second level, where the sound-and-light man was also situated, I noticed that the band's self-appointed groupie photographer—Celia had pointed him out to me earlier and said that he followed all the bands around—had moved over to our table, a much better vantage point for taking pictures. He had been sitting alone at one of the circular ledge-tables built around posts, but it had an obstructed view of the stage. He had set up his camera on a mini-tripod on our ledge. He had also taken my stool next to Hana, but I was able to find a spare one at one of the other posts, and I dragged it over and placed it next to Kevin's. He introduced me to the photographer, whose name, I think, was Theo. It got sucked into the Sluagh's thunderous sound, even at this distance from the stage. He was at the other end of our four-abreast line at the ledge, and it was impossible to have any kind of sensible conversation, even with the person next to you.

But Kevin was not really interested in conversation; he seemed fixated on a line of young women right below our perch. They were waiting to withdraw cash from the ABM, and as each approached the machine out of the semi-gloom, her face and torso were spotlit by its bright light—a lascivious slide show, or sideshow, for his viewing pleasure, as décolletage seemed to be much in fashion these days. Busty and daringly décolletée, the young woman whose turn came next first removed her bank card from her cleavage and then dropped her cellphone down in its place. Her short-cropped hair was streaked red and green, and she was wearing a black costume—it couldn't really be called a dress—with large multicoloured polka dots. She had no handbag or clutch purse or any other stylish conveyance for keys or makeup or other weigh-me-downs, so perhaps her bank card and cellphone were all she carried, all she needed. Ah, the unbearable lightness and rightness of being young—to the old, at any rate—a night on the town with just the barest of necessities, and not a care in the world. She craned her neck and squinched her eyes as she operated the apparently uncooperative machine. When she finished, she wrapped her money around her bank card and secured it with a plastic band, and, after removing her cellphone from where Kevin rather conspicuously longed to put his rough old sea-dog face, put the card and money back in its place.

When she walked away, I saw that she was wearing high red sneakers and black stockings with holes at the calves. Perhaps it was just this ragged Orphan Annie feature of her dress (though it was probably as deliberate as the ubiquitous jeans with torn knees), or the fact that she could have been my own child, my only child (indeed, she looked like an overgrown, well-endowed child), but, far from feeling sexually excited by this young creature, as Kevin seemed to be, I felt instead a righteous fatherly protectiveness. When a stray beam of light caught what might have been a house key attached to the laces of her sneakers—a trick that Celia had learned from one of her friends after losing her key many times and having to wake us up in the middle of the night—my guardian urge intensified, as if the flash of light from the key had awakened me to the fact that I was sitting next to a sexual predator.

Yeah...and our neutered bobtail cat is a lynx, I thought.

Of course, I knew next to nothing about Kevin's sex life, which he had never talked about, neither bragging of prosperity nor complaining of austerity, but then we had seen each other only off and on for the past thirty years. Grim had once described him as sexless, but had not gone on to explain just what he meant by that, and I didn't really want to ask. Not that he had a complete lack of desire for women, I don't think, or that he was sexually unattractive to them. Perhaps all Grim meant was that the so-called life of the mind—certainly Kevin's primary life—had a way of becoming the only life: an enervating quotidian fever.

I did know that he'd once had a fairly long-term relationship with a woman from Grand Manan, New Brunswick, whose name was Melissa ("Honeybee," he called her), but whether this had been an intimate relationship or not I couldn't say. She was a fellow lecturer who had come down with MS and, eventually, ended up in a wheelchair. She had gone back home to be looked after by her family, who operated an organic dulse operation. I had never met her, but Kevin had mentioned her many times. (On one of his trips to Toronto, by way of Grand Manan, he had arrived with half a suitcase of dulse for my delectation.) No doubt he would have been totally useless in caring for her, for he seemed oblivious or indifferent to the fact that he himself had a body, and an aging one, that needed looking after, and would be all at sea with a badly deteriorating one.

Perhaps a sad case of late libido, I thought—like some melancholic composer's late sonata or quartet, into which he pours all the mellow anguish and regret of a tragic life—as Kevin, from the shadows of our unseen vantage point, stared down into the valley of another innocent display of décolletée.

"There are knitters at the bar," I announced loudly, to distract him.

He turned and looked at me as if this were a Zen koan I had pulled out of my spiritual hat.

"Whereabouts?" he said, after a thoughtful pause.

I raised my arm and pointed to the bar on the right. "Down there," I said, "just before the men's."

He stood up and looked out over the crowd.

"I used to knit," he said. "But only on airplanes, mind you—the only place on earth I can't read. It's good for the anxiety. Then at some point the needles were no longer allowed...I can't see any knitters. Oh yeah, I see them...three of them...always an ominous number. You're not feeling spindly, are you?"

"What?"

"You know, the Three Fates, spinning the thread of our destiny around a spindle. But maybe they're witches, or sirens, or muses."

"So what are you gentlemen discussing?" said a high-pitched but melodious voice above the din, behind Kevin's back. Hana was smiling brightly over his shoulder. The photographer had apparently deserted her, perhaps to go down on the floor near the stage to get some close-ups. He was doing this for nothing, Celia had told me, and not just for the Sluagh but for a slew of other alternative, unknown bands. He taught winds at the music school— his instrument was the oboe—and photography was just an avocation. He posted the photos on his website and invited the bands to use them for PP, as long as every photo was credited to him. Was he hoping that one of these unknown bands playing in some obscure hole-in-the-wall downtown, like the Beatles at the Cavern, would make the Big Time and take him out of his even more obscure classical slough, where the possibility of fame was even more unlikely (though the whole musical universe was tuned to the "A" on the oboe)?

"The Three Fates," said Kevin, turning towards Hana. "James may have spotted them in our midst. I think I'll go down and have a look. Drink, anyone?"

"I'm fine," I said.

"No, thank you," said Hana, smiling at Kevin as he walked away, and then turning and smiling even more broadly at me. She took a sip from her glass of Perrier and lime.

"What does he mean?" she asked.

"Oh, I saw some women knitting at the bar," I said. "He thinks they might be the Three Fates. Just a poet's fancy, no doubt. Not the sort of place you'd expect them."

"Kevin is a poet?" she said.

"Oh yes. He's published quite a few books, though he has to teach for a living."

"I must read his books," she said. "I read much poetry. Do you know Szymborska, a Polish poet?"

"No."

"My favourite poet," she said. "She has written a poem about this problem. 'Poetry Reading' is the title."

She recited a verse, in Polish, then translated it for me.

"'O Muse, where are *our* teeming crowds?/Twelve people in the room, eight seats to spare—/it's time to start this cultural affair.'

"But she is ironic, of course. For the Polish poet, the South American poet, the South African poet, poetry is not just a 'cultural affair,' but a political affair. The poet is more engaged than in the West. She speaks out against the state. A resister, no? There is Milosz, there is Mandelstam—a Russian, but born in Warsaw, one of the disappeared. In another poem, Szymborska says: 'Whether you like it or not,/your genes have a political past,/your skin, a political cast,/your eyes, a political slant.'"

As I looked into Hana's soft, grey-blue eyes, they seemed to be reflecting the political cast of my own skin, and a resistor tacked to a beige cardigan was perhaps a fitting symbol of *my* politics, I thought, a fashion statement of my political past as a pacified pacifist, a socialized socialist, a self-satisfied satirist.

"Kevin himself is a political poet at heart—a resister, an agitator," I said, perhaps feeling the need to offer my long-time friend as a fitting substitute for my own failings, but at the same time not wanting to elaborate on this subject. Indeed, I wanted to stop talking altogether, for we had to shout in order to hear one another.

"I will read his books," she said, as the music stopped, and we both looked toward the stage.

"How is your work going, Hana?" I said, much too loud into the silence.

"Oh, there is much trouble at Mistaken Point," she said. "People are stealing the fossils, cutting them out of the rock with chisels, destroying them. They have to limit access now—guided tours only—or all will be lost."

As I tried to think of something sympathetic to say, on stage all eight band members seemed to be huddling like the offensive side of a football team before the next rush. Hana was looking very distressed.

"Why are they taking them?" I asked.

"These are diamonds, you must understand," she said. "Maybe they will sell them...maybe just for souvenirs. Scientists would not do such a thing. We must protect them at all cost."

The music was starting up again, but not the full-bore blare of the eight-piece band. Celia was playing solo, a soft, slow air on the fiddle, and in the great vacuum of silence after all the noise it was like a sound at the birth of music, an eerie aeolian sound, the wind through the reeds, and then through the strings of the ancient mythical aeolian harp. It was one of the most plaintive tunes I'd ever heard, but as it grew louder I was drawn in by an undertow of muted rapture. Then the drummer began to play along, with a sort of arrhythmical beat, as if he couldn't keep time. It was a funeral march for a defective heart, a broken heart; an uplifting lament, a dirge-like anthem, but not of any particular nation; a love song for the loveless soul, the pilgrim soul, the refugee, the exile, the spiritual diaspora of all nations. To ask whether it was folk music or Western art music or so-called world music, whether it was carol or spiritual or aria, seemed entirely beside the point. What had begun as softly as a murmur was now an intense rapturous moan.

"'I'll Hang My Harp on a Willow Tree,'" said Hana. "A song from your country. Do you know it? Celia has been playing it for me, and it makes me cry."

She was crying, and I had to turn my head away, for my own eyes were filling up as well.

"No, I've never heard it before," I said, as the drum became more insistent and the fiddle louder and the other instruments began to join in, and as I looked toward the stage I saw a body floating above the crowd in the centre of the room, above the mosh pit. No, not floating, but crowd-surfing, defying mosh-pit etiquette, raised upon the hands and arms of the moshers like a martyr on a bier, the bodies and arms of the whole throng swaying as they moved it along. And whose body should it be but Thomas Kevin Keough's, raising and swaying his own arms with a sort of swimming stroke in the air high above the crowd—a resurrected Lazarus, and the music itself like some ancient, resurrected thing, an ur-music, plaintive and joyful at the same time, a hopeful resignation, the musical equivalent of Beckett's *I can't go on. I'll go on.*

Yes, *this music crept by us upon the waters.* It had not only quieted the crowd of onlookers, but soothed the savage mosh-pit beast, whose arms lifted Kevin gently onto the stage when the music ended, and he stood up and embraced my daughter the fiddler to concerted cheers, whoops, and applause, then disappeared down the stage steps into the crowd.

22: ON THE OLD BURMA ROAD

Grandy himself called me on the day before the launch. Charmingly apologetic, he was. He asked if I would "terribly mind" doing a signing he'd arranged at Chapters on Kenmount Road—"the Old Kenmount Road," as he called it. I didn't like the inauspicious sound of that; it might have been a tour of duty, a war assignment on the Old Burma Road he was sending me on—"one in theatre right now on the present tour." As it turned out, my sensitive antennae were right, and not just about the signing but the launch as well.

The signing was from three to five in the afternoon, and the launch was at five at the Southside Press.

"I know it's short notice," Grandy said, "but it's the only time they can fit us in."

Though I did terribly mind, I reluctantly agreed, not wanting to ruffle his feathers at this late date. He was, I reminded myself, reissuing my book, and on his own initiative, not mine. But gratitude for Grandy was hard to summon up. It was not so much the short notice that bothered me, but the fact that big-box signings for me were the PP equivalent of what the DRE was for Kevin.

Grandy seemed surprised at how acquiescent I was, and I guessed that he had some ingratiating strategy at the ready, just in case.

"It's one of the great Newfoundland novels, *The Ropewalk*," he said.

"Arguably," I said, coyly deploying my favourite floater of a word.

"Only time can tell you these things," he added, "but thirty years should be enough."

"Did it make any money?" the ingrate asked. Hard to summon up, as I said, gratitude for Grandy, and even harder to sustain. No royalties, not even royalty statements, ever came my way, if I recall. But it was a long time ago.

"No, my son. It was one of my losers—as bad as poetry," Grandy said.

No doubt he meant the writers as well as the books, I thought.

"But we might get it on the curriculum this time round," he said, "if I can twist a few arms here and there."

"A pilot project, perhaps," I said, recalling Kevin's ordeal, and there was silence at the end of the line.

I waited for a click, but he said, overenthusiastically, it seemed, changing the subject, "There's a fine young fella in there at the bookstore—the manager, Bill Brokenshire, used to work for me in marketing, matter of fact. Just ask for him when you go in. He'll set you up."

Inauspiciousness settled on me again at the sound of that—being set up by a man named Broken-shire.

And set me up he did, along with another "writer" at the same time. An "unfortunate scheduling conflict," I was told, upon entering the big-box shop-shire the next day and asking to see the manager, but I began to suspect that there was more to it than that. This was no mere scheduling conflict, no mere coincidence, but more like synchronicity—and synchronized by the gods, no doubt. *As flies to wanton boys, are we to th' gods;/They kill us for their sport.* Aye, *sport.* My competitor was none other than a former hockey enforcer promot-ing his new book on a national publicity tour, on a tight itinerary, Bill said, and thus he would be given precedence. (And a celebrity as well, I thought, which took precedence over just about everything these days.) I could still stay, of course, he immediately made clear, but I would have to be stationed at the back of the store, and Bobby Clobber would be signing at the main table up front.

Was I to meet in the flesh, then—on the ground, in theatre right now on his present tour—the once safely distant and abstract object of my smugly virtuous attack in the newspaper? Had my turtles come home to nest? Did I know how to turtle? An unlearned, instinctive defense mechanism, I hoped.

During our simultaneous signing session, the celebrity-enforcer's presence in the store was announced over the intercom at regular intervals, along with his penalty-minute totals (I kid you not)—his "body of work," as hockey reporters now refer to such statistics, and with no pun intended. In this case, in over a decade playing in the NHL, our man had set franchise, season, and career records for penalties that would probably never be beaten, considering that a veritable army of *sooks*—even some hockey writers—had been campaigning for years to have fighting banned from the NHL, as concussions had reached critical mass and alcoholism, drug addiction, and suicides were now well-reported phenomena of the enforcer's trade. And for this body of work, the announcer informed us, our man had been given, as a retirement gift, the bench from the penalty box of his team's old arena after a new arena had been built and the old one had been torn down and its seats and benches auctioned off.

My presence was ignored by the PA announcer, and by the customers as well. I had a bit too much time to think—daydream, imagine, *fantasize*. I imagined going down to my competitor's table and confronting my fate head-on, challenging him to a fight as a publicity stunt. A mock-angry sweep of his books off the signing table would certainly incite him, as if an enforcer needed incitement; he had a short fuse, no doubt. I could forewarn him, perhaps, with a little handwritten note: *This is just a joke, now, don't be alarmed—a publicity stunt arranged by the bookstore manager.* But perhaps he wouldn't get the joke, I thought, and I might get something else besides publicity.

Other, safer strategies occurred to me. Where was my Palm Buzzer, my handshake shocker, now that I really needed it? As a kid I'd ordered this so-called novelty item from the back pages of a comic book. (*Have fun at parties!*) It was a battery-powered device which, inconspicuously strapped to the palm of your hand, delivered a shock to anyone who shook hands with you. I would go down to his table and introduce myself. Shaking my hand across the book-laden signing table, he would pull back in alarm, but I would hold on and be dragged across the table, sending books and everything else on it flying. But not having this prop for my theatrics, I could simply collapse dramatically over his signing table with the crush of his introductory handshake. I would end up in his arms, be lifted up by the shoulders, with me grasping the lapels of his jacket. Flash! Photos! Front page! "Local writer fights enforcer."

Another possibility occurred to me. I looked underneath the table I was sitting at, one of those long portable tables rented for dinner parties and wedding receptions, with collapsible legs at each end that could easily, accidentally, be kicked out—*yes*. I had seen it happen at a drunken wedding, sending a whole tableful of dishes, glasses, food, and wine sliding to the floor.

After the first, dismal, solitary hour, under the depressing cloud of these ridiculous ruminations, these clownish, pratfall fantasies, I went over to the Starbucks and bought a coffee. On my way back, I browsed briefly, masochist that I was, through the remaindered fiction in the Discount Books section. And what should catch my eye but a diminutive hardcover copy of *The Humbling* by Philip Roth, himself humbled for years by the Swedish Academy's withholding of the famous prize. An obvious sign, I thought, an appropriate denouement to this sad afternoon, and I should have picked up a copy and left. Instead, I asked a clerk nearby if she could ask the PA announcer to inform the customers that I was waiting patiently for their patronage at the back of the shop. She very apologetically agreed, and within five minutes my name and the name of my book resounded reassuringly in the noisy air, but, alas, it did no good.

So, around four thirty, I got up from my table and slowly made my way down to my competitor's, arriving, coincidentally, just as another announcement for my book was being made. I had expected a lineup at his table, but there was no one there. I stood at one end of it, my feet close to the collapsible legs. My own legs felt weak, eminently collapsible. He was sitting behind the table, reading his book, probably for the first time, I thought; ghostwritten, no doubt, or a *with*-book, written with some sportswriter or other. (A sad irony for us *writers*: we never have the esthetic pleasure of reading our own books. We only have the *pleasure*—I'll let it stand—of writing them.) Then he looked up, turned his head, and cast an ominous gaze toward me. He looked to be about forty, but was still a sandy-haired pretty-boy—brutal, blue-eyed good looks— albeit with a face squared by a savage brush cut and jutting jaw.

"That's me, I'm at the back, James Nightingale," I said, breathlessly, pointing to the ceiling as the announcement ended and extending my hand across the table. He stood and clasped it, with more than enough strength to give me the excuse that I needed, and the necessary impetus, to carry out my pathetic slapstick attack. But the look in those cold blue eyes stopped me cold, an expression that did not fit those fearsome features. It was not an aggressive or guilty look, not the hard look of a cold-blooded fighter, as I had expected, but something much deeper, beyond belligerence or guilt—an innocent fury, an unfathomable hurt, a sorrow and pain that made you turn your prying eyes away. It was the look of a lost and lonely child, which, in the blink of an eye—though of course he didn't blink—turned my insidious, ridiculous *ressentiment* to ash.

"Congratulations," I said feebly, feeling a bit lost and confused myself. "I'll have a copy of your book," I added.

"You bet," he replied. "Already signed."

"Thank you," I said, and made my way back to my lonely post.

I left with no sales whatsoever, but, my emotional tables turned, with something more than 120 big-box penalty minutes to my credit.

I took a taxi to the Southside Press—on the Old Southside Road, where else. For another tour of duty, I was sure.

∾ ᔓ

The walls of the so-called Great Room at the Southside Press did not display the artwork that I had expected, given Kevin's oft-repeated tale of his storied last visit, many years ago, to publisher Alonzo "the Virus" Grandy's office, but a selection of artifacts that Grandy had been collecting all his life. He had invited us, in a brief welcoming address, to admire these treasures as we mingled, met, and conversed, purchased a book or two if we wished, sipped our wine and nibbled our hors d'oeuvres prior to the evening's formalities: the launch of six new Southside Press titles, along with my reissued first novel, *The Ropewalk*, none of which had been listed on the invitation postcard. Expect at least a baker's dozen, and a long, long evening, Kevin had warned me, so I was relieved, if somewhat underjoyed, to see only a baker's half-dozen on the "spring" list. Spring had come and gone, as had the June launch date; it was moved to mid-July, then to mid-August. I was glad I wasn't on the fall list—I'd be here till Christmas.

There was a large crowd, perhaps a hundred or more, among whom were some uninvited guests; namely, Kevin and Grim. Fearing a contretemps, I had invited Kevin to stay away from the launch, but here he was, looking as mischievously aglow and well established as a dandelion. No doubt he had already been drinking before he arrived.

Besides my book there was a cookbook, a bird book, a political memoir of the Smallwood years, a community history, a biography of a curler, and a mystery novel set in St. John's. All the authors—all first-timers except me, I noted, while browsing at the display table—would be introduced by Mr. Grandy himself, his assistant had informed me. Presiding *in propria persona*, as Kevin had put it, exercising his Latin—here in person, especially for me. He usually sent a proxy for fledgling authors, he said, who had to earn the favour of the royal presence. After the introductions, we would say a few words about our books, read a short excerpt, and answer any questions the audience might have. I was to be last, but not least, the climax of the evening, the assistant said, with some of that false Grandy charm.

Though Grandy was drinking from a regular wine glass, the liquid in it was not the colour of the wine, the plonk, the rest of us were drinking, but was of a more golden hue. And he had more than half a glass of it, whatever it was, and was swirling it around inattentively with the bowl of the glass in his palm, as if he were holding a brandy snifter. It was brandy, I guessed. *In propria persona*, indeed, and not without the honourable persona's perks.

About two dozen objects were displayed on the walls: in frames, in glass cases, in slings, or simply hanging from hooks. There were various

Beothuck artifacts, including a birchbark cup and bowl, trident-shaped ornaments, combs, and a soapstone lamp. There was an ancient map of the
New Founde Land; a one-hundred-year-old Newfoundland flag, the Tri-
colour; a devil's purse; an Innu tea doll; a great auk's egg; a Mistaken Point
Ediacaran fossil (didn't Hana tell me it was illegal to collect those?); and, on
the wall above the spot where Grandy was standing right now, sipping his
brandy, a three-foot-long walrus penis bone that looked like a weapon—a
caveman's club, perhaps. When I had first looked at this object—"Baculum
with carved walrus head, finely detailed vibrissae," as the information card
described it—I had a premonition, perhaps because Kevin was standing
right beside me. I remembered Chekhov's playwright's dictum, if I may call
it that, expressed in a letter or in conversation, which had later found its way
into a friend's memoirs: if you mention in Act I, he said, that a weapon is
hanging on the wall—a pistol or rifle in this case, but surely a walrus penis-
bone club would do—you had better make sure that it is used by Act III.
He himself had followed this advice in *Uncle Vanya*, if I recall, but I guess
he forgot to hang an axe on the wall in Act I of *The Cherry Orchard*.

I was now standing next to the man who had written the bird book—I'd
seen him signing a copy for a woman who looked to be in a hurry to get away—
as we both examined the egg of the extinct great auk, *Pinguinus impennis*, "the
northern penguin," quietly and thoughtfully sipping our wine. He looked really familiar: a big man, perhaps six foot six, with a big bushy beard and long
hair, both greying, wearing khakis, a black-and-green chequered shirt, and a
hunter-green vest with lots of pockets and slots for shells.

A large egg with a spintop-like shape, standing on its end in a glass case
against the wall, with markings like obscure geographical features seen from
space, it looked like a doomed planet, shrunken and misshapen after a great
catastrophe—a nuclear war or a collision with an asteroid. Up close, the markings resembled some indecipherable calligraphic script: Chinese or Arabic or
Cyrillic; or van Loon script, my editor's tiny, illegible, handwritten, single-
page critiques of my manuscript submissions, Dr. van Loon's prescriptions for
everything that ailed them.

The great auk egg's warm, golden-ochre earth tones—had it been painted?—made me think of a Grecian urn, though I had never seen one in the flesh, in the clay, only pictures. Of course I had read many times Keats' euphoric "Ode on a Grecian Urn," shards of which came back to me now: "bride of quietness… foster-child of silence and slow time…not a soul to tell why thou art desolate…" And I suppose it was an urn in a way, this abandoned egg, though not with the remains, but with the undeveloped beginnings, of a life inside it.

"Something sad about an egg that never hatched," I said, "especially when the bird itself is gone." The bird man turned and gave this bleeding heart a pitiless look, red in tooth and claw, not attuned to my naive philosophical musings.

"Problem is the pelagics are one-eggers," he said, "like half of *Homo sapiens* these days."

He said this in an all-knowing, though not unpleasant, tone, but one that said, emphatically, *I* am the bird man, *I* am the egg man, and you're not. He seemed to be the epitome of all the scientific types I had ever met—not a lot, mind you, perhaps not even a sample large enough to be statistically, scientifically, significant. They were superficially sociable, but underneath, cold-hearted, amoral, ruthless beings who talked about "doing the science" of this or that as the be-all and end-all of human activity. Nothing you said was ever true or right unless someone somewhere had done the peer-reviewed science to back it up. Perhaps they saw something amoral and ruthless, not to mention irrelevant, about "doing the art." Imagining, inventing, pretending, impersonating, imitating, and performing were subjective misrepresentations of reality, in their view, all in the name of the great god Art. You're just imagining things, my friend. If they could see this as theory, hypothesis, experiment, inquiry—the same process they themselves followed—it was a practice without parameters, rules of procedure, due process. There were no rules, to put it bluntly. But surely this made it the biggest and boldest experiment of all.

"That egg, by the way," he added, "is one of only seventy-five in existence. Alonzo won't tell me where he got it. Found it in an old fisherman's house he bought around the bay, he says. Auk-feather mattresses on the beds, down-filled pillows."

"You must be the author of the bird book," I said.

"Yes...and you're...?"

"James Nightingale," I said, offering my hand.

"Yes...I think I've heard the name."

"Novels," I said. "*The Ropewalk.*"

"Right...Jack Doody," he said, still holding on to my hand, but with a surprisingly feathery grip for a big man.

"Howdy, Doody," said my ludic elf to myself. Then I remembered where and when I had seen him before—just last week in the cafeteria at the Veterans' Pavilion, when I'd been having supper with my father. He'd been sitting at the same table, wearing the same quasi-hunter outfit he had on now, talking rather loudly to a man I assumed to be his father, who may have been hard of hearing. It was a long table, and though we'd exchanged glances a few times, we hadn't spoken, and he obviously didn't remember me.

"Did I see you at the Veterans' Pavilion last week?" I asked him.

He looked surprised. "My father's a resident there," he said.

"Mine, too," I said. "I think we all ate at the same table one evening. Perhaps they know each other."

He nodded his head, but didn't seem to want to pursue the matter.

"Is your book for birdwatchers?" I asked him.

"No no no," he said, laughing. "You never see most of the birds I'm interested in. Strictly seabirds, and my main interest is the pelagics—petrels, puffins, shearwaters, kittiwakes, dovekies—birds that never come ashore except to breed. They spend most of their lives upon the water, and some of them live to be thirty or forty years old."

"Are you at the university?" I asked.

"No, not any more." He paused. A wry smile seemed to be lurking in his beard. "You don't want to know what I do for a living," he said. "You writers tend to be sensitive types." He paused again, and his expression darkened. "I shoot birds," he said. "Wildlife control out at the airport. They can bring down a plane easily enough. It's already happened in other places. I used to rescue them in my former life, from oil spills and the like. I got called on to do a lot of that, and in a way I'm still doing it, but on a bigger scale—a preemptive rescue, you might say, of whole populations. I was investigating the oil-drilling venture as a research project, what might happen if there's a blowout offshore, and things got a bit hot for me at the university. I'm still doing it, but freelance now, you could say."

"You think there'll be a big spill out there?"

"Without a doubt. It *will* happen. It's a sure bet with the sea conditions out there, the depth of those wells, and they're drilling deeper, farther out. There's no plan in place to deal with a blowout. It's so far offshore they think the oil will never reach land—that's the plan. That's all they think people are worried about—the oil reaching the coast—and maybe they're right. They don't give a damn about the birds—the largest populations of seabirds anywhere."

"And what about the cod?" I asked.

"The cod, too, of course—goes without saying. What's left of them. That's all that tiny biomass needs—the final blow. When I began to post this information on my website, things got a little hot, as I said, and I was asked to stop or put a disclaimer on there. I think, therefore I must be censored. Academic freedom, it's called. Research funding from oil companies is big business these days, and research itself is the university's top priority. It brings in the money."

"They fired you?"

"No, I resigned in protest. But they probably would have. I didn't have tenure. It's scarcer than cod at the universities these days. It gives you the freedom to say what you want. Besides us, only judges and senators have it. But I don't need the university. I'm renowned in academic circles, as they say. I can get a job anywhere in the country.

"They'd love to have me in Alberta," he snorted. "But I want to stay here, where the birds are. I have kids here, too. No wife now, but two marriages and three kids. All in university themselves, and costing me a fortune. So I need a job."

"You must feel strange, though," I said, "an advocate, a protector, killing birds for a living." I hadn't meant it to sound judgmental, but I guess it was.

"I'm not an advocate, I'm a scientist," he said firmly. "I just gather the facts, the evidence, and report it. I don't tell people what to do with it. It's mainly scavengers I'm killing out there, anyway—gulls and crows. You may see a few ducks and geese, a scattered owl or hawk, the odd migrant blown off course, a few flocks of starlings. The problem is that the airport is right between the dump at Redcliff and Windsor Lake, the town's water supply, a big body of water way inland that's like a Black Sea resort for birds and…"

I was staring at the strange markings on the unhatched great auk egg and listening to Jack Doody trying to publicly reconcile his two lives when I began to feel a distancing anxiety and was no longer listening very closely. His voice was echoing inside my head in the impersonal, voice-over style of one of those television wildlife show narrators, and I imagined him driving around the airport perimeter back roads in his pickup with a shotgun—would he use a shotgun?—on the seat beside him, or perhaps right on his lap—a sawed-off shotgun?—stopping every now and then to peer out his side window through his binoculars into a patch of greenery or the branches of a tree where a hoot owl was dozing on a lazy summer afternoon, a deranged modern-day St. Francis with the clear conscience of a madman on an overriding mission. He picked up the gun and pointed it out the window…but then, instead of a shotgun blast, I heard the piercing sound of microphone feedback. What Grandy's assistant had called "the formalities" must be starting up, I thought. Then I heard a voice above the natter of the crowd, and it wasn't Grandy's, but Kevin's. Eyes blazing, body in spastic motion from having drunk at least a bottle of plonk, no doubt, and God knows how much before he came, he had seized the microphone, seized the spotlight, before Grandy had laid down his brandy and deigned to address us. Kevin announced that he was going to read a few poems.

"'Dead Doberman,' dedicated to my favourite publisher," he said ominously. He read it in a muted histrionic voice.

> Black snout quivering between the palings;
> red eyes watching me root in the soil;

his body a steel trap.
I warn him with a handful of worms;
his last day on earth; it is raining…

It was clear that the assembled guests, unaware of the history, as they say, between Kevin and Alonzo "the Virus" Grandy, didn't quite know what to make of all this, and what an appropriate response should be. But there was a hesitant clapping, even a whoop or two, as Kevin shuffled a few pages he was holding above the podium, during which Grandy made his way to the front, stood close beside Kevin, and switched off the microphone. There was an expectant hush, an undertone of nervous talk; Grandy whispered in Kevin's ear as he kept shuffling his pages. Then Kevin abruptly vacated the stage, and Grandy turned on the microphone again.

"My favourite Newfoundland poet, ladies and gentlemen, Mr. Kevin Keough," the despised, dispatched Doberman, the inadvertent onlie begetter, lied, if not as cleverly and elaborately as Kevin, to loud applause and more whooping.

"Let me continue with the festivities this evening, ladies and gentlemen, by introducing our first author, and a first-time author, Dr. Jack Doody, whose book will no doubt become a classic of ornithology for the layman, a classic of natural history like Harold Horwood's *Foxes of Beachy Cove*, like Franklin Russell's *Secret Islands*," said Alonzo Grandy, and went on and on in this vein, though never mentioning the name of this landmark new book, till Doody himself was at the microphone introducing *Seabirds of Newfoundland*, and making a plea for said seabirds, whose lives were in peril from the reckless pursuit of offshore oil, well documented in this book, he said.

He read a moving passage in a deep sombre voice—he could do the art as well as the science—about the solitary lives of the kittiwake, the sooty shearwater, and the dovekie, the smallest of all seabirds. "How adorable," said a woman beside me, beside herself with love for the dovekie, whose picture was on the cover of Doody's book. Except for the cover, the book had no pictures; he wanted us to imagine the birds and their lives, he said, though he had included detailed descriptions—the dovekie's, the only one I'd read, was surprisingly anthropomorphic—based on numerous sightings, photos, and sound recordings. They lived their lives miles from shore, he said, and who could blame them. The great auk, Newfoundland's member of that most iconic trio of extinct birds that included the dodo and the passenger pigeon, had only ventured to land for a mere two weeks of the year to breed, and look at the end result of that.

"That's all we have left," he said, pointing to the egg in the glass case by the wall.

What I had read as heartlessness was dissipating by the minute, turning into its very opposite, in fact: sentimentality. A good storyteller, old Jack; his voice had an enchanting quality. He told us about a blind colleague of his, also an ornithologist, though more well known as a sound recordist, whose first-hand knowledge of birds had been acquired almost entirely through sound. He had used his recordings of seabird songs—or cries and calls, as Jack referred to them—to "compose" the world's first "birdsong symphony." "A Seabird Symphony" was a computerized pastiche of themes from the choral movement, the popular "Ode to Joy," of Beethoven's Ninth Symphony and the sounds of seabirds. It had premiered at the St. John's Sound Symposium in 2000 to usher in the new millennium, enlarging Beethoven's "all men shall be brothers" theme to "all creatures shall be sisters and brothers."

This man, he said, had spent almost as much time upon the water as the seabirds whose voices he had recorded, but though his friend had never seen a bird in his life—landbird or seabird—Jack Doody felt that he knew more about birds than any person he'd ever known.

"What are we to make of this?" he wondered aloud. I think we were all wondering, too. He left a pause long enough after the question for me to conclude that this was more parable than story, for one thing—the Parable of the Blind Birdwatcher, if I were to give it a title—and that some moral was meant to be drawn, perhaps something about that problematic pair, seeing and believing. We reflected like a pious congregation and awaited his answer, but the question was all he had a chance to propose.

The congregation began to part like two halves of this Red Sea of reflection, as Kevin made his way to the front of the room like a parliamentary sergeant-at-arms or an Usher of the Black Rod. He was not holding the ceremonial mace, however, but the three-foot-long walrus penis bone that had been on display at the back of the room, and not carrying it on his shoulder but brandishing it straight out in front of him like the practical weapon the mace used to be. Behind the royal bodyguard was Grim McGillvray, in royal regalia from his *Shakespeare in Carbonear* show, but wearing a Republic of Newfoundland T-shirt underneath. They proceeded to the platform, Jack Doody graciously conceded the microphone to McGillvray, and without any introduction he intoned:

> *...this scept'red isle...*
> *This happy breed of men, this little world,*
> *This precious stone set in the silver sea...*
> *This blessed plot, this earth, this realm...*
> *This land of such dear souls, this dear dear land...*
> *Is now leas'd out—I die pronouncing it...*
> *...is now bound in with shame,*
> *With inky blots and rotten parchment bonds...*

He stopped and covered his face with his hands. He shook his head. He abruptly removed his hands from his face to reveal eyes wide with alarm, then described a prophetic, apocalyptic vision of death and destruction, and not just of waterfowl and fish, but of the inhabitants, the happy breed, the dear souls of the scept'red isle itself, the whole fishing, fowling, seafaring, jigging, trawling, sealing, and now oil-drilling *race*, as we like to call ourselves, whose blind accumulation of oil wealth—black gold—was nothing less than a pact with the Devil, and would mean the end of us all:

> *O, I have pass'd a miserable night,*
> *So full of fearful dreams, of ugly sights...*

O Lord! Methought what pain it was to drown:
What dreadful noise of waters in my ears;
What sights of ugly death within my eyes!
Methoughts I saw a thousand fearful wrecks;
Ten thousand men that fishes gnaw'd upon;
Wedges of gold, great anchors, heaps of pearl,
Inestimable stones, unvalu'd jewels,
All scatter'd in the bottom of the sea.
Some lay in dead men's skulls, and in the holes
Where eyes did once inhabit, there were crept—
As 'twere in scorn of eyes—reflecting gems,
That woo'd the slimy bottom of the deep,
And mock'd the dead bones that lay scatter'd by.

Yes, Shakespeare had everything, as Grim had said to me on more than one occasion, even a prophecy of doom for this dear, dear land. At least, that's what I read into it. I wondered now if it was Kevin or Jack Doody who had put him up to it. Or perhaps it was Grim's own idea, after listening to Jack speak and realizing he had the right words at hand for the occasion.

When Grim stepped away from the microphone, Kevin took his place, the walrus penis bone-mace now resting peaceably on his shoulder. He began to read a poem, but quickly stepped sideways when he noticed Grandy coming toward him, and he brandished the baculum in Grandy's face, preventing him from ascending the platform.

"Hats off, stranger," Kevin shouted, and when Grandy made a grab for the penis bone, he pulled it away. "Hands off, stranger," he said threateningly, and poked Grandy's chest with the weapon, pushing him back. Grandy grabbed at it again, got a good hold of the carved walrus head this time, and tried to pull Kevin from the platform, but again Kevin managed to pull it out of his grasp. Grandy turned and walked back through the crowd toward his office.

I moved forward and stood next to Kevin and Grim.

"He won't call the cops," Kevin said to us. "Half this stuff on the walls has been stolen, or illegally bought."

The lights went out, followed by a great intake of breath in the Great Room, then silence. There were no emergency lights, but the room had three big bay windows, almost from floor to ceiling, and as it was still light outside, after a few minutes everyone began talking and drinking and eating once again, not caring in the least, it seemed, if the official ceremonies resumed or not. What Grandy had once said about book fairs could also be said about book launches, it seemed: no one goes there for the books. The books are the last thing on people's minds.

But it was dim enough in the Great Room for Grandy to creep around from his office at the back, and he appeared out of nowhere behind Kevin and very quickly had his arms around him in a sort of Heimlich manoeuvre-cum-bear hug embrace, lifting him off his feet. Kevin was still gripping the walrus penis bone, using it like a staff or ski pole to keep his balance, as Grandy kept lifting him and dropping him, both of them uttering swashbuckling, scato-logical grunts and groans, threats and curses. Kevin managed to jump down off the platform, which was only about eight inches high, in an effort to loosen Grandy's grip, but he held on, though his face was swollen and red, his head perched on Kevin's shoulder like a lit pumpkin. Then they fell back onto the platform with a loud thump. Kevin was lying on top of Grandy and still hold-ing on to his staff, but Grandy's hands had released their grip and his arms had fallen back, cruciform-like, against the wood.

Kevin got up off Grandy's lifeless body and looked down at his face. His eyes were closed. It looked as if he had been knocked out. More people gath-ered around and looked down at him.

"Jesus," Jack Doody exclaimed, and bent down and took his pulse. "He's still alive," he said, standing up. "Call an ambulance," he shouted over our heads toward the back.

Kevin tugged at the arm of my jacket. "Come on," he whispered, and against my better judgment I followed him and McGillvray out the door. We got into Kevin's car—he threw the penis bone across my lap in the back seat—and he drove to a Ye Olde English Pub that had more artifacts on the walls, albeit more hokey, cutesy, and kitschy ones, than Grandy's Great Room. We sat at the back, and Kevin stood the penis bone on a shelf in the corner behind a tall harlequin-figurine lamp. A waitress came by and we ordered three pints of the pub's own "handcrafted" stout.

Before we could even get on to the subject, Kevin directed the conversation away from the unfortunate scene we had just left behind to a discussion of the walrus's sexual apparatus.

"Who would have thought the walrus would have evolved way beyond us," he said. "And perhaps seals, sea lions, hippopotami, whales...perhaps the whole lot of them...some land mammals, too."

"It is a land mammal, isn't it?" said McGillvray. "I always thought it had a rather superior look on its hairy old face. Look at that moustache... and those tusks," he added, as if there was one to observe right at the very next table.

"Always at the ready," Kevin said, with a wry grin. "And here we are still relying on *hydraulics*. Make no wonder high blood pressure is so common in men. But it can't always be sloshing around with a rigid three-foot rod projecting from its body, can it? I mean, that's kind of awkward and uncomfortable, and a bit of a handicap in the wild."

"I'd say it's probably tucked away in some body cavity," I said, " and not brought out till it's needed, in the breeding season."

"Maybe with gear like that they breed all year round," McGillvray surmised.

"Viagra...*virga*," said Kevin, his eyebrows erect with a sudden illumination "The word *virga* means 'rod,'" added the Latin scholar. "The clever bastards!"

McGillvray let out a laugh. "Anyway...," he said, raising his pint for a toast, "long may his big jib draw," and, having exhausted our wild speculations on the sex life of the walrus and other wildlife, we three mateless, soft-membered mammals, biologic ignorami, heartless artistes, toasted the walrus and forgot completely about poor old Grandy, who may have been lying on his back in an emergency ward, may have been taken immediately into the operating room to remove a blood clot on his brain, may have died, for Chrissake, may have been launched into oblivion, or up into the Great Room of the afterlife, even before we had shamefully snuck out the door.

23: ON BLUEBERRY HILL

It was early September—the worm had left the partridgeberry, according to the old man—and we were off to the berry grounds, to his favourite partridgeberry patch, high up on a barren hill that he called "the Bluff," a topographical term he must have picked up from the hundreds of Westerns he'd read in his seventy years and some. (He had always refused to tell us what his real age was.)

I had always thought that this fruitworm, like the snake in the Garden, was a myth, an old wives' tale, a piece of folklore; but in an old field guide, *Edible Fruit of the Island of Newfoundland*, in the closet-like library of the Veterans' Pavilion, whose tiny collection I had browse-read my way through over the summer, there was a picture of this minute larva and the moth *Grapholita libertina*. It looked and sounded like something noted butterfly stalker Nabokov might have gone after with his net; indeed, even something that might have inspired a certain book.

Though the partridgeberry was my father's favourite wild berry, this was the heart of the blueberry season, and blueberries were my favourite. No worries about worms, for one thing. Who could depend on a worm to emerge when an old field guide, or even a veteran berrypicker like my father, said it would? And blueberries were sweet enough to eat on the spot, didn't require cooking up with lashings of sugar, as partridgeberries did, though the old man claimed they tasted sweet.

He disliked the partridgeberry's twin cousins, the worm-free cranberry and marshberry. These were picked later in the fall, preferably after a frost, which sweetened them, and when boiled up for jam were indistinguishable from partridgeberries, as far as I was concerned. But the old man, with his more experienced, more sensitive palate, vehemently disagreed with that. In his younger years, he had always picked enough partridgeberries to last through the winter, storing them in the old-fashioned way: in barrels of rainwater in the basement, instead of in a freezer.

He had refused to buy a freezer—and a dishwasher, a clothes dryer, a microwave, a vacuum cleaner. Except for the floor-model TV, fridge, stove (a coal- and wood-burning dinosaur), and wringer-washer (a light-year leap forward from the scrub-board), our domestic environs had been a technological vacuum. What's wrong with the stove, the kitchen sink, the clothesline, the broom, the scrub-board? he had often asked. None of us, however, Mother included, were ever brave enough to point out that he himself never used any of them: never washed the dishes or swept the floor, never rubbed his knuckles raw on a corrugated-glass scrub-board, never slaved over a hot stove in summer, or, worst of all, never stood on top of a slippery iceberg of a snowbank and hung heavy wet sheets on a clothesline in winter—and at the end of the day removed board-hard frozen ones. He had pretended to barely tolerate the television, sitting in front of it with the rest of us, but always with a paperback Western up to his face to make his point, over the top of which he kept an eye on the activities of Ralph Cramdom, Joe Friday, and Matt Dillon.

∾

But before we set off for the berry grounds in the four-wheel-drive Jeep I'd rented once again, before taking him out on what I thought might be our last outing together—I was returning to Toronto the following week—I had to meet with Dr. Payne, the psychologist, and the new social worker for an update on my father's condition. Apparently, he had been acting up; he was refusing to participate in some newly organized therapeutic social activities.

When I arrived for the meeting around ten o'clock, the old man was sitting on a chair outside Dr. Payne's office reading a book, and he nodded at me very solemnly as I approached.

"Are you coming in?" I asked him.

"No. You talk to them," he said.

"Why are you sitting here?" I asked.

"I'm reading," he said. He raised a thick paperback out of his lap to show me the cover: Larry McMurtry's *Lonesome Dove*, which I had mentioned to him in the spring. He looked like a pale grey lonesome dove himself, seemed to have visibly aged since I had last seen him, less than two weeks ago.

"Do you like it?" I asked.

"I'll tell you when I'm done."

"What's this about the Book Club?" I said. "They say you won't take part. But you love books."

"Not kindergarten books," he said.

"What do you mean?"

"I don't read kindergarten books," he said vehemently, standing up, and then strode off down the hallway.

I opened the door to Dr. Payne's office, spoke to his receptionist, and was asked to take a seat.

Agitation, Anxiety, Aggression and, finally, Apathy, the biggest problem of all, Dr. Payne had informed me, outlining his patients' aberrant behaviours, the classic dementia "A-list," as he called it, at our first meeting, in May, not long after I arrived. It occurred to me now that I was feeling all of these things myself, a raw aggregate of emotions that I hoped was more *cementia* than dementia.

After introducing me to the new social worker, a Mrs. Foster, he went through the A-list again today, focusing mainly on Apathy. To overcome the dreaded Apathy, he said, they tried to create a meaningful physical environment, chock-full of patients' mementos, cues to memory and identity, connections to their "former lives," and meaningful activities like the Book Club, instead of the ubiquitous TV watching. This amounted to about fifty hours a week in personal care homes, he said, double what it was in the general population, though they slept through a lot of it and so could not sleep at night, leading to even more Agitation, Anxiety, Aggression, and Apathy. Especially Apathy.

"But 'the Interpreter' continues to work," said Dr. Payne. "There is a consciousness still interacting with its surroundings, and it needs meaningful objects and activities, like the Book Club."

And though Apathy didn't seem to be a problem for my father, Dr. Payne admitted, he had exhibited outright Aggression toward the other Book Club participants.

"What kinds of books are used in the Book Club?" I asked. "Maybe they're not all that meaningful for *him*. He's an avid reader. He calls it the Kindergarten Book Club."

"Well, they're group-appropriate stories," said Dr. Payne, " about ten pages, in large type."

I tried not to laugh. "Well, there's the problem right there," I said. "That's not a book—it's hardly a short story. He probably feels insulted by that, with the large type and all. He's reading an eight-hundred-page novel right now."

Mrs. Foster spoke for the first time since she'd been introduced, and just as she did, as if on cue, as if making a contrary gesture, I heard the old man begin to whistle—it was unmistakable, I had heard it often—"Tumbling Tumbleweeds" by the Sons of the Pioneers. He used to have a poster of them in his workshop, on which the name "Len Slye" had been crossed out and "Roy Rogers" written in. I wasn't sure if Len had adopted a stage name later on, or if Roy had been using a pseudonym earlier.

"We'll make him the leader," said Mrs. Foster. "He can help the others. He tells them amusing stories. They think he's very funny."

Mrs. Foster herself seemed to speak in a fixed kindergarten tone and rhythm.

"He can be very warm," she continued. "He hugged me when I visited him."

"He probably thought you were my mother," I said, and she smiled patronizingly.

"They need adventures," said Dr. Payne, "in spite of their handicaps. Adventures are important. Even leading the group discussion can be an adventure."

I was surprised to hear the word "handicaps." Even the old and frail and demented were said to have only "issues" and "challenges" these days.

The old man had moved on to "Cool, Clear Water." *Keep a-movin', Dan, don't ya listen to him, Dan, he's a devil of a man...*

"I'm taking him berrypicking today," I said, proudly.

"That's good," said Dr. Payne. "But remember, they're prone to wander, and out there in the wilds there are no familiar signposts, which can be a problem, so be sure to keep a close eye on him."

"It's not really wilderness, where we're going," I said. "We won't be far from the main road, I don't think."

"Talk to him about the Book Club," said Mrs. Foster, and I pursed my lips and nodded.

There was a pause in the conversation, during which I expected to hear the old man whistle something like "The Wayward Wind"—a *restless wind, that yearns to wander*—one of his Whistler's Top Ten, though I wasn't sure if that was a Sons of the Pioneers tune or not. But there was only silence, and as it appeared that our discussion was over, I stood up.

"Thank you both very much," I said. "I'm going back to Toronto next week. I may not be down for a while, but my sister and my daughter will be in to see him when they can."

"He's in good hands here," said Dr. Payne. "You don't have to worry."

He remained seated, but Mrs. Foster stood up and was now smiling very motherly at me. I resisted an inappropriate urge to give her a hug.

"Thank you for coming in," she said, still smiling warmly.

"Thank you," I said. We shook hands. I turned and shook hands with Dr. Payne, who managed to raise himself a few inches out of his chair.

∽ ∾

I found my father in the cafeteria having a cup of tea and staring off into space. He was already dressed to go, in multiple layers of clothes: a blue nylon parka, a red hunter's vest inside that, though he had never hunted, and beneath that an old grey fisherman's knit sweater that Mother had made him. He was probably wearing his long johns underneath all that.

"Aren't you hot in all that clothes?" I asked. "It's boiling hot in here."

"We're goin' out, aren't we?" he said.

"It's eleven thirty now," I said, looking at my watch. "Do you want to have some lunch before we go? What time do they serve lunch in here?"

"Time?" he said blankly, as if this were some exotic mineral he'd never heard of. "Lunchtime…noon…high noon," he added.

"We may as well wait, then. Why don't you take off your coat."

"Naaw, I'm all right," he said, and picked up his teacup.

I noticed what looked like white handkerchiefs hanging out of his coat pockets. He had always used handkerchiefs instead of tissues.

"You're losing your handkerchiefs," I said, pointing at his parka.

He pulled his coat forward with one hand and pushed the white cloth inside the pocket with the other; then he did the same on the other side.

"Pillowcases," he whispered, with his hands around his mouth. "There's bound to be lots of berries this year."

"How do you know?" I said, choosing the more neutral question, ignoring his rifling the institution's linen closet. Pillowcases and flour sacks had been used in the old days for berrypicking, plastic containers not being as commonplace as they are today.

"Now, look," he said, ignoring the question. "What were they sayin' about me in there? I don't like that woman Foster. She's been pokin' around in my room. She's lookin' for my keys."

"What keys?" I asked.

"My car keys, b'y…for the Dodge," he said. "How do you think I get back and forth? She don't want me drivin'."

What point in pointing out that there were no keys, no car, and no licence to drive even if there were one? No point, I thought.

"We'll take my car today," I said. "I rented a four-wheel drive. You said we'd be going on some rough roads."

He frowned slightly, but before he could say anything I said, "So what way are we heading?"

"Toward Cape St. Francis," he said. "There's a road turns off left at the top of a hill, about a mile from the Cape. I don't know the name of it, but I know where it is. It leads right in to the foot of the Bluff, and we'll climb up from there. Don't you remember me taking you and Sheila over there when you were a boy? You tripped up comin' back down the hill and lost a whole bucket of berries in the bushes. Broke your mother's heart."

"You got a good memory," I said to him, as I thought to myself, Now if you could only remember what you did this morning—if you took your pills, ate your breakfast, had a bowel movement, a bath.

"I can even remember what you were wearing," he added, as if taunting me. "A red wool sweater your mother knit you, and a pair of breeks. I yelled at you and you started bawlin'. You were still holdin' on to your empty bucket. Then you threw it in the bushes and ran on ahead of us down the hill."

"How old was I?" I asked, as if testing him.

"Eight or nine, I guess. Sure, you must have come with us more than once."

"No memory of it at all," I said, "but I do remember those breeks I had to wear to school, with the leather patches on the knees and the laces at the bottom. Some other boys had them, too. Like riding breeches, they were. We were dressed up like little Royals, but without the riding crops and ponies."

He was gazing off into space again. I laid my hand on his arm.

"Listen, Dad, I have to go to the bathroom," I said. "I'll be right back."

There was veterans' graffiti in the bathroom. *Work Family Fatherland Crap Vichy Nazi Shit*, it said, a cascade of angry black words from the top of the cubicle wall right down to the toilet paper roll. A disillusioned veteran of the French campaign, I thought.

When I got back to the cafeteria, the old man was dozing in his seat, and I let him doze till a bell sounded for lunch.

∾∽

He had no trouble finding the gravel road that led to the berry grounds—
Keatings Road, with no apostrophe, of course. *Be gone, satanic Mark, offspring of Hell first-born,* I apostrophized to myself, but the old man heard me
and gave me a worried look. About two kilometres down Keatings Road, a
narrow, tortuous, deeply potholed track, named after a local family, most
likely, we came to a sign that actually said BERRY GROUNDS, but the old
man gave it a dismissive flick of his hand when I stopped and asked, naively,
"Right here?"

"No no no," he replied derisively, as if this were so obvious a trick only
someone who had never picked a berry in his life would fall for it. "I suppose
you think they got stones, too," he added.

"What?"

"Berries, b'y."

I didn't reply to that.

The road got rougher—torturous, in fact—but I ventured on, over boulder humps and down into deep, water-filled potholes and sharp-angled mini-
crevasses for another two kilometres or more before we reached the foot of the
Bluff, the top of which looked very high and far away. To my great surprise,
there was a parking space on the right side of the road.

And it was a very gradual climb up the hill, on good hard ground. With
two light, empty salt-beef buckets each, and no trees or thick brush to fight
our way through, just low bushes and tuckamores and scattered glacial debris
on both sides of a clear path, the walking was easy enough. About halfway up
the hill, the old man spotted his first patch of partridgeberries; such a deep
dark red, this berry, and so close to the ground. He dropped his buckets and
actually got down on his knees, as if to worship; but, to his great dismay, when
he cracked open a partridgeberry between his thumb and forefinger, he found
that the fruitworm was still in there.

"Goddamn," he exclaimed, but in a whisper. "They said we had frost," he
added. "That should've drove 'em out." He squeezed another and another, with
the same result, flinging berries and worms back over his shoulder each time.

Chuck Berrys, said the Punster.

"Can I see one?" I asked, eager to see the offspring of *Grapholita libertina*.

"It's just a goddamn worm," he said, but he proceeded to produce one for me anyway. He sat on top of a downturned berry bucket, reached down beside it to pick a few more partridgeberries, selected a choice one, and discarded the rest. He held the squashed red berry up to my face. Writhing on top of it was a naked and near microscopic white worm.

"Ahh, what odds," he said, chucking it back over his shoulder as he'd done with all the rest. "There'll be lots of blueberries."

We came across what seemed like a plethora of blueberries right beside the path, in fact, near the top of the hill; but despite my frequent appeals to stop and pick, he just kept right on walking, dismissing them with the same contemptuous wave of the hand with which he'd dismissed the BERRY GROUNDS sign. His energy and stamina were amazing—I could hardly keep up with him. He had removed his nylon parka and stuffed it in one of his berry buckets.

"Wait'll you see what's on the other side of this hill," he said.

It was cool and breezy at the top, but the sun was bright and strong, still high in the sky at three thirty. The view was spectacular, in all directions, though the old man was only looking at the ground. To the northeast was a broad expanse of blue ocean; in the opposite direction, the shadows of clouds were moving across a dark, undulating evergreen sea. And from where we stood, all the way down to the treeline, covering the entire southwestern slope of the hill, more blueberry bushes than I had ever seen, and so laden with berries that even from where I stood I could see small inviting blazes of blue in the bright sun. There were a few other berrypickers scattered about, indicating where, exactly, the really good patches might be, but I knew even from my limited berrypicking experience that it was bad form to go anywhere near another berrypicker's patch.

"Okay, let's get at it," the old man ordered, and immediately set off down the hill.

"Do you want your water?" I shouted after him, but he gave me his patented dismissive wave of the hand.

I was glad that he was so active, so mobile, had so much energy and enthusiasm at his age (whatever it was), but it worried me nonetheless. Dr. Payne's warning, *prone to wander*, was always in the back of my mind, and I was glad that the old man was wearing a red hunter's vest as I watched him zigzag through the rocks and brush and berry bushes toward what was perhaps his very special patch of unsigned berry grounds, the memory of it filed away in one of those "havens of memory" that Dr. Payne went on about, in an uncorroded circuit of his deteriorating brain.

I removed my knapsack and took out one of the two bottles of water I'd bought at a convenience store en route, along with a couple of Mars bars, his favourite, two apples, and two bags of peanuts. If for some reason we got stuck out here, I thought—always this urbanite's pathetic fear, even in a big urban wilderness like Toronto's High Park—at least we'd have something to eat and drink. And perhaps we should have taken a tent. The sightlines were comforting, though. Behind me, far below, I could pick out the gravel road winding through the woods and ending at a small pond. There were cabins in there, perhaps, but no rooftops or chimney smoke was visible. We could even walk in there, or out to the main road, if it came to that, if we cracked an axle or ripped open the gas tank on a rock.

I sat down on a rock and had a drink of water. The old man was already about halfway down the hill, bent over in his usual berrypicking posture: knees slightly bent, bucket between his legs, one arm on a knee and the other one picking, frequently switching arms and knees. Just a half hour of this, though, I found to be awfully hard on the back, and I preferred to crouch or kneel down while picking. Sometimes I lay down and started eating. As a youngster, I used to eat at least half of what I picked, which had sometimes resulted in a bit of unfatherly, i.e., threatening, advice. "Stop stuffin' your gob before I go over to you" comes to mind. If I were out of his line of sight, though, I would lie down in the berry bushes in the sun and stop picking altogether, a pleasure-seeking sultan on his divan, dropping plump sweet blueberries into my mouth from my half-filled bucket as I looked up at the clouds drifting by.

In belated defiance, I grabbed a handful of blueberries from a bush right beside me. They were large and sweet, and when I had eaten those I picked and ate some more, feeling not only adolescently defiant and utterly disinclined to get down to the hard berrypicking work that I knew the old man expected of me, but adultly indifferent to the rout of free radicals by the crack team of antioxidants that blueberries were said to contain. Instead, I let myself take in the mind-clearing distances, the restful vistas of blue and green, the mindless drift of clouds.

Having crawled out of the murky depths long, long ago, and having watched other creatures take to the air, I guess there is something—not déjà vu exactly but palimpsestic perhaps—about *height, altitude, elevation* that frees all care. Terrestrial height, at least, height with my feet still on the ground, without the anxiety that comes with being trapped in a flying sardine can for several hours, marinating in sweat with a hundred other canned creatures, worrying about turbulence and bombs and metal fatigue and air traffic controllers dozing at our destination. Not to mention startling observations in mid-flight: *Is that duct tape on the wing?* Not to mention the dangers we may never consider: those unfortunate, high-flying creatures of the air, for example, that sometimes get sucked into the big metal bird's maw. But it was Jack Doody's duty to see that this didn't happen; in short, it was his job to shoot them, as he had informed me at the book launch last month, with an odd mixture of shamefacedness and nonchalance.

About a week after the launch, Jack had taken his father out of the Veterans' Pavilion to spend a day with him on the job, as he had done several times before, and, on this occasion, he very kindly took my father along with them. He'd had such a good time, he told me—a meaningful adventure, as Dr. Payne would have it—that he couldn't wait to go out again. Little did I know when he told me this, that his second airport adventure would occur a lot sooner than he thought, and under rather traumatic circumstances for all concerned. The prelude to this misadventure was to begin right here, in fact, this very afternoon, on the Bluff, on the sublime but vertiginous heights, on the bountiful slopes of a mini-mountain that I would always think of as Blueberry Hill.

24: BERRYPICKERS' VERTIGO

Ironically, even the trustee, the caretaker, the responsible son, in charge of a father whose memory was failing, cannot remember exactly and entirely what happened on Blueberry Hill that distressing afternoon and evening. To partially account for the event, I had even proposed to Dr. Payne (and not entirely in jest), with whom I discussed the ordeal at some length, a new entry, or sub-entry—Berrypickers' Vertigo—in his professional bible, the *Diagnostic and Statistical Manual of Mental Disorders*, always close at hand on his desk, but he was less than receptive to the idea.

Now, as I've made clear, I am not an inveterate berrypicker like the old man, but I've had enough experience at it to know that there is a sort of trance or mesmerizing effect, an in-the-zone fixation, that takes over even after an hour or so of intense berrypicking. It can result in dizziness, disorientation, loss of balance and direction, and, if you happen to be out on some barren, rocky headland with steep ocean cliffs, where berries are often to be found, especially partridgeberries and cranberries, there may be tragic consequences. Berrypickers in this vulnerable state of consciousness, unaware of their physical surroundings, fixated on finding that incredible patch of berries that everyone else has overlooked, *have* been prone to wander—to wander right over cliffs, in fact, and fall hundreds of feet into the ocean, their bodies never to be recovered.

This had not been a danger for my father and me, of course, for we were a long way from the ocean, high up on a hill, and though heights could induce vertigo in some people, the experience of vertigo had nothing to do with heights per se, or a fear of heights, as Hitchcock's *Vertigo* has led many to believe, myself included. As I listened to Dr. Payne patiently explain this to me, I could tell that he felt certain that it had nothing to do with berrypicking either.

But though there were no precipitous cliffs, there was that deep, dark, fairy-tale-like woods that began at the foot of the hill, and, as I got down to some serious berrypicking that afternoon, at the foot of my conscious mind I could still hear Dr. Payne's warning, as earnest as a Swiss alpine horn: *prone to wander.* But even when he had wandered, I thought, to reassure myself, he had not gone far, a mere half kilometre or so from the Veterans' Pavilion down to Quidi Vidi Lake to watch the rowers. Many times, to be sure, but always to the same place.

Those had been my final thoughts before I picked up my berry buckets and walked a short ways down the hill. My father had already worked his way down almost to the treeline. I turned my back to the sun, which was blindingly bright. As soon as I got to work, crouched down and focused my eyes on the ground, I could see that the blueberries were everywhere, in great profusion, though the slanting ground and the thick brush and rocks made it difficult to move around. But before long I was picking in earnest, nose to the grindstone, eyes to the coal face. After about an hour of conscientious berrypicking—no eating whatsoever—I do recall straightening up out of my crouch much too quickly, feeling dizzy, losing my balance, falling sideways, catching my foot in a thicket of alders and falling on my back...but everything was a blank after that.

When I woke up, it was almost dark. I was still on my back in the bushes, but looking up at the moon now instead of the sun, with a bad pain in the back of my head. I raised my right hand and looked at it. The fingers were stained purplish blue, a few squashed blueberries stuck to the palm. My left hand was blue as well, and the face of my watch was smashed, the hands bent and unreadable, but sort of twitching. When I felt the back of my head and looked at my right hand again, it was red and blue. *The old man*! I thought suddenly. *Where's the old man?*

I struggled up out of the bushes and got to my feet. I felt queasy and sat down on a large rock nearby. My head and my heart were pounding. I felt the back of my head again—a rough crusty patch, but there didn't seem to be much blood coming out of it. I stood up again and looked down the hillside. I wanted to shout out his name, but thought better of it. I was feeling dizzy. I sat down again and tried to think. I was awfully thirsty. I needed water. I stood up again, felt a bit steadier and less queasy.

I spotted one of my overturned berry buckets in the bushes and took a few steps toward it and found my knapsack. I sat down on a rock and had a drink of water, which made me feel a bit calmer. *Holy fuck! The old man*, I said in a frightened whisper to the silent, empty, moonlit hillside, which looked like a stage set for *The Twilight Zone*. I stood up and shouted, "Hello! Dad!" I waited for a reply, but there was none. I shouted louder, "Dad! Malc! Dad! Hello!" like a lost and frightened child, but it was the parent, the father, who was lost. "Hello!" I shouted again. "Hello! Malc! Dad! Hello!" Only silence, not even an echo.

I felt weak. I sat down again and drank some more water, then got up, put on my knapsack, and began to walk slowly and carefully down the hill, right to the bottom, where the woods began, shouting "Dad" and "Malc" with almost every step I took. The moon was bright, and I could see in among the trees for quite a long ways. They were spaced well apart, paths were visible, but I saw no point in going in there and getting lost myself. *The woods are lovely, dark and deep, but*...I shouted his name into the woods a few more times, then I thought that perhaps he had not wandered into the woods at all. In any event, if he had gone in there, I would never be able to find him in the dark. Perhaps no one ever would. And wasn't that what he had said he wanted the last time we had been out in the country, on the barrens—to be left out there among the berry bushes and rocks and peatbog and brooks?

No, no, no, I said to myself. What he had most likely done when he finished picking and was unable to find me was to make his way back to the car and wait, perhaps till dark, then walk out toward the main road, stop at the first house, and call the police. They might be on their way here right now.

I decided to climb back up the hill and make my way down the other side to the car. When I got to the top, I sat down and drank more water, bit into an apple and ate most of it, threw the rest in among the bushes.

My head was clearer and not paining as much. I looked down the other side of the hill and could make out a clear path almost to the bottom, the moon shining on a descending dreamlike ridge of white limestone rock. It struck me for a moment that I might be dreaming, and I couldn't quite rid myself of that sensation until I reached the bottom of the hill and saw the car. I was hoping against hope that I'd left it open and that my father was sitting inside, awake and waiting, or stretched out on the back seat, asleep and dreaming, or perhaps sitting on the bumper with his berry buckets beside him, giving in to eating a handful or two, something he had always refused to do.

But, alas, the car was empty, and he was nowhere to be seen.

The car clock said nine fifteen, and it was almost ten by the time I reached the first dwelling on the rugged and winding gravel road—a trailer, brightly lit, with an extension at right angles to the original living quarters. There was no doorbell, so I knocked on the chocolate-brown aluminum door. When there was no answer, I knocked harder, shaded my eyes from the overhead light and peered in through the glass, through the teardrop lights of the inside door, but I couldn't see anything. I thought I could hear a TV playing, and it sounded like a hockey game; but in early September? Then very suddenly an angry-looking man in a plaid shirt opened the inside door and looked at me suspiciously through the glass of the aluminum door. I could tell he wasn't going to open it, so I said, loudly, "Can I use your phone? It's an emergency."

"I don't have one," he shouted back, but I didn't believe him.

"My father's lost in the woods," I yelled pathetically.

"I don't have a phone," he repeated.

"Okay," I said, raising my arm as if to fend off his uncharitable blow.

I walked out the empty driveway and across the road toward a house that was lit up behind a line of spruce trees. Looking back over my shoulder,

I could see that the trailer man had come out onto his front step and, with his hands gripping the railing, was watching me as I entered his neighbour's driveway.

A thin, frail-looking man, tall but stooped, who looked a lot older than my father, answered the doorbell of his small bungalow and, when I quickly explained my predicament, led me silently and nonchalantly, as if I were his familiar phoneless neighbour, to a rotary phone on the kitchen wall. His almost spectral appearance seemed to personify the identity of that anonymous addressee whose name, or descriptor, sometimes appeared on an envelope in my mailbox: Occupant.

I phoned 911 and told my story to a man whose calm detachment and formality made me feel all the more alarmed. Occupant was having a mug-up at the chrome kitchen table right beside me, eating toast and drinking tea from a china cup with the tea bag still in it, the string tab hanging over the side. The man on the emergency line told me he would contact the appropriate authorities—the RCMP and Land Search and Rescue—give them the details, and they would send out a crew first thing in the morning.

"In the morning?" I shouted. "Why not now? It's only ten o'clock."

"They'll assess the situation, sir. It's dark now, hard to find a missing person in the dark. I've got all the details, don't worry, they'll be along before daylight. You just hold on there till they arrive."

"It's only ten o'clock," I said again. "It won't be daylight for another eight hours. What's he going to do till then? He might die of exposure."

There was silence at the other end of the line.

"Tell them my father has dementia," I pleaded. "He probably has no idea where he is."

"I'll let them know, sir. They'll assess the situation. You just hold on there till they arrive," he repeated. "It's a warm night, sunrise is at six thirty," he added, "and it'll be light by six."

After I hung up, I thought of calling Land Search and Rescue myself, but could only find Marine Search and Rescue in the phone book. I called the Veterans' Pavilion instead and reported what had happened to the night desk clerk, who seemed as detached and unconcerned as the man on the emergency line.

Occupant had been watching me and listening intently, and after I finished and thanked him for the use of the phone, he said, very kindly, if somewhat pathetically, "You can stay here if you like. You can sleep on the daybed. There's no one here but me."

How strange life is, how unpredictable, I thought, perhaps a bit melodramatically, as I was feeling overwrought. You can go from being the object of suspicion and rejection, complete indifference to your plight, to being offered a room at the inn, a bed for the night, simply by crossing the road. Perhaps that's *why* the chicken crossed the road.

Pecking at his toast crumbs, Occupant looked a bit like a bewildered chicken himself, and his invitation was perhaps a casual plea in disguise. Where was the emergency line for this kind of existential predicament, I thought, the 911 number for isolation and loneliness, being left behind, forgotten, lost in a house that had once been a home? Perhaps the suspicious, hard-hearted bastard in the trailer across the road was his son, just waiting for the father to die so he could live in a real house.

"That's very kind of you, sir, but I don't want to impose," said the indifferent, cold-hearted man who had merely used him to use his phone. "I better drive back and have another look around," I added. "I wouldn't be able to sleep, anyway." As he had been listening to my every word when I was on the phone, I didn't think I needed to fill him in.

I drove back as far as the BERRY GROUNDS sign and parked the car in a large open area I hadn't noticed in the daylight. It looked as if it had once been a gravel quarry, but had since been graded for public use by berrypickers who didn't want to venture farther on, or, fooled by the sign, saw no need to. I got out of the car and urinated against a large spruce tree on the edge of the lot, looking up at the full moon and feeling like an old dog about to howl.

I stood leaning against the car door, mulling things over, not wanting to get inside. It was a warm night, as the 911 man had said, bright, with hardly a breeze, and I told myself not to worry. Close to my feet a flattened, white pizza box, though covered with dust, shone in the moonlight. Beside it was a used condom, another one nearby, evidence of desire going its merry way, *the young in one another's arms*, heedlessly reproducing the sad pageant of life and death, despite the many losses and regrets that awaited: loss of youth and desire among them; loss of love, beauty, parents, partners, children; your mind, your soul, your so-called creative powers. Perhaps mine were on the wane already—the dreaded "mid-list list," as van Loon refers to it, having witnessed it often over the years among his loyal crew of mid-listers, his ship of fools, as he likes to call us. Though doggedly loyal both to him and to ourselves, to that intractable thing called Literature, and to that Beckettian motto of despairing hopefulness, hopeful hopelessness—*I can't go on. I'll go on*—chronic discouragement, dejection, and rejection take their inevitable toll, the consoling ballast of critical and collegial praise unable, in the end, to stabilize a reader-less ship, a royalty-less voyage. *I can't go on. I'll go on.* Sometimes I'm not sure which is worse.

I got in the car, had a drink of water, and ate a Mars bar, meagre sustenance against all those dark thoughts, but I was so hungry I ate the other one as well. I ate some peanuts. The remaining apple, however, exuded such a ruddy cheerfulness in the moonlight, such a sappy sanguinity, an unappealing goodness at that sad moment, that I put it back in the knapsack. I had a last drink of water, then tilted the car seat back, zipped up my jacket, and closed my eyes. My body was a dead weight, and the night was so unusually quiet that I must have fallen asleep right away. But though my body may have come to rest, my mind was still in motion, running a reel of restless dreams that seemed to go on all night long.

In one dream, I was on a moonlit path in deep woods, and I saw my father coming toward me with a bucket and a red-stained white sack in each hand. Ignoring or defying the fruitworm, he had picked the partridgeberries after all. The sacks looked like swollen, tie-dyed T-shirts. He laid his burden on the ground and began rubbing his hands together.

"Dad, are you okay?" I said, when I got up close to him. He was still rubbing his hands together, and grimacing.

"What's the matter with you?" he said. "Where'd you come from?"

"I thought you were lost," I said.

"Lost? What kind of foolishness are you gettin' on with? Take these buckets of berries, will you?"

"Where'd you sleep last night?" I asked. I could hear the sound of sirens in the distance.

"In a tilt, where else," he said. "I never sleep better than in a tilt. It's the smell of the var, and the frankum I was chawin' on. Where'd you sleep?"

"In the car," I said.

We were now sitting in the car, with his buckets and sacks of partridge-berries on the floor in front of him.

"Are you hungry?" I asked. "Did you take your pills?"

"I'm after havin' breakfast," he said. "You can guess what." He scooped up a handful of berries from a bucket and pushed some into his mouth.

"See if your pills are in your jacket," I said.

The sirens sounded much closer now.

"Did you find them?" I asked.

"Yeah, I got 'em here. What are they for?"

"You had a stroke, Dad. You don't want to have another."

He popped the plastic pill bottle with ease, didn't have the same trouble he always did with the childproof lid, looked down into it and then over at me. He put his finger in and slid something to the top, and as he looked at it on the tip of his index finger, it began to move. It was a small white worm, and he stuck it into his mouth.

In another dream, I had parked the Jeep overnight in the middle of the road, facing into the woods, so that I would have a clear view of anyone walking out. Looking through the windshield in the half-light of dawn, half-awake, I saw something moving—a creature coming toward me on the gravel road, a wild animal I thought at first, but it was a lone, two-legged creature, and I got out of the car and began to walk down the rutted rocky road toward him.

This time he was carrying only a red-stained white sack in each hand—full of partridgeberries, I thought—but as I approached I saw that the sacks were dripping blood.

"Dad!" I shouted, and I tripped in a rock and almost fell. When I looked ahead again, the sacks were dripping insects instead of blood, and the road between us was covered with them, all crawling toward me—and not fruit-worms this time, but maggots.

Fiction, of course, is notoriously ideal for conflating things, but perhaps it's not as good as dreams. I was not one to analyze my dreams—I rarely re-membered them—but being the sorrowing, self-blaming, regretful, and nos-talgic kind, I was easily led back into memory's mausoleum, an overstocked storehouse of dissolution and loss, wherein dwelt the invisible worm and the visible remains of Alicia and me. I awoke knowing clearly where the maggots had come from—a hotel in Montreal where Alicia and I had once stayed.

But my dark thoughts were interrupted by a tapping on the car window, and I looked out to see a man in uniform, a police officer. I rolled down the window.

"Good morning," he said. "Constable Hanrahan, RCMP. Your name, sir?"

"James Nightingale," I said.

"You reported a missing person last night?" he inquired.

"Yes, my father," I said. "You found him?"

"Yes, I think we have," he said. "Could you please step this way, sir," he added officiously.

"Is he okay?" I asked, opening the car door, but he had walked away. With my heart thumping and my throat tight and dry, I followed after him. His car was parked directly behind mine, almost bumper to bumper, as if to block my escape, and not far behind his, two men dressed in firefighter-type hats and heavy-duty clothing were standing beside a large, white, squarish vehicle that looked like a courier truck—a Search and Rescue unit, I guessed. Constable Hanrahan opened the passenger door of the police car and walked around the back to the driver's side. We got in and closed the doors almost simultaneously. My tongue and mouth were too dry to speak a word, but he said, to my great relief, "A message just came through on the radio. Your father's been found at the airport, we think. He seems to be okay."

He reached for a clipboard on the dash. Resting it on the steering wheel, he said, "I just need to ask you a few questions."

I had a few questions for him as well.

25: POETRY OF DEPARTURES

Celia had persuaded me to fly back to Toronto instead of taking the bus, boat, and train again—or a boat all the way. Kevin said he knew the captain of a container ship that did a regular run between St. John's and Montreal, and he could get me a berth. But in the end I agreed to try to overcome my irrational (in Celia's view) fear of flying by flying headfirst into the prevailing anxieties with the assistance of a mild tranquilizer provided by her housemate, Hana. As the plane rose above the tarmac in the late afternoon, from the very runway perhaps that my father's wandering feet had trod, I looked out the window and tried to imagine all the missteps that had led him there.

∾ ᔍ

I didn't need to imagine much, of course. The reports from the police, Search and Rescue, the taxi driver, airport security, and Jack Doody himself had put most of the pieces together for Dr. Payne, Mrs. Foster, and me. And though they had told me that people like my father still needed adventures, they were quick to point out, as if I might think they were to blame, that this was not quite what they had in mind. The "story" had even made the VOCM radio news.

There was a reason—two, in fact—for my father's being at the airport, if not actually on a runway as a plane was coming in. First, I had told him I was leaving in a few days and asked if he wanted to come out to the airport to see me off. Second, as I've already mentioned, he'd had such a good time with the Doodys, Jack and his father, Wilfred, two weeks ago, that he couldn't wait to go out there again.

It appears that on the day of our blueberry pick he had, first of all, followed a path into the woods below the Bluff instead of coming back up to the top. He had walked a long way in the dark, several kilometres, it seems, and he must have been very tired and confused. When he came across an abandoned tilt, I guess he took refuge there for the night, just as he'd told me in my dream. He got up at dawn the next morning and continued on this path until it came out to the main road.

Now imagine, if you will, that you are a taxi driver coming back to St. John's from Pouch Cove in the early morning fog, just past dawn, after dropping off a boisterous crowd of drunken adolescents who'd spent the evening and wee hours of the morning downtown. You are feeling slightly drunk yourself after breathing the confined exhaust exhaled by this intoxicated crowd. Your headlights spot an old man carrying two white buckets and two white sacks, walking on the pavement on the wrong side of the road, the side you're driving on, so you decide to pick him up before someone runs him down, and give him a free ride to wherever he's going. Home to Whiteway Street, he says, but as you near the city, he changes his mind. Passing the road to the old airport, RCAF Road—the airport was a Canadian Forces base during the war—he asks you to turn in there. He directs you to an old hangar, where, two weeks ago, he may have sat in an office having a cup of tea with Jack Doody and his father before Jack took them out in his pickup on his daily rounds, shooting birds around the perimeter of the airport. But Jack, though on duty this morning, is not at the hangar; he is off somewhere in his truck.

The taxi driver leaves, but not before reporting this odd person to the police on his two-way radio, just in case he's been reported missing or has escaped from some institution.

Now we've all heard news reports of egregious breaches of airport security; well, here's another to add to the list. Prone to wander, as Dr. Payne warned me, my father goes looking for Jack Doody, carrying his precious berries with him.

He takes a stroll along the narrow road that runs around the perimeter of the airport, and eventually wanders out onto the runway itself.

Now imagine you are the pilot of a giant aircraft, an Airbus 340 or a Boeing 767, carrying over a hundred people whose lives are in your hands, arriving at St. John's in the early morning hours. From Toronto or Halifax, perhaps—I might have been on this flight myself. It is foggy, as usual, at the St. John's airport, and you have to circle the runway for half an hour; but you have now committed yourself to a landing—you are too low to pull up—and, as you break through the fog-clouds, there, on the runway, your most cherished strip of Mother Earth, walking right down the middle of it, in fact, is a man carrying two beef buckets and two pillowcases full of blueberries.

You do not know what he is carrying, of course, let alone that the buckets were once filled with salt beef and the cases with pillows, but it is enough to give you the equivalent of berrypickers' vertigo. They are not strapped to his body—he is holding them like a man carrying water from a well—but who knows what might be in these buckets and sacks. Your aircraft is descending slowly but surely; you are coming in for a landing, an explosive obstacle, perhaps, right in your path; and just as it seems as if the worst is going to happen, a pickup comes speeding down the narrow road along the edge of the runway, driven by the very man whose job it is to shoot creatures that are a danger to your aircraft. He does not shoot this lost creature, of course; he jumps out of the truck and whisks him out of harm's way, gathers him up like a child, along with his buckets and sacks, as routinely and efficiently as a garbage collector.

∞

For his part, the old man didn't know what all the fuss was about, and he seemed to have experienced no ill effects whatsoever from his ordeal. He recalled being picked up by the taxi driver, being picked up (literally) by Jack Doody on the airport runway and taken back to the Veterans' Pavilion (though he hadn't been aware that he *was* on the runway), and being out berrypicking and sleeping in a tilt (he had a load of berries and a large wad of frankum to confirm that); but he didn't remember that I had accompanied him, though I still had blueberry-stained hands and a crusty lump on the back of my head to confirm that when I arrived at the Pavilion later that morning. My own berry buckets, though, were unavailable as evidence; they were still somewhere out in the bushes waiting for some lucky berrypicker to find and fill.

It was a good thing, in a way, that he couldn't recall that we had gone berrypicking together, for it meant that I wouldn't be subjected to the usual attack on my lack of berrypicking and outdoorsman's skills, not to mention my leaving him to fend for himself in the wilds, such as they were. But I felt a small hurt for being the only forgotten character in this adventure story, even though I knew why he had forgotten and why he would continue to forget, which made me feel less guilty about leaving him permanently to fend for himself, like the sad old man whose telephone I had used. In a few days, my old man would forget that he even had a son who had abandoned him, as many sons and daughters are wont to do, sons especially, if the anecdotal evidence is to be believed.

Perhaps dementia has a positive dimension, I thought—and not for the first time. It's an evolutionary mechanism, perhaps, cruel but kind, a coping strategy to help us deal with the long dreary remains of our lives, the bitter butt-ends of our days, when even the palliative butts are denied us; when, alone in our empty houses, or placed in a *home* (an even bigger and emptier house), we spend our time waiting for a letter, a phone call, a visit from the children to whom we devoted our lives, but who are now so engrossed in lives of their own they go about them as unaware of our lonely vigil as the demented themselves.

Yes, dementia may have a very positive side. This notion struck me forcibly when I visited my father at his *home* this morning to say goodbye and found him assembling or dissembling an alarm clock. Not one of those small, squarish, plastic, battery-powered quartz clocks with illuminated hands and numbers and a loud, irritating chirp instead of a ring, but a large, round, weighty, old-fashioned, spring-loaded number with an alarm bell on top, a bell that really sounded like a bell, as loud as some fire-alarm bells these days.

I had grown up with the sound of this clock. Though it had never been in my room, it awakened the whole house when it went off, which was always early, even on weekends. Sometimes it mercifully stopped working, but it didn't take the old man long to get around to fixing it. (He refused to throw anything out.) He loved fixing it, taking it apart until it was totally unrecognizable as a clock. Scattered across the kitchen table, despite frequent admonishments from my mother, it looked more like some kind of mechanical puzzle. The thing was ancient; his own father had owned it, had brought it back from the USA, where he had gone to find work in the early 1920s, but had come back home within a year.

This morning I entered his room to see all the parts of this clock-puzzle spread out before him on a small table by the window and him sitting at the table staring at them with his hands folded in his lap. He turned his head and looked at me as if he had no idea who I was, as if I were a stranger interrupting his work, or his contemplation, for he didn't seem to be thinking about the workings of the clock. Perhaps he had no idea what it was, could no longer form an image in his mind of what all these pieces represented; or maybe he had entered a place where fixing this clock no longer mattered, where this commonplace mechanical thing was no longer necessary. His mind had delivered him beyond remembering or forgetting; beyond waiting for me or Sheila or anyone else to visit; waiting for a phone call, the mail to arrive, supper to be announced; beyond clocks, beyond watches, beyond time. Perhaps dementia was another dimension altogether.

"Dad, I'll be leaving this afternoon," I said.

He turned his head and squinted at me. The light in the room was dim, but he didn't want any lights on in the daytime.

"Don't forget to say goodbye to your mother," he said.

"No, I won't."

"Did you get the licence plates for the car?"

"Yes, I did," I lied. "Sheila said she's going to bring you something for supper," I added, to change the subject. "I had supper with her and Loyal last evening. You must get tired of that cafeteria food. They don't change the menu very often."

"I don't mind the grub," he said.

"She said she'll be here around five. Don't forget now. They'll be serving supper here around four thirty."

"Don't forget, don't forget...Is she bringing the children with her?"

"Sheila?" I said. Something wouldn't let me go along with this. "Sheila doesn't have any children, Dad."

He looked at me and squinted again, opened his mouth and began to probe one of his lower molars with his tongue, as if this riddle might be solved this way.

"He's still holdin' out, then, is he?" he said.

"Loyal?"

"You got a good memory for names," he said.

I laughed in spite of myself. Then I put my hands over my face and began to rub my eyes, but I remembered that he hated this gesture.

"Cecilia's coming over to see you this week," I said quickly. There was a long pause.

"Grandfather will be pleased," he said, as if beginning some grand, impersonal, omniscient narration, someone else's story rather than his own. He lifted his right hand out of his lap and began to move some of the clock pieces around on the table. I felt a strong impulse to leave, and I walked toward the door; but I turned and went up behind him and put my hands on his shoulders.

"I've got to go now, Dad," I said. "My plane leaves in a couple of hours."

"Yes, you go on ahead," he said, as he leaned toward the table. "I'll be along the once."

Both of his hands were moving the clock pieces around now, as if it were coming back to him how they were to fit back together. I moved around to face him, then sat down at the other side of the table.

"Dad, I can't take you with me," I said, "but I'll be back soon. For Christmas, maybe, for a couple of weeks or more."

He looked up, but not directly at me, then began to speak as if to someone else in the room.

"I was worried about him when he was young," he said, "how he would get along. He was a dreamy sort of youngster. All he wanted to do was pick flowers—not from his mother's garden, mind you, for a funeral or Mass in the graveyard…something useful…but wild ones, weeds, down in the meadow… dandelion, daisies, buttercups, clover. He'd press them under cellophane in old photo albums that were only half full. I was worried about him, if you know what I mean. None of the other boys, his friends, were doing things like that. But I guess he turned out all right in that regard. He didn't have many friends, spent most of his time wandering around by himself. I had to go off and find him in the woods more than once. He liked school, if you can believe that, loved reading those big schoolbooks he brought home every fall, especially the English readers. He could recite poems by heart, and he wrote some, too. He was losing his eyesight by the time he was ten—real thick glasses, 'four-eyes,' they called him. Even after that sleet storm in the winter of '59, when just about every light pole on the Island was knocked down and we had no power for three months or more—January to March month, it was, the coldest time of the year—he was still reading by cod lamp most of the night. To get him to stop when it was late, freezing cold or not I'd send him out to the coal shed to get a bucket of coal to bank the stove for the night, and if he came back with big frozen lumps, which was useless for banking, I'd send him out again to get some slack. Flowers and books, flowers and books. I don't think he was much interested in anything else. Birds, maybe. He knew the names of all the birds in the garden. I tried reading those books he wrote, and so did his mother…"

He trailed off. I'd been sort of mesmerized by this third-person talk, and when he turned his head and looked me right in the eyes, I felt as if a hypnotist had woken me up. He looked as if he himself had woken up.

He lowered his head and opened the drawer of the table and took out a folded piece of yellowed paper.

"Here's one of your poems your mother kept," he said, handing it to me. "She found it among the stuff you left at the house when you moved away."

I unfolded the greasy, creased rectangle and read a handwritten poem that I remembered writing only because I had stolen the title, "Poetry of Departures," from Philip Larkin, my favourite poet at the time:

There are still no nightingales here;
just the gulls and starlings
you left years ago
on your journey down the thirteen ways
among the twenty snowy mountains.
Crumbs and garbage
keep them alive
through the long winter.
And in a spring that never comes
I've strained to sing
a song I've never heard.
And the year has turned around again;
still snow in May, ice on the lakes—
this fire in my throat.

And here I was, departing again, though it didn't feel so final this time. "I've got to go now, Dad," I said again, "or I'll miss my flight."

He was looking at me and I was waiting for him to speak, but he just raised his eyebrows, as if in mild surprise, and didn't say a word.

I put my hand on his shoulder as I walked past. I stood by the door and looked back at him, then opened and closed it as quietly as I could; but as I walked away the doorlatch caught and made a hollow, belated click.

∾ ∽

When the plane had levelled off at cruising altitude and the steady drone of the engines became a calming mechanical OM (assisted by the tranquilizer, perhaps), when the brat brace of young businessmen in my row stopped loudly speculating and became quietly immersed in the financial graphs and tables on their laptops, I looked out from my window seat to see—yet again—a duct-tape patch on the wing of the airplane. Not a big patch, mind you, but big enough. (Anxious flyers can spot even transparent tape; they've done perception/anxiety studies showing this, believe it or not.) I immediately thought of Dr. Zuckerman, the young American podiatrist I had seen last month, who had excised my callouses with a scalpel, one on the ball of each foot, and recommended inserts for my shoes. They would be custom-made, he said, using a state-of-the-art process (though actually a very old one)—a handmade plaster-cast mold for each foot.

But as he worked lovingly on my feet, one hand caressing a foot and the other expertly manipulating the scalpel, Dr. Zuckerman talked non-stop about airplanes and their capabilities and vulnerabilities, and specifically about the ones that had been flown into the Twin Towers and the Pentagon. The expatriate Dr. Zuckerman was a George Bush despiser and a conspiracy theorist who believed that the ruthless Bush regime had actually planned the 9/11 attacks and engineered the destruction of the Twin Towers. Architects and engineers had confirmed, he said, that only buildings meticulously rigged with explosives could collapse the way those towers had gone down—a controlled demolition, a common and now refined practice in the construction industry.

If Newfoundland had been Bushland, I thought, looking again at the duct-tape patch, the land of Homeland Security and the Patriot Act, anti-terrorism central, if the old man had been spotted strolling down the runway of some major US airport with his bags and buckets full of who-knows-what incendiary substances or devices, *Act first and ask questions later* might have been the patriotic call to arms, and when his remains were sent back home, cremation would not be necessary. (*Cremation has taken place*, as the obits say.)

Dr. Benjamin Zuckerman was from the Bronx and had met and married a Newfoundland girl from Little Heart's Ease who was studying music, piano performance, in New York City. A pianist himself, he had gone to high school with Murray Perahia, Alicia's favourite pianist—I must remember to tell her this, I thought—her favourite performer of the Mozart piano concertos, to be more specific. Alicia had highly discriminating tastes, need I say, and had a favourite pianist, violinist, and violist not just for every composer but for every opus and opuscule of every composer's oeuvre.

And though Perahia might have had the perfect touch for the Mozart piano concertos, he might have been a pariah as far as playing Chopin was concerned. Only Rubinstein could play the Chopin concertos, and the nocturnes. But it was the sublime Lipatti for the waltzes—"the Keats of the piano," as she called him, hoping to sharpen my undiscriminating appreciation with reference to the literary canon, perhaps—though he had recorded very little, having died almost as young as Keats. It was Lipatti for Bach as well, but the ghoulish Gould for Bach's Goldberg Variations; Klein for the Mozart sonatas; Kempff for the Beethoven sonatas, but not the late sonatas—Pollini *owned* those; De Larrocha *was* Granados...and on and on it went, for almost every piece of the recorded classical music repertoire.

Thinking about Dr. Zuckerman and Murray Perahia had not only reactivated my flying anxieties but the maggots crawling around in my dreams. In our late period, Alicia and I had gone to Montreal on a July weekend to see Perahia perform at Place des Arts, his only Canadian stop on a North American tour. Alicia seemed offended that he had chosen Montreal instead of Toronto. We stayed at a small family hotel, which comprised two large brick houses, a duplex. There were garbage cans in the hallways, some uncovered, and we woke up on a hot humid morning in midsummer to an army of maggots crawling up the hall and under the door of our room. Alicia was the first to encounter them, having gotten up early, as she usually did, and the sound waves of her terrifying screech probably still hang in the air of that hotel room.

It was the first time we had been alone together for a long time, and though it had been a pleasant trip up to that point—it was a self-conscious pleasantness, however—this was our late period, as I said, and I saw the maggots as an omen, confirming my earlier premonitions. She had booked a room with two single beds, and the night before, at the concert, Perahia had not played a Mozart concerto, his forte—no Mozart at all, if I recall—but mainly melancholy Chopin, which perfectly suited my mood that evening.

"He's lost his way," Alicia whispered, and I looked at her and frowned. She never spoke in the concert hall, and had subtle ways of chastising those who did.

It turned out that I was right about the omens and premonitions. We were catching the fast train back to Toronto the next day, and at lunch Alicia broke the news about her and Richard. The ensuing argument, though replete with the expected—and heartfelt—recriminations, felt merely rhetorical and theatrical, as if we were watching two old enemies involved in a staged, pre-arranged engagement, an emotional duel. Though we seemed to be merely spectators, however, I'm sure we were still suffering collateral damage from this unfriendly fire, and these wounds, added to the many others that we had inflicted and suffered of late, would mark the end of us.

∾ ∽

Perhaps I would agree to sell the house, I thought, as I looked out the airplane window into the clear blue alien air, the still-expanding universe of vertiginous space in which, as I usually, anxiously, perceived it, we seemed to be stalled, becalmed—not moving, just hanging there, waiting to drop. I had heard of so-called elevator drops of ten thousand feet or more, straight down an empty chute of traitorous air.

Perhaps I would move away from Toronto the Good for good. It hadn't been all that good for me, and there really was nothing to keep me there now. To British Columbia, perhaps—I could look up Beulah in Vancouver. She had left me her address and telephone number. She had decided to take an extended vacation—her annual summer holidays plus a month's leave of absence (stress leave)—and spend some time with her daughter, Tansy, who was now living alone in her father's condo. Beulah's ex had been temporarily transferred to Australia.

I had never been to the West Coast, only as far as the BC interior, for Canada Council readings in the Okanagan earlier this year: Vernon, Kelowna, and Penticton—the Fruitbelt, Vinland, Peachland. I had taken the bus down there after an overnight stay at Banff, where I was to do a mentoring stint for a few weeks on my return.

I had arrived at Banff by a most circuitous route. The train no longer went to Calgary from Saskatoon, and then on through Banff National Park, but on a route one hundred miles farther north—to Edmonton and on through Jasper National Park. I got off in Jasper, then hitched a ride with a wild-looking wildlife officer down Highway 93. It felt like Highway 61, as he played homemade cassettes of Bob Dylan songs from the sixties all the way to Banff. None of the old weary nostalgic tunes that I was fond of, however, like "One Too Many Mornings," "Girl from the North Country," or "Boots of Spanish Leather," just up-tempo numbers like "Highway 61 Revisited," "Rainy Day Women," and "Leopard-skin Pill-box Hat." He didn't talk much, but he identified the various areas of wilderness—"the Wildland," as he called it—that we were driving through, solemnly naming each in turn as if it were a pristine piece of God's Creation: "the White Goat Wilderness…the Siffleur Wilderness…the Ghost River Wilderness." Sometimes, hearing Dylan lines he loved, he could not contain himself and would burst into song: "'How does it feeeel?' 'Where do you want this killin' done?'"

"Where do you want this readin' done?" I myself sang during a third repeat of "Highway 61 Revisited."

"Out on Highway 61," he drawled in reply.

Alicia had had no interest at all in seeing Canada—cities or wilderness. The Prairies, the North, British Columbia, Quebec, the Maritimes, and the New-found-land and Labrador were mere geographical abstractions to her, as alien and empty as the air and space outside this plane. New York, London, Paris, Buenos Aires—these had been her destinations of choice, and almost always with other musicians, not with me. I had made a single trip with her to New York City, by train down through the Adirondacks to Grand Central Station. The Fires of London had been invited to play in some avant-garde hotspot that was the musical equivalent of an off-Broadway theatrical venue.

I had not attended the concert, however. I had gone to a reading instead, for which I was subjected to constant rebukes on the train ride back. On the ride down, I had read in a copy of *The New Yorker* that Joseph Heller would be reading at the 42nd Street Y on concert night. When would I get another chance to hear, and perhaps meet, Bombardier Heller? I thought. Had he finally written another book? As it turned out, the place was so crowded I had hardly been able to see him, let alone meet him, and his new book was the second one since *Catch-22*. "It was love at first sight," that first book begins, and so it was for me as well. How had I missed the follow-up? I bought them both, but decided to forego the mile-long signing queue.

Yes, I would go out to BC, to *British Columbia*—it sounded foreign and exotic, distant in both time and space. I also had a standing invitation to go to Salt Spring Island. Last year, while serving on a Canada Council jury in Ottawa, I had met a poet with a house on the island who invited me out for a month-long visit, a residency of sorts, though I would work for my keep as an apprentice printer. Her home doubled as a publishing house, with an old-fashioned printing press used to produce poetry chapbooks. She had sent me a selection of them on her return home. They were typeset by hand, hand-sewn as well, and letterpress-printed on Hahnemühle Ingres papers, with delicate Somegami endpapers and Fabriano Roma covers. If this sounds more like Pre-Raphaelite art and design, or a William Morris-type fashion statement, instead of publishing, well, fear not, Dear Writer, this esthetic will not be coming to your trade book anytime soon. Perhaps paper, glue, and covers will be unfashionable very soon.

There might be therapeutic saltwater hot springs on Salt Spring Island, I thought, like the freshwater hot springs in Banff, where I had been unable to take the 100° F waters because some members of the World Wildlife Fund were there, protesting the destruction of the Banff Springs snail, attributable, they claimed, to human use of the hot springs. The first mollusc to be listed as an endangered species, its habitat had once included all nine of the hot springs in the area. Now it could be found in only five, and these were the only places in the world it *could* be found.

Perhaps I would return to Banff en route to Salt Spring, establish myself for a few weeks in one of those longhouses reserved for established writers, big-listers and mid-listers. They were set way back in the woods away from the main camp of creative endeavour. Then I would finally get to take that train through the Rockies—the older and more spectacular southern route— which, I had found out, ran only in the summertime. A private company had taken over the CPR line. But I would not establish myself for long in any one place. When the house was sold, I would not use the money to buy a new one, or a condo, or even to rent an apartment, which could easily come in at over a thousand dollars a month. I would bank the money and take to the road, travel around like a blind Irish harper of old, living in the houses of friends and patrons. Perhaps I would start out close to home, at the Gibraltar Point artist residency on Toronto Island, and end up at the Pierre Berton House in the Yukon. Or abandon Canada altogether, steel myself and fly off to the Fundación Valparaíso artist colony at Mojácar Playa, Almeria, Spain. Several writer friends had recommended that.

And if I really wanted to get away from it all, I had friends in Chilean Patagonia who had been asking me to come down for years. A climatologist friend had gone down there to study the glaciers in the Southern Ice Field— the Pius XI glacier, in particular, the only one of the forty-eight in the field, perhaps the only one in the world, that was still advancing (the Vatican hierarchy must have raised a few eyebrows about this). But he had abandoned his research, and his university job, and married a beautiful Chilean woman who ran a restaurant in Punta Arenas, on the Strait of Magellan, a major shipping route before the construction of the Panama Canal, but not much used any more. He was now a sous-chef and part owner of the restaurant.

And now there was also the prospect of coming back home for good and moving out to Random House on Random Island. McGillvray had written to tell me he was moving back to town and offered me the house, rent-free, and his cargo van, too. Someone had made him an offer he couldn't refuse: to set up an in-house theatre company, the Newfoundland Shakespeare Company, as it would be called, in the Basement Theatre of the Arts and

Culture Centre. The newly appointed, "more enlightened" manager of the centre, a former actor himself, who was replacing a "bourgeois visionless functionary, a political appointee from the Smallwood years," had seen the St. John's production of *Shakespeare in Carbonear* and had been "mightily impressed." It would not be long, proclaimed McGillvray, before his new company would vacate the basement and take over the main stage of what would eventually become, perhaps even in his lifetime, "the McGillvray Centre for the Performing Arts."

Grim seemed to be bursting with generosity and magnanimity. He had burned his "Denunciad," he said, his bitter *summa theatrica*, his diatribe against critics, directors, producers, even other actors. (I had, you may recall, considered burning it myself, but who was I to cast the first stone.) "Writing it," he said, "felt more and more like self-immolation than any kind of therapeutic retribution."

Yes, perhaps Random House was the place for me. (Mainstream after all!) The old man needed me—perhaps Celia and Sheila still needed me—and I would be close but far enough away not to be at their constant beck and call. Of course, it was not like either one of them to beckon or call. But could I survive out there in the Newfoundland outback? I didn't want to do it by way of the usual seductive technological intravenous—cellphone, Internet, satellite radio, cable TV—which was as well established out there now as it was everywhere else. My soul would live on peace and quiet, silence, solitude, and my body on wild and homegrown food: blueberries, partridgeberries, and bakeapples from the marshes and barrens; wild mushrooms from the woods; vegetables from my own garden, from a root cellar in winter; and capelin from the beaches in summer. I would get myself a dory and catch a few fish: lobster, crab, and herring in the spring; cod in the summer during the so-called food fishery; mackerel in the fall; trout from pristine ponds most of the year. I would get a few hens, maybe a goat and a cow. I would merit a "story" in *The Random Sounder*, which would, in the usual journalese fashion, begin: *Writer James Nightingale walks from the henhouse next to his carefully tended vegetable garden to the back door of his one-hundred-year-old saltbox carrying a bowl of*

*free-range eggs to prepare an omelet for his breakfast before sitting down to a day's
work at his desk overlooking the Sound.*

Who was I kidding? I was romanticizing things, as usual. McGillvray
had lasted only a year out there. Besides, I had no Thoreauvian or Emersonian
philosophical reflections on nature or self-reliance, simplicity or solitude, to
impart. If I opted for the *vita contemplativa* and turned my pen to something
like that, I was, like McGillvray, more likely to contemplate producing a bitter *summa literaria*. And thinking about *summas* and bitterness and regrets,
I remembered Lillian LeBlanc's manuscript, about two hundred pages of "A
Life Unlived," nestled in my leather bag, and I reached in and took it out.

She had given it to me about two weeks ago, and I was now almost halfway through. The cherry blossoms (or apple blossoms) under which she and
Vernon (or Howard) were married, and which had caught my fancy the first
time she read a passage of the manuscript to me, had by this point in her
story become a leitmotif, had led her back to the apple-blossom summers of
her childhood when she would be sent to live with her grandparents in Great
Harbour Deep, to which she would have to travel by boat. Out on the deep,
rough water in that small, open boat, Lillian would hide down in the tiny gal-
ley and refuse to come up. Upon arriving at her grandparents' place, as if to
recover her equilibrium, she would climb up inside their big, sprawling, cav-
ernous womb of an apple tree, innocently intoxicated by its scent, imagining
herself inside a sunlit room with "billowing curtains of apple-blossom lace,"
as she describes it, listening to the songs of the white-throated sparrow and
the black-capped chickadee, whose cheerful little heart, she tells us, beats a
thousand times a minute, and the wild canary, whose song goes *sweet sweet
sweet sweet sweet.*

And Lillian's apple blossoms had led me to the back pages of my own
childhood, to the *Classics Illustrated* comic books, perhaps the first graphic
novels, in which I had read about Johnny Appleseed. Precocious little reader
that I was, I had also discovered Shakespeare by way of these comics, but
it was the legendary apple orchardeer, not the playwright, who had captivated me. For forty years Johnny Appleseed had wandered the orchardless

landscape of New England, planting apple seeds he had gathered from cider mills. He gave the apple seeds to travellers, settlers, and farmers wherever he went, Eden-like orchards blossoming like alleluias in his wake. He had been a real person, I discovered later on—born John Chapman in Massachusetts in 1774—but he had been much more real to me as a legend.

Though he might have had another reason for visiting those cider mills, it was not something I had considered at the time. I had been so captivated by his calling that I had never wondered about his reasons for doing what he did. What caught my fancy, I suppose, was the pure, childlike, pastoral simplicity—not the unaccountable mystery—of the task. Surely I wasn't thinking in metaphor at ten? The seeds of the craft and sullen art already germinating in my heart? Childhood, the unexamined life, was the life worth living, I thought. The *vita literaria* could make you long for that.

Lillian's apple blossoms and cherry blossoms had a poignancy and mystery of their own, and perhaps she was gradually leading us to the fruit—partaking of which, unlike the fruit of Homer's lotus blossoms, we would be induced to remember instead of forget. But whether it was the bitter apple of the tree of knowledge we would be biting into—a crabapple, perhaps—or something like Montaigne's somewhat less acidic, more philosophical fruit—*Que sais-je?*, "What do I know?"—or perhaps just a plain old McIntosh—*la vie quotidienne*—no doubt it was Lillian herself who had first tasted it. As had Eve, she pointed out, before offering it to Adam (read: husband Howard), contrary to popular myth.

High in the air, in my sterile, off-white, canister of a room, with only the white noise of a mechanical bird and the mere memory of the scent of apple blossoms, I settled uneasily into my seat and turned the pale blue pages of Lillian's childlike, handwritten script.

ACKNOWLEDGMENTS

The author would like to thank his astute editor-in-chief, Patrick Murphy, who has since departed Nimbus for medical school, where no doubt he will learn to master a different, but just as indispensable, sort of medicine; his meticulous copy-editor at Nimbus, Whitney Moran, now replacing Patrick as senior editor; readers of this novel in manuscript (in whole or in part): Don Austin, Glenda Ellsworth, Anne Hart, Doreen McCarthy, Gordon Rodgers, Paul Rowe, and Adrian Turpin; the Newfoundland and Labrador Arts Council and the City of St. John's for financial assistance during the writing of this book; poet Don McKay, for the perfectly perspicacious phrase "the work/work work of art," from his poem "Early Instruments"; and, last but not least, the long-time friends whose allegiance to the artistic life and dedication to the workworkwork of art have been both bedrock and inspiration.